NORMA ASHE

BY THE SAME AUTHOR

Novels

THE MORNING IS NEAR US
BROOK EVANS
AMBROSE HOLT AND FAMILY
FUGITIVE'S RETURN
THE GLORY OF THE CONQUERED
FIDELITY

Plays

ALISON'S HOUSE
INHERITORS
THE VERGE
BERNICE
TRIFLES AND OTHER PLAYS

Biography

THE ROAD TO THE TEMPLE

SUSAN GLASPELL

Norma Ashe

A NOVEL

J. B. LIPPINCOTT COMPANY

PHILADELPHIA : *1792-1942* : NEW YORK

PART ONE

*I*T WOULD have startled Mrs. Utterbach to be told she was living in a time of memorable prosperity. Were there a sprite let loose
in time (happily there is not), darting way ahead, then coming
back with the news, and were this mischievous one to pause at the
desk where Mrs. Utterbach fussed with papers to say: "I am speaking from 1942. You, as I presume you know, are in 1927. This
instant finds you nicely settled in the rich twenties. For years to
come this decade will be known as the time when money grew on
every bush. Madam, I leave you in your era of stupendous wealth,"
Mrs. Utterbach would have found the time-demon not very funny,
neither sane nor kind. She did not know about the money on every
bush, having no such bush herself. Perhaps it is ever so: consider
the people who were very bored, or terribly sad, or even extremely
earnest in the Gay Nineties; and at the peak of the twenties were
those who did not know how to keep roofs over their heads.

Such a one was Mrs. Max Utterbach, at the moment concerned
with the roof over her head; or, more precisely, so much of a roof
as there was over the head of her lodger, Miss Doloros Pettibone,
who threatened to move before tomorrow's sun had set, "Unless,
Mrs. Utterbach, steps have been taken." She meant steps on the
roof, putting on shingles over her bed. The rains of heaven had
had the effrontery to fall right into bed with Miss Doloros Pettibone.

"And when you consider that I have been with you thirteen
years," Miss Pettibone had said in that tone of hers which was an

accomplishment: acid without ceasing to be genteel. "Had **you** thought of that?"

Had she thought of it! They seem thirteen hundred, she'd like to have said.

"And when one considers the circumstances," the lady had—oh so delicately—reminded.

Not that it was at all delicate—this reminding; not that there was anything delicate or decent about her being here at all, and at times Mrs. Utterbach would like to have set her right out in the street, as she had George Mack, who got drunk and destructive once too often—and that one with the incredible hair, who actually got a man right up to her room! It wasn't *that* kind of house. And perhaps this was one reason the refined insults of Miss Pettibone were tolerated: her presence marked it not that kind of house.

It was hard, it grew harder, as the district became less desirable, and the whole place sagged into a run-down look, to have it understood by those who hadn't known her of old that "Mrs. Utterbach's" was morally above reproach. The plumbing wasn't above reproach, one might reproach the food and the furniture; but the morality was technically correct. And this was important to Mrs. Utterbach as her daughter Lorna—nineteen—lived in the house. "Miss Pettibone is still with us, you know," she would say, thus, she felt, surrounding Lorna with an aura of security. Not that Lorna could bear the old snifflebones, as she called her.

But as to why Miss Pettibone stayed—"the circumstances" to which she would refer in the war for her ends. The old lady had lived in this house almost all of her life. Long before it became Utterbach property it had been the Pettibone home. She said it was sentiment; "something in her" couldn't leave and never would (though always threatening to). Mrs. Utterbach took no stock in this sentiment. She saw it as revenge, a long-drawn-out spite.

Mrs. Utterbach's husband had taken the house from the Pettibone family by way of a mortgage. And why *shouldn't* he—and how could he help it? she would demand of herself, very impassioned about this, secretly not happy in the idea of taking a family's home. They weren't too good to take the money from Max in the first place, were they? Glad enough to get it, weren't they? Then as good as laughed at him for expecting them to keep up their payments. They were Pettibones. He wouldn't dare do anything to Pettibones.

Soon after the Pettibones were forced out Max Utterbach died. They then alluded to God's ways and a justice above the laws of man. The very old ones died just about then, causing some unfavorable comment against the Utterbachs, even though at three-score-and-ten the best of families, according to natural law, begin to thin out. Only Miss Doloros remained in town when Mrs. Utterbach, left the Pettibone place on her hands, and left with little else (except two children to support), decided to use the unsightly mansion as a boarding-house. It was then Doloros Pettibone came and said: "I want to come back home. I'd like my old room: this southwest corner with the bay-window. I have enough to pay my way, and here I shall live until I die."

Mrs. Utterbach was moved, embarrassed, and very soon resentful. She couldn't live up to Miss Pettibone and make a living. She would find her examining a spot on the wall as if she could scarcely believe her eyes. "Do you remember the condition in which you left it?" she would sometimes be goaded into asking.

As factories moved in nearer, and what had been "a fine residential section" more and more became working-class district, the personnel of Mrs. Utterbach's tenants changed and she had to see Miss Pettibone draw away in hurt surprise before inflections to which her ears were unaccustomed. Maybe she thinks *I* like it, Mrs. Utterbach would say hotly to herself. If it isn't good enough for her why doesn't she move out? she would a hundred times ask herself and sometimes ask Miss Pettibone. But it was as if the last of the Pettibones were seeing something through. Just what, perhaps the lady herself could not have said.

And Mrs. Utterbach, though irked by the constant implications and reproach of this "better element," had her own compensation for Miss Pettibone's sorrowful disdain. Life was one long mean struggle against alcohol lamps in the bedrooms and washing of underwear in the bathroom. The fine consideration and beautiful speech of ladies and gentlemen did not prevail; goodness knows what they did when they went out and some of them came home scarcely able to find their beds, but "Miss Pettibone is still with us." As good as hanging out a sign, "The place is moral."

But the roof. No use calling Jim Towne. He'd say, "What? Patch those patches—*again?*" And Ferd and Ferd would say: "It will have to be roofed, Mrs. Utterbach. Now shingles are rather expensive, that's true; but here is a nice composition . . ."

So she was fussing with papers, pulling out odds and ends from pigeon-holes as if some happy surprise must lurk in a corner long unexplored. But all she turned up only made matters worse. Taxes must be paid next month. And here was this notice from the bank —interest by the fifteenth.

The mortgage was on the other side of the ledger now; the bank held it this time, and commented on depreciation of property. They feared—they knew she'd not had any easy time, but they really feared a payment on the principal might have to be asked. "I can't!" she had cried. "And how can I earn my living if I lose my house?" "Well, perhaps not this time," Mr. Osborne had finally said, but doubtfully, as if questioning whether he was doing right by other people. And so there it hung, over her head; and it was terror which hung over her head.

Now she knew why Max had that strained look the last months of his life. She could understand it better now that it was she who had to say: "I can take care of it next month,"—all those things one tries to say with a confident smile, as if taking care of it next

month, when five months overdue, was nothing need give anyone a moment's concern. A few nights before her daughter had
asked: "Mother, if you could have one wish granted, what would
you ask for?" "The money to pay my bills when they come due,"
she had answered so promptly that Lorna laughed as she said that
wasn't a very exciting wish. "It would be heaven," she had replied
—for, oh, how she hated it: standing them off, afraid to hear the
doorbell ring.

She'd simply have to get in a little cash she wasn't counting on.
Everything she knew was coming in was as good as spent for what
would have to be paid out. That was the trouble: she could just
make it. What came in would enable her to get by—by the skin
of a cent. But not if anything unforeseen happened. Roofs must
not leak. Yet in an old house something was constantly giving way.
"It's its age," Willie Haines had said the month before about the
toilet. It had become a nightmare. She'd wake in the morning
wondering what that day's demises would be.

Well, some cash; or else some credit. Once she'd had credit, and
how gracious it made life. All the tradespeople had been friendly
when she decided to start out in the business of running a big
boarding-house. "Anything we can do, Mrs. Utterbach." Nor had
she abused this, she wasn't the sort to do that. But what had meant
something to her was the sense of security in not having to pay
instantly. She really felt all those people were her friends and she
was surprised, she was hurt, when the reminder letters began coming in. The first collector was as if a friend had turned against her.
This was after things began going less well, but in the days when
she still thought she could "get it all straightened around." How
in the world had she ever expected to do that? It would be like
straightening around fate. A candy factory went up in the next
block and hid the view of the river from the best of Mrs. Utterbach's rooms. She could no longer say, "Here you have a nice view
of the river."

"It just isn't a desirable place to live any more," Mrs. McElvoy, whom Mrs. Utterbach had trusted for two months when her husband was out of work, said after McElvoy got a little windfall from relatives and they paid up and moved to "a nice *clean* little apartment in one of those modern buildings." Clean—clean—how Mrs. Utterbach had struggled to keep the dingy place clean, she couldn't bear the thought of hers being a dirty house. She didn't know which she hated more: having the house dirty or that constant driving, scolding, cajoling and firing of the help in the struggle to keep the place clean. "*This* old paint?" that saucy Maggie had said when she told her it wasn't clean. "You clean that paint or get out!" she had cried, then backed away—startled, ashamed of the sound of her own voice; it seemed to be saying to her, you are becoming a shrew.

She was used to collectors now. The tradespeople grew worse in proportion to her need of them; and perhaps that was the way of the world, she had many times thought bitterly. So easy to be friendly when it isn't going to cost you anything. Very rare is a kindness that means taking a chance.

People get afraid of you. They see a few things: unpainted house, a cheaper lot of people going in and out, and they smell out all the rest—that you can barely make it at all, aren't going to make it much longer; and *they* aren't going to be caught. "I have my own family to think of," the butcher had said. Credit is what you have when you don't much need it.

Thinking about it wasn't getting her anywhere. She wasn't coming out even this month, even leaving off the roof. . . . Of course, there was Ethel Evans. How long did the girl expect to stay in her room, get her food too, without paying a cent? *Six weeks.* Why, she could have rented that room twenty times over. Probably could rent it tomorrow—week's rent in advance—enough, perhaps, to patch the patches over Miss Pettibone's bed. And Ethel Evans just sitting there talking about getting damages soon!

Chances were she'd never get them at all. More than likely she knew she wasn't going to get them—just kept on saying that, getting her living for nothing. She's living off me, Mrs. Utterbach thought, out of her own desperation, for until the roof began to leak she had felt sorry for Ethel Evans: alone in the world, injuring her knee like that. But what a shaky case it was, she hastened to think, trying to shut out that picture: alone in the world. It wasn't as if she had been an employee of the place where the steps gave way. Did we ask you to come here looking for work? they might very well say. Do I have to support her? Mrs. Utterbach demanded of herself. Why, I might be saddled with her months and years! I have my own children to think about.

She shoved receipted bills and those unpaid into one heap and got up to go and tell Ethel Evans she'd have to do something about her rent.

CHAPTER TWO

*M*YRICK PETTIBONE, who back in the seventies built this house known now as Mrs. Utterbach's, must have heard that a man's home is his castle and sought to make his look as much that way as possible. There were turrets wherever one could possibly be worked in—or rather, bulged out. The house looked like a body with a lot of swellings. But this had been advantageous in renting rooms. "I can give you a tower room," Mrs. Utterbach would say, commenting brightly on sun, view and air. So she thought now, working up indignation against Ethel Evans, she even has a tower room!

It was a third-story room, and Mrs. Utterbach's shoe caught in a hole of the stair-carpet, nearly sending her off balance. It would have to be mended. But what was the use? Take it up and the whole thing would go to pieces—this carpet an area of holes or holes about to be. As the plumber had said of the toilet, "It's its age." Another thing to throw out, and no way to replace. Well, let them walk on bare boards! They'd make a great clatter, but better that than one of the roomers falling downstairs—damage suit on *her* hands.

Ethel Evans sat in the pleasant bulge of her room and smiled as Mrs. Utterbach came in. She's done that all along—kept on smiling. At first this had seemed so brave, but today it was irritating; Mrs. Utterbach couldn't think of Miss Evans as brave and go ahead with what she had come to do. Why, she has morning sun and afternoon sun too—sitting there in the sun, smiling as if she hadn't a care in the world! *Six weeks.*

"You look very comfortable," she said; and something in her, betraying her self-interest, couldn't help being glad the girl was comfortable in the long chair she had put in for her after the accident, the two soft little pillows she had thought might help to ease. She was studying Spanish, wanting to "improve her chances." Certainly Ethel couldn't count on her looks to help with her chances. A plain girl—broad face.

"I love the sun," she said. "It's almost enough in itself, isn't it?"

Enough in itself? Mrs. Utterbach stood there just as she was: one hand on her hip so that elbow crooked, the other arm lax at her side; one shoulder a little hunched—a very bad posture, but just so she stood, as if so arrested. Oh, that went a *long* way back —someone who used to talk about the sun. . . . The brain with which we thought of it—tenderest love and highest hopes—the brawn and the dream, dream of a better world, because we'd been made by the energy of the sun. Impatiently she moved, loosening herself from what for the moment had taken her. Not that now! That was another world. Long gone.

Answering the girl, "I'm afraid it isn't enough to pay the bills," she said.

Ethel Evans looked as if she'd had a sudden twinge of pain. Perhaps she had been having pain all along, but knew it more acutely now. "You're worried, Mrs. Utterbach?"

"How can I help but be?" She said it desperately, as if she were the one who were being dispossessed; as indeed she felt she were. It was one of those times—this coming to demand money of a girl penniless and crippled—when she felt dispossessed of her birthright. What she should have been she was not let be.

"Everything's going to pieces," she said. "Things wear out and there's no money to replace them. How can I *help* asking you for your rent?"

"Why, you can't," the girl said. "You've been wonderful about it. And that's why I'm so glad."

"Glad?"

"That Mr. Gorman really expects to have some money for me next month."

Did she believe it? She was an exasperating girl who lived in a trust that everything was going to be all right. She drew life from that, as well as from the sun. Perhaps there was some truth in it: money from this lawyer next month; and even if there weren't, how could one break it down—belief in which she lived?

That by which we live. . . . Something down deep in her, something of long ago, was pulling her away from what she had to do. She *must*—be practical. If she told the girl she'd have to give up her room, surely she could get money from—from—oh, *somewhere*.

"I am so grateful to you, Mrs. Utterbach. And now it's just a matter of a little time."

Time. Time was just what there wasn't enough of. It would all fall to pieces: her property, her chance. Then what about Lorna? And what about Fred, who like as not would be in trouble again, sending for money any day now—her own son.

"Haven't you *anybody* could help you?" she demanded; then suddenly thought suppose someone were to ask me that. I'm alone too. It made her feel near to this girl, nearer than she wanted to feel just now.

"I seem to have nobody but you and God," Ethel said, and smiled.

"Then you'll have to count pretty heavily on him," she replied sharply. Better be sharp than cry. Fine landlady *she* was—wanting to cry when asking for the rent!

"Do you really believe in God?" she suddenly asked.

The girl considered carefully. "Do you know, I really do," she brought forth, with a sort of earnest surprise that made them both laugh a little.

"I'm sure I don't know why you should. What has he ever done for you?"

"Why, Mrs. Utterbach. Don't you feel that God ever did anything for you?"

"Does it *look* like it?" she cried. "Use your *mind*," she said harshly—for, unfortunately (very unfortunate it seemed), her own mind was working, and not as she would have had it, but getting away from her, as at times it did. A wonder of long ago . . . Wonder as it had once visited her . . . Wonder . . . God . . . Were they akin?

"Where are your parents?" she demanded, as if this were a monstrosity—someone who had no one. "Where are your brothers and sisters—uncles, aunts? Haven't you girl friends—a young man somewhere? You can't be *all* alone. We don't live that way."

"My mother died having me. I was the first, so there are no brothers or sisters. My father . . . he seemed to get tired of me. When I was two he left. I did have an aunt," she went on brightly, as if glad to qualify to this extent. "I stayed with her until I was ten and then she—well, she had other plans. Mr. McGuire. She married him and went to Nebraska. Then I lived with someone who was a relation to her but wasn't any to me. And then—"

"Never mind!" cried Mrs. Utterbach. "That seems quite enough. But I don't know why you go on talking about God!"

"You make me believe in God," the ridiculous girl said.

"I do nothing of the kind!" she retorted sharply, felt the glass of water on the stand by the chair, dumped its contents into the washbowl and let the tap run for colder water.

She looked through rooms on that floor to check up on Sadie. And as she found things: a rimmed washbowl, a bed not properly made, her spirits rose, or at any rate her energy did. Here was something to attack—a just cause and she could work retribution. She went sniffing things out—wasn't this what the mistress of the house was supposed to do? Yesterday the girl had asked for a dollar a week more. Enough dust in corners to smother that request.

In this room were two of *them,* those so-called students the town was over-run with. Mrs. Utterbach resented them, for reasons she wouldn't dare go into very deeply. She had to keep right in her life as it was now—keep going—not think of things that had once been: other students, another college. . . .

The college in this town had to do with curing all human ills in what seemed a suspiciously simple manner. Her son called it the joint racket, and one did hear a good deal about joints. Certain manipulations of the body could correct anything whatsoever that might be wrong. With this went a whole culture, as if a new school of thought were being founded. One heard about the Greeks and the Norsemen, ancient rites, rhythm of the ages. The students became believers—fanatics—an earnestness and exaltation worthy profounder learning. This last was what Mrs. Utterbach resented (though at pains not to look closely into her reasons for being disturbed).

The students came from little towns all around, spent two consecrated years in The School, then returned home to manipulate the human bodies and establish the spiritual rhythm of their immediate neighborhoods—possibly doing some good, Mrs. Utterbach didn't know. She didn't often agree with her son, but was disposed to concur in his judgment, "it's a phony." They seemed to feel all of learning was gobbled up while they were here, that they carried away with them everything the human race could possibly need. It seemed to leave a good deal out, and of this they appeared quite unaware.

Mrs. Utterbach didn't like them in her house: bent over their books, earnestly talking. It was a travesty on something she had once had, and had no longer. It was the more disturbing because there were things about them it was hard not to admire. They came from poor plain people and they seized upon this as their chance to become more. It became a religion, though there seemed a good deal of confusion as to what the religion was about—whether it was bettering one's self, serving one's fellow man, finding the long lost key to the universe, or getting ahead of the rest of the human race by grabbing a truth that had escaped the centuries, bearing it off at a price it was possible, with sacrifices, to afford. They were very arrogant about the medical profession and all the rest of the unenlightened. Mrs. Utterbach didn't feel they were entitled to their exaltation. You had to win exaltation. It was not so easy. Once she had known . . . Never mind! Never mind any of that now.

Sacrifices these students certainly did make, all of those who dwelt with Mrs. Utterbach. None of this going away to college and squandering the old homestead on reckless living. Most of their "pleasures" were provided at the school, so there wasn't even much going to the pictures. They lived meagerly and made every cent count. It was so worthy one would like to have seen it in a larger cause. . . .

But if they didn't spare themselves neither did they spare Mrs. Utterbach. They beat her down on the price of rooms—seemed to think they should have a cut rate because they came in droves; then, in droves, began their campaign for "privileges."

They didn't want to board in the house, their idea was to cook in their rooms. This was something Mrs. Utterbach had never permitted, she had had pride in not having the class of people who cook in their rooms. In the beginning all of her roomers had been boarders. This was the idea of "Mrs. Utterbach's." But after a time there were too many vacant rooms and she had to take in people who wanted—perhaps only breakfast. "We like to eat around," some would say; others said it was cheaper, or they got tired of meals at any one place. Still others bluntly told her they didn't like the food.

In the beginning she had taken considerable pride in the food. Then she found she spent too much on it. She made an effort to get cheaper cuts and still have the table attractive. She shopped around for the best values, so she could offer her people a table she wasn't ashamed of, pay grocer and butcher, and have enough left over to clothe the Utterbachs. And because she really put a lot of thought and effort into this it hurt her to overhear the remarks of her boarders. Perhaps it was just a boarding-house convention to deride the food—something to be witty about, or as witty as natural endowment permitted. She would have liked to be allowed to feel she was providing for them as best she could, that she looked after them. This had been her honorable intention in the first years. But she got hardened by their hardness, until she came to feel it was good enough for them—all they paid for and all they deserved. Now the meals were just routine. Why should she try to think up anything different? Would there be any gratitude? Miss Pettibone had a few luxuries: sometimes a tenderloin steak, broiler or lamb chop, which she paid for herself. This could be managed because Miss Pettibone had her own little table when she ate in the dining-room. Often she had a tray in her room. Sometimes the other boarders would smell the steak going through the hall and pretend to faint, or go running after it with outstretched hands. They behaved as if Mrs. Utterbach had no feelings at all. This so changed her feeling toward them that instead of enjoying making them comfortable there was a satisfaction in getting the better of them any way she could.

And she was bitter that she should feel this way, knowing if there was any such thing as intention, it was not as it had been meant she be. She knew that something was lost. Not that she thought much about this. Her thoughts had to keep right in the groove of the days: marketing, cooking, cleaning; taking a great deal of "back talk." Keeping from being cheated, or as little as possible. And always the struggle to keep the place as decent as she could and pay her bills.

And Lorna. There was the real struggle, to have Lorna "keep

up," not sink to the level of this boarding-house. When Lorna was born no one would have foreseen any question about her position in the town. She was securely among the "nice people."

But now Lorna's mother kept a run-down boarding-house in a neighborhood the best people had left. She herself hadn't the time or spirit for her old friends. Nor the clothes. She tried to keep neat, but she certainly hadn't clothes for bridge-parties, luncheons and teas, to say nothing of the evening parties she sometimes read about in the papers: Rachael Day, Mr. and Mrs. Frank Fielding, Lucy Naegal, the Dick Meisters. Once that had been her life—those names. Strange how you could drop out as completely as if you had gone to live in China, or were dead. For a time some of them had "been nice." But it had been effort on both sides, and now she had no position save as the woman who ran Mrs. Utterbach's. Once in a while she'd meet old friends in the stores. They were cordial, but there was an awkwardness. The other day she'd run into Helen Fielding in Horton's. Helen was wearing a simple smart suit; chic little hat, gloves, shoes, bag—everything right. "Why *hel*-lo," she'd said, so warmly it almost shouted at you, seemed false. And Helen Fielding's old friend, Mrs. Utterbach (what good times— how many good times they'd all had together), was very conscious of her own out-of-style brown dress, stiff felt hat that was blue— not that she liked blue with brown, but she got it for a dollar ninety-eight. Quite a difference, she thought grimly, turning away as soon as she could.

There is a certain way of living. When you are out of that there is constraint between you and those who are in it. Is friendship then no more than that? one might well ask. Yes, sometimes it is. But a common way of living makes for ease in relationships—a lot of things you have which I have too: the cook, the car, the children's schools and parties; the fittings, the beauty shop, the trips. Friendships go an easier way when people have very much the same kind of lives.

For herself Mrs. Utterbach didn't care; she had had to let it all go because her life couldn't include it. But now she was worried about Lorna. For Lorna everything was ahead: friendships, her social life, marriage. It made all the difference in the world for Lorna. Perhaps I should have tried to keep up a little more myself, she would think, so Lorna would have some connections, something back of her to carry her along. But how *could* I? she'd ask, and the picture was quite absurd: hurrying through her work at Mrs. Utterbach's (she did a lot of hard work herself), seeing that the last of the lamb was made into a casserole dish with canned peas, racing through all that to go, on the streetcar, to have lunch with Lucy Naegal or Rachael Day. How would my hands look? she thought now, as she took up the dress she was going to alter for Lorna to wear to a dance that night. The dress was satin and the stuff caught on her rough hands. For a long time she had tried to take care of them. But now . . . so tired at night, and, oh, what difference did it make?

A tap at her door—the Pettibone tap—gentle but insistent.

"It's all taken care of," she said at once. "A man is coming right over. And anyway it doesn't look a bit like rain tonight, does it?"

"Ultimately," said Miss Pettibone, "it will rain."

This there was no denying. Mrs. Utterbach murmured assent. It was well to agree with Miss Pettibone, even in the most obvious matters.

"The question," continued Miss Pettibone, "has to do with the roof, not the weather."

"A man is coming right over to fix it."

"A man?" Miss Pettibone asked coldly.

"Why, yes," said Mrs. Utterbach, and kept herself from asking —What was it you wanted? A monkey? A woman?

"*A* man." The emphasis located the seat of Miss Pettibone's discontent. "*A* man—to fix it! I'm tired of all your silly fixing! Half a dozen men should be coming—to *roof* it!"

Miss Pettibone was going to over-excite herself, forget she was a lady. Then she'd be sick and have to be taken care of.

So Mrs. Utterbach talked soothingly of how it wasn't possible to get half a dozen immediately. One man would at least bridge the gap.

She had grave doubts of her own words. It was true Albert Henry was coming over to do something about the leak over Miss Pettibone's bed. He said he could do it like falling off a log. Albert was a Negro who had a sunny attitude toward his own powers, a comfort when better workmen gave no hope. "Leave it to me!" he'd say, and if there was anything Mrs. Utterbach wanted to do, after thirteen years of running a boarding-house, it was to leave something to somebody else. But leaving things to Albert was like leaving the sane sound workmanlike world behind one—evading an issue, hiding your head. What Albert fixed didn't stay fixed. He would blithely undertake the unfixable, then a few weeks later sorrowfully shake his head at the ingratitude of inanimate objects. "I never thought it would act like that," he'd say in hurt reproach. "Well,"—forgivingly, "now I'll fix him again."

Calling in Albert was saying you are beaten and won't admit it. But it will give me a little time, was what she always thought.

Lorna—oh, the poor child! She should have a new dress. Shirring in this red chiffon wasn't going to fool any of them. Lorna Utterbach was wearing the same pale green satin she'd worn to the dances last year. And indignation at the way things were took hold of Mrs. Utterbach, as it would at times, though she tried to ward it off—where did it get her, how could she change anything, and why spend yourself against something you can do nothing about? But it just wasn't right! When you worked as hard as you could, were nice to people you didn't want to be nice to, spent your whole life trying to keep things going, there just *ought* to be money for your daughter to have a new dress for a dance! It wasn't right and she didn't care who said it was! But all this rebel-

lion came to was a snarling of the thread. She made it worse in
impatiently trying to untangle it. Became angry at the thread itself; then tried to treat it delicately in order to placate—had to give
up and make a new start.

It was while in this mood, having to be gentle when it would
have been a satisfaction to be rough, that she was sure she heard
Lorna's voice, laughing. She couldn't locate the laugh, but had a
suspicion it was coming from a place where Lorna had no business
to be.

She hadn't known her daughter was in the house, didn't know
she was home from school. Lorna went to business college, having
finished high school the year before. Her mother had wanted her
to go to the normal school, then get a position as teacher. There
seemed something safer about this—"the people you would be
with," she had said vaguely. "Meaning more genteel?" Lorna had
laughed, for in her struggle to keep her daughter apart from the
people who lived in this house she had been known to use that old-
time word. "A *real* teacher, that would be the most wonderful
thing in the world to be," she had found herself saying; and didn't
even hear Lorna's: "A school marm? Oh, Mother, have a heart!"
for right there it had opened back—way back—something of long
ago from which she had been shut out for what seemed more than
a lifetime. A glory that was gone. Just once in a while it lived for
her—for its moment. It couldn't live with her through her days,
these days at Mrs. Utterbach's, that one would not expect and could
not bear. But once in a long while she was visited—touched, as
from afar, and made to know this wonder had really been.

Lorna was taking a secretarial course. It helped her mother to
think it in that phrase, seemed to open up a better future than studying stenography. Perhaps she would get one of those really nice
positions: in charge of the office, entrusted with responsibility,
treated with confidence and respect.

She had gone to her door and stood there listening. Could it be that Lorna was down the hall there, in the room of the one they called Doc, who taught in what her son called the joint racket? Time and again Lorna had been forbidden to go in any of the men's rooms. Oh, she wanted to keep her so much *nicer* than that, not sinking into the common life of her mother's boarding-house. She'd give anything if she could have sent her to college, away from this house for the next few important years. But they needn't think the landlady's daughter was easy game—these uncouth men who lived in her house! To her it was terribly important Lorna keep aloof from it all; of another world she wanted her to be. Lorna didn't seem to feel the importance of this. She'd stand around laughing and joking with them. She doesn't seem to have any *pride*, her mother would think, and not always think that through to the end: pride, in what? Lorna had known little else. Since she was about six she had lived at Mrs. Utterbach's. Always the struggle, her mother's struggle all the time she was in high school, to have Lorna "keep up"—be with the nicest crowd. Since childhood Lorna had known no gracious living that was her right. "I like to have fun," she'd say, and as if it weren't very important to her where she had it.

That *was* Lorna's voice, behind the closed door of Doc Stanton's room. Why, how *could* she—lowering herself like that! The man was flashy—common; so glib and second-rate. Oh, what was *happening* to her little girl—sinking into this—this . . . She stood before his door, a little bent, her head twisted so that her ear was close to the crack: attitude of the eavesdropper, a posture always avid, mean.

Without any warning noise a door across the hall opened and Miss Summers came out, followed by a girl who a little while before had come to see her. They had so unmistakably caught her eavesdropping that they stood stock still; and she did too, only her head moving around to them. Then she straightened and with absurd dignity said: "How do you do?"

They couldn't hold back their giggles and as they moved down the hall she heard Miss Summers say: "She does that."

She wanted to scream, "It's a lie!"—wanted to call out, "I'll not be called *she*," but instead she knocked loudly at the Stanton man's door.

He called carelessly, "Come in."

Lorna had her shorthand book and pencil, as if she were taking dictation. But she was sitting on the bed, and the man sprawled in the old morris chair, a posture much too relaxed to seem, to Mrs. Utterbach, the gentleman in the presence of a lady.

He did pull his feet in a little, but didn't rise. There! I should think she could *see*, Mrs. Utterbach thought.

"What are you doing here?" she asked sharply of Lorna.

"I'm taking dictation,"—and they both laughed, the easy intimacy of knowing just what they were laughing at.

"We're both practicing," he explained—not as if he had to explain, but was just being good-humored. "I want to learn to dictate and Lorna wants to learn to take it."

"I want to speak to you, Lorna. In my room."

"I'll be along in a few minutes."

"You will come *now*." (Oh, she knew she wasn't doing this right, but she couldn't stop.) She turned to the man. "My daughter is not to visit you in your room."

And then it was she who flushed hotly, for as she heard the words she knew she was giving the very implication that was the last thing in the world she wanted to put upon it. By her unfortunate words she had brought about a horrid intimacy among the three of them.

"*Mother*," Lorna gasped. "Why, don't be—*idiotic*." She tried to laugh. Her mother knew she was shocked and furious.

"Oh, I don't think I've done the little lady any harm," the man said—so easily that to Lorna's mother it seemed insolent.

CHAPTER THREE

*N*ow Lorna was storming at her; and as her daughter stood before her, hands clenched in anger, she suddenly saw—so clearly she didn't know how to bear it—another Lorna, another gesture. A Lorna much younger—a baby. She wanted to be picked up, held out her arms, and the curve of her tiny hands was so tender and supplicating. Countless babies have done it, and Lorna herself did it time and again, but something in that one moment was to live on. Her own response to it, perhaps, for as she took her baby up her heart was tender with the wish I hope I can always give you everything you want! Everything you want that is right for you. That she had not been able to do this—only in measure so meager —was her own saddest deprivation.

"I should think you'd be ashamed of yourself—prying around after me like that! Acting as if you thought we'd gone to bed together!"

"Lorna!"

"You *did*. You make everything horrid! You just make everything horrid for me!"

She couldn't speak; only looked at her daughter, as if hoping to see she had not heard right.

"Well, I don't care! And you needn't look like that! Why can't you let me have a good time here in the house? What else do I have? You're just a *snob*. And it's ridiculous to live the way we do and be a snob!"

Now she had to speak. She couldn't let that go by. Even in this hurt moment of "You make everything horrid for me," she couldn't let that go by—a snob.

"It's something else, my dear. I want a life for you—" (Oh, how could she say it—*now?*) "Once I knew a life . . ." (No, *no*— not that!) If only Lorna would *unbend* perhaps she could say it. But rigid there before her, rigid in anger against her.

"Well, whatever you want, I haven't *got* any such life. So why should I act as if things were too good for me when I haven't anything else?"

"Oh, you have something else. You have your own friends, your social life." She tried to speak more lightly and took up the dress on which she had been working.

"Well you might as well know I haven't! And you can just put that dress away. Give it to Sadie. She'll think it's swell."

"Oh, come now, Lorna. I'm sorry I embarrassed you. Perhaps I didn't do it right. It seems not. But my idea was right—I do stick to that. I don't want you in the room of a man like that. The door shut and you—"

"There you go again! Door shut! Do you have to be in bed because—"

"Stop talking about bed!"

"It's because you think he isn't anybody. You *are* a snob, Mother. And terribly—well, on-the-make."

Was *that* what her daughter thought of her? The make? On-the-make—*for what?* Couldn't she do something? Couldn't she make Lorna understand her mother was not . . . ?

"I have tried to—" she began unsteadily.

"I know you've tried," said Lorna sullenly, resenting finding herself in the position of seeming unfair. And as her mother turned her face away, shielding it, "Oh, hell, I'm sorry," she said.

"Don't say hell." It was so funny, coming through the gasps with which she tried to control her breath, that Lorna had to laugh. She laughed too, a little wildly. Yes, that was better, for, oh—how she did want to laugh with her daughter.

Again she took up the dress.

"Listen, Mother. I'm not going to wear that dress tonight. I don't suppose I'll wear it again ever. It's enough out of style now, and by the time I'd be wearing it— Give it to Sadie."

"Oh, you don't mean that."

"I *do* mean it. It's all over—see? Finished."

"What is?" She asked it sharply, afraid of it.

"My life with that gang. What you'd call my social life. They don't want me and I'm not hanging on any longer. I don't know what my life is going to be," said Lorna, "but it's not going to be any hanging on to the fringes. I am what I am and that's all there is to it."

In her dismay there was something else: a sudden new admiration of Lorna. But instantly she was afraid again: what did she mean, and where did this leave her? Safety. She wanted safety for Lorna, wanted her to be one with the boys and girls of a protected life. That in itself seemed protection. And then she remembered she hadn't seen Bert Allen for several weeks. She had just assumed Lorna was going to the dance with him that night.

"That's a fine way to talk." She made it as gay as she could. "And what about Bert?"

"Oh—that's all off." She picked up the red chiffon her mother had let fall to the floor; flipped it aside, discarding. "Don't look so dismal, Mother. If I don't give a hoot, why should you?"

"But just this morning you told me you were going to the dance."

"Yes. I was going with Allie Smith and her brother. No thank you. I'm not having any."

She didn't like to ask, what about Bert? But Lorna offered that. "Bert's got a new girl."

"Well, and what if he has? That was nothing but a school affair. Kid stuff you'd call it. As soon as the other boys see you don't go with Bert any more— Oh, you'll have plenty of invitations to the next party."

"Like fun I will! You know better than that while you're saying it. I just don't *belong* in that crowd any more. And you know why."

"I know nothing of the sort," she said firmly.

"You don't? Well, where's your old gang? They have a lot of fun. It's always in the papers. I don't see your name there."

"Of course not. I'm much too busy. But it's different with you. You're young—just as attractive as any of them! I don't want you to—drop out."

(Oh, no, she was saying to herself in panic. Don't *you* drop out. That would be defeat indeed. Submerged in the life of this boarding-house. Lorna taken too. *Everything* gone.)

"The other girls have homes to entertain in," Lorna was saying, and perhaps with no idea how cruel she was. "Oh, I'm just different—that's all."

"You're as good as any one of those girls you know! Why your mother and father used to—"

"What do they care about 'used to'? It's now that counts. It's a car and snacks at night. Having them in to eat and dance—stuff in the icebox, lots of records. And it's *where* you live. Nobody lives down here any more."

"Miss Pettibone does." It was so feeble a straw that she laughed, hoping Lorna would laugh with her.

"One half-cracked old woman isn't going to— You know as well as I do this isn't a place I can ask them to."

She was thinking hard. "I'll put the Johnsons out. They can take an upstairs room or leave. We'll take that back as a sitting-room for just us. I never should have rented it to them, but I—I was rather worried just then. Well, we'll take it back, and you can have it for your friends whenever you like. There! Now isn't that a good idea? Of course a girl has to have her own place to entertain,

not where the riffraff can come. We'll get it furnished so nicely.
I'll take the best pieces in the house and if they don't like it they
can just—Don't you think it's a good idea?" she asked, so anxiously.

"No," said Lorna, wearily. "Don't hold *on* so, Mother. I'm just
not one of them. Every time I'm with them I feel it. They *do* things
differently. Their mothers and fathers—"

"Yes? Their mothers and fathers?"

"Oh, you know darn well what I mean! And why do you have
to act as if you didn't—be pathetic and hurt and put me in the
wrong? *You* can't help it—and I never said you could. But let's
not *try* to be what we aren't. Next year I'll be through school and
probably get a job. And meantime I'm going to have some fun with
people who don't think they're better than I am. Tonight I'm going to the movies with George."

"George?" Her mother couldn't think who George was.

"Mr. Stanton—Doc."

"Oh, no! No! You can't do that!"

"What's the *matter* with you, Mother? He's not a criminal, is
he? Heavens! You act as though he were poison!"

"He is! I mean he would be—to you. Lorna! It would be the
end of everything!"

"Why that's just *silly*. The end of what—for heaven's sake?"

And as Lorna went on—never heard anything so silly, such a
fuss, what was the matter with him, Pete's sake? she was desperately
wondering if she could find words for what was almost gone. If
she could summon—if it would come to her now—save her—
what once had lighted her life.

"The light," she said. "The light is not in him. He was never
taken. He will never be taken."

Lorna was staring at her, looking a little frightened by the
strange words, the tone in which they were spoken.

"What does he know of—the miracle? . . . Wonder." She

spoke the word slowly, repeated it, as if again coming to know it herself. "Did anything ever—*part* for him? Did he ever—look *through?*"

"Mother! Stop it! What's the matter with you? Don't *look* like that!" Lorna cried, really frightened now.

It all left her then—what for an instant had trembled there as of old. It *was* there. Still there. . . . But as she looked into her daughter's horrified face she at first wanted to laugh wildly, and then there was anger, anger for something betrayed: betrayed by herself because she could not give it words, by Lorna because its presence frightened her. And as what she had almost come into withdrew itself from her, she felt stripped to the commonest things of life, and in those terms spoke.

"Can't you see he's just nobody at all?"

"*Well,*" said Lorna. "I'm glad you're yourself again."

Herself again? Oh, but it was the *other* way. For that one instant it had trembled there . . . herself.

"You had me worried," Lorna was saying. "George never pretended he could run the world, so I didn't know what you were raving about. He gets on very well at the school, and I guess that's enough." She picked up her shorthand book and pencil. " '*Part* for him—'! Honestly, Mother, you oughtn't to let yourself go like that."

Her mother stood between her and the door. "You are not going to the movies with him tonight. You are not going anywhere with him—ever. I'll put him out of the house first!" And suddenly she cried: "Oh, Lorna—don't do this!"

Seeing Lorna's face she laughed: "Now I've got you worried again, as you say."

"Well—yes, Mother; to tell the truth, you have."

"You see, there's Fred. Or rather, there *isn't* Fred. I've almost let Fred go."

Fred's sister was silent.

"I mean—in my pride. Of course I'd still do anything for him I could, because he's my son. But—"

"He's sort of a sneak," said Lorna.

"Oh—don't say that!"

"For heaven's sake who began it? And what's the use beating around the bush? He'd cheat and lie just as easy as—"

"Don't talk that way! Don't say those words—about your brother. I only meant—it's been a loss, a hurt, about Fred. Trying to show you I *have* to have pride in you, Lorna. Now it's going to be all right," she went on quickly. "I'm going to do some things differently. We'll have it much nicer here. You just wait. You'll see. We'll take that room from the Johnsons and—"

She was interrupted by Freda's loud call from the hall. "Miss Utter*bach!* You in there, Miss Utterbach?"

"What is it, Freda?" she asked impatiently.

"Man's here with the coal. Says he won't put it in till he has the money."

"What are you talking about—won't put it in till he has the money?"

"That's what he says. First you give him the money, *then* he puts in the coal. *After* you give him the money he—"

It was Lorna who stopped her. "All right, we get you. No money, no coal. You've told us now, what are you hanging around for?"

"For what I'm to tell him. Does he get the money or does he take back the coal?"

Mrs. Utterbach found her voice. "Why, this is out*rage*ous. It's an insult! They can't *do* this."

"Yes they can, Mother. Have you got the money?"

"I have the money, and I'll give it to him *after* he puts in the coal!"

"Oh, what's the use? What's the use having a fight about it? We have to have the coal, don't we?"

"I see it like Miss Lorna does," said Freda. "We have to have the coal—I know *that*. If you got the money, what do you care whether you give it to him ten, twenty minutes sooner—ten, maybe fifteen minutes after?"

"Well I *do* care!"

"I don't see it makes so much difference whether you give it to him first and *then* he puts in the coal or whether—"

"Stop it! Just keep out of this, will you?"

"The doorbell's ringing, Freda," Lorna said quietly.

"What'll I tell this man that's—"

"Answer the door!" Mrs. Utterbach cried shrilly.

For a moment mother and daughter stood there without speaking. Then the mother began to laugh. "What was I saying—just before Freda came in? Going to have it so nice here, wasn't I? Had some big ideas, didn't I?" She kept on laughing.

"Now Mother—pipe *down*. It's a dirty trick, but people are like that. Always be mean to the poor. That's the way life is. What good does it do to get all upset?"

Mrs. Utterbach was going over it. "He said he had to have cash. Well, *that* wasn't very nice. I've *always* had credit for coal. Of course it was a long time last time, but I did finally—"

"Mother," Lorna broke in, speaking patiently, "what about the man?"

"Finally he was paid—every cent. Then I need coal again. 'I'm very sorry, Mrs. Utterbach, but this time I'll have to have cash.' I didn't like it—it wasn't very nice, but what could I do, and I said, all right, he'd have the cash. And now—"

Freda reappeared. "There's a lady to see you, Miss Utterbach. I don't think it's for a room. She looks so *nice*."

"I'll go and attend to the coal, Mother, while you—"

"Why, it's an insult! Doesn't he believe my *word?* I told him he'd have cash and here—yes, right here—" She took bills from a drawer of her desk. "I was taking him very literally. He doesn't even have to risk a check. Cash he said and cash— And now he's saying he doesn't believe me! He thinks I am going to get the coal in and *not* pay for it, after I said—"

"Well, maybe if you just showed him the money," Freda suggested. "Maybe then he'd—"

"Be quiet, Freda," said Lorna. "That lady's waiting, Mother. You go down and see her and I'll—"

"I won't stand it! I won't be treated like that! I'll tell this man—"

"He says it's not him," said Freda. "It's the boss, he says, not him."

"I shall call the office. They needn't think—because I am poor—think I'm a cheat because—" She was on her way down to the telephone.

"*Mother*," Lorna called in subdued voice over the banister. "She's *waiting*—that lady. She'll *hear* you."

"What do I care who hears me?" she called back in a voice that certainly did not care. "They can't *do* this to me. They're saying I'm not honest! Nobody has *ever* said—"

Once she looked up from the telephone to see a tall woman step out from the little reception room near the front door—look at her, stand there hesitating, then turn back into the room. It passed through her mind she's thinking of leaving; but nothing took any hold on her mind just then, nothing but fighting this insult she was going to fight if it was the last thing she did in her life! She'd taken a great deal, her pride had been hurt time and again, but this was an out-and-out saying she couldn't be trusted!

She was saying into the phone: "You can't say I would cheat and lie! Right here in my hand as I talk to you I am holding twenty-two dollars." She counted it out. "Ten, fifteen, twenty, twenty-one, twenty-two." One bill slipped to the floor and Lorna, who had come down and was hovering around, stepped forward and picked it up. She looked frightened. And down at the back of the hall, in the dim light she saw Freda and the man who was waiting to put in the coal, or take it back. But she scarcely took any of them in, any more than she had the lady who'd hesitated in the doorway. She *had* to do this and nothing could divert her. "Here it is, right here on the table with the telephone. If you were here you could see it. If he took twenty steps your man who is standing down the hall could see it. I will give it to him at the proper time. But I will sit here and *freeze*—I will let everyone in this house freeze before I'll be called a liar and a cheat! Do you hear what I'm telling you?"—her voice rose even higher. "I am not the kind of woman you can—"

Something was said at the other end; she hung up the receiver. She sat there bent over, her hands on her stomach, moving forward, back, as one does when there is a cramp.

Lorna stepped up to her, put a hand on her shoulder. Her mother nodded toward the man. "Tell him to put in the coal," she said, but there was no triumph in her voice, only exhaustion. "Give this money to Freda. She can give it to him after—" Her voice came to life. "And get a receipt! If they think I'm not honest how do I know what *they* are? I wouldn't put anything past—"

"Yes, Mother—yes," Lorna said hastily.

She wanted to lie down. She never did that in the daytime, the days too busy. But now she had to. She started for the stairs, then remembered the woman who was waiting, remembered how she had stepped out into the hall, stood there looking at her, hesitated, then gone back. She must have overheard the angry talk at the telephone. Well, what if she did? she thought, and a residue of anger remained in her, ready to flare up. Who was she—that woman? She looked well-dressed. In that glimpse she had of her (the hall wasn't much lighted through the day, lights to pay for) she had an aloof and elegant look. *Pained.* Yes, that was it, pained to find herself in such a place—vulgar wrangling about paying for the coal. Well, what did *she* know? Had she ever come up against a world where you had to pay for things before they are put in? Fight your way. You are stepped on and step back. What if you do raise your voice? Let *her* be a lady in a world that wouldn't believe she was honest! What did she want here, anyway? Not a room, Freda had said. "She looks so *nice*." If she was too good for the place what was she doing here at all?

She'd have to see her.

She turned and walked along the hall toward the front door, stood in the doorway of the little room where men friends sometimes waited for the women to come down, where people looking for rooms waited for her. It had always been a formal cheerless little room, and its stiff furniture that made some pretensions to the grand life had an ashamed and wholly discouraged look now.

The room had one of the bay-windows, an absurdly small one, and that was where the lady who was waiting to see her stood, her back turned to the room, looking out. She gave an impression of not having wanted to overhear the commotion in the hall, not being able to escape, but retreating as far as she could. Pained—that word came back to her. Probably sorry for herself for having gotten into such a place, Mrs. Utterbach thought.

Very handsomely dressed. Groomed. Here was a woman people took care of. A husband—or someone—had paid plenty for that ensemble, perfectly fitting back. A good hairdresser. Breakfast in bed. Massage.

The woman was so withdrawn that she didn't know she was no longer alone. "Did you want to see me?" Mrs. Utterbach asked sharply.

She turned and stood there regarding the woman in the doorway. "Norma?" she asked diffidently. "Norma Ashe?"

$\mathcal{A}$ND then it was the woman in the doorway, proprietress of Mrs. Utterbach's, who stood quite still. Norma—this lady had said. Norma Ashe, she'd said.

The stranger stepped forward a little. "You don't remember me, Norma? Of course—we've both changed; so many years."

Norma. Norma Ashe. *She* was Norma Ashe. And this was . . . ? School. That year. *That* year.

"You aren't—Rosie?" Her voice was faint.

"I was Rosie. I haven't been called it for years. Now I'm Rosalie. But the truth is—I'm Rosie." She said it with a little tremulous laugh, and stood there waiting to be accepted.

But . . . it was like something that just couldn't be. The one who had been called Norma did not move nor speak.

As the pause grew long Rosie ventured: "You have a little time, Norma? I wanted to see you. Could we—sit down and talk?"

Sit down and talk . . . Norma and Rosie . . . sit down and talk *here?* She looked helplessly around the inhospitable little room, spindly gilt chairs that gave you no room to sit. What a place to visit, see your room-mate, dearest friend, after . . . ? *Twenty-eight years* since Norma and Rosie had sat and talked.

"It's a little better in here," she said, leading the way to the shabby living-room. Perhaps none of the boarders would be there; yes, it was empty. At least you could sit *in* these chairs, not on edges.

She plunged right in. It might become real if she spoke of

things that were real. "I keep a boarding-house now. It's not very successful. It was better at first. Really it wasn't such a bad idea to start with. But the neighborhood changed. And then the house is running down—terribly, and no money to do anything about it. I don't like the class of people I have. But what is there to do? I'd never have taken this house except we got it on a mortgage. Miss Pettibone, one of the original—"

She came to a halt. *Rosie.* This was Rosie who sat there before her. She was beginning to recognize her, through all the things that were different: hair so different now, her manner of holding herself. But the way she would open her eyes wide, then slowly close them again. Now Rosie was looking at her so strangely, as if bewildered; but waiting: waiting for something that would be familiar.

She was bewildered herself. What was all that she'd been saying? And looking at Rosie, who timidly smiled a little, as if wanting to bring them together—Rosie, so well-groomed, correct, she was suddenly conscious how *she* looked.

"But it's been different with you, hasn't it, Rosie? You haven't had any such worries, I can see." She thought of Lorna—dropping out. No heart to try to keep up any longer. Rosie looked as though she had everything. Her old friend. Perhaps Rosie would help Lorna!

Such things happened. Why, she might even *take* Lorna. Away from this boarding-house—Doc Stanton. Into the life she should have, chance to meet people—clothes—a good marriage.

"I suppose there are—different kinds of worries," Rosie was saying, speaking very carefully, it seemed. And there!—how familiar *that* was: knitting her brows, turning her head a little aside, waiting to say it just right. Rosie . . . still there.

"I'm sorry you're having a difficult time, Norma. All these years you've been very real to me. You must remember—surely you remember—how much you meant to me? And then—what we went through together?"

All of it as if she were asking something: asking Norma to remember. And so afraid—afraid she wouldn't.

The appeal in Rosie's eyes almost captured her, almost reached to that in her which hadn't been hers for years. It could take her home to the most her life had known.

It trembled there as if gates were about to swing and what had been closed would open.

But the last hour had very nearly destroyed her, beaten her down into a life from which she had little power to emerge. All the time was sound of the coal going in. Hard to disentangle herself from that rasping sound, all that went with it, be freed for a glory she and Rosie had once shared. And all the while thinking of Lorna; as she looked at Rosie, so beautifully dressed, she thought of Lorna giving up the life that should be hers. *Sinking*. They were sinking—she and Lorna; and almost visibly she pulled herself away from an old beauty Rosie's voice could summon, back to this thought of what she could perhaps bring about for Lorna. She could no more afford the luxury of things gone than she could afford the beauty treatments which made the difference between Rosie's appearance and her own.

"I've always remembered you too, Rosie," she said. (Where did Rosie live now? Lorna. Where would Lorna live if . . .) "My, what good times we used to have."

Rosie seemed to withdraw herself a little, as we do from a further hurt. But she tried again, bravely. "I was thinking more of —of the other thing ," she smiled; that smile of Rosie's which asked you to help her go on from there—how well she remembered it.

But she *couldn't* (all the time sound of the coal going in). "The ideas, you mean," she said. And knew at once just what she had done, making it so much less in naming it like that, as if disposing of it. Why must she suddenly think of Judas the betrayer, the disciple who betrayed? More than one disciple—who betrayed?

Where was Lorna? She had been terribly upset: first the quarrel about the Stanton man, then all that about the coal. Could she have Lorna meet Rosie now? She wouldn't be looking her best, or acting her best. Such things were going through her mind in the pause before Rosie spoke.

"You do remember them, don't you, Norma? What you call— the ideas?" It seemed to hurt Rosie to put it like that.

And did Rosie think *she* liked it? Rosie—so elegant, who could afford everything, even the wonder of that time long gone—did she think one would *choose* to have the vision fade from one's life?

"Oh, yes," she said; "yes, I remember. We lived in a dream, didn't we?"

"It was more than a dream." Rosie spoke hastily and with spirit, defending. Then she sat looking at her old friend as if she couldn't believe what she saw and heard. Yet again she tried. "I was always sort of dumb, you remember." She paused, with a smile: smiling and pausing to help Norma remember. "I followed you, because you were so wonderful to me. There seemed—a glory about you, Norma. To me you really were—inspired."

Me, thought this woman who now ran Mrs. Utterbach's. A glory about *me?* Inspired at the telephone perhaps. She was about to laugh when assertion, in deep loyalty to something gone, rose in her to affirm— There's truth in what she says. There was a time when the light was in you. You moved in it and it could have—

The room was at that moment invaded. Miss Summers, who had caught her listening at Doc Stanton's room, who had giggled and said "She does that," came in with another lodger.

Oh, how *horrid* not to have her own sitting-room! She should never have let the Johnsons take it. That was when the furnace broke down—desperate for money—selling her birthright—hers and Lorna's. No place for Lorna to take her friends, no place for her and Rosie, dearest friend she'd ever had, the closest—here, after twenty-eight years.

Miss Summers worked as a milliner part of the time and now

she was staring at Rosie's hat and clothes. The landlady stared back at her tenant, trying to make her get out of the room. How could she talk with her there?

Should she take Rosie up to her bedroom? There hadn't been time for Sadie to get in to do it that morning. "I'll attend to it myself," she had said. Then the roof leaked—Ethel Evans, Doc Stanton, Lorna, the coal. And she'd already moved Rosie once; it would be getting ridiculous.

Miss Summers, as if not liking Mrs. Utterbach's unfriendly looks at her, began talking in low voice to her companion, giggling as she had when she'd discovered her landlady eavesdropping. She's telling the story, Mrs. Utterbach was sure, and felt she'd like to *kill* such people. She ought to walk right over and order them out of the room!

She hitched her chair around so her back was to her roomers, and thinking too that so she might hide Rosie from them, protect her. She said in a low voice: "The class of people I have—"

She was stopped by what she saw in Rosie's eyes: shock beyond belief; and sorrow.

Oh, nonsense. She was making things up. "We were speaking of—?"

"It doesn't matter," Rosie said.

And Norma knew that it did.

"Things come in between," she said.

"Yes," said Rosie.

"Not for you, so much," she said, dropping her eyes from the smart quill in Rosie's hat to a perfectly shod foot. Rosie's feet used to seem too big. They didn't now. Those shoes cost money, went through her mind as she said aloud: "It's easier to be your best when you look your best."

It had been such an upset day she hadn't even changed her dress; almost always she had done so by this time of afternoon. She wasn't wearing a trim house-dress, but an old thing she was wearing out: too fussy, and discolored in spots so it looked as though it weren't clean. How she had struggled about that; she couldn't bear not to be clean.

"I always loved the way you looked, Norma." How gently she said it. Was that all part of the grooming? Rosie used to have outbursts—high spirits, enthusiasms. An idea would strike her and it was not in low voice she'd excitedly bring it forth. It was evident Rosie was very good form now. If Lorna could be in an atmosphere like that!

But Rosie was saying? Hard to keep her mind on what Rosie was saying; and not that she didn't want to! Why she hadn't seen an old friend—one who went far back like this—oh, the many many years. Rosie was *here*. Rosie . . . She had thought little about her in recent years, so many things to keep her thoughts from those vanished days, but she had truly loved her, gone through something with her—*known* something. Together with her, a few others, had known the highest moments of her life. And now, in this hour Rosie was here, when something wanted to come to life between them—Miss Summers whispering and giggling; exhausted by the coal, Lorna. So that she was hardly with Rosie at all. Not really.

"I don't mean just because you were beautiful," Rosie was saying. "And I suppose other girls were more beautiful, as a matter of fact." She smiled. "If there is any such thing as fact about beauty. But you had that radiant look. It would come and transform you. You were so . . ." She waited for the word. "Dauntless!" she brought forth with triumph. "As if you could know life face-to-face and not be afraid. You weren't even afraid of—the wonder of things. I used to think it was because you were part of it."

She was moved by what Rosie said, almost captured. Dauntless!

And Rosie felt this for she cried: "There! It's there again this moment—in your eyes."

Miss Summers, rising, said to her friend: "So he'd better look

out. He's mistaken if he thinks he's safe in his room. Ears are everywhere, round *this* place."

She meant me to hear that, thought Mrs. Utterbach—half rising,
flushing angrily.

And so it was gone: what Rosie had evoked and seen for an
instant in the eyes of her friend. Resentment was in those eyes
now, and then something a bit calculating, as she thought, I'm not
doing this very well—trying to interest her in Lorna.

"I fear I seem much changed to you, Rosie," she said. "I don't
care, for myself, but—"

"You don't *care*, Norma?"

"And what good would it do me if I did?" she asked sharply.
"Can you imagine what this life is—the kind of people I have to
deal with—the mean little—"

Rosie had turned her face away—looking sidewise, and down.

"I'm sorry," Norma said. "After all this time, when you come
to see me—I talk of things like that."

Rosie looked back to her, and smiled; but now it was a smile trying to cover up. She's disappointed, thought Norma, and for an
instant was bitter about this; can *I* help it? she thought. Can I
help it my life is like this? But quickly she again felt warmly
toward Rosie, who had remembered her, held a picture of her all
those years.

But there was Lorna.

"For myself," she said, "I've let it all go."

"I find that almost impossible to believe," Rosie said slowly.

"But I've had to, my dear. How could I do otherwise and go
on living?—day by day meet the mean little things that are done
against me. Well, I won't talk of that. But I do want a different
life for my daughter. She's just nineteen, and only today she told
me that *she* had—let it all go."

"Let what go, Norma?"

"Her social life. The crowd she's always been with. *You* know:

the *nice* crowd. They all have more money, they can do things differently: cars and all that. She feels they're letting her go, and today she told me she wasn't going to *try* to be one of them any more. And it's not right! She's just as good as they are—even if her mother does run a boarding-house!"

Rosie was silent.

"I'd like to get her out of all this. Some place where she would have a chance."

After a moment Rosie asked slowly: "What kind of chance?"

How silly to talk like that! "Why—*her* chance. A chance to *be* something."

"Once we had a chance to be something," Rosie said sadly.

"I must go," she added, before Norma had quite known what to say. "I just—stopped by to see you." She took up the handsome purse that had been lying in her lap; gold monogram. R—and what was that other letter? She didn't even know what Rosie's name was now.

"Oh, no. Why, this is awful. Rosie! I'm so sorry. Here you come to see me—and everything is so wretched. Let me get tea," she said hastily. "Yes, it won't take—"

She was about to rise, but Rosie's gesture stopped her. "No, Norma dear. Please don't. Truly, I don't want tea. I just—wanted to see you. And in a moment now, I must go."

Rosie had come to see her; remembered her and seemed to cherish the memory. Not for a long dreary time had she been with any friend who really cared about her. Rosie had come, and now she was going away again. Before it had really begun—their meeting, it would be over.

"I remember our room," she said.

"The long table where we both studied," said Rosie.

"You sat on one side, and me, at the far end from you, on the other. That gave us the most room, we thought."

"We had so many books and papers," said Rosie.

"Our teacher—" But this halted her. That led right back. She *couldn't*—not the way things were, things inside herself, all the mean little things she had to live with. She wasn't worthy. If you were very religious you wouldn't enter the church, approach the altar, with filth clinging to your shoes.

But Rosie had taken this up. "Yes; our teacher. Do you sometimes—think of him, Norma?"

"Of course," she said hastily. "Oh, yes."

"The things he told us? What he wanted us to be?"

No. Now this she *couldn't* do.

"Yes indeed," she said, in the manner of one who ends it there.

She felt Rosie looking at her, and at last had to look up and meet her eyes. And Rosie's eyes were not trying to dissemble. They were incredulous and wounded. As if she had lost her last friend, thought Norma. As if she had lost the friend she had never expected to lose.

She simply had to get away from her for a moment. And she must really *try*—make the effort—about Lorna. "I want my daughter to meet you," she said, and went in search of Lorna, leaving Rosie alone there in the living-room—with her thoughts. She hurried fast as she could, not wanting to leave Rosie alone with those thoughts.

Lorna had gone out. "Soon 's she give me the money for the coal," said Freda, "she shot right out this side-door 's if hell and high water was after her. She was some scared! And that nigger! You had that black boy scared white! Miss Utterbach—you was *wonderful*. The grandest back-talk I ever heard all my days!"

"Where did Miss Lorna go?"

Freda chuckled, "She didn't wait to say."

Rosie sat there and did not hear her enter the room. There might have been a funeral, thought Norma, and she sitting on here after the others had gone. Back there in school, in that other life, Rosie used to get her feelings hurt—she was so trusting, out-going, generous. And then it was her friend Norma would laugh her out of it and make it right for her. Rosie was more disciplined now—oh, much—but she did seem again that girl who needed her friend.

So when she said now, after learning Lorna was not there, "I must be on my way," (it sounded so sad, "on my way," though what could be especially sad about Rosie's way?) Norma said, with something of her old command, "No! Why, Rosie—this is terrible. You looked me up, found where I lived, and we haven't really had our visit at all."

They were standing and Norma put her arm through Rosie's, drew her over to the sofa. It was only dimly she noticed that the tapestry was wearing through—the good old things all going—what would she do about new covers?

"Now Rosie Major, you sit right here and tell me something about yourself. How old you are I know—though nobody would believe it and I don't suppose you tell it much."

Rosie smiled; but it was as if she had let go of what she cared about and would play this game for a while, just to please.

"What's your name?"

"Stephenson," smiled Rosie.

"Is he living?"

"Oh, yes," she said. "Yes indeed."

"Mine isn't, you know."

"I know, Norma. I'm sorry."

"You happy?"

Rosie thought. "I really don't know. Some ways—it's all right. In other ways . . ."

"I suppose that's the way it always is," said Norma. "But you haven't had it hard," she added, a shade less sympathetically.

"You mean—?"

"You've had it easy, I mean. About money," she added impatiently, as still Rosie didn't seem to know.

"Oh—that. Yes. Everything is all right—about money." She'd

said it as if thinking of something more important.

"That's considerable to be thankful for," said Norma dryly. "If anybody asked me, are you happy, and I had plenty of money, the answer would be *yes*."

"Don't! *Please*," implored Rosie. And her face was so distressed it was quite gently her friend said: "You don't know what it means to be without it. And have your children without it. You have children?"

Rosie nodded. She was looking at Norma as if still searching for the thing she couldn't bear to give up.

"Tell some things without being asked," Norma said. "Let me know you a little, Rosie, before we separate for another twenty-eight years."

"I wanted us to know each other again," said Rosie. "That's why I came."

"And you found things—not very nice here."

"I don't care anything about the place," said Rosie. "Any place where you were—no matter how rich, how poor—to me it wouldn't be a place. It would just be—where you were."

Then she asked anxiously, "Did I say that right?" and they both laughed, and were close to tears, for Rosie used to ask her, "Did I do that right?" She never had enough confidence all by herself.

Norma put her hand on Rosie's; Rosie's so smooth, her own coarsened by work. That didn't matter just then. Rosie had said— No matter how rich, how poor, it would just be—where you were. She held Rosie's hand close; as if she would hold on to something.

"I never would have believed we could have lost each other as we did," Rosie was saying. "With me, my life just took me, and I never really got out of it again."

"It was that way with me," said Norma. And they were silent, each wondering if now that they had seen each other, they had found one another again. And, despite the closeness of this one moment, each knowing she had not. Their lives were too different; and what had given them a life together—oh, that was gone from the lives of both. And from the world, it seemed.

And of all the things Norma would like to have asked, "Where do you live now, Rosie?" she asked, for the other things—there wasn't time, and it was all too far back, far down—buried under living.

"In New York," Rosie said. "My husband is an investment broker there."

"And they will put in the coal—before you have paid for it?"

They laughed; but not as they had once laughed together.

"And how many children have you, Rosie?"

"Two girls. Laura has been married two years. Evelyn came out last winter."

"Came out? Oh—I see." So *that* was the way it was with Rosie. And she thought of the old green satin upstairs—the red chiffon—which Lorna would *not* wear to the dance that night. It wasn't fair! —the difference between her life and Rosie's. "Came out." Society. New York. Everything. And Lorna couldn't even keep up with her old high-school crowd in a small town!

"Well, my dear," she said, "I don't see that *you* have much to worry about."

"You don't think money is everything, do you, Norma?"

"I think it can get practically anything."

"Oh—*Norma. You.* Oh, my *dear*—what has happened to you?"

"Plenty has happened to me," said Norma grimly. "The trouble with you, Rosie, you don't know what you are talking about!"

"Can it buy—faith? The vision and will to make a better world? Can it buy what once was ours?"

"It can buy security," she said doggedly. "And when you have that all these other things can be added unto you."

"Our teacher didn't have money. He had only 'an endless fountain of immortal drink.'"

"You don't *know*, Rosie. You were able to bring your daughters up in a nice world. You have—"

"Nice world! It's *you* don't know what you are talking about! Does your daughter come home drunk every night?"

"Well I should say not!" boomed a fatuous voice. "*That* little lady doesn't get drunk, does she, Mrs. Utter? We see to that! *We* do."

It was Doc Stanton, coming forward and waiting to be introduced to Rosie.

CHAPTER FIVE

*G*ETTING ready for bed that night Mrs. Utterbach was stopped just as she was pushing down her stocking. One instant she was noticing a hole in the brown cotton stocking, and then something cut in. *Who am I?* cut in. It came with the suddenness of a flash or a stab, but simply and clearly, simply as one would say to a child, "What is your name, my dear?"—and clear as a bell in a night quite still.

"Know thyself," someone had said a long time before. But which self? It didn't seem possible she could be both Norma Ashe and this woman who ran Utterbach's. How, in one lifetime, could you be two people so different? When had she ceased being Norma Ashe? Did anything of her remain? Did she live *at all* in the woman who now sat on the side of the bed taking off her stockings?

Well, there was no great mystery about it, she tried to tell herself as she went ahead with what she was doing. It was sad, but life did that to us, to other people as well as her. We were one thing, and then life changed us. That self was gone then— buried under living. We could be buried under living just as, when living was over, we were buried by something else. Twice buried; or perhaps buried a thousand times.

Undressing was slow for she kept being stopped by thoughts that came. Where had Rosie gone after she left here? They never spoke of that. (Oh, how much there was of which they did not speak.) Rosie wanted to get away from Doc Stanton, though really not as much as she wanted to escape Mrs. Utterbach. "Good-

bye, Norma," she said at the open door, trying to smile and looking as though she might burst into tears. Said quickly, "It was nice
seeing you,"—looked horrified when she found she had said that,
and with a rather desperate final goodbye was hurrying down the
steps.

Hurrying away—where?

Somehow it was very very strange not to know where those
swift footsteps were taking Rosie. Almost stranger than her having
come was not knowing where she had gone.

She'd try by actual movements: getting her nightgown from
the back of the closet door, opening and shoving shut a bureau
drawer, to shake herself loose from these thoughts. What was so
strange about it? Rosie said she lived in New York; then more
than likely she had gone back where she lived. New York was a
long way from Illinois. What was she doing out here at all? Was
she on her way West and thought, "I'll stop over"? In Chicago,
perhaps, and it occurred to her "I'll just run down there"?

But how did she know where to come, she wondered. How did
she find me? We never spoke of that. How little we spoke of!

And suddenly she thought suppose she is still right here in this
town! Perhaps no train out tonight, not where she wants to go;
or perhaps tired and not wanting to travel—wanting to think, to
weep, that very instant in a room at the Midland Hotel, right
down there on Fourth and Main. Or perhaps restless and taking a
walk. Which way would she go? Out toward Clearview Park?
Just suppose that were true—she and Rosie—Norma and Rosie—
meeting after twenty-eight years, talking for an hour (less than an
hour) and then in the same town, as apart as they had been all
through the years.

Oh, what nonsense.

And yet she wasn't making it *all* up. Rosie had been here; that
much was true. She had appeared, after twenty-eight years; then
she was gone again.

She belonged in a different world now, Rosie did. She was what is called of the world, worldly. Smart, and yet better than that: gracious as well as fashionable. Rosie Major. She came from a farm in South Dakota. Her winter coat had been made at home, by her aunt. Norma's coat was bought at Clarence and Robbins and had fur on it. She didn't want Rosie to be unhappy about this; and Rosie didn't want *her* to be unhappy about having something better. They were both like that then. How far, in every way, they had both gone from those days.

Taking the pins from her hair she met her own eyes in the mirror. And stood there looking at herself, to see what Rosie had seen. This is a wretched light, she thought, glancing resentfully up at the bulb which swung from the ceiling, taking the place of her bureau-lamp, which she had had to put in one of the rooms, replacing a broken one there. There'd been so much of that. "But I must have a comfortable chair," a new tenant would say. Or again it was a bed-table. And when she couldn't buy those things she'd try to manage by shifting around, robbing herself when there was nothing else to do: a cushion, a rug, until it was a room without grace she lived in now. For a long time she had clung to her own rights in this, telling herself she must have a place that was her own, shut the door and feel among her own things. But first for Lorna, then for the roomers, she had stripped her room. Nothing belonged with anything else: no pattern, no harmony, not a room to which tired body and spirit would gratefully retire.

She wondered what Rosie's dressing-table was like. She could imagine it from pictures she'd seen. Though she didn't have to fall back on pictures. Her own dressing-table in their lovely home in this very town. Max used to stand before it, teasing her. "Do women have to have all these things?" he'd say—proud that she had them. Crystal, silver, ivory. As she stood now before her crude dresser she looked down from the unkindly globe to the face it lighted in the poor mirror. Can *I* help it? she thought, as she had more than once through that wracking day. Her skin and hair hadn't been taken care of. Her neck had not remained firm and proud, like Rosie's. And the bills—the constant bills—they'd marked her face almost as though it were pocked. "A beautiful spirit will shine through the most worn face," she'd read in someone's mushy column the other day. But what if the spirit weren't beautiful, and how could it be when you lived among people whose one thought was to get the better of you? It made you canny and calculating and that was what "shone through" in the worn face.

Rosie needn't have been so surprised, not quite so dismayed. She might have kept a little common-sense, even if she did live a life of luxury, she thought now, defensively. For she herself didn't like the face that looked back at her, as if accusing. What did Rosie expect? If she'd learned anything about me—and she had learned enough to know where I live—well, what *did* she expect?

She expected Norma Ashe. Older, of course—much older, and not unmarked by what the years had been, but there. Yes, she expected Norma Ashe to have been constantly there, to be there now and to the end. No doubt Rosie had been quite sentimental about this. Nothing could destroy Norma, she had thought. Nothing could change her—not really.

So that was all Rosie knew about life! But suddenly it was only a blur she saw in her mirror. Tears because she was sorry for Rosie. Oh—my dear, you shouldn't have come, she thought. If you hadn't seen me you could have gone on believing I was there. You needed to believe that, didn't you, Rosie? And now you're poorer.

This more loving thought of Rosie made real the girl Rosie remembered. Norma Ashe. Everything about her was vital, as if she grew in the sun and from roots that were rich. Someone had said that of her once, and this woman who ran Utterbach's could think it without self-consciousness, as she was thinking of someone else.

The hair now drab and brittle then had vitality to defy any number of years. That was back in 1899, when hair wasn't short, but hers was rather short. Just to her shoulders, because she had an idea she didn't want her head weighted down with too much hair. Her head must be free! It bothered, restrained her, to have her hair always pinned up, and when she was studying at home, and often when they were walking in the country, she would let it down —loose, free. It didn't hang straight but curled up crisply; not red, not gold, something of both. How often she'd wished Lorna had it —Lorna's hair was unlighted brown. That other girl's hair— Norma Ashe—glowed in the sunshine, and when there was no sun it was luminous in the gray day. Some freckles, and not rosy cheeks —Rosie had those—but a good deal of color that came and went with excitements within. Eyes gray—flecked with the gold of the hair, and very deep when what she was thinking had strangeness, and loveliness. "Challenging eyes," their teacher had said. "I see by Norma's eyes," he would smile, "that she has something to say to us."

She was strong—that girl: she could run, she could fight— how they used to tussle in the snow! She was brave, and gay in her courage. The whole of her deeply devoted to what she believed, her energy was boundless to seek out the truth and the beauty. No meanness, no guile—candor, and faith. Always expectant: open to the wonder of it all; moved by high feeling but not abashed before it, never afraid. With clear eyes she looked and in her strong young hands . . .

She couldn't bear it! Shame of what had happened overwhelmed her and she fairly welcomed it when there was an uproar in the hall, some of them coming home shrieking and laughing—running up the stairs, chasing each other down again—*shameful*, after eleven o'clock! A door opened and a voice called: "For Christ's sake, pipe *down*."

She hurried into her robe and out into the hall, leaned over the banister to see those two boys, the youngest from the school, rolling around wrestling.

"Now this will *stop*," she called down shrilly, her hair once more hanging loose around her shoulders—unsightly now. "Such things can't go on in this house! Either you behave yourselves or you get out!"

The one with curly hair looked up. "Sorry, Mrs. Utterbach. We were just fooling."

The other one wasn't so nice. "Thought we'd liven the place up a little. This dump is one long funeral."

She started down the stairs, clutching her robe around her. "If you don't like my house you know what you can do! I don't want you here anyway. You're nothing but a lot of—"

Another door had opened and Lorna was at the banister imploring: "Mother—*please*. They'll stop now. *Please*."

Lorna followed her into her room, stood there against the door. "I just can't *stand* it. What's the *matter* with you, Mother? Why you're acting—you're acting like—"

"I am acting like an old shrew," she said.

"Well why do you *do* it? Honestly, you make me—" But Lorna didn't want to say it.

So she said it. "Ashamed."

So *that* was what it had come to. Her daughter ashamed of her.

"Maybe it could be done," she said; "run a cheap boarding-house and remain a lady. I—I don't seem able to do it. I get so *sick* of this riffraff!"

Lorna sat down by her on the bed. "But Mother, they aren't riffraff, especially. They're not rich, they're not in society—does that make them the scum of the earth?

"Other people have to make a living too," she went on. "It isn't just you. These are people with jobs; or people getting themselves ready for jobs—like me. We're right in the class with them. Then why do you have to despise them so?"

"We are not in the class with them! This—this just happened to us."

"Oh, what's the difference?" Lorna asked wearily. "What's the difference how we got here? Here's where we are. Some of them have it pretty tough. Why don't you be a little kind to them? Then maybe you'd like them better."

"Don't talk to me that way! I can't *stand* it—not tonight."

"I'm sorry, Mother. You're tired. You're worn out."

She looked at her daughter, something beseeching in the look. "Once there was a girl—there was a girl who said . . . believed . . ." She couldn't put it into words. Not tonight. "I wish you'd known that girl, Lorna. You wouldn't have had to be ashamed of her. You would have liked that girl. I really think you would." Elbow on her knee, her head lowered and averted, she shielded her eyes with her hand.

Lorna reached over and took the free hand, though she almost never did anything like that. "I'm just worried about you, Mother. You get so upset. Gee, I know you've had it tough. Don't think I don't know how hard you've worked and all you've had to swing. Maybe it will be better soon," she said with resolute brightness. "Fred just *might* do something; and before long I'll have a job and can help."

"Oh—my poor little girl," she murmured brokenly.

"I'm *not* your poor little girl! I'm O.K. What about that lady who came?"

Lorna had kept away from her since the storm about the coal. And she hadn't gone out with the Stanton man. Afraid to, probably. Afraid of the scene her mother would make.

"Did you used to know her?" she went on, trying to keep her mother's mind engaged for there was some giggling in the hall. About her, probably.

"Yes," she said. "I used to know her."

"When?"

"Oh—a long time ago. It was very long ago," she added, to herself.

"Is she nice? Were you glad to see her?"

"I don't know," she said. And added slowly: "I don't know whether I was or not."

Lorna laughed, uncomfortable, for now her mother was strange again. "Then I guess you weren't. You look awfully tired, Mother. Aren't you going to bed now?"

The house quieted down, even the trips to the bathroom were about over. A few late-comers slipping in furtively, as if they'd been doing something they were ashamed of. Oh—maybe not. They weren't bad, most of them. Just—hopeless. You could use the word two ways, meaning not acceptable, impossible; or, more literally, as those who were without hope. And these people who lived in her house were without hope, though not knowing it. They'd say— Oh sure, we have hope. Golly, we live on hope. Hope for a job—a better job; new clothes, more dough. Get my man, get my girl. Home of my own some time. Kids, maybe.

And what was wrong with that?—home of one's own, children. Oh, nothing—nothing was wrong with that; but even this best of it left so much out. And they didn't know the miracle was left out.

Vision of what life might become . . . Oh, the stirring valiant words he had once said to them of what life might be. She associated it with the snow—up there in South Dakota; breasting the wind, sting of the cold on her face—running, and feeling the blood running within her, and thinking of it: the life blood in one's veins. Thinking of why it was there, how it had all come about: the centuries that made the man of today. First forms of life that were behind us and brave human lives behind us. The lives ahead! —what might come into being because we now were. How did he ever impart it? How had he been able to infuse it into them—as blood of life itself?

She had thought then that nothing could daunt her. Though in fact she had scarcely thought of it at all, as she'd never questioned it. She would have laughed, a confident youthful laugh, at the idea she could ever forget, that it could ever die down in her. But I *am* this, she'd have said in strong golden confidence. This is my brain and heart; this truth is my very blood.

And now it was a dim past, buried under another life that was gone. Ever since she'd been running this boarding-house, when she thought of the past it was her life with her husband she meant: those fifteen years they had together. What went before that was too far back now—remote, detached. She was separated from it, not only by years, but by what she herself had become. Just as there are buried civilizations, so in the span of one lifetime there are buried selves. It was not only too far back, but too alien to what she was now. Like an inaccessible country, a land one no longer knows, lost world. When it would sometimes come into the moment: a line she read, the stars when she opened her window at night, it was but a remote and impossible beauty, life is not like that she would think. All she could do was hold on. She had to stay right *in* her life, not go out from herself, even to remember. And almost with resentment she would push down what threatened (beauty and truth can threaten too) and she was like the other people who said of anything outside their lives, "I have no time for that." Time . . . They used to consider the marvel of time.

She must get to bed; another day would be beginning soon. Lorna's green satin dress still hung over the chair where she herself had flung it when the demand came to pay for the coal. At this very moment the girls Lorna knew were wearing their pretty new dresses, dancing with the boys Lorna knew too. She began folding it up to put away. "Give it to Sadie," Lorna had said. It wasn't fair! All those old things trying to haunt her tonight, wanting to get to her, what had they to do with the world as it was? The dream and the daring, fairer world they were to help bring to birth—what place for any of that in *her* life? All very well for Rosie. Rosie could afford such luxuries, she thought bitterly.

But it wasn't easy to be bitter about Rosie. It didn't last, and even while there it wasn't real, but forced—used, trying to protect herself against something, trying to defend. And helplessly she sat there in the straight-backed chair from which she had taken Lorna's dress, holding the discarded party frock in her lap, and now could not completely withhold memories of what she and Rosie had shared.

She remembered much they had not spoken of that afternoon. How little they had said in the short while they had together. She herself talking of the difficulties of running a boarding-house, "the class of people." Those very words she had uttered to Rosie, when once they had believed that in all people—*all*—was the life that once awakened could go toward the better world which waited to come into being.

All people? Miss Pettibone? Miss Summers and Doc Stanton? The man who would make her pay for the coal before he put it in? Old friends who let one drop out when one was poor—her old friends, now Lorna's? The banker who talked about taking her house?

No. It was a dream dreamed in youth, in a cloistered youth where they lived in the light of an inspired man. It had the beauty of the uncorrupted; but, alas, of that which has not been put to the test. Their teacher believed it, for he had come through uncorrupted, and what he believed shed a light, as from the power of its own truth. They were his disciples, and he believed in his disciples. And when he died they were not lost, but what came from him seemed to grow stronger in them, as if so it must be, for it must go on.

She and Rosie used to study together, not just to learn, but that they might be more worthy and have more to give to what life might become. What serious young people we were, she thought, trying to think it more lightly, not very well succeeding in thinking it more lightly . . .

And suddenly she knew so clearly just why Rosie had come. Once there had been a rift, and together they had looked through. And now Rosie was lost. She knew it as well as she knew in what chair her old friend sat that afternoon. And she came to me—why? Oh, very clearly she knew why. Because she thought I still had what once we shared. Why, she always came to me. Why wouldn't she come to me now? The husband who made money, the daughter who came out; clothes, manner—that had nothing to do with it. She was searching; she sought a way back into what had once informed her life. Why, Rose has *nothing*, she thought. She is destitute and alone, and she came to me believing I still had what we had together. How did she find me? It may have been hard; but she came—timidly, but trusting, wanting to be taken back home. "I must find Norma," Rosie had said; "then I will be restored, and can live."

$\mathcal{T}$HERE was a change in the Utterbach house: the voice of the landlady was not as much heard and when she spoke her tone was preoccupied rather than harassed. She didn't now fly off the handle, as so often in the few months just before, those months of mounting worry, not knowing where to turn. There was just as much to worry about, but Mrs. Utterbach seemed to be thinking of something else. Freda would say, "Here it is eleven o'clock and they've not sent the meat," and she'd reply, "I suppose I might call them up," but as if it weren't very important, as if not really thinking about it.

Miss Summers made a long complaint about the hot water; she was so surprised by the lack of interruption that she went on and on. And the pause that followed went on. Finally the landlady seemed aware there had been a flow of words and this flow had stopped. "What? What did you say?" she asked.

"You heard me," said Miss Summers.

"I didn't quite follow you."

Her roomer laughed, not very agreeably. "You must have something on your mind."

"Yes," she said.

"Don't you feel well, Mother?" Lorna asked her.

She felt quite as usual she said.

"Somehow you don't seem yourself," Lorna persisted.

"I suppose not," she said. "But then, I haven't been, for many years,"—went back to her thoughts, not seeing Lorna's perplexed frown.

One day Miss Pettibone stopped her in the hall. "Please come into my room, will you, Mrs. Utterbach?"

She pointed to the place over her bed where there had been a leak.

"It is not very pleasant," she said, "to lie in your bed looking up at a place so—so soiled." Miss Pettibone used the word daintily.

And Mrs. Utterbach said: "Miss Pettibone, why do you stay here at all?"

Miss Pettibone immediately sought her easy-chair, speechless.

"I just wondered."

"*Well*—" was all Miss Pettibone could find to say.

"I don't seem to understand people," Mrs. Utterbach went on. "Myself, or anyone else. I thought if I could understand just one person it might—clear it up."

Miss Pettibone found voice, a quavering but indignant voice. "I think, Mrs. Utterbach, that it is your business to make me comfortable, not—not *understand* me. I have remained here with you all these years—"

"Yes; and I wonder why."

Without giving Miss Pettibone time to reply, "Is it spite?" she went on. "Do you stay here to be a reproach to me? That seems such a sorry way to spend one's life; especially as I am reproach enough to myself."

"Have you forgotten," Miss Pettibone asked, in her manner of firing an icy but refined gun, "that this is my *home*?"

"Oh—that's nonsense," she replied dully, and there Miss Pettibone flared up. "Is it indeed! My father built this house! Planned and paid for it. I remember the day we moved in; though I was only five years old I remember—" She was searching in her crocheted bag for a handkerchief. Into it she murmured: "All those happy years."

"It was always a gloomy house," Mrs. Utterbach said prosaically, not meaning to be cruel, bent only on getting the truth about some one thing; "I should think you'd be glad to escape from it."

"The trouble with you, Mrs. Utterbach, you have no sentiment. You're *hard*, and so you can't understand."

"Understand is just what I was trying to do," she said wearily, on her way to the door.

"You never will!" Miss Pettibone called after her, triumphantly.

"I wonder," she said to herself.

Rosie shouldn't have come. What good could it do—bringing to life the past, when you had to live right where you were at the moment? There isn't *time* for anything else. Time. . . . And with the thought of it she was in the stream of it, and knew it wasn't true the moment was all.

Her bewilderment wouldn't let go of her. How could one change like that? Where had it gone—all that had lived in her? Once it was the whole world. Once it had been her whole self. She could understand how one might take leave of oneself through a confused hour or day, a week or even a month, and then feel with a shock—What happened to me? Myself wasn't there at all. But not to be your own self through most of the years of your life . . .

As she went on running Mrs. Utterbach's her mind wasn't on the food or the bills or the voices of her lodgers. Things that had so recently upset her didn't get to her now; something else engaged her. Days long gone now filled her days. She remembered what she thought she had forgotten. And yet there were guards, there were limits. As if something in her tempered her memory to what she could bear, it didn't go all the way back, to the thing itself, that brief high moment from which it had seemed all the rest of her life would open. That was not there for her again—fluid; it was way off and inaccessible, shrouded, as high places and distant beauty are shrouded. Those veils would never part for her again. She was not good enough. How simple and pure they had been, those few who had shared what was like revelation: she and Rosie, Austin Wurthen, Virgil, Helen too. And there was one other: that strange boy Emil, a little younger than the rest, who sort of hung around because he did the work at their teacher's—fixed the fires, cut the grass. She didn't know whether he was really one of them or not; he was just around, in his clumsy way hovering there, seeming anxious. "Sit down if you like, Emil," their teacher would say. "Don't worry," she remembered his sometimes saying. "Everything is all right." Why had he said that to Emil? Why should he reassure him? She had wondered then, wondered now; and wondered what ever became of Emil. He was like someone who looked in upon it all. And she had a curious feeling of Emil as guide, though there was no reason she could have given for the feeling. As if he could perhaps take her back where she could not go by herself.

For she could not take her weary footsteps back to those heights; she would not know the way. That would be more light than these eyes could bear; and she could no longer stand erect, as one must upon the height. Leave it—just leave it there in its distance, what had once been, and was perhaps there still, and forever, but not for her. Somehow—somewhere along the way, she had betrayed.

Where? She had no idea why it was so important she find this out. How would it make any difference just to know? Whether it would or not, she had to know. Where had she begun to deny faith? Where was it sprung—that leak in her courage? That flame so pure, so strong, where was the moment, the very instant, it choked, yellowed, beginning the sad change from flame to ashes. She wanted to find that time, place, and the fact it would do no good made the need none the less.

Her life hadn't been what is called bad. She had loved her husband and helped him. When the necessity came she had been self-supporting, self-respecting, done the best she could for her

children. That would be said of her by another. But ah no, she
knew: knew that somewhere along the way she had betrayed.
Something in her that should have been stronger than any circum-
stance had been killed in its golden youth. Many years ago it had
happened, for she had been long bereft of what made her once
splendid world.

And so Mrs. Utterbach was indeed preoccupied these days, ever
since the fine lady came to see her. It was a very good time to
loaf on the job, as the girl who did the rooms was not slow in
finding out. Smell of bacon and coffee from a room brought no
hurrying footsteps, and the bill collectors were discouraged, they
made little impression. Lorna laughed and talked with Doc Stanton,
though not very happily: the fact her mother didn't seem to notice
troubled her. She would have felt more at ease had her mother
continued her objections. This was strange, and seemed all wrong.

Her mother was living with another girl. She was trying to find
out what ever became of Norma Ashe. She really did not know,
and for some reason she could not have given, she had to know.

PART TWO

*N*ORMA ASHE was on a train that made its way through the wheat-fields of South Dakota, taking her from Pioneer College to her home in southern Iowa. She had graduated the week before, and a week before that she was twenty-one years old. The Nineteenth Century—with its achievements and defeats, all the love and hate of a hundred years—would soon add its weight to the past.

There were no school friends on the train because she and Rosie had stayed over those days to dust all the books in the library. They had used these books and some of them had made life what it had not been before; so they wanted to do this for them, as no one else was going to do it. They thought their teacher would like it; between him and the books was something, not just him, not the books alone, but a living relationship. He had, to the measure they could accept it, taken them with him into this limitless world.

He had taught them how to take care of the books; here is extension of your life, he had said, and one is not careless of what is more precious than diamonds. When they dusted they weren't to drive the dust into the bindings, but *out*. They knew about the spreading and slapping shut, leaving a loved volume as free as one could of what would corrode.

All the reaching and twisting did make their backs ache at times; they would laugh and say, a good thing they hadn't gone to a big college—many more books. It was slow going because they would linger over certain volumes, recalling when they'd read them, things their teacher had said. Some of them were his own books, he had left them to the library when he died two months before. That was why they had begun doing this, and then they hadn't wanted to leave the clean books among dusty ones.

"Now they're ready for someone else," they'd said. And they wondered who'd come, and whether they would have the wonderful times with the books they had had. They were sorry for these strangers who would come: they wouldn't have him, their teacher.

They had other teachers, to be sure, but they always thought of him as "our teacher." He taught philosophy, but in their evening sessions with him, at his house, he made it include many other things: poetry and history, anthropology, religion—what man has been and thought in his life on earth. All of this he related to their own lives: their heritage, obligation. His name was Joseph Langley. They addressed him as Professor Langley, but in their minds, and when they talked together, he was "our teacher." In their hearts he was our beloved teacher. He believed in them and they were not going to disappoint him. His having died made no difference in this high resolve, except to make the obligation the more deeply rooted. What had lived in him must live now through them; not to make themselves more learned or cultured—that was only a means to an end. The end was a better world.

In the fall Norma was going to the University of Chicago, that wonderful new place, dedicated to learning. Their teacher had arranged this. He had a friend, he said, who would send one student, the one Professor Langley selected, and he had chosen her. The day he told her the air became so rare she could scarcely breathe. Even now it was hard to believe this was happening for her, and his death made it a high obligation. The very fact she could not report her progress to him made the obligation to all of life, thus including him. She was going to study to become a teacher. This seemed to her the most wonderful thing in the world. So would she pass on the torch.

But how she would miss Rosie. . . . Two years they had been

room-mates, fellow-students. They went through so much together. All the things of their lives were shared—big things, little:
darning their stockings and washing their hair. "We ought to go
to bed now," and "It's time to get up." The occasional happy surprise at the boarding-house table—"the same old thing." Wrap-
ping up when the room got cold at night, happy when the sun
shone or the air had a tang that made them want to run; bracing
against the wind, hurrying through the rain—slipping on the ice,
and laughing.

Giving the room its thorough cleaning on Saturday morning;
dressing for church. "Now where are my gloves? Goodness!—
have I lost my gloves?"—all of it not one of them alone but the
two of them together. Lighting the lamp, bending over their
books. "I wonder if it means . . ." "Do you think he meant . . . ?"
Sharing that fine moment when light broke and they understood.
Reading together a line too beautiful not to share; tasting, testing,
lingering over a word which hadn't been one of their words and
now was theirs. The problem of chapped hands, other problems
with which girls are beset.

All of this, part of a world called actual, and looking together
into a world they had not known was there, wonder at what they
glimpsed. A rift. Seeing *through*—released from their individual
lives, taken. Resolution: resolve not to fail life that waited to be
moulded by the dream of what life might be. That hour in their
teacher's house—he not there and yet there as never before, evening of the day they had seen his body lowered into the earth—
it was like having been baptized together in the waters of what
was to be; like being born together. . . .

Never could she feel as close to anyone else as she did to Rosie.
Even though they were in different places, years and years apart,
even though they *never* saw each other again (though she couldn't
imagine *that*), something that was Rosie was her and what was her
was her friend.

It didn't seem right she go to the University of Chicago—that wonderful place—and Rosie not go. She had spoken of this to their teacher, though it was hard to do, it seemed greedy, as if asking more for herself. She said it timidly, but had to say it: "I suppose Rosie couldn't go too?" He shook his head. "No, I can only do this for one of you." "Perhaps it should be Rosie," she had said. "There's something about Rosie . . ." (How could she say it: this something about Rosie?) "Rosie is so *good*. Rosie *is* goodness." She frowned; it sounded awkward, and she had meant it to mean so much.

Again he shook his head, smiling at her, for he always understood, and knew now her perplexity in not putting it as she would like. "No, Norma, you are the chosen, and you must go."

She was the chosen; and yes—she would go. Perhaps she could somehow make it up to Rosie. If she could become enough, as much as his belief in her, that might in some way be for Rosie too.

Rosie was so happy for her; not just trying to seem happy, wanting to be, but happy as if it were great good fortune for herself.

She was going to Minneapolis—Rosie; she would live in a rich house there and teach the children. She did not feel this was any stepping-down; she looked forward to it, with timidity, to be sure, humility, but eagerly, as her own great chance. What could be more important than teaching children, Rosie would say. "Perhaps, very young, they can begin to care about the things we care about, and that will make their whole lives different." With a good deal of excitement (there were so many fine excitements) Rosie would consider how she might awaken these two children as their teacher had awakened them.

And she would go on studying. Norma would tell her what she was working on and Rosie would get the books from the Minneapolis library and study too. That way they wouldn't really be apart.

What Rosie dreaded was the house. Unfortunately she'd seen a picture of it, and it overwhelmed her. "You've been to our house, Norma. You know how we eat in the kitchen, and go outside, and hardly ever open up the front room. I was even afraid here at school at first."

Norma would reassure her. "Now Rosie—what is a *house?* Somebody had money to build it. And what is money? You know as well as I do there are things more important than money. And some of those things you have and will bring with you to that house. That house is just a big pile of rocks and you—" Then they'd laugh about this mansion being a pile of rocks. And go on talking about what Rosie would bring with her. They could say things to one another without being abashed, not feeling foolish, for they had a common language and knew they were understood. Never did they feel sheepish about what they felt was important. They were their teacher's pupils. They were in very truth his disciples.

But they did worry a little about Rosie's clothes; the dresses her aunt made for her hadn't the right style, and as Norma sat now on the red plush seat, looking out at the maturing grain, she wondered if she couldn't save something out of the money her grandmother was going to give her for clothes to go to Chicago and get one really nice dress for Rosie. Clothes did help, and right at first, before they knew what she really was, it would be easier for Rosie if she had one dress not made by her aunt. Something like her own blue silk, perhaps—Rosie just adored Norma's best dress: high collar, sleeves full at the top, shaping to the arm; shirring around the waist, long full skirt. Yes—something like that.

And then her brows puckered: Virgil liked that dress too, and it disturbed her to think of Virgil. He pretended he didn't like the dress, would back away from it as if afraid—silly things like that. But expecting you to know what he meant; his eyes as he regarded you expecting, sometimes daring you, to know what he meant.

Often he seemed to be protecting himself with a mocking manner, as if there were too much there to let it be exposed. There was indeed much there, in Virgil. He always startled something in herself; an ironic twist of his, a denial that was a test and a challenge, could make her know what she felt and hadn't been aware of feeling. His eyes seemed somehow veiled, as if he were too sensitive to let his eyes always be giving him away. This slim fair boy of whom their teacher had once laughingly said: "Virgil is very fortunate; there was an oversight and they forgot to leave any room for the grooves in his mind," was always surprising something in you. But she knew how he could be hurt, had reason to know the tenderness which escaped the mocking, self-defensive manner.

Was she in love with Virgil? Certainly she loved many things about him . . . his power to see, that gift for seeing was a poet's gift. He had given her eyes she had not had before she knew him: absorbed in what she was trying to think out, or carried high by a rush of feeling, she might often have missed the pattern of the trees on the grass, bright-tipped wing of the bird on a topmost branch. He knew the differences in the quality of the days. The seasons were his to savor. But what most of all drew her to him: the feeling that she understood him was always immediately followed by a sense of there being more than she understood. That would never let one—come to the end of him. Life with Virgil would have perpetual zest. Well . . . in the mind it would. He would be—good for her. (What a way to think it!) She could never slip into emotion for emotion's sake with Virgil, nor into easy accepting. His surprised eyebrows would pull her right up, she thought with a smile. Fellow-students with enough difference of approach, and quality, not to let any day be the end of the adventure. What more did one want? Was that all one could ask and all there was to it?

That wasn't all there was to it in drama and poetry, she thought, looking perplexed, a little rueful, as her eyes swept the wide country through which she was passing. Perhaps, she thought with a slight smile that had a remote wistfulness, they just heightened it to make it drama and poetry. Take Shakespeare. Certainly she didn't feel for Virgil as they felt in Shakespeare. Could she feel that way for someone else? She didn't know; how could she know? She didn't want to! There was so *much*—so much to know and feel. She wasn't going to have her life taken away from her!

She knew that their college days had been unlike life in most of the colleges. In many of them love affairs were just a part of going to college. It hadn't been that way at Pioneer, not with their little band. There were five of them (their teacher's disciples) and together they cared so much for what had opened to them that they became almost as one. Perhaps their teacher took the place of the love affairs: what he made them feel, the *stir* of it! Like the frosty morning—tingling as the frosty morning; like the stars—opening to the limitless. They were happy explorers together; this so engaged them that they didn't scatter into the usual way: pair off and fall in love with one another. They were in love with it all, and that brought them together, and that was enough. Perhaps this was strange; yes, it *was* strange. All of it exciting and beautiful and strange.

But after their teacher died, as the time drew near for them to separate, Virgil wanted to be with her more, be alone with her. He would come and want her to go for a walk, when she and Rosie were studying. Sometimes she would go. At times he'd put his arm around her as they walked, and she didn't feel so near to him then. When they stood still he'd take her hands. One night he said, "I love you, Norma. Don't you see how it is?" Another time he stopped as they were walking and said slowly, all his guards down now: "I worship you."

She was shaken by this, as if suddenly, for the first time, she had come face-to-face with him. And as if she had come a little nearer something she hadn't known: an unknown beauty and danger. She was somehow thrilled by his manner—awed, and proud too, that he was now letting her know him as no one else knew him. And yet, for all that, it was little more than an intimation of the mystery; only a sense of its being there, an inkling. She let him kiss her, for she couldn't hurt him in that moment. It was a gentle, reverent kiss, and she was touched, but not greatly changed—only a sort of trembling before what might be.

When the others knew about her great chance, that she was to go to the University of Chicago, Virgil was the only one who seemed to have reservations in his gladness for her. He was fearing where it might take her, and troubled by his own divided feeling. He wanted, she knew, to be wholly glad, as Rosie, Austin and Helen were, but his pleasure was shadowed by this fear of how far she might go from him. She was sorry he was divided, not as he would be, for they were so close anything not happy for one of them was shared by the others.

He wanted to talk of the future: not hers in the University, but their future together. He was going to study law ("In your study of the law do not forget justice," their teacher had smilingly said) so it would be a long time, quite aside from her going to the University, and she told him this the night before he left, when he urged they be engaged before they parted. "It won't be so hard to be apart," he said, "if I know that after these few years we are going to be together all the rest of our lives." "But I am going to be a teacher," she said, and he had replied, vaguely, that that would all work out some way.

She didn't want to say, but that is what I care about most. "I am counting on you, Norma," their teacher had said. He had looked at her gently and profoundly, and as if there were more he wanted to say. "I like to think of it," was all he had said.

Now he was gone, and she wanted to do for others what he had done for them. So how could she leave it to "work out some way"? She could not imagine her life outside this stream: full strong stream into which she had been taken. It was what the very devout felt in being called to the church. She was as consecrated as that.

But that last night, really sorry to say goodbye to Virgil, and not wanting him to go away unhappy, had she said more than she meant? She didn't say yes, but she hadn't said no; she'd said something like we'll see. And when he said he thought he could come to see her late in the summer, before she went to Chicago, she said how nice that would be, and he seemed very happy about this. Too happy. She hadn't meant it to mean so much.

Wanting to stop thinking about it now, she took from her grip her little volume of Plato; in a moment of realizing she was really leaving, she had slipped it in there. She would read a little in it as she journeyed, thus what she was leaving would attend her on her way. For here, too, was a meeting of minds, a wrestling with thought, an engaging of all one's powers in struggle for the truth. One's powers must increase!—so high an energy demanded for thought. Energy engendered again, and ever again—always freshly. The truth was not something won and held—a thing accomplished, fixed, passed on. We were on our way. We did not rest in what we knew; no, constantly won or forever lost. Not a graveyard— an arena.

As she turned pages of her little volume, reading marked passages, she thought how long ago these golden words were written, living now in this moment, as she, Norma Ashe, rode on a rumbling train through the wheat-fields of South Dakota. In that longago Greece they had not known about South Dakota, but had they suspected there might be a living mind—centuries hence—to meet their minds? The great companionship . . . bridging the centuries. These words not only made alive that long-ago hour they were spoken, they made more alive this moment (bending of the wheat in the breeze, white clouds racing gaily). Thought—and the word that conveyed it from one to another: soul of the world.

The young man who was sitting across the aisle from her, two seats ahead, suddenly turned as if she had spoken. He kept looking at her, as if bewildered. He appeared unembarrassed by his own staring, and somehow it didn't seem rude. Then he turned away again, as if not knowing what to do.

She had wondered about him. He would sit for a time utterly still: hands clasped, head bent. Then spring up, in that same abrupt way he had turned and looked at her, walk to the front of the car and stand there looking through the door. Once the conductor came in and spoke to him, but he didn't seem to want to talk.

The train had stopped. She looked out but could see no station, only a shed and a couple of excited men there. The young man across the aisle was looking from the window on his side, then crossed to look from her side of the car, opening a window to peer ahead.

Two of the passengers went outside and one of these men came back with the news. "There's a wreck ahead. We can't get through."

The young man turned swiftly upon him. "What?" he asked sharply. "What did you say?" And when the news was repeated he demanded quite wildly: "Well, what will they do? What are they going to do about it?" The man said like as not they'd back up and send them around the other way. "*What* way?" he asked roughly.

His glance fell upon Norma. He kept looking at her—why, it seemed *savagely*. Though that was ridiculous. What had she to do with it? "Do they think they can move us around like a lot of cattle?" he demanded of her.

She only shook her head. What was the use of talking to anyone so unreasonable? Did he think *she* was pleased with the wreck? Well, she wasn't. Back up—back toward school. The main line, the way East, was almost as far back as the place she had left.

Everyone was crowding out to hear about the wreck. She thought she would go too, put on the jacket of her pongee suit, pushing down the full sleeves of her shirtwaist, but as she was about to rise this young man came and stood by the seat, blocking her way. "What will I do?" he asked her, helplessly, and sat down facing her, the seat the conductor had turned back to give plenty of room for her things.

"It will delay us," she said; then drew in her breath: that quick look from his dark eyes was as if accusing her of something; as if she had done something to him and he *hated* her.

But no sooner had she thought this than he was different. He seemed looking at something that tortured him. "*Horrible,*" he murmured.

He bewildered her. "You think people were hurt in the wreck?" she ventured.

"I don't care whether they were or not!" he retorted, and she drew back, she had never heard anyone speak just like that.

But he had been hurt—somehow; she asked gently: "What is the matter?"

He didn't say anything at first. Then, "I'm not travelling alone," he said.

"I didn't see anyone with you," was all she could think of to say.

"No," he said, turned and looked from the window, hand shielding his face, as if the better to see out, or as if not wanting her to see his face. When he turned back he said, "You'll never see her. No one will ever . . ." He seemed stopped by his words, realization of what they meant. "She's up there ahead. In the baggage-car. In a box. My mother."

"O—h," she said, lingering over it, for it had so much sympathy to carry.

"But that isn't it," he went on, in a rush. "It isn't just *now.* That wouldn't be so bad, maybe, not for her. Anyway, she doesn't know. But she *did* know—before."

"Before?" she repeated, at a loss.

"She's been shut up in a box for *five years*. Waiting for me to get money to come and get her out! *God*, it's rotten! The whole damn world's rotten!"

"No!" she said, almost involuntarily; she couldn't let that pass, even for one who was hurt.

He looked her over: her nice suit for travelling. It was almost insulting the way he looked from her suit to her shoes and up to her little brown hat. And it wasn't at all polite the way he laughed as he said: "I'd say you don't know much about it, young lady."

But she did know! She certainly did! "You're hurt and angry," she said, "but that doesn't make it a rotten world." Her faith had been attacked, she had to speak. Life had come from far—by courage and faith; life was beautiful and brave.

"Don't stop talking to me," he said, as she was with her own thoughts. "I can't be alone."

She smiled at him to reassure.

"I am the one ought to be shut up in a box!"

"But you aren't," she said. "You are alive, and so you have to live your life."

"Why?" he demanded.

"Oh—you know why. That's something we know, no matter what we say."

"That's just talk," he said, and it would have seemed very rude, and she would have turned away from him, if he weren't a tortured human being needing one of his fellows.

"I lost my mother too," she said. "When I was fourteen."

"But that was different," he said quickly. "Because you were good to her, I mean."

She thought, and was troubled. "I don't know whether I was or not. I was . . . careless about her. I'm afraid I just took her for granted. I didn't know, until after she died, how much she did for me, or how much I cared for her." She thought I wish I could remember telling her I loved her. Why, I *must* have, she thought, but couldn't remember.

"I didn't know it was going to be so long," he went on, somewhat as if talking to himself, yet looking at her as if to hold her, as if she mustn't get away from him, even in her thoughts. "We were poor. *Damn* being poor!" he burst out angrily. Then, "What's the matter?" he asked.

"I guess I'm just not used to people swearing."

"Well you'll have to get used to it with me!"

Then: "What? *What* did I say?" he asked, and seemed honestly bewildered.

She had barely left school, and already she was in a different world: violent, angry, tormented world. There had been a wreck. Things were happening all around her. And this young man, unlike anyone she had ever known. Why, I don't even know his name, she thought.

"I'm sorry," he said. But immediately demanded: "How can you talk if you don't say what you mean? Do you want me to say My! What a beautiful world it is?"

"Not if you don't think so," she smiled. "And of course you aren't feeling that way now." There has to be something underneath, she thought. Something we don't lose even when we are hurt. But how could she say this to him? He might throw it right back in her face. She didn't know how to talk with him. She had been used to talking with people who felt much as she did.

"It's true," he said, and it was all the time as if he were trying to catch hold of her, not let her get away into her own thoughts. "Being poor *does* make a rotten world. You can't do the things you want to, kind things you'd like to do. You think you will later on. And then you—sort of forget about it; so busy trying not to be poor."

He had said it bitterly and she had to answer it. "The poor are very kind to one another," she said, and then flushed: it sounded prim and she knew he would be right back at her.

"Which Sunday-school did you go to?" he taunted; then in his quick way leaned forward and put out his hand as if about to take hold of her. "You won't stop talking to me, will you? You won't, will you," he repeated anxiously, "no matter what I say?"

"No," she said, and was immediately startled by her promise. It was as if she were promising not to go away from him.

The conductor came through the car and stopped to speak to him. "Awful sorry about this, Mr. Utterbach." (Utterbach. So that was his name.)

When they got back to the junction his mother's coffin was taken from the baggage-car and carried into the station. She was standing by him and heard his tortured "*Christ,*" when they swung it down and one man almost lost his hold. "I couldn't even do this for her," he said, turning angrily upon Norma. "Moved all over the godforsaken country! Jostled around by hoodlums!"

It wasn't godforsaken country; they weren't hoodlums; it wasn't his fault there had been a wreck. But how could she say any reasonable thing to this young man? What could she say to him— and why was she with him at all?

Because it seemed he had to be with her. When they got off the train he had taken her arm, saying: "This way," and as if there were no question about it hurried her with him to the baggage-car.

The other passengers were going to a restaurant up the street. Now the conductor came up to the boy and girl. "Better get something to eat," he said kindly. "It'll be three hours to wait." As the young man (Utterbach—what a strange name) didn't speak, "Everything will be all right here," the conductor assured him. "The station won't be left alone," he added, as if he understood.

"It would be better for you to get something," she agreed.

He shook his head. "You go," he said. "That is—if you want to." His eyes seemed asking her not to go.

Then she remembered Mrs. Moss had put up a lunch for her.

"Never can tell what will happen on those trains," she'd said—and how true that was! "I have some sandwiches," she told them, and the conductor said he would have coffee sent over from the restaurant.

They sat on a bench outside the baggage-room. This was late June and the day was warm but there was a fresh breeze. The station was almost at the outskirts of the little town and she could see a long way across the country—"the godforsaken country." How wildly, unreasonably, he talked, this young man beside her who was now absent-mindedly eating a roast-beef sandwich. Something was very wrong with him—more than the death of his mother. Something more like guilt than grief was making him hate the world. She wondered how she would like him at a party, say, when nothing like this had happened. Perhaps he would even be fun, though that was hard to imagine now. She liked the quick way he moved, the abrupt swift changes, his concentration, fire. This made him very alive, but that aliveness was on the wrong side: damning the world and wishing people harm.

It was early afternoon. She tried, by the sun, to get her directions straight, that she might look, as accurately as possible, toward Pioneer (when they'd named it did they know how right the name was going to be?). She was so near she could actually walk back: not more than ten miles. Her journey hadn't been at all as she'd expected; she would be very late getting home—good thing she'd been able to send the wire, so they wouldn't worry. But it wasn't only the delay. There had been so much of the unforeseen. Her feeling about leaving school had been interrupted, as her journey was. She had been sad about leaving, but her feeling was strong, and in a serious way happy: setting forth to do her part. . . . Then a wreck—people hurt, and they had gone back, until she was close to the place she had left. Close to it, but farther away. If she went back now it would be different, and not only because the others had gone.

She thought of the books they had dusted, waiting there so serenely, as in calm confidence: what man had thought, aspired to be. Back there was a world she knew: dear familiar place that had been good to her, where she was valued and loved. It had been like leaving home, or a convent, and going out into the world. She had known life would be different in the world, but hadn't known it would be different so soon, so rudely. Her teacher was buried back there, and as she unfolded a little packet of salt for her egg she felt resentful toward this young man who was so abruptly making things different. One should have acceptance; from the very hardest things of life was something to be won. She knew this to be true, they had come to know it when they lost their teacher. What would he—their teacher—say to this young man? He had wisdom; he would understand and know what to say. She felt very young, and not as confident as she had an hour or two before. Perhaps it was very silly her staying here with him at all. "But, Norma, you didn't even *know* him," Aunt Nettie would say, and she could smile a little at this: her aunt would say it so firmly, and it left so much out.

There seemed to be a great joke in the baggage-room, a sort of brawling laughter burst from there. Her companion sprang up, tipping over the cover of the lunch box he had been using as plate. "Why the *louts*," he said furiously.

"They're just having fun," she said hastily, fearing he would go in there and make a fuss.

"*Fun?* Is it any place—" Then he sank down. "I suppose so," he said. "I can't expect *them* to care. Why should I expect anybody to care?"

"I care," she said.

He turned and looked at her. "I just don't know what I would do if you didn't," he said, and his voice . . .

So he wasn't all anger and hate—this stranger she seemed to have linked herself with.

He continued to look at her, and even when she flushed and her own gaze wavered, his eyes were still holding her. Something she had never felt before in her life—not for Virgil, for no one—she felt now in response to his nearness.

She moved a little away from this sense of nearness, but as if bringing her back he reached out and touched her hand. They sat just so for a moment: his hand on hers. She was perplexed by what she felt. Other hands had touched her hand . . .

"Listen," he said, in low urgent voice. "I don't want you to think I'm just a boy crying because his mother is dead. That's not very nice—your mother. But what I can't stand is something else. It's . . ."

CHAPTER EIGHT

*W*HEN she looked back on it she was always a little breathless in sense of how swiftly it had moved; like those swift movements of his: a tempo that is set. As if she were on an imperious river—carried along. She would try to see where she was caught into this surge, taken.

There had been the wreck; going around the other way (not the way it had been meant she go). Talking at the junction as they ate the lunch her good landlady at school had put up for her because you never can tell what may happen on those trains. . . . His torrent of words—his mother in her coffin in the room just behind them.

"She'd worked to put me through school," he told her. "She did anything—cooked for people and cleaned for them. I got what jobs I could, but I couldn't have made it without her. The great idea was my education, my start. She was so cheerful about it; brave." He puckered his brows. (How heavy his eyebrows were: thick and dark.) A moment he closed his eyes and shook his head—just a little, but very definitely. "Though it didn't seem brave. She was too good to want to seem brave. Just did it. As if it made her happy.

"She finished her job; and then . . . couldn't do any more. Health gone. I can see now she went on long after she should. A long rest, the doctor said. But you see she didn't want to be a burden on me, just getting my start. Now I can look into her mind. I can see now just what went on in her mind.

"She said she'd like to go up and stay with her sister. And I thought—well, all right, for a little while. Then *I* could take care of *her*."

He had a crust of bread in his hand and savagely threw it away. "Well, I didn't. Time went on and I didn't send for her. Though I could have; we could have managed. I'd send a little money to pay her way with her sister, help a little. But I know now I didn't send enough. My aunt didn't hesitate to tell me that—just day before yesterday she told me. And I can see they made my mother feel she was a burden. *My mother* . . . a burden."

He turned fiercely on Norma. "Don't try to tell me she didn't go through hell!

"And I didn't go up there." (Was he going to cry?) "Oh, I *meant* to," he laughed harshly. "I'd *think* about it—if that does anybody any good! But always put it off; wait till you have a home to bring her back to, I'd think. Left her there in a godforsaken place where she wasn't wanted!"

He was so unhappy Norma tried to think of something that might help. "Perhaps you really didn't have enough money to—to manage it," she said.

"I did too have the money!" he retorted rudely. "I was spending more than I needed on myself, thinking I had to keep up an appearance for business, making that excuse to myself. I'm in the real-estate business,"—his manner changed for a moment, he told her this in more usual way. "With Saunders and Saunders—Des Moines. It's going pretty well. I think I can make money." He said this with some zest, but immediately he was back at himself again. "And what good will it do me? Do you think if I had a million dollars (and I *might* have a million dollars), do you think I could ever forget?"

He was looking at her—demandingly. There was something so insistent in his eyes it made her uncomfortable, a little resentful, and she had nothing to say.

"Can I ever forget my drinking with the fellows?" he went on, as if accusing her as well as him. "Going out with the girls, spending money on— Yes!" he broke in upon himself, "and running off to Florida—hero stuff—thinking *that* was so smart—while all the time my mother, alone and sick, shoved into a little back room that didn't look out on anything but the privy and the hen-house!"

He turned away. "*God,*" she heard cursed under his breath.

He turned back to her. "And then you try to tell me it isn't a rotten world!"

"Perhaps you didn't do it right," she said. "Perhaps you were thoughtless and selfish. But that doesn't give you the right to speak for all the rest of the world. I know something about the world too, the goodness and courage. And so do you! For you knew your mother. Was it a rotten world *she* made?"

"And look how she was treated!"

"By you. Blame yourself, if you think you should, but don't get out of it by throwing it back on the world. The world is where *she* was, as well as where you are."

He seemed more surprised than anything else. He laughed a little as he said: "You aren't very consoling, are you?"

"Consoling? Oh, but you want more than that, don't you? You want to get it straight, don't you?"

"I suppose so," he said rather sullenly.

"All this damning of the world is just another way of getting *out* of it. Your leaving the truth of it behind the way you left your mother behind. Oh, I'm sorry," she said quickly. "That wasn't very nice, was it?"

"Not very," he said.

As he considered it he grew angry. "I don't know why you think you can talk to me like that!"

"If it's a rotten world, why isn't it *your* fault? Your mother did her part. What have you ever done to make it a better world?"

"I never thought anything about it," he said. "And you needn't jump on me like that! At—at this time."

This honestly surprised her; to her any time was the right time to see as far as one could. But . . .

"I see what you mean," she said.

As he did not speak she went on, a little timidly: "But isn't there another way to look at it? You're feeling something—perhaps for the first time in your life. You've been shut in with your little ambitions, your own selfish—"

"Look! Is that any way for a girl to talk to a fellow? And *you*. To look at you, a person would think you were kind." He laughed.

"I think I'll go over to the restaurant and get something. You've eaten up all the sandwiches."

"Well don't leave me here. I mean, I'll go with you."

How awful of me, she thought afterwards. Talking like that to a stranger. But something she held high and very dear was violated in that damning of the world, people who did nothing to make life better cursing it for not being better. And it had come to her so soon, right after she left the place where life was good and hopes were high.

In the restaurant she saw a man who lived in her college town: Mr. Jenks, the blacksmith. "Oh, how do you *do?*" she cried, and he seemed surprised by the warmth of her greeting. He would have been more surprised had he known she wanted to say, I'll go back with you!

"I guess I was hungry," she said, eating a good plate of stew. He said he was too; "Even if I did eat all the sandwiches.

"You know," he said, cocking his head around toward her, teasingly, "I don't believe that—me and the sandwiches. You just made it up."

"I did not make it up!"—and perhaps hot food was what they needed, they talked of more usual things, a boy and girl getting acquainted.

When they came to the place where they would go different

ways it seemed they had known each other for some time. But he hadn't seemed to realize this moment would come when she would go one way and he another. "You're *leaving* me?" he cried, after the conductor told her she must get off at the next station for her branch line. She told him she must go home—said it laughingly yet gently; to her too it seemed—well, it seemed strange that they should part. "But what will I do without you?" he went on, in his tumultuous way. "Don't you *see?* With you—I'm all right. Without you . . ."

(Through a good deal of her life that was to go: "With you—I'm all right. What would I do—without you?")

"Listen—" She stopped, laughed a little, though half wanting to cry, absurd though that might be. "I was going to say your name—after I said listen. You know? The way you say, Listen, Jack—or—"

"Listen, Max," he told her in his prompt imperious way.

"Max," she said. "Max. That's nice. I like Max."

"You do?" he asked swiftly. "You like—Max?"

"I meant—the name," she said, looking down, a little coquettish. But she wasn't really coquettish; she raised her eyes to his: honest eyes, so clear and deep now with concern for him; tender eyes, for she did seem to be leaving him alone. "And I like you too, Max."

"Oh—" he breathed; then broke off, laughing as he demanded, "Oh, *what?* Oh, Ann? Mary?"

"Oh, Norma," she told him.

"*Norma.*" He said it as if it were too wonderful to be true. "Oh —*Norma,*"—and that moment was intimacy such as she had never known.

As he was helping her from the train they scarcely spoke, as if some wonderful thing had happened and there were no words.

And then he came shouting after her. "Norma! Norma!"—running away from his train, which was about to pull out. "Quick! This is *awful*. I don't know your last name or where you live!"

His train was starting; laughing, she ran back to it with him, telling her name and where she lived. Waving from the platform he called: "I'll be there! Just as soon as— *Norma!* Can you *hear?* I'm coming for you! I'm—" The rest of it was lost in the whistling and the rumbling, and she was afraid he would fall off—swaying, leaning far out and waving.

A little unsteadily she sat down to wait for her train. Why, what has happened, she thought. Why, I don't *know* him, she thought. Don't know him? She knew him in a way she had never known anyone else. All through her she seemed to be singing. Things around her—men thumping trunks, a child with a banana —weren't quite real.

Back home she'd keep telling herself to be sensible. What is the *matter* with me? she'd think angrily. What had happened, after all? She met someone on the train; he was in trouble and she was sorry for him; he was grieving about his mother and didn't want to be alone, so he clung to her because she happened to be there. But it was hard not to remember his eyes when he knew she would leave him, how they clung to her—incredulous, hurt, imploring. His voice spoke in her mind as if it were now part of her mind; his touch was on her hand, part of her hand. She would tell herself she didn't approve of him, that he really wasn't the kind of person she would like; but find herself dreaming, living it over and over.

She lived in a small town, in a white house with her father, her grandmother and her Aunt Nettie. Her father had a hardware store, which included many things, and he sold most of the supplies to the farmers thereabouts. It was because of her grandmother, or rather her grandmother's husband, Norma's grandfather, she had been sent to Pioneer, instead of one of the colleges in her own state. He was a minister, his parish up there in South Dakota just before Pioneer was founded. He hadn't lived to see the school open, but had worked to bring it about.

"When it is time for Norma to go to college I'd like her to come up here," he had said. "I believe something very good is going to happen up here." How grateful she was to him for that belief! Had she gone elsewhere she would not have known her teacher. How different her life would have been if she hadn't known him. . . . She might have gone through all the years of her life her eyes not opened as now they were open; not awake, as she was awake now. He brought it all to life for her. Now she had a heritage and a vocation. She would work, she would learn and think and feel; the life that was Norma Ashe must be *for* life, and to her utmost she would give herself toward making a great dream come true. Long long years that dream had been in the life of man—in the poets, the philosophers, the great religions. But it did not possess the world. More people must know, and knowing care; so would their kingdom come, what man's life might be on earth. She was not abashed by this feeling, not embarrassed before what she aspired to be. "If only a few are different, then life is different," her teacher had said. "Never think it makes little difference about you because you are but one. If life changes one unseen iota, the balance changes, and where there is change there is the great chance. You—I mean *you* —may inject into life what can reach the blood stream of the race. You have eyes: why not see? You have minds: why not know? And why have you hearts if not to feel? Any one person can make life a little less blind and cruel. Never fear that others are not equal to sharing what it is in you to become. They want to! Man is ready."

The day after her return home she got out her notebooks, all the records of her work with him. She would go through them this summer, amplify from things remembered and not set down here, try to go farther, see meanings that had escaped her; at the same time studying the books he had told her would make her better prepared for her work in the fall. He himself had left life now, but he was living here in his thoughts; and if she could find something he had meant which she had not grasped—that would be being with him all freshly, as of that moment. And if (though this she scarcely dared hope) she could carry some thought farther than he had taken it, then the very life of him was going on after his death.

Her Aunt Nettie laughed indulgently when she came in Norma's room and found her working with these notes, her books around her. "It's vacation, Norma," she said. "You're going back to all that soon enough. These are the days to have a good time."

"I am having a good time," she said.

"Nonsense," her aunt said. "How can you be having a good time all by yourself?"

Her Aunt Nettie couldn't; for her a good time was being with people. "What a lonely day it's been," she would say if friends had not dropped in.

"Bert Lord is home from Iowa City," her aunt went on. "I suppose that will liven things up."

As Norma made no reply, she thought Bert Lord a conceited, empty-headed fellow, Aunt Nettie asked: "What about the boys up there at school?"

Virgil. He'd said he was coming to see her before summer was over. Oh, he mustn't! What could she say to him—now? And what do you mean by *now?* she thought, disturbed and vexed with herself. What was there now to make things any different? Someone she met on the train—how did that make things different?

But something was different; before she hadn't been sure and now she knew she could never care for Virgil. She didn't—feel that way about him. And they had so much in common, had shared—oh, so much. She knew him and liked what he was. But something wasn't there. . . . She never felt different when his hand touched hers. His voice did not live with her when she was not hearing it. His eyes only looked at her when—

"Didn't you like any of them?" her aunt interrupted.

"Of course I did. I liked some of them very much."

"Well—?"

"Well *what*, Aunt Nettie? Do I have to be silly just because I know a few boys?"

Her aunt laughed. "You wait, young lady. Your time will come. Better be silly than an old-maid," she called back as she was leaving the room.

Aunt Nettie was a little silly herself. What an old-fashioned way to talk! Did you have to be an old-maid because you did what you wanted to do with your life? All right then—*be* an old-maid. What of it?

Resolutely she opened her *History of Philosophy*. "Norma," he'd said. Said it as if it breathed from his heart. Max. His name was Max.

Of course she wasn't going to spend the whole summer studying. There were lots of things here at home she liked to do. Bess Ainsley was visiting her cousins in Omaha, but would be home next week; they'd play tennis, go to Carlson's for sodas. Bess had her phaeton and they'd drive out in the country. There'd be church sociables and picnics on the river and parties. She'd play with Elsie's baby, sometimes take care of the baby so her sister could go out. She'd visit old Mrs. Michaels, shut in with her bad hip, such a jolly old lady who liked company. But just now she wanted to stay right *in* this; it fortified her, made her know who she was and what her life was going to be. She would *not*—be interrupted. She was not going to do anything she didn't want to do! All this remembering: just how his mouth would shape a word, how his dark eyes grew even darker, voice that could say more than the word it spoke—she was afraid of all this that had become part of her.

He's forgotten all about it by this time she would tell herself. (Oh, *no*—he couldn't, could he?)

"What are you studying?" her family asked. "German philosophy," she told them. "In *summer?*" her aunt protested. "Why, that's ridiculous!"

No doubt she was a little ridiculous, but she had to be very *sure*, sure that even if he came (of course he wouldn't) it could make no difference.

He arrived the following week. Her grandmother came in where she was studying. "Norma," she said, "there's a young man downstairs to see you."

"One—one of the town boys?" she asked, rather faintly.

"No, he seems to be a stranger. He has a very odd name. It's Utter something. I think it's back—yes, Utterback—though I never heard the name. Your hair is all mussed."

She said all the reasonable things. (What a very little way "reasonable things" go at times.) She said they scarcely knew each other, wouldn't have known each other at all if it hadn't been for the wreck. It just happened and wasn't really a part of their lives. He *could* get along without her; if he'd never met her wouldn't he be getting along without her? He just thought that *now*. We all had to learn we couldn't have everything we wanted—and after a time we didn't want it anyway! And she had her own life—oh, yes, indeed she did! She knew just what she was going to do. That was her *whole* life; anything else would be just a little part of it. She was committed. If she had taken her vows in the church would he expect her to turn aside?

"Lord, *yes,*" he replied. "I'd fight the church or anything else on God's earth for you. Norma! Can't you see there is nothing we can do about it?"

Well there certainly was, she'd said. She had her plans all made. In the fall she was going to the University of Chicago. She was going to be a teacher.

"Norma! *You*—a teacher."

And what was the matter with that, she'd demanded furiously.

Why be so furious about it? Why couldn't she just calmly say no? She didn't *have* to—marry this man. Nobody could *make* her. And what was she *crying* about for heaven's sake?

"Norma"—a caress, the way he said her name. "Don't fight it so. Don't fight, Norma. Something happened between you and me. I know that. Don't you know it? What's wrong about it? Why does it make you angry? I know I'm not worth you, and you saw me in a terrible way—so weak I must have seemed. But it's all different now. Don't you see how everything is different? With you I can do anything! Will you honestly answer one question?"

"No! No, I don't think I will! I don't have to answer questions!"

"Do you love me, Norma?"

"That would be ridiculous. I don't know you. I've only just met you."

"And we were never introduced. Is it polite not to answer a question? Do you love me, Norma?"

"I could," she said slowly. "But I can't," she quickly added.

"Why?"

She wondered if she could make him see why. Were there words for it? Oh, there would be words in a moment that was calm. But now? When it was other things she was feeling—things that had taken her unawares? *This* she hadn't known—what nearness could do; the way he spoke her name and looked at her seemed to make her his, as if she had let him do all the things she'd not let him do: hold her to him, hold her in his arms and kiss her. She was afraid he would hear her heart-beats and know all she felt which she didn't understand and told herself she didn't want to feel. Was it a *trap?* she thought angrily, when the touch of his hand, ardor of his eyes, made her think of being in his arms?

They had gone for a walk. She couldn't very well sit there with him in the parlor, all the things she was used to, everything just as it should be in the parlor: family album on the center-table, picture

of Elsie's baby in the little easel, on the walls those solemn pictures—her grandfather, Uncle John.

He didn't want to stay there either. "Last time we saw each
other we took a walk. Shall we take another?"—so eagerly, and
yet something a little bashful about him now, and that was too
bad: it made him nicer.

"Is that one of the boys from school?" Aunt Nettie had asked
when she went up for her hat. "I met him up there," she evaded.
"He didn't let the grass grow under his feet," Aunt Nettie said
triumphantly.

No, not a young man to let grass grow under his feet. . . .

It wasn't a very nice day, and what a good thing *that* was!
It was heavy, rather stuffy, and there were mosquitoes. Some days
made you too happy. This wasn't a time to be any happier than you
could help. He linked his arm in hers as they walked along. She
felt him so close to her, all through her knowing he was close. He
would almost come to a halt, looking at her, then hurry along, as
if hurrying her somewhere.

They just followed that street and it became a country road.
She had known well enough it would. Why hadn't she proposed
going downtown? But then people would be wondering who he
was—a stranger in town—ask questions. That was the reason, she
told herself. And if they asked who he was what in the world
would she say? For that matter what was she going to say to the
folks at home? "I met him on the train." That would sound *nice*—
for a girl like her. What kind of girl did he think she was? she
said to herself, working up indignation against him—for, oh, she
was *happy*, and that was ridiculous and all wrong. Where was she
going, anyway?

She was going with him. Going along with him. And he was
talking to her. He was telling her it had never been like this with
any other girl. So earnestly—with wonder—he said it. He had
been thinking of her every minute since she left him. He'd remem-

ber just how her hair waved round her ears, how her chin went up when she called him down. If he'd had to go another day without looking into her eyes—"I would have died," he said, so solemnly they both laughed.

He turned off the road into Cutter's lane—so she did too, she going where he went. "Why, what a nice tree," he said, for it had fallen and made a seat. On this seat sat Norma Ashe and Max Utterbach, two people who had happened to meet. Off in the meadow were Mr. Cutter's cows, some of them lying down, two of them switching flies with their tails and at the same time lazily nipping clover.

A breathless day. Was the world really holding its breath? What was waiting in this silence, broken only by the rather perfunctory barking of the Cutter dog, outcry of a crow that seemed displeased about something. He had asked her a question, and she was going to tell him why she couldn't go along with him through life, as she had gone with him from her home to this lane. No matter what you feel in this moment—be true! Be true to the best you have known in your life. She waited, trying to see her teacher's face. Max waited. It all seemed breathless as the day.

CHAPTER NINE

*I*F YOU were trying to make real sunrise on a mountaintop to one who had never seen a sunrise or a mountain, you would halt in your words, feel inadequate, helpless. I am making it less, you would feel; belittling. Perhaps I should not speak of it at all. And thus Norma Ashe would halt at first, feeling inadequate. Yet no . . . we could communicate; and that was a miracle great as the sunrise. It lighted, transformed, as the sunrise. Hope of a better world was in man's power to communicate. But you must speak from the truth and not about it. She almost prayed to the great vision to be there now, itself speaking. She was trying to speak for life that waited: the dream we could make come true. "Into your hands it has been committed." The time was at hand; only the awareness was lacking: awareness that we could make life what we would have it be.

And it was not easy in this moment for his nearness was there too: sense of his nearness all through her. If light of the vision would not transfigure her words what unreal and pretentious words they would seem: she wanted to study; come into knowledge. The past bequeathed us and the future ours to shape. That we must know all we could of life and each day see it as if we had never seen it before: freshly, a miracle. Man was on his way, and had only begun. How she had a great teacher who had initiated her into this, and now it was for her to prepare herself and to the measure she could do for others what he had done for her.

All of this, not coming from the very heart of its truth, would sound like an earnest but pretty exalted girl. "Exaltation without knowledge is a dangerous thing," their teacher had said. "The dream must be as strong as the mind of man. The mind of man must become more, and ever more, to be worthy the dream." And she had gone such a little way. Small and unworthy she felt now, trying to speak for what life might be had we the knowledge and the faith and the daring. Were we *aware* . . . no door closed to awareness of what waited to come into the life of man.

She would halt as she spoke, but in trying to look upon it the light on her face was from that toward which she looked and his eyes did not leave her face.

"Something happened. We were taken. Oh, I know that to be true. All the words for it have been used for lesser things. We use great words for little things, belittling them. So perhaps we shouldn't try to speak of it at all."

"No. Yes, I mean, speak of it," and his tone was tender, as if he wanted to go with her.

It released something for her; her feeling for him was not fighting her, and she could tell him a little of what that wonder had been, how she had dedicated her life to what might come to be. "Why is the dream there if it could not be made real? Where did the dream come from? Always the dream has been ahead. The dream is what some Great Will wants us to make come true. I want to be closer to all the great brave men of the past. I want to know them and let them live in me and, if I am good enough, speak through me. Great voices need not be silenced by death. Thus we conquer death—for life."

"Yes," he said, with an emotion that made her remember he had just felt death. As she looked into his eyes she put her hand on his, not with motive for herself, but to take him with her—from hurt to himself into this wonder of life that waited.

He raised her hand to his lips, and the gentle touch of his lips on her hand was not for possessing, but in tribute to something he felt in her.

"Tell me more," he said, after they had been silent a moment.

"Our teacher," she said slowly, "he seemed able to do a wonderful thing. He was able to take us—where he had been. Ahead of our own experience, he could—project us. There were five of us," she told him.

"And something in him—he had to do this. What he could do for us was the most important thing in the world to him. It was as if—why, I never thought of this before, but as if he were racing against death. And life was to win! Through us."

Again she was silent, thinking of their teacher: that feeling in him that was life itself working, the deep and imperative necessity.

"Your face is so beautiful," he said softly. "I'll never forget your face as I see it this moment."

His words made her happy; then troubled. Had she failed? Was he thinking of just her?

"Do you know what I mean, Max?" Almost timidly she asked, "Do you feel truth, if not in what I say, somewhere near?"

"This is all new to me," he told her. "You mustn't expect me to understand all at once. But if ever I felt truth I feel it in you now."

"Oh, Max!" she cried. "Max!" She hadn't known he would understand: understand why they must part. It made her love him—freely now, now that he understood.

He felt this love in her, and his arms went round her, his cheek against hers. He kissed her. "I love you for all that you are," he said. "My wonderful Norma! Beautiful Norma Ashe," he murmured. "I'll love you as long as I live." His voice was low and strong. Passionate, tender and reverent. There was a long moment of no words. Communion: now that she needn't fight, now that what she felt she could feel with him.

She didn't want to speak of it any more that day, she didn't need to now. But he seemed to want to call it to life in her, watch her face in wonder and touch her in adoration. And so she would talk for him, though now it was because he wanted her to, rather than herself speaking because she had to. Perhaps, though not knowing this to be true, she wanted not to lose that wonder and adoration in his eyes as she talked of those moments when it seemed a veil had parted and she had looked through. "He thinks," she said of her teacher, "that it could so easily come, here in this new country. The soil itself was so recently virgin. Here men are not going old ways. Here in this western America they have only begun to make new ways. It is not all shut-in—fixed. That leaves openings, you see."

"I suppose so," he said, looking perplexed. "It sounds a little like business opportunities," he added; then seemed concerned, as if fearing he had hurt what was between them.

But she laughed, and it was more just a boy and a girl, so that he laughed too, quite loudly, then seemed a little abashed by his loud laugh.

"Now Max, you know I wasn't talking about business opportunities. Though they're all right too."

"They have their place," he said, smiling at her sidewise, mischievously.

"Sometimes life—makes a leap," she said. "In this new country perhaps . . . Think of it! We may be just on the *brink* of this great forward thrust!" She was captured by what she had said. It was from herself now.

As she paused, "I don't know what you mean," he said. Then, anxiously: "You don't want me to pretend, do you?"

"Oh no—no," she said hastily, and fervently. "Not that. Never that—between us."

She flushed at what she had so impetuously said. He agreed softly: "No—never that, between us."

Hastily she went on talking, to get past this: beautiful and dangerous, almost as if she had said their lives were going to be together. "It's a biological term—the leap. Did you study biology, Max?"

"Not enough to know much about it," he said ruefully.

"That's just the trouble with me! I don't *know* enough. I just know *about* a good many things. And that won't do. To understand you must have knowledge. That's what I mean about the University, Max," she said, stoutly yet with wistfulness, for it was the University was going to part them. "Why, my whole lifetime is so short a time for all I must know. Even then so much will be left out. Our lives should be longer," she said.

"They're long enough for a good deal of happiness," he told her, smiling tenderly.

"Perhaps we think too much about happiness. It takes the place of too many other things," she went on, trying to run away from happiness. "Though *that* is happiness too: understanding all we can while we are on earth. And leaving life—perhaps leaving it a little more than we found it."

The face she turned to him had such beauty of conflicting emotions. "I am sure you will do that, Norma—whichever way.

"I still don't understand about the leap," he said, to keep her from saying that for her there could be only one way.

She frowned. "I wish my teacher were telling you instead of me."

"I don't."

"Oh, yes. He would—capture you."

"I'm captured already," he assured her.

She smiled but said, "I have so much to learn. I want to teach and—"

"I am your first pupil," he told her.

"Max," she asked, "do I seem righteous and conceited and horrible to you?"

"I am a person," he replied in his quick way, "who when asked a simple question will willingly and honestly answer. I think that is polite, and only right. Norma—Miss Ashe—you do not seem righteous and conceited and horrible to me."

"About the leap," she went on, knowing he was going on to tell her what she did seem to him. "It has happened with plants, and with primitive forms of animal life too. There's the long slow process that is the history of life on earth. And then there are the rare times when a form of life *does* make a leap, skips the in-between and is a form of life a long way ahead. As if . . . as if the design of what was to be was there in that existing form of life, and an urge to realize it without the long waiting. It's an achievement of life that is like a miracle. But it's *in!* It's in the stream of life, don't you see? It *has* happened, so it can happen again. The design is there in us—waiting. We could— Oh!" she broke off. She turned to him and like a solemn little girl she said, "I just thought of something."

"What did you think of, Norma?"

"You don't see an unborn child, do you? You don't *see* it." Her face flushed but she'd said it steadily. Her eyes were big with marvel, marvelling at what you do not see.

He held her hand close, thinking his own thoughts. . . .

"But the unborn child is really there," he said gently. "A reality, I mean."

"And so is— Don't you *see,* Max? *There.* Waiting to come to birth. . . ."

She sat very still, as if indeed waiting. . . .

"I like it," he said at last, "because it makes you so beautiful. But darling—" It stopped everything: his words, her thoughts. "Darling" he had said.

"Did you hear what I said?" he asked softly.

She answered tremulously: "Yes; but you—shouldn't."

"Yes, darling, I should. Because that's the way it is between you and me." And then, as if to forestall: "But what you were just saying, Norma. Why does it mean so much to you?"

With a beautiful simplicity she answered: "I suppose because I feel it there in me."

"You feel—?" he asked uncertainly (she was so beautiful—so lovely and wonderful; so *good*. All his life he would cherish her!).

"The design that waits. What we are one day going to be. One day . . . If one day—why not now? If a flower, a worm, can break through its form—anticipate—realize—then why not the mind of man? We've heard so much about the long slow process—"

"I haven't," he said.

"Now Max, you *have*," she laughed. "That's just what we do hear: that life can't be changed, can't be hurried. The long slow process, and sometimes going back, going wrong. This is inevitable, we are told. But that's not true! There's the miracle too: the casting off and the coming to birth."

He considered it and laughed, "You'd find people wouldn't like it. They like it the way they are."

"Poor? Do they like it poor? Did you like it, Max, the way it was for your mother?

"Oh, I shouldn't have said that," she said, seeing his face and remembering the coffin carried from the baggage-car. "I'm sorry, Max. I get so excited. Forgive me."

She had put out her hand and he took it and held it. "No," he said slowly, "I didn't like the way things were for my mother. And you know I'll never forget it."

I'm afraid you never will, she thought. He held her hand hard, his face was taut.

"But all you do about it is hate," she said gently. "Hate only makes the world—go back."

"And how could I—*me*—sort of dumb and not any too good— make the world any better? I won't hate now, not that same way, now that I have you; but I don't for the life of me see how I could make the world any different."

"Everyone makes it different—one way or the other. It's the idea it can't be different that is keeping it from being so. That's all that is standing in the way: an idea; a wrong idea. If a wrong idea has that much power—what couldn't the right idea do?"

"And what would that right idea be, Norma?"

"That we *can* change life. Can make it what we want it to be!"

He brushed a mosquito from her face. They both laughed a little at the interrupting mosquito.

"You spoke of people being poor. Are you a socialist, Norma? Something like that? You want it all to be evened up so nobody will be rich and nobody poor?"

"That isn't enough to want. We must want so much more than that."

"Well—gee, I don't know," he laughed. "Seems to me that's a good deal. Most people think it's so much it's crazy. And you want more than that?"

"Differently. I want differently. If I had five dollars and you had five dollars, couldn't we still hate each other?"

"Not on my side," he said. "Leave me out of this hating game."

"Yes: leave hate behind . . . Max! Do you know what you said? You said: *Make a new world!*" She sat there trying to see it: the world that had left hate behind. "I wish my teacher were here."

"I'm not missing him at all," said Max; and then, remembering what this teacher meant to her, he smiled as to say, You do understand?

He has the nicest smile, she thought; then frowned. Here she was trying to think something out, and stopping to think about Max's smile. But there never had been a smile just like it, smile that could say so many things: teasing, tender. He could speak through his smile.

"Why, what was that?" she said, looking down at her hand.

"I was hit too," said Max, "on the head."

"Goodness," she cried, looking up at the dark clouds, "sitting here and letting it rain!" They had to scamper for it and reached home wet, laughing and breathless.

"Now isn't this awful," Aunt Nettie said, following Norma up when she went to change her dress. "Here your young man has come to see you, but I didn't know he was going to stay and we've nothing for supper but codfish-cakes."

"He won't care," laughed Norma, but Aunt Nettie threw a raincoat over her head and went next door, coming back with a chicken all cut up for frying. "I knew Mrs. Sands had it, so I told her it was an emergency and got it away from her. It's all right—I gave her the fish-cakes and I'll get her another chicken tomorrow."

She was glad she had to change; now she could put on her pink gingham. Max would like her in the pink gingham, she thought in happy excitement.

All the family seemed to take to Max. You can't help it, thought Norma; and that's just the trouble. He told her father things about himself she hadn't known; but for that matter, what *had* she known about him? "Then I went to war," he said. "You *did*, Max?" she cried; could have bitten her tongue out! Her grandmother and aunt were looking at her in surprise: her not having known Max went to war. They'd be more surprised, she thought, if they knew all I don't know. (Of course—Florida. He did speak of running off to Florida.) Was it dangerous, the war, her grandmother was asking solicitously.

"Well—yes," he said. "The mosquitoes attacked us without mercy. We were wounded time and again and suffered horribly." "But what did the Spaniards do?" her grandmother pursued. It seems they had never seen a Spaniard. "They just kept us in a Florida swamp."

"And what good could you do there?" Aunt Nettie asked.

"We used to spend hours wondering about that," he said, and her father laughed loudly and seemed to be having a good time with Max.

He had to go back to Des Moines on the ten-o'clock train. It was fresh after the shower and she and Max sat out on the porch. They were quiet as the time drew near for him to leave. "I'm coming back, you know," he said.

"Max, I don't think you should." She had to say it because—oh, she wanted him to so much.

"I'll never give you up, Norma," he said, so quietly there seemed no answer to it.

She *must* answer. "But you do understand—"

"I understand that I love you. And I believe, way in your heart —you love me." He looked at her and there was no denial in what he saw.

"All those other things—it will arrange itself. It's *got* to, for when two people love each other—*well*, for heaven's sake, what is more important than *that?*"

She couldn't think—at the moment. Her hand was in his and she was happy and seemed part of the fresh gentle night, smell of the earth after the rain.

When they stood up for him to leave he said, "Will you remember that I am your first pupil? Your first pupil needs you. Would it make the world any better for me to be cast into outer darkness?"

"Oh, Max," she laughed, "you wouldn't be cast into outer darkness."

"Norma," he said, so earnestly, "outer darkness is just where I would be. Though it wouldn't make much difference—for I couldn't live."

"Now that really is *silly*."

"I mean it and I say it. You are the light to me now. You are my life and all my hopes."

"Max—Max—what have I done!" She buried her face against him and she was weeping.

"Yes—cry," he whispered. "I want you to cry."

She lifted tearful surprised face. "You *want* me to cry?"

"Would you cry—if you didn't care?"

She walked with him to the gate and stood watching him down the street. From quite a little distance he turned and called, "I'll be back!"—a confident and a joyous cry.

CHAPTER TEN

*N*EXT MORNING she told herself she must get right to work, go ahead as though her work started that very day; and indeed it did, she had a schedule to follow.

But she had never found it so hard to study. Her mind would slip away from her . . . sense of his nearness there as a presence.

All her family liked Max and wanted to talk about him. Such a nice young man, they said. So pleasant and bright; so easy to know. (Quite true!) Probably they wouldn't care much if she didn't go to the University at all! They had been pleased when she wrote them about it, proud that she had been chosen, but of course nothing in the world was as important as having a nice young man come to see you, getting married, perhaps.

She knew better! She knew what her life was going to be. But she hadn't made this clear to Max. Looking back she could see she had done it all wrong; in trying to show him why they must part —how close they had come. It was as if her feeling became a part of their love. That was not my intention, she told herself now. She had let him kiss her, hold her so close. This, too, had not been her intention. . . . She shouldn't have done it, she told herself, but unable to be really unhappy about the wrong she had done. It was the sadness of parting, she would tell herself.

Next time she would do it differently. Next time . . . dreaming again. *No.* Next time she would make it clear. Though really there shouldn't be any next time. She would write him he mustn't come. And then she smiled, and the smile lingered. He'd come anyway.

Come on the next train, if she wrote him that.

"*Norma*," she heard her Aunt Nettie say.

"Oh—?"

"I spoke to you three times." She laughed indulgently. "Dreaming of your young man."

"I am *not*. I have *plenty* of things to think about!"

"Tsh—tsh," said her aunt to these protestations.

"Norma," wrote Rosie, "I miss you just terribly. The world seems different when we aren't together. It makes me feel so by myself. I need to be with you. I lose something when I'm not with you. You *have* it, Norma—what I lose when I'm not with you. I cannot imagine your not feeling secure, not—"

Oh—Rosie, she thought with a pang.

"What our teacher wanted us to be, most of all it rests with you. With all of us to the measure we can, but you are more than the rest of us. That was what he felt when he chose you. He knew what was in him would not be lost because it is in you. That must have helped him when he was about to leave it all behind."

Nothing will be lost, Norma affirmed. But felt loss as she said it. When she went on with her life—Max out of her life—oh, something would be lost. Something she had to try very hard to stop thinking about: so sweet, dear, so happy.

Resolutely she told herself: very well then, *sacrifice*. Had no others sacrificed? In the long history of the world had there not times without number been sacrifice for what man believed? That was the courage, the denial, belief, had brought us where we are. She had been out of school less than two weeks—why did she need to be fortifying herself with these thoughts!

"Last night I milked for Father," Rosie wrote. "He works so hard; he looked tired when he came in from the field and I wanted to help him. I learned to milk when I was quite a little girl, so it came natural to be doing it again. I thought of things—*our* things —there close to Bossie and Nell, who had this good milk to give and seemed glad to be giving it. I didn't feel just myself, not separate, but part of all that was life. It all seemed so *good*. They were content, Bossie and Nell, and the milk was to help life go on. You can feel that about so many things on a farm, or I suppose anywhere. I mean, things are related; giving does not make you lose but makes you more. All around me, everywhere I turn, is evidence our teacher didn't *make it up;* I know, a hundred times each day, that what he revealed to us is there. It was there before, but we did not have eyes to see. I shall always be grateful to him for giving me eyes to see."

Rosie is good. . . . No door of self closes her from the life around her.

She wrote Virgil the letter it would be useless to write Max (Max would not heed such a letter). She must clear the way ahead. She could at least begin with Virgil.

But it wasn't easy, once she began, for she was not telling him the whole truth: why she knew now, better than in their goodbye at school, that even a long way ahead, she couldn't marry him. She paused long over the thought: I am bound to Max. Even though I never marry him (I will not marry him: how can I?) it would not be possible to marry anyone else, feeling as I do for Max. That would be being unfaithful, doing wrong. So it was Max, to the measure it couldn't be anyone else. Its own kind of union: beautiful and frightening intimacy.

It was a wonder which she was unable to understand. How many hours had they spent together? Couldn't she count them on the fingers of her two hands? Almost. One hand you might have to use twice.

So many hours she had spent with Virgil. All those hours at school that meant so much to her—many of them they had shared. Walking home from the evenings with their teacher; the library, class-room. Picnics. All of it. Here was someone she knew; knew and respected and liked. Their teacher had liked him. He said there was challenge in Virgil. Much went on in·him. This old friend of hers thought about things Max had never thought about at all. Her first hour with Max he was calling it a rotten world; swearing and saying blasphemous things. Not like them—way outside the things they had felt together up there. How surprised their teacher would be that she should be thinking of Max, not Virgil. Or—would he? So little surprised him, looking at life with eyes kind and wise.

Of course she wasn't going to marry anyone at all, going on with her work, but she must tell Virgil that even if she were to marry, it couldn't be him.

Well—no, she needn't tell him that; certainly she couldn't tell him about Max. How could she—even if she thought she should? "I met someone on the train; we just got to talking and—" How preposterous it sounded. How beautiful, and somehow inevitable, it was.

"I don't have to tell you, Virgil, how much it means to me: this chance to go to the University, all it may open up. I feel my whole life must be given to what I hope to do." (As she wrote she was trying to feel she was saying it to Max as well as Virgil.) "There cannot be a divided interest, part of me absorbed into a life with someone else. I can't have that kind of a personal life. My whole self is not enough—falls far short—for what I want to do.

"We went through a great thing together, and *that* is a bond, and more beautiful than any other could be." (Is this true? she thought. It didn't sound right, feel of the truth was not in it. But as to Virgil, between her and Virgil, it was true.) Oh, it was a hard letter to write; between her and Virgil had been something that was pure: truth felt together, beauty shared, and was she hurting that now, not telling all the truth? Between them up there, their teacher's disciples, had been openness, not evasions. Was she . . . ?

But she had to finish the letter, as best she could. He mustn't come, nor go on thinking, as he'd said that last night, "It will all work out some way." He was too good for that. She couldn't do him that wrong.

So hard to see it straight: right; wrong. Just such a short while ago she had seen right, had seen wrong, and had known they were different.

Max wrote her: "Darn it all, I wish I'd paid more attention to my English course. I don't know how to write. I can't write what I feel. What I write isn't good enough for what I feel; and when I write it it sounds like something that has been said before. And this is *new*, Norma—nothing was ever like it before! Oh my darling, I know what it is, but how can I make you believe that if I'm too dumb to say it? You know so much, will you be good and just *know* all I can't say?

"I suppose it's because I know I'm not good enough for you. It ties my tongue—I mean my pen. When I see you I can tell you, won't need the damn pen. (Excuse me, and I've tried to cross it out, but excuse what's under the blot. Though maybe you'll get used to my swearing a little? Can't you, Norma? I seem to need it at times. It expresses me, as you would say.)

"When I see you— Now I can't even *think*, let alone write. Just dream of 'when I see you.'

"I loved you when we sat there on the log and you talked; loved you for the wonderful things you said, and your face as you said them. I had never thought much about the world—only my own part in it, I'm afraid. But you—you *took* me somewhere, Norma; took me into places I'd never dreamed were there. Like having a new country opened to you. And *you* did this for me, Norma. You said to me, 'This is ours!'"

Why, no, I didn't, she thought. It was just the *other* idea. What other idea? That he was to be shut out? Is that what you gained from your teacher—that *anyone* was to be shut out who could come in? Had you meant to say, This is mine, you can't come in here?

I seem to be very confused, she thought. I wish I could talk, even ten minutes, with my teacher.

Then events took a hand. It was like a conspiracy, the way things

kept happening to draw her and Max together; as if something behind events *wanted* this: the wreck first, now this new excitement
about Texas and his changed plans.

"Something has happened," he wrote in the next letter. "Something that may mean a lot to our future." (*Our* future; she paused
to think, registering objection with her mind, and all through her
something that was like a happy humming.) "I'm going a long way
from you—and that part of it I don't like one little bit, but what is
it they say—longest way around the shortest way home? Doesn't
seem to make sense, does it?—but in our case going a long way
from you may be the short-cut to being together forever. Forever
—hear what I said? I mean as long as we live."

Max is sort of crazy, she thought happily. His company was taking on a lot of land in Texas. They would take people down there
from the Middle West: Iowa, Illinois, South Dakota, Nebraska,
and sell them tracts for their homes. Max was taking a party down
the very next day. That was why—darn it all—he couldn't come
to see her first. But when he came back—oh, he wouldn't lose much
time getting there when he got back!

"Mr. Saunders thinks I'll be good on the job," he told her. "He
thinks I can persuade people."

(I haven't a doubt of it, she thought rather grimly. Couldn't he
persuade anybody of anything? Well—most anything.)

"This is a wonderful idea," he wrote. "New country. Opportunity for people who wouldn't have much of a chance up here. I'll
tell you all about it. I'm so excited because it's like those wonderful
things that means so much to you."

Selling land? Is that the wonderful thing means so much to me?
Max has it all mixed up, she thought. There's no connection. Well,
perhaps, in a way—a remote sort of way. New country; a chance.
It had a stirring sound, and anyway she was glad for Max.

She found herself telling her father about it with some pride,
and her father was much impressed. "They must think a lot of

him," he said. "He's young to be getting such a start. That young man will go far—shouldn't wonder a bit if he did."

She turned with great resolution, and no little effort, to getting her clothes ready for Chicago in the fall. "What I think," said Aunt Nettie, "you'd better go up to Des Moines, a little later, and get yourself a really nice suit."

"I'm not going *near* Des Moines," she said heatedly.

"Why, I thought it might be kind of nice," said Aunt Nettie, insinuatingly.

How awful her family were! They certainly weren't much help. Her father saying Max would go far, Grandmother always wanting to know if she'd heard from him, and now Aunt Nettie trying to push her right into— Well, push her. I have to do the whole thing, she thought. All by myself.

When Max returned, and came to see her, he was triumphant. A number of them had bought; it was the start of a big thing.

"Norma," he asked wistfully, "are *you* happy about it?"

"Of course I am, Max," she assured him. "I am happy for you."

"I hope so," he said rather sadly; "because, you see, my mother can't be."

She had to be happy for Max doubly. It was as if he couldn't be happy about it if she weren't. She must be proud of him, she alone, his mother not there to be proud of him.

This visit it was Max who did most of the talking: the country down there; proposed developments; riches of the state and what the future could be. He was so engrossed in it he didn't seem to realize their time was going by. "*Lord*," he said in disgust, "here it's time for me to go—and I've talked *business*."

"But I wanted you to," she laughed.

"I'd like to talk to you days and days; years and years. Well, I will," he said, more contentedly.

"Max, you do realize I am—"

"Maybe this is our new home too," he went on. "Perhaps that's where we'll be. If it opens up as—"

"Max, will you listen now? I'm going to Chicago in the fall."

"I don't think you'll like it, honey," he said with his mischievous smile. "It's all too built-up—the stock-yards and everything."

"I am not going to the stock-yards. I am going to the University."

"You know enough already."

"That's a *ridiculous* thing to say. I've told and told you that I haven't begun to know the—"

"Poor Norma—so ignorant. You spelled a word wrong in your letter to me. I was awfully glad."

"What word did I spell wrong?"

"It's a very simple word. You really should know better, my dear. Slipping; you slipped on slipping—only one p."

"I certainly do know better than that," she laughed. "I must have been excited."

"What about?" he asked quickly. He put his hands on her shoulders, searching her eyes. "Could it be you were a little bit excited because you were writing to me?"

"It—it could be," she granted, and his arms went around her and as she bent her head against his shoulder he kissed her hair.

She made herself draw away—after a minute. "Max—please listen now. I *am* going to the University. That's my life."

"Maybe you are going to the University—for a little while," he said; "learn to spell and all that, till I get this opened up. But my dear—my darling and my dear—that is *not* your life.

"No," he said softly, before she could speak. "I may not know many things, but this one thing I know—and you'll just have to take my word for it. Your life is with me. I know it as I know nothing else in God's world." He said it so gently, yet so surely, that just at the moment she didn't know how to say no.

It was almost September when something happened to change the whole course of the life of Norma Ashe. "Something happened"—and to her who wouldn't have believed, so short a time before, that anything could send her from the way she was to go. As easily she could have believed the star up at which she looked would suddenly cease to be.

Max arrived without letting her know. "Couldn't wait to write," he cried. "Norma, I'm going down there! I mean to stay. They've given me the whole job—that end of it. You understand, Norma? I'm manager down there! That's my headquarters."

It was hard to speak. She wanted to be glad for him, but how could he be happy when it meant they would be so far apart? Texas. Texas was a long way from Iowa; miles and miles away from Chicago.

He was waiting, looking at her so expectantly, needing her to be happy with him.

"Max, that's wonderful for you," she said. "I'm sure it is a great thing for you. Only—" She stopped. Didn't he *see* it? Didn't he even *think* of it?

"Only—? What only?"

"Well—it seems so far away."

"And what difference does that make?" he demanded eagerly.

She had thought it made a difference. She couldn't help being hurt.

"But darling," he smiled at her, "you don't think I'm going *alone*, do you?

"No—listen a minute, Norma," he hurried on, "that just couldn't *be*. Why, it wouldn't be right," he said, as if this settled it.

Right? But for her something else was right. She tried to cling to the word. "Max—I can't." But she said it falteringly, and as if it broke her heart.

Then quickly she was angry: with him, herself, most of all with the way things seemed to be conspiring to take her. "No! I will not! I *can't*. Can't you *see?* Can't you see *anything*—but yourself?"

All the bright strong happiness seemed to go out of him. "I thought I was seeing for you too. I thought you would want to be with me."

"I *do* want to be with you! Only—there's *my* life, too."

"I thought when it came to the show-down, being together, or separating, I thought you would want to go with me."

"Do you think it is just what I *want?*" she cried.

"Yes, I do. I don't see why not."

"Well *I* see—why not. Why, I'm all ready to go. I'm ready—next month—to begin. Then how can I run away to Texas? What would there be for me in Texas?"

"There'd be me," he said. "Doesn't that count—at all?"

"You *know* it counts. But you won't know the other things. You just won't know—anything else."

"I don't think there is much else to know," he said, with a rather wan suggestion of his smile. When he looked at her like that, as if she were hurting him and he didn't know how to bear it, she didn't know how to bear it herself, didn't know what to do.

But it wasn't the words they spoke; their argument went on, their battle, and in that battle they hurt one another bitterly, yet it wasn't the words with which they tried to say what they meant, nor the hot words which said what they didn't mean, but at the last what brought them together so they couldn't go apart was the passion that grew between them in this conflict—all sweeping into the passion of man for woman, woman for man, the hot sharp need to weld into one that frightened them both, making them so nearly one it was almost the same, almost as if already they had merged their lives and there could be no drawing back before what was and had to be.

They were back at their old place: the fallen tree in Cutter's lane. They had walked there as if not knowing where they were going, but instinctively—desperately torn, each terribly needing the other to make it right between them; now angry, again so un-

happy it was as if life were lost. And when they stood there where
that first day they had sat talking, he just put his arms around her,
kissed her with so much love, at first dear love. She quivered all
through her, sobbing in his arms. He kissed her wet eyes, the tears
on her face—tenderly at first, and then from the tenderness all
that had been engendered between them in the hot conflict, desperate thought of parting, it mounted and his lips clung to hers,
hers to his, until they knew what it was to be one and it was then
as if it could be no other way.

She had given herself to Max; it was as much to her as that, and
she was not one to give herself without meaning. Whether it was
right, or be it wrong, she was his. Life had taken her and there was
no turning back. It was as simple, as devastating and wonderful, as
inevitable as that. If she were married to him it could be no less
irrevocable. Again—something had happened.

They were married and went South the following week. She
wouldn't have believed it; so how could she tell it to anyone else?
But there were a few letters she had to write. She wrote Mr.
Howells, the man who was sending her to the University, would
have sent her. "It isn't that I do not appreciate—" Why, she *couldn't*
believe it—even yet, couldn't believe the words she wrote. "But
my plans have changed. I am going to be married." She spoke of
Rosie: a good student, wonderful person, one of the little group
to whom their teacher had given (she could barely write the
words) had given his very self. Could not Rosie go in her place?

She wrote to Rosie. "You will not understand, Rosie. I don't
myself. I have fallen in love. I didn't mean to, I don't know, even
now, how it all came about. But it has happened, and now it can be
no other way."

The words seemed curt, and always like something that couldn't
be true. Was it then no more than that, Rosie might well ask. Oh,
no, she replied for herself, it is none the less: what we knew there
and what I will always know. Only—I have to go another way. I

have to do it differently. Already she felt she knew more of life than in those days she and Rosie had together. It will all come together, she thought. If I know life more fully—can that make me less?

She was packing her books. She was giving up the University, but she would not cease to study. Perhaps her teacher, who understood so much, would not have felt she was betraying. "All right, Norma," perhaps he would have said, "you have to go your way. The way we didn't foresee may be the better way. Only—don't let it swamp you. You are Norma Ashe. Be that to your utmost." She could almost hear his voice as he thus assured her.

She held a notebook she was about to put in the box that would go. She opened it; her pencil was there, and she sat with her pencil poised over the page; not reading the page, but in familiar position, in a world she had known and in which she had been so secure. All those dear hours of the fine enthusiasms and great resolves, companionship of the books and the friends with whom she read the books. That had been her true home and she was leaving her home for a world she did not know at all. There was no use going on saying I wouldn't have believed it, but that was the way she felt, and it was as if she had had so little to do about it. She had seen her way so clearly, and now it was another way she was to go. Was there some design in it: this the better way, even for realizing what had been revealed to her up there with her teacher? Was it all part of a progress? Seen for her though she herself could not see? Max had talked glowingly of that new country, the chance for people who had somehow been left out of the chance up here. Change, an openness—would that mean too an openness of the spirit? She was not going to the University; she would know less through books. She would not be a scholar, one of that great company. But was she to be used—another way?

She could not believe she was denying; that would give her a feeling of the traitor, and though bewildered, she did not feel a

traitor. The world could not be so beautiful to her were she denying life. Max needed her. And yes—she needed him. It made her
more humble than she had been before, when she felt she needed
no one because what she was to do was the whole of her life. Now
she was *in* life, and surely that was good, and good must come of
it. She would be more—not less; only the way was all unseen,
where before she had so clearly seen the way ahead.

Aunt Nettie came in and found her packing her notebooks with
her books. "Goodness," she said, "I should think you could leave
those behind."

"I am not leaving anything behind," she said.

Aunt Nettie's husband had died the year after they were married. That was when Norma was a little girl. She liked her aunt, but
had secretly thought her a little silly, not much to her. Now she
thought—how lonely she must have been.

When her grandmother gave her her own most cherished quilt
(the red-and-white) she thought of her grandmother's early days,
a pioneer out here in the midwest. She used to tell Norma stories
about it. "I'm going to be sort of a pioneer too, Grandma," she
said as she dried her hair in the sun at the kitchen stoop, and she
and her grandmother laughed and talked like two girls who have
something in common.

They had all been so good to her, and she had thought so little
about it. "Could I take Mother's gold chain?" she asked. "I'd just
like to—have it with me." She wished her mother were here to say
"Be a good girl." Oh, I will, she said, as in reply to the old words
which meant so little then, so much in memory now.

The night before Max came she and her father sat out on the
porch, he in his rocking-chair, she on the step. "Think it's going to
be cooler tomorrow," he said, and she remembered how many
times he'd get up from the dinner-table, saying: "Well, better be
getting back to the store. Got to keep a roof over our heads."

He had kept the roof over their heads, and how little she had thought about his long days in the store. He would come home tired at night; she could see him now, turning the corner up there. "Supper ready? Glory be—what a day *this* was."

Now that she was leaving—or now that she loved?—she could see him, see all of them, as she'd not seen them before. It was as if she had been apart from them before and was one with them now.

In the letter she'd had that day Max talked of all she was doing for him. She thought now of what Max was doing for her. . . .

She said to her father: "It is all one, isn't it?"

"What's all one?"

"What we are. We are not split off into compartments, are we?"

"Goodness, I should hope not," he laughed. "Sounds terrible. You think of the funniest things."

He sat there regarding the daughter about to be married. He wished her mother were there. He could only say: "You're a good girl, Norma."

Swiftly she looked up at him, her eyes shining through a film of tears. "Am I, Father? I want to be."

CHAPTER ELEVEN

*I*N TEXAS she had a feeling of living at the top of the world, but surprise that the top should be so wide and flat. It was very sparse here on top of the world, luxuriant things left down below. She wasn't actually in high altitude, but the air gave you this topmost feeling.

The Panhandle—funny name. How large the pan must be if the handle had to be as big as this.

It didn't take long to walk through the little town, low wooden buildings of a new town, a few stores and houses and offices, and when you left this behind you could see a long way: the air clear and the horizon far. But there wasn't much to hold the eye within this horizon. It was like a vast room that hasn't been furnished to live in. Some of the land in wheat, much alfalfa, here and there cattle. Far apart there were houses, but not standing in any relation to one another they looked lonely. They were small poor houses, built for shelter and with no thought of beauty. There were practically no fences and no roads traversed the tract. People just rode through the open; at night you could very easily get lost going to call on your nearest neighbor. There seemed no shelter and no guides. It gave Norma a feeling of being let loose in space: space unsurveyed, undiversified. Everything was unformed, unframed: no hill sheltered a valley—only the one big openness.

Perhaps she could come to orient herself in this openness: certainly it was uncramped! ("There's plenty of room if room's all you want," an old fellow said as he took the train back to St. Joe.)

If just once a week, or even once a month, she could go up a hill and look down on something unexpected: an old house nestling in a valley, a beautiful tree. One's eyes wanted something to focus on. . . . And the wind blew almost all the time. "Pay no attention to it," said Max. "It likes to do this in the spring and the fall." But the wind coming over so vast a plain seemed telling you to get out of the way.

She didn't talk to Max of what she missed, but tried to take on his feeling: big new country, a great future. "You know something? If you were to take Texas and tip it up at the southeast corner it would fold over into Canada. When you're in Dalhart, Texas, you're closer to Chicago than to Brownsville, Texas." Oh, it was big—no doubt about that. It wasn't intimate; this idea of tipping it over into Canada didn't make it any more cozy.

But she was going to like it! If it was making homes for people, a new start, that was good. Max said he liked its openness, all laid out there for you to see. "No secrets," she smiled. "Ah, but you're wrong," he quickly told her. "Texas has plenty of secrets—under the ground. There's natural gas, and I'd bet my bottom dollar there's oil! Did you know they found light oil at Corsicana in 1894? *Well*—I'll bet you're *standing* on oil this minute! All we need is the money and gumption to get to it! Do you know what that *means*?"

She didn't, exactly. "It would be useful, wouldn't it?"

He laughed. "It would be millions," he said.

He would say other things she liked better, things about the land. "It's been a long time alone. Can't you feel in this land that it's been waiting a long time? Now people have come. I think the land's glad."

How nice of Max to give feelings to the land. Yes, that made it less lonely.

Each room of their house was like a square box; same shape and size, as if that had been the easiest way to build a house: a parlor, dining-room, kitchen, bedroom. They had the furniture of the people who had lived there before they came. "What happened to them?" she had asked. "Oh, they went back to Illinois." "They didn't like it here?" (Illinois. Illinois was like Iowa: woods, hills, rivers. They had missed the rich earth of the upper Mississippi Valley.) Max said he guessed they weren't much good. The woman got homesick. "Imagine! Imagine getting homesick down here!" He looked at her, smiling, and she smiled too; not for anything would she spoil his pleasure in it all, hurt that driving energy and confidence in the future.

When she wrote home she would find herself using his words: open country, you could see so far; the land waiting for people who would come to make it their home. And when she wrote those things it made them more real to her, until for her too Texas had its own excitements and beauty.

She wished Rosie were here. Much of the time no one to talk to, not of the things she and Rosie used to talk about. Max was away a good deal, around the country; and when he came home he was full of things he wanted to talk about: sales he'd made, the people he didn't sell to, and why. "The darn fool said dry-farming wouldn't work. He just didn't have the nerve. Where in the world will you get if you don't have nerve?" She was happy with him when he had been successful, and would bring her love and sympathy to his disappointments, thus making him sure of himself and strong again. Busy and engrossed as he was, the things he had once loved to hear her talk about, there on the log in Cutter's lane, did not come into their days. Only in her own thoughts that lived now, as she went about doing her work. So how nice it would be if Rosie were here and they could talk as they used to.

Rosie was in Minneapolis, teaching the children in the grand house she'd been afraid of—"the pile of rocks." She had not been given the opportunity at the University which Norma had foregone; Mr. Howells had not given it to any of their little group. He had written her—briefly, rather stiffly, she thought. He was sorry she had decided not to go to the University. Sorry because it had seemed to mean so much to Langley. Langley had thought she would go far. But he hoped she would be happy in her marriage.

She had a letter from Rosie the week they settled into this house. What fun they had that first day, finding places for their things. They'd laughed about the furniture. "Stiff as a ramrod," Max said. "Think we'd better carve it up a little—paint her red white and blue? Don't you worry, my dear. You won't have *this* junk long. I'm going to buy you— You wait! You'll see. This stuff is only to start out with."

Apparently all the furniture in the house had been bought at the same place. It was golden-oak; in the sitting-room two rockers, center-table and combination desk and bookcase. "A place for your books," Max said, wanting her to be pleased—and so she was pleased. (Later she almost hated to put her books in there; this thing was so shiny and didn't seem substantial, and the books were toned by use and so sound.) But she'd carried it on gaily that first day. "And in the drawers I can put my papers. And see? This lets down. Here I can work."

"Hey! Leave a little room for my papers, will you?" he'd called from the kitchen, where he was noisily opening a box.

"Do you want the top drawer or the bottom or the middle?"

"Put me in the middle—then I'll have you on both sides."

Max was so sweet—such fun. "Happy?" he'd ask. "Happy," she would assure; and she was.

That first day it was all too exciting to mind the furniture much, but she did come to feel these things in her house weren't very companionable. A chair can be company for you—a footstool, work-table where there's room to put down both elbows if you want to, like the big table she and Rosie had used at school. She thought of the little low chair that had been her great-grandmother's, where she used to sit and put on her stockings. At home their things didn't much match; they were the things the family had accumulated through the years and they all had in them something of the past. She hadn't thought much about that at the time, and it was true some of the pieces were ugly, but together they made something; living was in them, and they took you in. This seemed like furniture in a store, and not the things she would have chosen. They belonged to that other woman, who got discouraged and went back home. But then she, that woman from Illinois, hadn't had Max. No furniture at all—with Max, would be better than the best things in the world and Max not bursting in: "Honey—where are you?"

"Why, *Norma*," Rosie had written, "I was never so surprised in my whole life! I had to read your letter over and over, and even then I couldn't believe it, and still can't, not quite. How *sudden* it was. I can tell how much you love him, giving up the University and all. I wouldn't have believed— But it's all right, because you did it, and anything you do would be right."

"*Rosie—*" she murmured, so warm and grateful; this seemed that shining past telling her it was all right.

"One of the great things about life," said Rosie, "is that you can't plan it all ahead, because it is greater than you are. So I think it was *meant* you were to do this, Norma—only we hadn't seen that, and how could we, because it was ahead. I think it was brave of you, anyone less brave might have thought she had to go the way she had intended to go."

She shook her head over the impetuous words. I don't know that it is brave to do what you can't help doing, she thought.

"Do you remember what our teacher said?" Rosie wrote on the next page. " 'Wherever you are, whatever you are doing, what is you is there, and it is from that place you can make yourself felt and make life more because you live.' You must remember now those things he said and they will comfort you when sometimes you think back to what you gave up."

How good of Rosie! It was as if, through Rosie, her teacher was speaking to her.

"It seems you were to go to the virgin country he talked about —country even newer than ours at school, or our homes; you were to turn your face there, rather than to the world where so much has already been done. You were not to go the way of others, but your own way. That is what I believe." And Norma had to smile as she blinked back a tear: memories of the many times Rosie had said, in a way sort of hushed and solemn: "That is what I believe."

(To think she didn't lose faith in me. . . .)

"How happily things are going for us," Rosie wrote, "because I am happy too, here with Claire and Ann and Robert. I teach them and go with them on their walks, eat and play with them and put them to bed. Claire makes me think of you. She's seven, and in her I can see you when you were seven. She's eager to learn, so excited when I tell her things that are wonderful, any of the many things in our world that are wonderful: the trees losing their leaves now in the fall—how the life is all there in the tree, waiting, strong, the very pattern of the leaves of next summer there in the tree. Her eyes grow big and bright when we talk of the birds going their hundreds of miles because winter is coming, and knowing how to come back—from Mexico, South America, to *this very tree*. 'Oh, *how* do they know?' she cries. 'There are so *many* trees. How can they find *this* tree?' And I don't know what to tell her—how *can* I? —*I* don't know either. I say, 'Life is full of things like a miracle. Many of them we don't understand, but we can be thinking about them, and when we do understand a little more—that's like going somewhere! Going into a new country.' 'Yes!' she cried, picked up a leaf that had fallen, ran her fingers round the edges (it was an oak leaf). '*This* is the pattern,' she said, and when we got home she drew it, as if she must draw it because she wanted to know it better.

"When I was opening his window last night Robert leaned out, pointed up to a star. The cloud had just parted, as if to show Robert the star. 'How long has it been there?' he asked. 'And how long will it stay?' The things they ask are one with the wonderings of long ago, when our race was young, and they are knocking at the door of knowledge, asking of what man has learned. It is all there in the questions of a child. We must know more, the child must be answered. Such trust that he will be answered.

"I don't mind the house much—not the way I thought I would; it's tremendously grand but I love the children and I think they love me. I feel at home because what could be more important than teaching children. They are not shut-in, but so free and happy in their openness to the world. When I look into Claire's eyes as she is eagerly asking, I could almost *pray* that I tell it in a way will make it a joy to know. That she will want to ask again and again— all her life ask and wonder and care. Our teacher did it for me, perhaps I can do it for her. She will do it, one day, for some other little girl; and so it goes on, on and on. . . .

"Only I do not know enough. I am reading Taine's *History of English Literature*, and I think it is beautiful that a Frenchman wrote so wonderfully about English literature, as if there are no separate countries in the mind. If we understood the great thoughts of each country then we would love every country—it would be *ours*, and then there would not be wars, our thoughts would draw us together.

"Oh dear, I go on and on, as if I were talking to you. How I miss talking with you. Norma, I hope you have children. You would be wonderful teaching your own children."

That was Rosie. Rosie herself. Dear, dear Rosie. The letter made her happy, it was indeed as if they had been talking. So Rosie wanted her to have children. . . . ("And so it goes on, on and on. . . .") Yes . . . Max would like that too. She went on dream-ing: the years ahead for her and Max, until suddenly she was called up short by smell of scorching and remembered the cake in the oven.

One thing Norma hadn't much knowledge of was cooking. Someone else had always done it: her mother, her grandmother or Aunt Nettie. This seemed rather awful as she looked back on it, but she, like the rest of them, had seemed to find it quite natural at the time. Norma was always busy with something else; the family had been proud of her because she was "the brightest girl in school," and when she wasn't in school, or off somewhere with "the crowd" she was curled up with a book, as they put it. No one had complained about this; Norma was "going on," they would have said. Anyway they wouldn't have wanted to eat her cooking!

But Max had to eat it—poor dear. (No, the cake wasn't ruined, after all.) She was used to being at the head of the class, now here she was in the role of the dunce. "You see," she said to Max, the day the pot-roast cooked so fast it was dry and tough (Aunt Nettie's was always moist and tender), "I hadn't expected to get married."

"Glad or sorry?" he asked, chewing loyally, smiling at her.

The book Norma pored over now was the cook-book Mrs. Sands, their next-door neighbor at home, gave her for a wedding present. She was the one Aunt Nettie snatched the chicken from that first time Max came. "You just might need it," Mrs. Sands had slyly remarked as she presented the book. "I learned other things," Norma assured Max, "so I can learn to cook. The best cook in our town is Mrs. Drummond, and she really isn't a very bright woman."

It heartened her to think of Mrs. Drummond, but the trouble with cooking was you should have been thinking about it when you were thinking of Max, or something your teacher had said; Rosie, or the rolling country of Iowa—why Texas had to be so flat, why the wind must blow all the time. When your mind should have been on the biscuits you were wondering what they were now doing at the University of Chicago. The Midway. The Lake. She had never seen Chicago, but she had pictured it. . . .

One day Max came home with the news they were to have company for dinner the following noon. "Oh—Max," she cried in dismay, before she'd had the sense to hold it back.

"What's the matter with that? We'll often have to have company. Entertain the prospects—make them feel good, like it here, buy land. That's all part of the job."

"I was just thinking—my cooking, you know."

"You'll get along fine," he assured her. "Roast chicken maybe; stuffing and all that."

"Don't you *want* them to buy the land?"

"What do *you* think?"

"But I haven't even tried stuffing on you."

"We'll have steak," he compromised. "Nothing to it. Just put her in the pan and let her fry. Now here's the idea, Norma," he went on seriously. "I feel this is all up to you. I'm practically putting it in your hands. *You* are to sell the land."

"*Me* sell land? Why I wouldn't know the first thing—"

"I want you to make this woman like you. Mrs. Clayton's her name. Her husband is for it, but she's holding back. It's awfully important. He has some money—more than most of the people we get; quite a bit, I believe. So don't you see, it isn't just the sale, but if he gets interested he'd have money to invest in developments we've got in mind."

"And his wife—doesn't like it here?"

"Says it's too flat. Seems to think it would be lonely. Imagine!" Yes, she could. She could imagine.

"Where are these people from?"

"Iowa. Your state—see? That's quite a bond to start with. You have to learn to use everything like that."

Iowa . . . In the spring you went into the woods for violets.

Big rivers and many little rivers in Iowa. Of course she had seen the Mississippi, majestic and opulent river: proud, knowing itself life source to the richest land in the world; but through her thoughts flowed a more intimate river: the Marquette, little river just seven miles out from the town of her childhood—little Marquette, her girlhood river . . . (tiny waterfalls and busy rapids; happy whisperings). They used to drive there for picnics, and in winter sometimes in bobsleds for skating (more often they skated on Jones pond, right out from town).

Was this Mrs. Clayton afraid she might miss a little river near her home? The hill she saw from her bedroom window? Or perhaps what you saw when you went up the hill: earth so black; grain golden and the sunlight picking out the reddening apples. Big barns crammed with plenty; proud cornfields and meadows magical in the twilight.

"I'm afraid I wouldn't be much good at selling land," she said.

Then he was trying to persuade her—earnestly, and laughing every little while, he tried to talk her into it. Didn't she want to be a good wife? Wasn't she going to be a help to her husband? "It will be no trick at all for you, Norma. You can make anybody like you without half trying. Just make her see what an advantage it would be to live near *you*. It *is* an advantage—honest it is," he spun her round and kissed her until she smiled. "Tell her a person likes it more and more all the time down here. Yes, that will be a good line: how it grows on you. Wonderful feeling of living in new country, opening it up for others. *I'll* tell you what you'll do, Norma!" He was suddenly all lighted up with a great idea. "Talk to her about the things you told me that first day we sat on the log and—

"What's the matter?" he broke off, for she had backed away from him and was standing there looking at him—stunned, it seemed. As if he'd struck her, or something.

He stepped nearer her, but she backed farther away, **and he** couldn't go to her for she was looking at him as if—as if she didn't know who he was.

"*Norma*—quick now! Now you can just *tell* me—before this gets any worse!"

"You mean you don't even know?" she asked slowly.

He shook his head, bewildered. Then suddenly light broke. "Oh," he said—relieved, for at least he knew now, thought he knew, what made his Norma so apart from him. "I see what you mean. Darling! I'm sorry. Of course. That was so intimate, you mean; just something between you and me."

"It was *not* just something between you and me!" She wanted to say that was the light I live by. But she couldn't say it to Max. Not now.

"Yes. Oh *hell*, I'm sorry. Sorry about hell too," he added with a little laugh, wanting to make her laugh with him. "Had you noticed I'm not swearing so much lately?"

"I don't care *how* much you swear! You might as *well*— Max— Max—how *could* you?" And suddenly she was crying, thank heaven, for now he had her in his arms, trying to comfort her, explain.

"I know, dearest," he soothed. "I see it now. Yes; how awful of me. But you see—well, in business you use everything. You get in that habit," he went on, holding her head securely against him as she was about to raise it and speak. "Yourself—your personality— everything you've got. I'm used to that—for myself. I just didn't think how it would seem to you."

"There are some things you don't *use*."

"Well, I don't know about that. Seems to me we should use all we've got."

"Not for personal gain. Max! If you were very religious would you use your *religion* to sell land?"

"I just might, honey," he told her.

"Love? Would you use love—to make money?"

"Not in any way that would hurt it. Yes!" he said, as if he'd done penance long enough and was for asserting himself now. "You use everything that becomes a part of you. That makes you *you*, and with that—what's you—you succeed."

"That's a pretty crude philosophy, I think."

"I never called it any kind of a philosophy! And listen, my dear wife, better not call me crude. Because you love me and married me, and if I'm crude that's not much of a credit to you, is it?"

As this didn't succeed, didn't make her smile, he went on: "Tell you what, if I'm crude—and I guess maybe I am—then you make me less crude. I was to be your first pupil, you know."

"Max—*please*. Please don't say any more about it. Some things I can't—make fun of."

"Who's making fun of? What was I making fun of for heaven's sake?"

"Well, can't take quite so lightly then. Not—not just now."

After a moment she told him, "I'll be as nice to these people as I can. I hope they can eat their dinner. I'll try. But I'm not going to say anything I don't believe!"

"Of course you're not. Who's asking you? I was only suggesting you tell them what you do believe."

She had moved over to the stove. She turned to him now, the pan of potatoes in her hand. "Why, you *don't* understand, do you, Max?" She said it at first in mere surprise. Then there was dismay; and suddenly she was angry. She set the pan down so hard a little of the boiling water spilled over on her hand. She stood there holding her hand, though giving little heed to it. Her eyes were hostile. "Do you think what I feel is just something to bring out and *show-off* with? Something to try to get *money* with? Do you think I would use the greatest things I ever felt in this world in a *scheming* way—try and fool people to get their money?"

"Oh, for God's sake who said anything about fooling them! What in hell's the matter with what you believe? Isn't it any good? That why you're afraid to talk about it?"

It was their first quarrel, and it frightened them both. They made it up in the night; made it up, in a way, in the way quarrels are made up, but it had shocked Norma profoundly. She tried not to think of it. Max just didn't see it as she saw it.

She was very busy with the cook-book next morning and their noonday meal wasn't bad. The Claytons were a good deal older than the Utterbachs (still seemed strange when she and Max were referred to as the Utterbachs) and when the older woman discovered their hosts were just married, Norma only learning to cook, she was "just lovely about it," Norma thought, and began to forget her idea of being nice to these people, but not too nice— keeping a good distance from Max's idea she was to make them like her for a purpose. Mrs. Clayton was telling her of good simple dishes she could make, and before she knew it she began to feel quite at home with her visitor.

After dinner the men went out to look things over again and Mrs. Clayton stayed on with Norma. They did the dishes together. "I remember so well," the older woman said, "when I began to keep house."

There was something deeply sad behind the words. All along Norma had felt in her this underlying sadness. Perhaps that was what had most of all drawn her to Mrs. Clayton: the something underneath. Even when she talked helpfully, kindly, about how to make meat-loaf—it was there. You saw it in her eyes, in her voice you heard it. You *felt* it in her—without seeing or hearing.

"Do you like it here?" she asked suddenly, after she had hung up the dish-towel and was looking out the window.

Now it had come! And she'd be honest.

"I don't think I would—if it weren't for Max."

"And you'd like the Sahara with Max," Mrs. Clayton laughed.

"He's so excited about it. I do take on a good deal of his feeling. I really do," she repeated, pleased, in spite of herself, that she could say this much. "And I think once I'm used to it I'll like the feeling of space—the openness. Perhaps it will come to seem like being free: your spirit free."

"Oh!" Mrs. Clayton stepped nearer, searching Norma's face. "Do you *think* so? You really believe that? Because, if I thought that . . ."

"I only mean it might be true," Norma said, speaking carefully. "Of course I've only lived here such a short time. So far I do miss the things up home. I'm not used to quite so much openness," she laughed. "Up home so many things are like friends. Just the way a hill slopes. A certain clump of trees or a brook that seems to be telling you something. I mean—"

"I know just what you mean," Mrs. Clayton said. "That's the country I've lived in all my life."

She stood there, thinking of the country she had known all her life, so deep in it Norma didn't speak. "Jim thinks I'd be better off down here," she at last said abruptly. "He thinks I *should* look at—something different. You see, I'm looking at things too much. The things I'm used to. How old are you?" she asked.

When Norma told her she was twenty-one she said: "Edith was eighteen. Or would have been—another week."

Then it was very still in the little kitchen. Norma had been putting dishes in the cupboard, but now stood there still, holding the plates. Mrs. Clayton was looking down. Then she raised her eyes. "Tuberculosis," she said.

Norma gripped the plates tightly. There wasn't any answer, not in that moment, to the anguish and loss in those eyes.

After a little Edith's mother said: "We didn't know in time."

Now she was swaying a little—forward, back. Norma put the plates down on the table, went to this mother and put her arm around her, gently steadying. And when she looked up again, looking at Norma, there were tears in the eyes that had been so hopelessly dry.

Norma led her to the sitting-room. "I wish I had a decent chair," she said. "I wish I had the nicest chair in the world for you to sit in —comfortable, and beautiful. And I wish you could sit there and remember all you have loved. And maybe the beauty of all you have had could help—the loss." She paused, not knowing how. "What is in my heart for you is better than this chair," she said.

"Why, my dear. How *good* you are. So young—and so good."

She wiped the tears from her face, and seemed surprised they should be there. "I haven't cried—oh, a *long* time. Not since the day we left her there on the hillside, and I went home—and she wasn't in her room.

"She wasn't in her room," she said again, pauses between each word.

"No," said Norma. What could she say? What *was* there to say?

She tried. "But everything she was lives." With dumb suffering the mother shook her head. "Yes. Why, it lives in you. It's living this moment."

"That isn't—the same."

"No. It's different. Do you think you could begin to think of it —this different way?" she asked timidly.

Mrs. Clayton had no answer. Norma had put out her hand and Edith's mother held tight to Norma's hand.

Feeling going from hand to hand, they sat there silent; Norma was afraid to speak, afraid of the wrong word on pain that could bear no more hurt. Yet there were words . . . words in which was the healing truth of life.

"She came from you," Norma began slowly, "and she came from all of life. And I think—something in you makes me feel it— that she gave to all of life."

"Oh, she did!" cried the mother, one with Norma now. "How did you know? For it's true—so true! She did give to life."

"What we give doesn't go. Each smile, every bright kind word become part of life. It's *in* the life that goes on. Oh, it's hard! I'm sure it is cruel and hard, and yet . . . as time goes on . . . loss won't be all. You will begin to feel her here in the life that goes on."

Mrs. Clayton was silent, but nodding a little to her thoughts. Then, as if this were disloyalty, "But *her*. Edith herself."

"I'm thinking of her too," said Norma. "Edith herself. Wouldn't she want you to find her in the smiles and the hopes and the sorrows of others?"

"She was going to college this fall. She was going to Grinnell."

"Grinnell is a good school. I went to a small college in South Dakota. A school with such an accurate name: Pioneer. And there I had a wonderful teacher. It was he who made me know. . . ."

She told about her teacher—what he had made her know. . . .

"We hadn't meant to be so long," the men said when they came in.

"Was it long?" Mrs. Clayton asked absently.

The two men stood there uncertainly. It was time now for the word to be said: whether they would close for the land, or return without buying.

It was Norma who spoke, and to Mr. Clayton. "I wonder if this would be the best place for your wife." She was just barely aware of Max, standing to one side, looking at her.

"We've talked," she said. "I know—how it is. I'm wondering if she wouldn't miss the things she is used to."

He looked very troubled. "She goes every day—*there*," he said, very low. "To the grave. That can't go on. I thought a change— something entirely different— But you think this isn't the right place?"

She knew just how Max was looking at her, though she refrained from looking at him she felt him standing there: incredulous, hurt, angry no doubt. The very fact he didn't speak up . . .

"I was just afraid, feeling as she does, this country might seem—desolate."

Mrs. Clayton had been standing by the window, looking out. Now she turned. "I've decided," she said.

"I want to stay, Jim. I'd like to be near Norma."

"I suppose it's one way to sell land," Max said drowsily that night. "It wouldn't have occurred to me—tell 'em they'd better not buy—might find it desolate. Worked, though. I guess maybe you're bright, Norma."

"Now you be still, Max."

"Why should I be still?"

"Because I don't want to hate you. I want to love you."

"You do love me."

"Yes," she said. But if he hadn't been so sleepy he'd not have been satisfied; she was thinking of something else. She was thinking of Edith's mother. Sorrow. All the sorrow of the world.

Faith. . . . Was there rescue there from sorrow? Faith in what? In the very life that hurt you? That asked so much. And promised more than it asked? Though not ours to choose. It was the way of life. We were hurt. We believed.

CHAPTER TWELVE

*M*AX COULDN'T be poor. Something in him drove him to make money. Most people want to make money, but Max had to. Perhaps it was because he hadn't done it for his mother. He had to make up for that now, and the fact it couldn't reach his mother only seemed to drive him the more. He said it was for Norma, and Norma was included, to be sure, but this was more than a man "wanting to have things nice" for his wife. He was running away from something, and that something was all involved with being poor.

He soon came to be known as the whirlwind. It wasn't only that he had energy and drove himself. He had ideas, the kind of mind that can look ahead and see where the money is; schemes, promotion. He was daring, and sometimes the men who had the money to invest were afraid of his ideas, but he was persuasive, he could communicate his excitements and often make them see it his way. In the fifteen years of their married life they were involved in a number of different things. He always smelled out the better chance, and was able—somehow—to get the connections where he wanted to go. He said it was a matter of personality; it was personality that counted.

After little more than two years in the Panhandle he got a job with one of the big promotion companies and they moved to Dallas. "But Max," Norma said, "I thought you liked it here."

"Oh, this is a much bigger chance," he told her. "Anything at all could open up from this. I'll be right in the midst of things.

Here was all right for a start, but you don't stay in your start,"
he laughed. "More money, darling. I'm going to buy you diamonds
and furs! I like diamonds better than pearls, don't you? And think
of the baby! Much better to have that young man put in an appearance in Dallas."

"I thought it was going to be nice having him right here: our
first place together, where we've been so happy."

"How funny you are sometimes, Norma. What's a place? Won't
we be happy any place we're together?"

"I shouldn't wonder," she laughed.

It was never easy to deny Max when he was so eager. You
couldn't look into his face and disappoint him. To be happy he had
to have her happy with him. That made him strong. And of course
she wouldn't hold Max back—not in anything that was right for
him. "It's for you, darling," he would say, when he made his dashing trips around the country, involved in more and more things.
"It's for you—and him." She knew this wasn't the whole of it; it
was also something inside himself. Once there had been something
she had to do. She knew what it was: that urge within.

She had come to like the breadth of it here. It seemed a right
place to have the baby. He would emerge into a world uncramped;
when he could first look he would look as far as he could see—
nothing to stop him but his own power to see, which would grow.
She had her plans all made for him: where she would put him in the
morning, where he'd be in the afternoon; it seemed he already belonged in those places. In Dallas it would be much more shut-in.
They were to live at first in one half of a double house—Max had
been there and arranged it all. Dallas was a city; she had never lived
in a city. She knew no one in this strange place Max told her was
just popping.

"Don't you worry," Max would assure her, "Mr. Johnson is going to get us acquainted right away. And he will! It's to his advantage. You'll make them like you, Norma; you have a way with

you, you know. And that will be good for me," he'd laugh. "I'm counting pretty heavily on my wife. Going to disappoint me?" he asked lightly.

She hoped not; of course she didn't want to disappoint Max. But she hated this idea of making people like her in order to use them, make friends that they might get along. She couldn't talk of this to Max. He said he simply couldn't see it.

"It doesn't seem right to leave Mrs. Clayton," she said.

"Oh, come now, Norma. You've been wonderful to Mrs. Clayton. It doesn't mean you have to spend your life with her, does it?"

"They came here because of us. We got them settled here, and now we go away and leave them."

"They have other friends here now."

"Not many. Mrs. Clayton will miss me. And I'll miss her too. She's so happy about the baby—almost as if it were her baby. Now we're taking him away from her; and she's already lost so much."

Max said this was pretty far-fetched. All very well to be kind, but we had to keep ourselves free.

Free? What was free? Free to move to another place where you could make more money? That wasn't all there was to being free. But she couldn't say this to Max, or it seemed she couldn't; it would hurt that happy energy. Many things she just thought about by herself, while going Max's way.

He said they'd make other friends, friends that would be better for them. One must have the right friends; these people here had nothing more to offer. ("These people here," who had nothing more to offer, had been good to them. . . .)

"You'll come to Dallas and visit me, soon after the baby is born. And when he's older I'll bring him back here to visit you," she kept telling Edith's mother. Mrs. Clayton said, "If it's better for you, I'm glad. And I won't talk about how I am going to miss you." But sometimes, a pause in their talk, her eyes were again as when she'd said of the daughter she lost, "She wasn't in her room." I wish I didn't have to leave her, Norma would think.

This was a hard time to move, in three months her baby would be born. They were going to call him Joseph. That was her teacher's name, and fortunately it was also the name of Max's father. So she could call him Joseph without saying too much about her teacher. Max would think it strange to name your baby for someone who had taught you in college; "far-fetched" he would call it. Now that she could feel her baby move inside her, things of late too often dormant moved again in her mind. Close to the intimacy of birth, she knew in a new and more intimate way what it was they had experienced in the days with their teacher. That, too, was conception; there was to be the growth within, the coming to birth. . . .

She knew that a great deal had been left out of her days. With her first pupil, as Max once called himself, she had made little progress—always other things he wanted to talk about, and many thing he wanted her to do, "be nice" to people. Had there been all too much of that? Had she succeeded too easily? People seemed to like her, and often she would succeed in ends not of her own choosing, and Max would say she was wonderful and what would he do without her? She loved him and wanted to help him, but what was she doing to make life more, as had been her dream and was to have been her life. She had tried, she had indeed, to be her own self in her contacts with people, faithful to what she was, not changing herself to gain ends. And yet . . . loving Max as she did, wanting him to be happy, had she done more than she knew? Things stole upon us . . . we did not always know what was happening. Had she all this time been selling something of herself when, just by being there, she helped him sell land? She would tell herself no, one's self was not a precious thing to be hidden away, kept intact. But why did she sometimes feel lost and dismayed?

The baby who was coming helped bring her back to herself. What wasn't realized through her would come through him. Nothing would be lost. *He* would go to the University of Chicago, she'd dream. She would be there to help him, see that he could go his true way. There was place now for everything she had ever felt and all it was in her to be. She remembered and dreamed and planned.

She hated to go to the new place because it seemed he should come into the world here where the first dreams for him had come. To live in a new house, be thinking about new people, begin another life, was an interruption. But when she told Max she didn't want to be uprooted, diverted, he asked anxiously if she were feeling all right. What a good thing they were going to Dallas. Good doctors there.

Again she was packing her books: opening, reading, remembering. They had not been the part in her days she had once resolved they would be. She had not gone further in her studies. How much more she would know now if she had gone to the University. But some things she knew now she wouldn't have known then: the life of a man and woman together, bringing into the world a new life. Having *him*. She thought "him" because Max was sure that to him a son would be born. If not, if not this first time, then they would have Rosie. She'd love having a little girl. Indeed she would like to have both Joseph and Rosie.

They'd been in Dallas less than a month when Max came in at noon one day bringing a bulging letter from Rosie. She stood there looking down at the writing she knew so well, smiling as she hefted the fat envelope—a good long letter from Rosie! It came at a time she needed it; she felt strange in this new place, and just holding the letter in her hand seemed to connect her with all her past. Of course she wasn't at all used to Dallas yet; she liked the house, but it didn't yet seem hers, just a place where she was staying. When she looked from her windows she could only see a little way. But here was Rosie; and that made her Norma.

They didn't write as often as they had at first. They would always assure one another: "Of course it isn't that I *feel* any different. Only, the days are so full, they go by so fast." Something like that she would say to Rosie, Rosie to her. Yes. The days were so full . . . went by so fast.

She hadn't even written Rosie the baby was coming. But that wasn't neglect, it was a temptation resisted. She wanted to surprise her. She'd picture just how Rosie would look when she learned the baby was really here.

Max said he had to eat and run. *Gee*, was he busy?—what a town! She didn't open her letter until he had gone. Then she sat in her largest chair, by the sitting-room window, and thought with a smile, if Rosie could see how *big* I am as I sit here opening her letter.

"Dearest Norma: There is something I think I ought to tell you, and I'd better begin with it, for if I told other things first I wouldn't really be thinking of them, so what would be the use?" Norma smiled. Just like Rosie.

"It's about Virgil." She wasn't smiling now, and didn't at once go on with her letter. About Virgil . . . She wished she didn't have to know it, wished Rosie hadn't felt she must tell her. It was hard to think about Virgil, and she didn't more often than she could help. Now, with the baby right here and all. . . .

She'd done it all so badly about Virgil. She had tried to write him as soon as she knew she was going to marry Max, began several letters, but never seemed to say the right thing. She did write soon after she got to Texas, but he had already heard, she had his letter the day after she posted hers.

It purported to be a better of congratulation; but so insincere and bitter it was hard to believe Virgil had written it. "Congratulations," he wrote. "All happiness and all that. I was a little surprised for I had understood you had it in mind to go to the University of Chicago. But then, love changes all, does it not? A short while before you had thought love played only a subordinate part in life. So quickly you saw the error of your ways, falling in love—and nicely into line. So congratulations again. I suppose he is very handsome? Dashing and worldly, no doubt, and with him you can have a good laugh at the greenhorns you knew up in the cornfields, all those things you once took so seriously. Strange how seriously we can take things—until we come to know better.

"Understand, I am just wishing you the best ever. Your mind can do very clever things—remember how it once persuaded you you were taking part in a miracle? That created quite a little excitement for you at the time. So I am sure that same mind, which serves your ends so well, will speedily let you forget all it would be silly to remember, and that you will be very very happy in your—may I say somewhat hasty marriage? Give my kind regards to your husband. I hear he is a businessman. That's splendid. How wonderful life is, as I seem to remember your having said."

Hurt and wanting to strike back. Angry and bitter—childish, not in the least like Virgil. But worse than that, it was as if in turning against her he was going to turn from all they had known together, must scoff at all of which she had been part.

This must not be, and she had written him a long letter, trying to make clear just how it had happened. Yes, she had fallen in love and that changed her immediate plans. It in no wise changed her feeling. She believed what they had believed together. She was sorry she had not been able to feel about him as he had thought he felt about her. His letter did not indicate his love had been very long-lasting. Perhaps that was as well, but what was wrong, "and you *know* this, Virgil," was that his feeling about life should be embittered. This was unworthy of him, and she was sure he now saw that for himself. "So please write me again—what you are doing and what you are thinking. It would help me so much. There is no one here with whom I talk as you and I once talked."

He made no reply to her letter; she had never heard from him again, and this was the first word that had come, even indirectly. She turned back to Rosie's letter.

"One day when I was in the park with the children two fellows came along. Robert was rolling a hoop and it bumped into one of them, spun and fell. The hoop did, I mean. He stooped to pick it up and rolled it back to Robert. (That part of it was nice.) And then I was so astonished and pleased for I saw it was Virgil who had rolled the hoop back. I called out his name, and just at first he was glad to see me, I think. 'Well—well—if it isn't Rosie!' he said, and we shook hands and stood there laughing.

"And then almost at once he began to change. He introduced me to his friend, but he began to make fun of things, Norma— *our* things. 'Rosie and I had a conversion together,' he told this other one—Mason, was his name. 'How is it lasting for you, Rosie?' he asked, pretending to be very concerned.

"I was so astonished I wasn't even hurt at first. I just stood there gaping, I suppose, as he went on talking to Mr. Mason, telling him we'd gone through a crazy period—like being drunk, he said. 'We had an exalted teacher,' he kept on. 'He more or less hypnotized us and we were to start right out and save the world. We were little Jesuses who would—'

"Next thing I knew I had hold of him and was shaking him— hard as I could. The children were frightened and Robert asked if he should go for a policeman (his mother had told us to do that if anything went wrong). But I couldn't even stop to think about the children, or how it must look—the way I was acting. I *slapped* Virgil—imagine! Then I sat down on the bench and began to cry. I heard this Mason say '*Gee*' and Virgil was sitting down beside me, but I turned away from him.

"He said he was sorry, and his voice sounded more like himself, so I asked, 'What has happened to you, Virgil?' He looked at me then as if perhaps he wanted to talk, say something real. But that passed (you could see it passing) and he said, sort of jauntily: 'Oh, I got a job and came to my senses.'

"I asked him to come and see me. 'You'll *have* to come,' I said, told him a person couldn't do things to another person—what he'd done to me, an old friend—and then just leave it like that. Mr. Mason said if Virgil hadn't the sense he'd come himself, and what was the matter with that? I said perhaps it would be nice sometime, but Virgil couldn't leave it like this. Virgil asked me if these children were mine. I just stared at him (what else could I do?) and he said: 'You young ladies do things so hastily, I thought perhaps this was more of the miracle-working.'

"So then I told him he needn't bother to come!—got the children started for home. He came running after me. 'Please, Rosie, I want to come.' I thought of him as someone who was sick—he looked that way then—so we arranged about the night.

"He's working on a paper in St. Paul. He says he does the police-courts and it has made him a realist. I said I thought he was going to study law, and he said he was sick of studying; where did it get you? He was through with all that stuff. I tried to talk to him about our teacher and all so dear to us. He'd listen with a kind of tolerant smile—sort of pityingly, it seemed, and amused too. But I went on. There were so few of us, I said. He broke in to ask where Helen was. She was a nice kid, he said; all that stuff hardly spoiled her at all. *What* stuff? I wanted to know, and he smiled in that mocking way as he said, 'Oh, *you* know, Rosie.'

"I tried not to be put off by his manner, but talk as if he were really there. Just Norma and me, I said; him, Austin Wurthen, Helen (I didn't know where Helen was). That was all, unless we included Emil, and I didn't know whether to or not. 'And you were one our teacher counted on so much. You and Norma most of all.' 'Isn't it swell about Norma?' he said. 'She'll probably have a pile of money," he laughed. He laughs too *much*.

"I told him my life was with children now and I knew how they acted. Often when they can't have a particular thing they want they turn against everything else. (Not mine; mine are so happy and interested, but I've seen it with their playmates.) They'll smash a toy they love because they can't have another ice-cream. I said he was acting like that. He talked about being a realist and grown-up—sort of *tough* and smarty, like his police-courts, probably—but what he was really acting like was a sulky child.

"This made him angry. He said I needn't worry about his not having you. He had plenty of girls and they'd show a fellow a much better time than you ever did.

"Oh—Norma, what's the use telling all this? Perhaps I shouldn't be writing it at all, but he's too *good* to be like that. He's lost, Norma. One of us is lost—and we were so close, and we are so few. So soon it happened after we ceased to be together. I think of our teacher: all he gave us; all he would have us be. . . . Do you think you could write to Virgil? At moments there's something in his eyes; it's still there: what truly is Virgil. He makes me think of a lost child, though how he'd laugh at *that* idea. It's disappointing that he should be so much less than himself, but perhaps we have to be many times disappointed and still not lose our faith, and our will. It happened because of you; forgive me, darling Norma, I don't mean it was your fault, but it came about because of you. So perhaps you are the one . . ."

When Max came home that night he started in with excitement about a man who was going to— But broke off, looking at her anxiously. "What's the matter? Been doing too much?"

"I tried to write a letter."

"If it tires you like that to write a letter—for heaven's sake *don't*."

"I thought I should. I wanted to, but . . ."

"You have to think of yourself now, Norma. You—and that fellow Joe. And then there's me. What about me?"

"Oh—*lots* about you. I love you! I couldn't help it! I'd do it again! I—" she was sobbing—"*love* you, Max."

"*Darling,*" he murmured, so tenderly, but surprised and worried too, not understanding. "Yes, Norma—yes—yes." He was holding her, and she was shaking with the sobs. "There, dearest—there."

She pressed close to him, as though she must come close as she could. She looked up, smiling and blinking back tears. "I can't get as close to you now."

"Something in between," he smiled back, wiping the tears from her face. "But the something in between draws us together."

"Yes," she said. "Yes!"

"Now I'll tell you one thing," he said, after a little. "It's the black queen's night out, isn't it? Then you're to sit right here. *I'm* getting the supper tonight."

"Max—you couldn't!"

"Couldn't, eh? Think you're the only guy knows anything around here? Who peeled potatoes in the army? Did Miss Ashe? What's good enough for the army—isn't it good enough for you?"

How *good* to have Max come home—just when she needed him so! "There's some—" she began, but her words were lost in a great clatter of skillets and pans.

He came back waving an end of ham. "Know something? Know what I saw today? Guess!"

"You saw a cow with bright red horns."

"I saw a *diamond*. Fellow's got it—wants to sell it. Norma, it's beautiful." He said it so solemnly.

"Now Max, you mustn't be thinking of diamonds. We certainly don't need a diamond."

"Honey, I really think we do. You know why?"

She shook her head, smiling at him. Max! He was so *dear*.

"Because it's like our love. Imperishable—and all lighted from within."

"My dear," she murmured tremulously.

"Well, it's a secret, so I'll say no more about it." He tossed up the ham and caught it; whistling, went back to the kitchen.

She'd have to talk Max out of this idea. Certainly they mustn't buy diamonds. Imagine! Max is sort of crazy she thought—oh, so happily.

As she went on making clothes for the baby ("How many clothes does he have to have?" Max would demand. "Is he going to change his clothes every five minutes?") she was sorry she hadn't told Rosie. Rosie would have loved making something for him. It seemed now she had deprived Rosie, not letting her be happy in advance. She even started to write to her, but she just couldn't seem to talk about Virgil, and that made it hard to write Rosie; and it was so near the time now this news would make Rosie sorry she'd written about Virgil.

She loved working on the things he was going to wear. He was so real now that his clothes were all here waiting for him. "I wish Joseph would hurry up and come," she'd say to Max.

"Give him time—give him time," Max would laugh. "You can't hurry the kid."

"And when we get him," she said, "we're going to have him years and years."

CHAPTER THIRTEEN

*B*UT SHE was wrong: they did not have him years and years. Joseph just breathed, then left a world he was not to know. They were all ready for him—and he didn't stay. He had been injured coming into the world. She never once held him in her arms.

She almost left with him. From way off somewhere she heard Max calling to her, needing her, and found her way back. The doctor had his explanations. They only knew they had lost their baby.

Max was so thankful to have her that at first their loss didn't get to him. Later he would sit brooding and couldn't believe it: that his had happened to him, defrauded of his son. First his mother—now his son. Why did it have to happen to *him?* His life built on the idea of knowing how to get what he wanted, there was anger in his grief, bitter resentment. What kind of a world *was* this? It was right to have children, wasn't it?—then your child taken from you! For no *reason.* They were decent people, weren't they? They were making their way, could have taken care of their boy. The riffraff had children; thieves and cut-throats didn't have their children murdered at birth! Where was the *justice* of it—that's what he wanted to know!

She had to try to help Max; because he didn't seem to know any way of helping himself she tried to hold back her own grief, comfort him. "We have each other," she would say. "I know—I know," he'd cry, "but he was to be *part* of us. Why did they *do* this to us?"

153

"Who, Max? It isn't a conspiracy. All who are born do not live," she said wearily.

"Don't ever talk to me again about God! *Fine* heavenly father —knows nothing about being a father!"

And then he'd say, as he saw her face: "Norma! Oh, I'm sorry. I must take care of you. You're all I have. Darling, I will take care of you,"—gently, loving. But after that he'd say, with hard resolution: "You'll see. I *will* take care of you. You wait—I'll show 'em! I don't care *who* I hurt now or what I do! I'm going to make a *lot* of money. They can't *do* this to us."

"Making a lot of money won't bring Joseph back," she said.

"I know, but I've got to stop thinking of that now." He'd pace up and down. "I'll not be beaten! I tell you I *won't*."

"I care very little about a lot of money."

"Oh, you will. You wait—you'll see. Didn't I tell you I was going to buy you diamonds? That other one I decided wouldn't do, not big enough. I ought to get you a diamond ring now! Remember what I said? Imperishable—like our love."

"Yes, dear. But we have our love, and it is imperishable." She smiled at him, refrained from asking what would a diamond mean to me now?

"I tell you I'm going to be on *top*."

"Max—oh, my dear, if you get on top not caring who you hurt, top won't be a very happy place. My teacher once said—"

"One thing, Norma—please don't talk to me about that teacher! What did *he* know? What would he have to say—about our baby?"

"I wonder a good deal about that," she said.

He was off into one of his schemes, began talking about some land where the branch line was going through and they didn't know it was coming. "I think I know where I can get the money." He sat there figuring it out, and her heart ached for him, though he was so wrong. He was turning to something in which he wouldn't be defeated. But what he left behind? It was part of himself he left behind; he couldn't live with the self that must be hurt, and accept.

"I'll have another baby," she told him. He smiled at her, but it didn't seem to mean a great deal to him then.

Norma was alone a good deal; alone with the baby she didn't have. Sometimes he seemed there with her. He had been so real he couldn't at once cease to be. She didn't know what to do with his things. They broke her heart: booties and bonnets he wouldn't wear, the diapers she had learned about putting on— just there in a pile now, not round him, not taken off, put on, she holding him on her lap.

How much too easy had been the things she said to Mrs. Clayton about the loss of her daughter. And Mrs. Clayton had had Edith for seventeen years . . . woven in with all the things of her life. Twice she started to write her; she *must* write soon, tell about the baby, every day now she would be expecting to hear. But it seemed she couldn't tell her she had lost her baby without saying so many other things. If I had something could comfort her, why can't it comfort myself, Mrs. Clayton might well think. What we believe—is it easier to give that as strength for another than let it come in to one's own dark hour? No, no, that was all wrong and couldn't be true. If faith in life were no more than that it wasn't of the fiber of life, but just something to say. And it *was* of the fiber of life, and the heart of it. Great dreams and a living faith must not go down before a personal hurt.

But oh—*such* a hurt. And it cut so close to all she had believed and dreamed. All she had given up to go with Max was to be realized through her child. Nothing was to be lost, it would come through him. All that was wrong in their lives, hers and Max's (she was more and more fearing a good deal was wrong: get ahead, ahead of someone else—make money, on top), all that she hadn't done herself would somehow be resolved through the life of her child. She could impart it to him, she had thought, see to it his life did not depart from the way it should go; and that would be *her* part in the brave fight for a better world.

Though she knew, in these days when she was weak and sad and somehow lost, that even this was evasion. *She . . .* this self that was Norma Ashe. Her teacher had said: "Come into this spirit of loyalty to life. Extend that loyalty to the yet unrealized . . . dynamo of energy for adventure into what is not yet but can come to be. Too pure for self-consciousness, and almost without conscious effort, the animating spirit makes itself felt." He talked of the power of direct communication (as he to them). "We are not shut away one from another, but being one, an individual has the power to feel in another what could be his. Disease can spread, and so can the good. Be this and what you are will flow into the lives around you. This is the glorious power of life for extension. Remember, we reach one another."

How she had believed it! But closest to her was Max, and how little of her reached Max. Only that in her he wanted to have. Anything else seemed to stand in the way. He knew so surely just what his way was to be; when she tried to speak of other things he was sometimes tolerant, more often impatient. It seemed she could be near Max only in the way he wanted her to be near, help him only as he wanted to be helped. Herself (save for the self he wanted) didn't reach him at all. Were she to say this to him he would be amazed and hurt. Then he would laugh it off. "Why, dumb-bell," he'd laugh, "I love every bit of you. I know you through and through and love you from tip to toe,"—and to prove it he'd kiss her and love her and make her, for the time, forget other things.

The woman next door had given her a little gray kitten. She hadn't wanted to take it: take care of a kitten now when she couldn't be taking care of her baby. But Mrs. Alfred brought the little thing over. "Thought you might have fun with it," she said. And the kitten immediately began to play, rolling an empty thread-spool around on the floor, crouching and leaping—so nimble and happy. "I've got two cats already," her neighbor said. "If you don't want this one it will have to be put out of the way."

Put out of the way . . . that meant killed. And now the kitten had settled down for a rest, sitting there purring so confidently, white paws protruding trimly; no idea that doom was just ahead, just as we have no idea of what can— "Oh, no," she said; "she can stay here."

She named the kitten Spool. And as she got milk for her, let her out and in, sometimes it seemed she just couldn't bear it. Milk? *He* was to have had milk. Sometimes she couldn't watch Spool play. *He* would have played in just a little while. *This* was what she had instead of her boy Joseph. And then she would pick Spool up and cuddle her, make her happy, and resentment would go into tenderness for the little live thing. "It isn't your fault," she'd say. "Must I hate you because you are alive and happy? No; I will not be like that," she would tell Spool. "If you are all that's here, then I will take care of *you*. You're safe with me, little kitten. Don't worry."

Spool didn't worry. She ate and played and slept. She grew. "My, how you've grown," Norma said to her one day—then put her down; her head burrowing in her arms, she was weeping bitterly. *He* would have grown. Already he'd be bigger. Day by day—

She began putting on her things; she couldn't stay here just then. She would take a little walk: see what people were doing, be part of the world. . . .

She had only been out in the yard and around her block, since the baby. She was still not strong, and going out had seemed like leaving him, her thoughts of him, which were all of him she had; as if she would be forsaking him in joining with the rest of the world, when he couldn't.

Perhaps she was a little stronger now, for it was good to be passing people, people hurrying along their way, and wonder a little about them: where were they going, what were they thinking?

A man untying his horse from a post rubbed the horse's nose, saying: "We're off, old girl." He likes his horse, she thought, and felt a little less lonely, a little as if taken in. She had to stand still because boys playing tag ran too close to her. She turned to watch them, smiling as she heard their whoops. Two women were gossiping over a fence. "And I told him, what's the matter with beans? They're nourishing, ain't they? I said."

All over the world people talking to their animals, playing games, chatting over the fence. She heard a woman call, "School's out! Got to get home and see what the kids are up to." People had so much the same interests; did very much the same things. You'd think it would make them feel close to one another, she thought. Strange there should be wars, for when you went to war it was to destroy someone who probably felt much as you did: wanted to get home to the farm, the store, the kids.

But there had been righteous wars: the fight for what we believe. . . . When what we know to be good is about to go down before evil: a time to fight! What was it Plato had said? "The creation of the world—that is to say, the world of civilized order—is the victory of persuasion over force." But if force of evil would not listen to persuasion? Should we keep peace and see the good go down? She did not believe that.

War could be gallant, but there was nothing gallant about the petty wars of so-called peace, this constant war between people, trying to get ahead of somebody else, when that someone else had a life a good deal like your own. If they would only stop and *think*, she thought—think how that other life is really your life, for both are part of a whole; when you destroy someone else you destroy a part of yourself. There could be so much happy life on the earth—the big rich beautiful earth, our home.

What kept it from being that happier world it might be? People . . . people who were very much like one another. Only the worst of them would do it to their own families, but they'd do it to the family next-door, in the next town, in China. And in China the common things of life—the dear common things of life—must be very much as in Texas. Food for the family, cooking and washing the dishes and sweeping the house; a little garden for crisp things to eat, a little place for the flowers that were bright and gay and made you happy. Keeping the children clean and letting them go out to play; terror when there was sickness. Why, we *all* knew it, had it in common the world over, and we should know that when we hurt any part of it we hurt it all. In all the world there could scarcely be a place where the good honest people didn't want very much the same things, didn't know the same love and the same fears. If only we'd stop and *think*, she kept thinking, as she walked slowly along this street in Dallas, Texas, United States of America, Western Hemisphere, a star called Earth.

Now here was she, thinking about it. Surely she was not alone in thinking about it. All over the world must be people who wanted to think it out, knew it was not what it might be, cared, dreamed of the better life we could make. Would fight for it too! but felt alone, bewildered, unsure.

What stood in the way? Only an idea that it couldn't be. And she thought, as in the days with their teacher, if a wrong idea has that power, what couldn't the right idea do! An idea . . . there is might in an idea. It was greed and dullness locked us into this wrong idea. But all over the world (she felt them as though they were walking with her) were those who would welcome the idea of what life might be as a man in prison would welcome the opening of a door.

What really *is* it, she thought (knowing she was walking a little too far, but keeping on, as if her thoughts would turn back if she did), in very simple words just what was it we talked about at school, that which I once knew and wanted, and want now? Yes—want now, even though now I know it's harder than I had known then. For we are captured; our lives wind chains around us. Things bad, and good things too, wind chains around us: love, loyalty, ambition, fear. Hard—not easy, to be free. But it has been done! There are the brave ones who have remained uncaptured. It *can* be.

She thought back to just how they had thought it up there in South Dakota—they, the then uncaptured. It must first be a reality in the mind. We don't know the power of our own minds. They *make* reality; a vision is as real as losing a job or having a baby. Only—we don't know that, think our lives must be determined by the events of the day. But if it came as a new wonder in the world that this flush in the mind has more beauty and more potential power than anything else on earth—oh, how many chains would fall away! An awakening to something in us we hadn't realized and haven't tapped . . . waiting . . . there for us to bring into the world called actual.

She passed two children and smiled at them and shyly they smiled back at her.

She had stopped to rest a moment before turning toward home and found she was looking in a store window. And in this window were familiar things: notebooks like those she used in school, pads of yellow paper, cards for recording, pencils for writing down one's thoughts. She and Rosie had loved to go and buy these things; something about having fresh supplies seemed to mean a new start. "Now we're all ready!" they'd buoyantly say. Or, excitedly: "What will be written in it—before it is full?"

Impulsively she went in the store and bought a notebook, pad of the untouched paper, pencils. It was a link with the old days, and again it seemed a fresh start. Why, I'm only twenty-three, she thought. I have all the chance in the world!

She'd study again! *Why not?* There was challenge curiously poignant in carrying home these things all virgin for recording; again she felt one with that great company who have striven after knowledge. Perhaps her thinking, walking along this street just a little while before, had been too soft. Labor . . . the way was exacting. Her teacher had always said: *prepare.* Nothing more shameful than not making our minds what they might become. They had been won for us by ages now dim in the past; the more we could make them the richer our gift to the mind of the future. She thought of the books she would get, hours of the day she could set aside for working. Best of all: she wanted to! Herself again! Strange . . . some things in a window, way down here in Texas. But they were reminders. . . . That was what we needed: reminders. Tonight she would write to Rosie: tell of her walk and her thoughts; seeing their old things in a window—her old eager self as she carried them home!

But her evening was not as planned; a man was coming to see Max and he was particularly anxious she "be nice" to this man. "He's very important," Max said in his excited way. "He's a Texan born and bred and knows the whole state. He's in on a lot of things. I'm in luck to have fallen in with him!"

They talked about the great resources of Texas: how the riches of the state hadn't begun to be used yet. And as Norma was interested he talked about the history of the state: how it had belonged to Mexico, for a time an independent region, the story of its being taken into the United States. He told of the fight there had been to keep slavery out of Texas and how that fight had been lost—the South wanted slaves. Told stories of the first white men in Texas, courage of the first settlers, men who had won and men who had lost. "But the fortunes are yet to be made! And not in the land business, my boy—not selling little tracts to people with little money. *Under* the sod—that's where the money lies in Texas." They were talking of natural gas, then of the oil-gusher that had come through at Spindletop. "*Oil*—that's the stuff. If it's there—why isn't it all over the region? Bet we're *sitting* on oil this minute. Keep your weather ear to the ground," he laughed. "Fortunes are waiting under this earth."

They went seriously into talk about the new company for piping natural gas north, a company now being organized in which Max was to have a chance. Max was excited and keen too; he asked sharp questions; Mr. Baxter seemed to like him.

But Norma was troubled. "It seems to me," she said slowly, "that any treasure which is under the ground—well, that's just something extra, isn't it?—something unexpected. It seems to me it should belong to *all* the people of the state. Why doesn't the State take it over, so it will be for all the people who live here? Many of them, you say, have had a very hard time. All the disappointments about crops—the droughts and things—here is something that could help them, couldn't it?"

"*Norma*," said Max. "What a crazy idea!"

"It doesn't seem crazy to me. Why should it be piped away by just a few men who've found it and have the money to start it off? If this were done right nobody in Texas need be poor! And it belongs to them, doesn't it, if it's right there under the ground?"

"My wife isn't very practical," Max tried to laugh it off.

"That's all very nice, my dear lady," Mr. Baxter said with a kindly smile for her, "but I'm afraid that isn't the way the world is run."

"Why isn't it?" Norma persisted. "I mean, why couldn't it be? If people were once roused to—"

"Now for God's sake, Norma," Max interrupted, "don't start out to rouse the state of Texas!" He tried to laugh, but he was far from pleased with her. "You're an outsider here. What do you know about how Texas should be run?"

"So are you an outsider, and why should you try to get what

belongs to the people of Texas?" She'd said it impetuously because she was excited about her idea and Max was trying to stop
her.

"I think this nonsense has gone far enough," he said.

Mr. Baxter was indulgent with her. "I'm afraid you're something
of an idealist," he smiled. "Oh, well—we all are when we are young.
I was something like that myself once; remember one time, just
a young fellow then, I saw a man get a pretty raw deal. They
took his land after he'd developed it a good bit; left him with
nothing and he'd worked like a dog. I stood up for him, not that
it did any good. It was too bad, but I've seen lots of things like
that. I've seen people go out of Texas like beaten dogs; people
who came believing it was their great chance, brought their
families, worked like slaves. One thing and another would go
wrong: the winds and the pests and the droughts. Lots of them
couldn't make it. I don't like it, myself, but I guess you have to
learn what the world is like."

"Mr. Baxter! *Why* need the world be like that?"

"Norma! I'm telling you now—"

"Please, Max. I'm talking.

"You say you were once an idealist," she went on, turning a
little away from Max. "Why did you change?"

"Oh, that's easy. Because I have to live in the world as it is."

"*Certainly*," said Max.

"But wasn't it at all your business, as an idealist, to change the
world that is?"

He scratched his head, his face puckered wryly. "Afraid that's
too big an order for me," he laughed.

"Because you gave up. You ceased to care. Oh, I hope that
doesn't sound rude. It's just that it means so much to me—tonight.
Isn't it true, Mr. Baxter, you ceased to care?"

"Might be something to it," he said, less at ease now.

"And where would I have been if I hadn't taken the world as

it is?" he demanded, rather harshly. "With a lot of crackpots! I wouldn't like that very well either."

"I wish to apologize," said Max. "I am very sorry. I have no idea why my wife is talking like this."

"Yes you have, Max. Remember? We were sitting on a log."

Mr. Baxter said he guessed he'd run along now and let them iron out their little differences of opinion. "Young people have lots of ups-and-downs," he said. "And don't think *I* mind anything that's been said. We all go through that stage."

"Max never did," said Norma.

"Now—now, don't you worry about Max. That young man is going to get on. And you'll like that. Come now—won't you?"

She shook her head. It was hard to say goodnight. She was afraid she was going to cry.

"Do you want to *ruin* everything for me?" Max demanded as soon as the door closed. "What do you *mean* by that crazy talk? He must have thought you were out of your head! Didn't I ask you to be *nice* to him? Didn't I tell you it was *important?*"

"It is important, Max," she said. "It is very important."

"*Fine* wife you're turning out to be!"

"I am more than a wife," she said.

"*What* more—for heaven's sake?"

She stood looking at him. It gathered in her and the word came as if it could be no other. "Myself," she said.

CHAPTER FOURTEEN

*T*HAT NIGHT, and other times in the years they were South, she thought, I should leave Max. Living with him while he's doing this, and living *on* it is as if I were doing it myself. We are too different, she would think. I can't be myself and be his wife.

Yet her mind couldn't make real the idea of leaving him. Between her and Max was life. Leaving him would be a tearing apart of the living—like taking up that kitten and hacking it to pieces. She loved him as her lover. She loved *him*, in spite of all that was wrong. There seemed something rather horribly righteous in the idea of deserting him for righteousness' sake. There would seem something invalid, ignoble, about a feeling that couldn't jostle against life, but had to withdraw before it.

And what would Max be if she left him? She didn't even want to form the picture. . . . And he wasn't that now. In spite of this—this *grabbing*, with her he was Max: warmth, charm, love. He had been terribly hurt: his mother, his son. Could she hurt him again, and more? He seemed almost innocent when she tried to talk to him. What was he doing that was wrong—for heaven's sake? He was only trying to make a good life for them. They would have other children and wasn't it a man's business to provide for his family? "But other people have children too," she said, "and you ride over them to get what you want. No—now listen! You *shouldn't* buy up the land of people who don't know what it's going to be worth! They're worried and discouraged and when you take advantage of that you *do* ride over them!"

"Ride over them my eye," he scoffed. "The best man wins. If I didn't do it wouldn't somebody else? It's a game, and if they aren't smart enough to play it is that my fault? Things are *popping* around here. Am I just to sit back and do nothing? I'll make the money while the making's good. The trouble with you, Norma, you're too unworldly."

"I don't want a world where people scheme to beat someone else!"

"It's just as Baxter told you—you have to take the world as it is."

"That's just what I hadn't intended to do," she said sadly. "My dream was—"

"Your dream! All right, my dear, keep it. You keep the dream and let me make the money. Now—now," as she was about to interrupt, "what do you *know* about business, anyway? Great Scott, you'd think I was breaking the law! I keep within the law, don't I?"

"Perhaps you do, Max. I don't know. But there isn't much virtue in keeping within laws that are wrong, not fair to other people. I haven't your respect for laws that keep people's lives from being what they might be!"

"You'd think I was robbing widows and orphans!"

"You took Judd Simpson's land."

"And what if I did! It was legal, wasn't it? He couldn't keep up the payments."

"If you'd given him time for another crop—"

"What you've got to get through your head—well, the world is *organized*. Things *are* this way."

Yes, she knew they were. She'd known that before she met Max, but she hadn't been as close to it, nor known it was as bad as this. And at that time her whole life had been in the vision of a world that could be different. That great hope—was it receding? It seemed farther away now, and if there were nothing she could do.

Once she had felt all energy, as if every bit of her: her body, her mind, was energy. It was Max who was all energy now, though so differently. "That boy's a live wire if ever I saw one," Mr. Baxter told her. "There's no stopping him—wants his finger in every pie," he laughed. Yes, a number of pies, and Max was happy, more and more felt he was succeeding and that made him ever more vigorous. Dallas was booming. "Anyone who can't make money here now is a fool," he would say. She couldn't always be pulling him down. He had to have her happy with him, feel her right there with him. It wasn't the way she wanted to live—always wanting more, but she loved him and didn't want to hurt him. Land, railroads, irrigation, gas—and finally oil. How men's eyes gleamed when they said the word oil!

In the nine years they were South they moved about a good deal. She met many people, mostly business associates of her husband, but none of them were close to her—oh, not at all as their little band at school had been close to one another. There had been excitements then; other excitements now—excitement of making their pile. She wasn't close to people because she was holding something of herself—best of herself—away. Only on the surface was she one with them in their frantic lives; there seemed no place in these lives for the things that had once been hers. Perhaps this wasn't altogether true of them. Possibly she did them an injustice. Once she had believed that in *all* people could be touched the spark that would make the better world.

She had her diamond now. Max was so happy the day he gave it to her that she was touched. He was so good to her—in the ways he knew to be good to her. "It's a symbol of our love," he said. "Lighted from within—imperishable." He was regarding her so tenderly; how could she ask him where the money came from?

"Promise me something?" He was turning the ring on her finger.

"If I can," she smiled.

"Promise you'll keep it as long as you live."

"I promise," she said; kissed him and he held her close.

They had another boy and Max wanted to name him Fred, for Mr. Baxter, who had let him in on so many good things. "Being a bachelor he'll be tickled pink to have a kid named for him. And it's not a bad idea; may give him a special interest in his namesake's future. I really owe it to him," he'd added hastily, seeing Norma's face. "You like the name all right, don't you?"

First there had been Joseph—named for Max's father, and to her, secretly, named for her teacher. Her teacher. . . . It seemed he had been dead a long time.

Fred wasn't a strong baby and her care of him, this anxiety, was the main thing in her life for a couple of years. They couldn't lose another baby! She couldn't bear it, and she didn't know what it might not do to Max. Their struggle to keep him drew them close, closer than they had been in this whirlwind of a life. And when the baby began to gain properly, grew rosy and played, it was as if they had won through together and they were triumphant and happy. Max would toss him up and cry: "See anything wrong with him?"

"Not a thing in the world," she'd smile.

She did the things for Fred she had planned doing for Joseph. She was happy with her darling baby. But the dreams for Joseph: how he was to do all the things she hadn't done, those same dreams didn't come to life for Fred. "Maybe we'd better send him to Harvard," Max said. "Good connections and all that. You're not going to be a hick, young fellow. Why, he'll have a chance to be all the things I never had a shot at. Isn't that a wonderful idea, Norma?"

She agreed yes—yes, it was a wonderful idea. She had been so frightened. Now her child was well. He would grow up. She had much to be thankful for.

She knew there were things about Max's business affairs he

wasn't telling her now, and she even felt this was perhaps just as well; what could she do about it, except make trouble between them? He told her things he thought she would like: how they were carrying some fellow along, even at a risk, because they hoped he could come through and wanted to give him a chance. As Max made more money, felt more secure, he was generous, would sometimes give her money to give to people they knew of who were having a tough time. "You have a way with you, Norma. You can get them to take it for the children. Must be awful, worrying about your kids." He wanted her to be pleased, and she was, though she knew how far short it fell and that it wasn't what she had meant by the better world of her old dream. She'd meant they had a right to it: the earth so rich. And social justice had been only a part of the old excitement and re-solve. The mind—the beautiful human mind—yet to know its beauty and its power, world there would be when we knew that what lived in the mind could come into the lives of men.

Of course she read, and when you read you think. She would have times of eagerly getting books, still knew some of the pleas-ures of the mind. But this seemed just something by herself. She no longer felt that oneness with great minds of the past or the hope that what came through her would communicate itself to others. The fact she couldn't communicate with the one nearest her seemed to cut her off from others, taking her out of the great stream.

The children Rosie had first taught were older now and went to school, but she was governess to another little girl and went to Europe with this child and her mother. The mother was not strong and wanted Rosie with her. How nice for Rosie. Norma would have picture postcards from places visited but there weren't so many letters between them now.

And then one day a letter came which distressed Norma. Rosie had come under the influence of some woman who had what seemed a hodge-podge of a philosophy: smattering of Oriental mysticism, a dabbling in German idealism, a so-called new thinking which added up to the idea we could make life very agreeable if we saw only what we wanted to see. "It's so exciting, Norma, because of course it takes me back to our teacher. The whole idea of this new religion—and it really is a religion to those who believe—is the power of the mind. Just as our teacher said, it must first have reality in the mind. You *see* what you want, what you feel should be for you. You refuse to let other things come into your mind.

"And while it is different from our teacher, don't you think it is part of what he meant? One phase, I mean. He was always telling us it is the mind can set you free. I feel it has brought me closer to him, to our old days. And it came at a time I needed it. I haven't told you, it is not easy in letters, but something has been troubling me very much. This is salvation! I'm sending you a wonderful article that tells it all much better than I have been able to."

Norma read the wonderful article—and it sickened her. She wrote Rosie in her first indignation, and soon felt she had written too sharply. "Rosie—Rosie—how *could* you fall into this? You who had the great *sound* teacher take up this clap-trap and call it him! For heaven's sake, don't do *that*. If you aren't equal to what we had from him—and I can understand that, for I'm not either—at any rate don't swim around in this *mush* and say it's what he gave you. Once the truth was right there, had we been equal to it. Apparently none of us was, but that doesn't justify us in lulling our minds to sleep in order to keep from knowing we've lost something. I've lost something, and I don't know what to do about it. But I know what's lost was *there*, and still is, for one who is equal to it. Life's done something to me. Even good things like love and children have done something. I don't understand this, I'm bewildered and ashamed, but I hope to God, and I say it in all reverence, I don't seize upon some maudlin thing and tell myself I have what might have been mine.

"Rosie, if you will stop and remember how our minds *worked*, how he taught us to see. Did he ever tell us to blindfold ourselves? Evil *is* there—and don't I know it now! But the good in the world could be stronger than the evil, if only we believed that with all our hearts and worked to bring it about.

"Do you remember how sharp his mind was? Things he would say could cut like a knife. There was no namby-pamby about it, no hocus-pocus, as in this stuff of yours. He talked of a miracle— yes, but not a miracle you get by lying down to sleep. The mind could be *more* was his cry, and a cry to battle! He was a man inspired, but it was a great mind that was inspired: a lively, tough, ever-active, ever-receptive mind undismayed.

"This thing of yours (we could always talk to each other, couldn't we, Rosie?—so can't we still?) seems so isolated and unsound. What once inspired us wasn't any sudden half-cocked idea. The world had been getting ready for it a long long time. The ages were behind it, the long slow getting ready which is the history of life on earth. He believed that now we were ready; but, resting in what is, we remained unaware of what we could do. He believed that to a few people this awareness could come now—he hoped to us (I am almost glad he is not living), and that through communication from one to another man could rise to new sense of his powers. How tragic to be ready—and miss the moment! We could rise from our inertia as those first forms of life (remember the light in his eyes as he talked of those brave ones, the fore-runners?) leaped from the water to try and live on the land. For them too—ages of making ready; and then the time was at hand! Many died in the adventure, but there were the highly-developed, hardy ones who survived; as if, mindless though they were, there was in them a faith and a premonition. . . . It went on and on—the adventuring, and so there is man, and so there is the human mind. We come from *courage*, Rosie; from believing and taking a chance!

"The chance for adventure is as great today—greater. But where are the adventurers? I do not find them in Texas; or in myself.

"Dear Rosie, I'm sorry if you have been troubled. You speak as if you had been unhappy about something, and you must know how it hurts me if all is not well with you. But wouldn't it help now to try and get yourself straight? Can't you find your way back to yourself? I fear this letter won't help. Try and realize my dissatisfaction is more with myself than with you, that I put it badly because I have been so far away from it and write as one unworthy. But through what I say, through words that may seem even angry, and certainly not eloquent, try to remember, Rosie —*try*—and remember.

"I think what made our teacher unique was that he was a great intellect and a great soul. The two are not always one. He had a cultivated and a profound mind, and there was in him much of the Christ. He sorrowed in the sorrows of the world and writhed in its injustices. What he would do was not for intellectual attainment, though that was used, but to light man into his kingdom: what life here on earth might be.

"Rosie, I wonder where he came from and just what he had been through to make him as he was. He never talked about himself. Do you realize that in one way he was almost a stranger to us? We only knew that Mr. MacConnell met him and brought him there. Why did he come to a little place like that, he who would have been valued in the most important place in the world? And why was he in such a *hurry?*—you know what I mean. Every day counted; each hour so immediate, so important. And why *us?* Why were we the chosen of all the world? I didn't think so much about it at the time. He was there for us, and it was wonderful. But now I think about it: where he came from . . .

who he was . . . this stranger who must give us all he had."

Stirred by this letter she had written Rosie (poor Rosie, getting such a letter) she wrote briefly to all the others. She wanted to know what the rest of them were doing, hoping that through some one of them it lived and was finding its way. "We seem to have lost touch with one another," she said. "Tell me how it is with you now. Do you think of the things we once thought about? Of our teacher? Are you doing any of the things he hoped we would do?"

Her first reply was from Helen Foster. "Yes indeed, Norma, I do think about the things that meant so much to us, and I think I can say that in my little way I am doing something about it. I'm with this social settlement here in Chicago; how often I used to wish you had gone to the University, and we would be seeing each other. I go to the University for some lectures. It's a wonderful place—so alive.

"I'm all wrapped up in my work here at the settlement. We take in the children while their mothers are working, and we have classes for the mothers too, trying to teach them about the children's health, better conditions for them. The hard part of it is the mothers are so tired in their spare time, and they're so poor they can't do much to make things better at home. It's a very poor neighborhood; the poverty is *sickening*. Conditions *should* be changed, far more than these poor women can be expected to do. Two of the girls here in the House are socialists. Perhaps I am becoming one too, seeing what I do every day makes me feel *something* must be done. What my family would say I don't know. They're all Republicans—but I can't help that. The only thing is, one of the socialist girls, Jane Hershey, gets so savage about it. She says the whole place should be burned down and she'd like to do it! She's so violent it rather scares me off, though there's a lot in what she says: some people in Chicago so rich they don't know what to do with their money, many so poor they can't give their children enough to eat. Now that's not *right,* and I often think of our teacher, and I hope he would feel that in doing just my little bit, I am doing something. I work very hard —often washing children's clothes, giving them baths, trying to teach them not to steal; anything that's to be done. It's all wrong, isn't it, Norma? Perhaps all we can do is the little thing that's at hand, even though it's only taking lice out of a poor child's head. I've seen so much lice."

So much lice—and Helen was such a dainty girl: always taking a bath, doing-up her shirtwaist, washing her hair. How good of Helen, she thought; and sat a long time thinking. "The little thing that is at hand." Yes, that was good. She loved Helen for it. And yet . . .

So much gets left out, she thought. We start to do our little thing, and in that we lead our busy lives. She felt acquainted with the girl who wanted to burn it all down. Yes; and perhaps some of these people grabbing treasure in Texas should be strung up! Violence. Their teacher hadn't meant violence, but she could see how it could come about, brought about, at times, by the magnificent anger of people who couldn't stand what other people were bearing.

Austin Wurthen wrote: "Grand to hear from you, Norma. What a good idea—sort of checking up on us. Here's the report on me: I'm in with my dad, who has this plant. It's growing, and we give work to three hundred and eighty men. Dad pays very decent wages (though of course some people never are satisfied) and we're working now on a development to build better homes for the men. The Company would own the houses at first—naturally, and the men could buy them gradually, so much out of wages each week. A great many like the idea, but of course there are some agitators who don't see it straight, seem to think we're trying to put something over. Well, if they don't like it here they don't have to stay, so what have they to kick about? It's the

union, which is in wrong hands. We're trying to make the men
feel we are their friends, that they don't need any interfering
union.

"Now don't get me wrong, Norma. Dad really has the welfare
of the men at heart, and I haven't changed, so you must know
I am thinking about what's best for them. Remember the inter-
collegiate oratorical contest I won? I've gone on with the speaking—talk to the men in a club we've organized, and it's taking
me into politics too. Dad thinks I should head for that, as well as
the business end of it. Maybe you'll come to see me in Washington some day.

"Yes, I think of our teacher, those days when we felt we could
go out and change the world. I'm a little more practical now,
though none the less an idealist. They call me that—an idealist,
because I am always thinking of how there can be this closer
union between owner and worker. Oh, I have lots of ideas. Even
now I'm trying to get a bill through the legislature that would—
well, can't go into all that in a letter.

"Often I find myself quoting things our teacher said; he always put it so thrillingly, didn't he? I can see now he was somewhat impractical, but we have to have people like that, and perhaps
it is for the rest of us to take the best of his ideas and incor-
porate them into the workaday world. A thing is of no value unless it can be made part of everyday life, and for that it has to
be—well, adapted, somewhat. He was on the heights, and I'm glad
I was there with him for a while. I know it did a great deal for
me, and isn't going to make me so visionary I can't meet the
world man-to-man."

I'm *sure* it isn't, Norma thought bitterly. Oh, Austin! What
are *you* doing to yourself?

She thought of the Austin she had known: vigorous, eager. He
was so open to ideas, had a hunger as for food. Nothing seemed
to stand in the way. Any thought from another which excited

him he could assimilate so quickly. Under a great influence there had seemed something flaming and good about Austin.

He had always had that ability to stand up before people and talk. She remembered one moment. . . .

When their teacher died it was arranged that one of the students speak at his grave. Austin was chosen, and it seemed right that he speak for them all because he felt what all felt and had the gift for expressing it. She could see him now, standing there on the gentle slope, the breeze stirring the thick dark hair of his uncovered head. "It is a great good man we give to this earth," he said. "If all of us who knew him are not more for having known him, then we were not worthy to sit at his feet. He had treasure; and a rare, a unique gift, in giving his treasure. He dreamed a great brave dream of what life might be. And now it rests with us. He has gone, but the dream does not go with him! Standing by his grave we know even more surely than when we listened to his words: we will carry the dream out into life. We will be, each one of us, the most, the best, it is in him to be. Thus we give him his due immortality.

"Though even as I say it, I know he would not want me to put it like that. He asked little for himself, and perhaps he would not ask even his own immortality. What he wanted was for all. Give to others and thus you give to me, he would say. We lessen our homage to him if we give it to him. Pause not here by me, he would say. Go forth and do your part! Be not afraid. Life can be more than man has yet dared to dream!"

It was so still on that hillside when Austin ceased speaking. He had spoken for them all and in silence they stood there as one. "Oh, he meant it!" she said to herself now. "I saw his face and heard his voice; I know he meant it."

And the saddest part of the whole thing was that he would say he meant it still. He thought so. He did not know what treasure he had lost. "Adapted"—"practical"—twisted to serve his own

ends! He was pleased to call himself an idealist, and on that platform he would make his way. Idealism: beautiful word, rare true
spirit—bandied about. And she wondered what the lives of people
might be, could not be, were their lives formed by the greatest
moments they had known. It closes in so fast, she thought.

In writing to all their little band she had included Emil, the
boy whose status she had never quite understood. Emil, who
wasn't really one of them but lived at their teacher's, did the
chores, and was often there with them in the evenings. He hadn't
had early schooling and wasn't in their class, but took a little work
at the college, along with other things he did.

He had always seemed anxious about their teacher. Why? "Sit
down with us, Emil," their teacher would say, and he'd sit near
the door, as if that was where he wanted to be. He never talked
in their discussions. Just—listened in.

She knew no address for him except the town at school, and
in all probability he hadn't remained there. She had never known
where he came from. She feared her letter wouldn't reach him;
and there was no response from Emil.

But she heard from Virgil, though not by letter. He sent her a
story he had written which was printed in an Iowa magazine.
At first the story seemed a slap in the face. It was about a barber
who was a great dreamer. But he'd be dreaming his dreams when
his mind should have been on shaving and he would cut people
and they would spring up in rage. Then he would say, "I was just
thinking how much better things might be,"—try to tell them
what he was thinking and this made them all the more enraged.
What did they care what the hell he was thinking! Let him think
and be damned! You couldn't be a barber and think.

Once he shaved a man's head way up to the top. The man
said by God he'd call the police! "I was just thinking the world
ought to be different," the barber explained.

The barber thought it would be better if we lived up in the air like birds. Or under the water, maybe, like the fishes. We wouldn't bump into each other so much. He thought rich men should spend all their money building a ladder way up to the stars. Maybe it would be better for us up there. His enthusiasm about life in the stars caused him to cut off a man's ear. He said it was too bad, and it really was because after that no one came in to be shaved. But he couldn't think if he wasn't shaving so he took to shaving himself, all day long. This did something horrible to his skin and he was taken to the hospital, where he died. His dying words were maybe we shouldn't have faces at all. Maybe we should just think.

She knew well enough just what Virgil had set out to do. But as she read it again she saw something else. The story got away from Virgil and defeated his ends. He really liked the barber. In its fooling way the story was very alive. At first disappointed, she became more pleased with Virgil than with any of the others. Something was going on in her old friend. He was making fun of the thing he had loved, but it was there in him, so strong he had to do something about it. He'd go on writing stories more or less like this (as you read it you knew he'd go on writing) and something would escape into them and they'd go on defeating his ends, just as there was tenderness in his scoffing at the barber. And perhaps, through this tenderness in absurdity, he'd say more than he might have said had he set out to say something. She thought of writing him this, but quickly knew that would spoil it all.

She read the story to Max who laughed heartily and said it was swell, good take-off on people addled in the head. "Yet it's sort of a tender little story, don't you think?" she said. About as tender as a kick in the pants, Max thought. But never mind: she knew what the story was better than Max did—or Virgil.

Emil wasn't the only one she had failed to hear from. There was one other: Norma Ashe. Easy enough to be critical of Rosie and Austin, kindly toward Helen and hopeful for Virgil, but what about Norma Ashe, down here in Texas? Virgil's story had given her a kind of zest; it seemed to waken her mind—though how *that* would annoy him.

They had been moving about a good deal, following "leads," but were back in Dallas now and she began going to the library. First she took out a book on the civilization of Ancient Greece. It was interesting, but it set her thinking about another civilization. How meager was her actual knowledge of her own great country, a civilization not of the past alone, but of today and the future. "Know your own country," their teacher had said, "and be proud and be ashamed. It is not patriotic to hide your head. Know what is wrong and *do* something about it. Are Americans of the future to be ashamed because of what you did not do?"

She delved into the great story of the American past, read the brave old documents: The Declaration of Independence—The Bill of Rights. Wonderful names for courage and hope purposefully put down on paper: Declaration of Independence, Bill of Rights —like noble music out of the past, like a clarion-call today. The Gettysburg Address—now men would be free. One kind of slavery gone—another to come. Where was the Lincoln for today? We need you, Mr. Lincoln—your grave and kindly face, your will to freedom. How would you free the slaves today? We must do it, you say? Yes. It seems harder. Why does it seem harder? Because we will not see that it is slavery?

She read of the westward movement; her own people had been of those courageous ones. Texas. She lived in Texas. If she knew more of the valor that opened the Lone Star State would she think it so impossible to right the wrongs that followed the white man?

She became absorbed in the story of immigration: brave dreamers who followed their hopes—came believing. The believers. . . . Oh, shame upon us, that many of them found, at the foot of the rainbow, a world of cruel greed.

It was good—oh, it was *good* to be back again: eager to know; caring; believing. It was good to be Norma Ashe again.

Then something came crashing in; something she never really understood shaped the years ahead.

CHAPTER FIFTEEN

*M*AX CAME home in the middle of the morning. Norma was surprised to hear his whistle in the hall, not having expected him before night. When he came in where she was he shut the door and leaned back against it. He seemed a little breathless.

"Surprised?" he smiled. "Well, you've got a bigger surprise coming. Could hardly wait to get home to tell you. What do you think? We're leaving!"

"Leaving Dallas?"

"Leaving Texas! We're going back North. Right away. Glad?"

Glad? She was dumfounded. "But, Max, why? I mean how can you? Everything you have is here; how can you go away?"

"Easy as falling off a log. It just—arranged itself. Here's the big news: I'm taking over a business in Iroquois City, Illinois. Just the kind of country you like. Furnace business—wonderful chance. I'll help you pack. Think we can get off tomorrow?"

"Of *course* we can't get off tomorrow! And why should we? Why all this rush? I don't understand it at all."

"Norma, we've got to." He had burst in in great excitement, as if bringing good news, but . . . She saw that he was terribly shaken, something desperate about it all.

"Max—tell me! What's the matter? Why are we rushing off like this?"

"But I thought you'd be tickled to death. It's a swell town —I was there once. About fifty thousand people—growing too— lots of business. We'll have the right kind of friends. Much better

183

for Fred to grow up in a decent town. You never liked it down here, and I'm sort of sick of it myself. Too much funny business, you were right about that. Why, Norma; what's the matter? Don't you see? No more of this moving around, dabbling in one thing and another. I'll throw myself into this and— Now where are the trunks?"

She sat down. "I just won't go if you don't tell me what it's all about. What are you doing with your—your interests down here? How can you wind it all up over night? And *furnaces*. What do you know about furnaces? You can't take on a business you've never even *seen*. What is this—another trade-in? Just another wild-cat scheme? I mean why do we have to *rush off* like this, as if we were being pursued? Why, it's as if we *had* to —get out."

He came over and took her hands; his own were cold. "I want you to leave all that to me. Just take it on faith." He searched her face; and then turned away from what he saw.

He stood a moment with his back to her; and she couldn't speak—so afraid. He whirled around. "All right then, if you won't you won't. *Yes*. Something *has* happened. Yes! We *do* have to get out. Now. Right away. The sooner the better."

"Max—tell me, dear. You haven't—done anything wrong?" She asked it faintly.

"They could make it look like that," he said sullenly. "Don't *drive* me so. Stop looking at me like that! I did it for them—now it would all come back on me. If you must know—I'm the goat," he said savagely.

"But they *can't* do that to you. Don't *let* them. Just stand up and face it! Oh, Max, *no*; don't *run away*—as if you were . . ."

"That's all talk," he said angrily. "You know nothing about it."

"Is it that business in Amarillo?"

"It all got—sort of mixed up. It would have straightened out

—another month. But some busybody interfered."

"But what difference will your leaving make? Won't it all— come out, anyway?"

"They got kind of sore at me. It will ease up if I'm not around. And don't you worry! I'm not getting out of it so badly. I saw to that," he said grimly.

"You mean they—bought you out? *Paid* you to go?"

"Norma!—you're not acting very nice. Asking all these fool questions, holding us up. Where in hell *is* that trunk?" He took clothes from a closet and threw them into a pile.

She was stunned. After a time she got up and began packing their things. It seemed Max had to go. She was afraid to ask any more questions.

She remembered things now: how wrought-up he had been in the last week. She hadn't thought much about it for he was so often in a state of high excitement. If she hadn't been absorbed in the things she was reading, thinking, she would have seen what she saw now: something different about this excitement. All the telephone calls; Max rushing out at strange hours, coming back very late at night. And when Mr. Baxter was here the other night, he and Max talking in low voice in the other room, what was that she had heard him say? "Well, Max, take it all in all, we're giving you a pretty good break."

She tried to tell herself it couldn't be too bad or they wouldn't let him go at all. Certainly people would know that they were leaving. But something about next week; someone who was coming next week.

Oh, she felt so sorry for Max. All his work. All his high hopes down here. Why, he was leaving *oil*. Getting out now, running away and leaving it. He talked of other things. How nice it was going to be for her: living in God's country again. (Once this had been God's country.) Living in a town she'd be proud was her home. They'd *get* a home—yes, by gosh, they'd buy. There was good society in a town like that. They'd be part of it. She'd know the right people now, good substantial people, not these fly-by-nights.

We're the fly-by-nights, she thought. But she *had* to help Max now. She couldn't look at him and not know that. Just at the last she heard a man say, "You haven't taken much of a beating, Utterbach,"—said it pretty sourly. Ah, but he had. She knew him and knew that he had. Again he was terribly hurt; and once more she had to help him. It broke her heart to see the way he was trying to carry it all off, bearing something alone.

"Thank God," he breathed, when they were over the Texas line. And then he looked so utterly tired, as though he couldn't move or speak. He rallied though, and soon his talk was all about the good life they were going to have in Illinois: furnace business, wonderful opportunity. He's really persuading himself, she thought; coming to believe this is what he wants. There was something pretty wonderful about Max. And surely nothing really wrong. She'd tell herself it was only that he had been too impetuous, gone too far in something. But he couldn't have thought it was wrong. He had thought it would all be—made right. And then there hadn't been time.

Under different circumstances she would be glad to be going back North. Her father and Aunt Nettie were still living in the old home in Iowa. Her grandmother had died. Illinois: the University of Chicago was in Illinois. . . . What a long time ago, not actually so long, but it seemed a very long time ago—all that about the University.

She would turn from her thoughts to play with Fred, keep him amused on the long trip. He was five now, and almost as strong as he should be. How much she and Max had gone through together: losing Joseph; all their fears about Fred when he was a baby. That was marriage: things shared . . .

She had other fears about Fred now, or at least worries. He

wasn't as straightforward as she would like. He wouldn't always tell the truth about things he had done; she didn't like the way he would take things and then say he hadn't. But he was only a little boy, children outgrew such things. Perhaps, as Max said, Iroquois City would be a better place for him to grow up.

It was all very strange about this furnace business. It seemed Mr. Sessions, who had put so much money in the Texas company Max was with, owned a considerable part of that Illinois furnace company; was now turning this over in exchange for Max's interests in Texas. She hoped it would be as represented; he mustn't have another disappointment!

There were some disappointments. "He told me—!" Max would storm, and there were days when she couldn't bear his troubled face. But he began to study it all, plan. The old energy came back— rather desperately at first, as if he *had* to make this go and by God he would! Soon he was full into it: conferences, reorganization, getting more money into it. That driving force was there again, and when she heard his voice once more confident, saw him buoyant and happy as he threw himself into his new work, she was so thankful she couldn't go back and dwell much on how it had all come about.

Almost nine years they had been in Texas. Things hadn't been right in their lives there. She had felt it all along and knew it now, insofar as she would let herself know. It had been the wrong idea: snatching what they could of the resources there, regardless of others who had invested of their toil and belief. She thought of the Lone Star State, the courage that had taken men there and wrongs that had been done from the first. Not only oil was buried under the sod of the Lone Star State; many hopes and dreams were buried there. As she thought back to that wide land now, somehow her heart ached, and she knew she hadn't felt it enough while she was there. In more ways than one they had failed down there. She and Max might have been for the *good*, in Texas.

But now she had to help Max forget. They never talked of it, only of the present, the good life and the good chance up here. And she would make it a good life! It was a beautiful town, their home.

Soon after they came north Lorna was born. It was Max wanted the name Lorna, as long as she didn't wish to call the baby Norma. He said he couldn't bear the name Rosie. Lorna was like Norma, had a good sound. Sounded as if she were somebody: Lorna. Not a common name like Annie or Minnie or Rosie.

They bought a house in a good part of town. "Important to live in the right neighborhood," Max said. And know the right people: he made a great point of this. "It's up to you, Norma; you can make anybody like you without half trying. We're new people here, mustn't fall in with the wrong crowd. It's terribly important—for business and the kids and everything."

"How do I meet them?" she laughed. "Do I knock on doors and say 'Pardon me, but are you the right people?'"

"Go to church," he said. "We'll go to the Episcopal church."

"Max! You can't go to church just to get *in* with people."

"Of course you can. Everybody does."

"No; they go to church because they believe."

"Well," he laughed, "can't we believe? You're a believer in almost everything. Why not the Episcopal church?"

"When I went to church it was the Congregational; and you went to the Methodist."

"They all believe in Christ, don't they?"

"I wouldn't bring Christ into it."

"Why not?"

"Because he didn't go to church to meet people!"

"Sure he did. Met lots of people there. I read it in the Bible."

"He went to *do* something for them—not get something for himself!"

"Norma," he said wistfully, "I want to go to the Episcopal

church. I used to go sometimes in Des Moines—had a girl went there. It's dignified; really I feel quite religious when I'm there. And I never felt religious at the Methodist—just sore because the sermon was so long."

She liked Grace Church herself: a stone building, ivy-covered. It seemed older than it could have been, as if it came from the past. And the service came from the past: thought about and formed through generations of believing. There they met the Frank Fieldings and Lucy Naegal.

The Utterbachs were a good-looking couple: the right clothes, good manners and lots of fun. They'd bought a house and Utterbach was building up a business. They were liked, and soon it was being said they were an addition to the town. Max joined the Commercial Club, where he met Dick Meister, people like that. Everyone liked Norma. She joined the Woman's Club; so bright, they said, and awfully attractive. Fred made friends for them too: he went to a play-school and the mothers would meet when they came for the children.

They became a gay part of the best crowd in town, as Max called it. They'd played some bridge in Texas, and now there were bridge-parties. Max took up golf; "good business, good exercise," he'd laugh.

He was a wonderful host, and when she saw him happy and gay with these new friends it seemed something had come right for him. What may have been wrong . . . for her too that came to be something left behind.

And she liked her new friends. Helen and Lucy were college girls, it was pleasant to be with them, often talking of things they were reading. Not as she and Rosie had talked. The things that had once informed her life, they were not forgotten, but somehow they did not come into these days, as once they had lived in all days. Their manner of leaving Texas had been a great shock; she was thankful now for a growing feeling of security: not for herself so much, for Max and the children. These present-day friends seemed so well-adjusted to their agreeable lives that she slipped into that adjustment herself, as if here were a biding place for the time. It was like getting your breath: other things are in abeyance. And when you have established a manner of living, day follows day, you a part of the days as they are. Later . . . she would say to herself when intimations of change would sometimes try to disturb her.

At times she was anxious about their affairs. "Aren't we spending too much money?" she'd ask Max. "It's all right," he would assure her; "have to keep up the right appearance. Things are moving now, soon we'll be on Easy Street. You've been *swell*, Norma. Be willing to lay a bet you're the best wife in the whole world," he'd affectionately tell her.

"Perhaps we should go a little more slowly."

"That's the very way not to go!"

Certainly it wasn't the way Max could go: slowly. She knew he had gone in pretty deep, injecting new life into the business; she had signed notes. "I hate to be in debt," she'd say. "Everybody's in debt," he would assure her. "That's the way business is done."

He got some money from Texas, land he'd held on to which was wanted for oil prospecting. "I got *that* out of the dirty deal," he'd gloat. He was speculating some, excited about what you could make money do for you. "It seems reckless, Max." "And where would you get if you never took a chance? Look at Dick Meister: how did he get Elmhurst? By plodding along? Not on your life!" Elmhurst was the Meisters' big place on the outskirts of town. "Don't you worry, my dear; we'll have a bigger one some day."

"I love this one," she said. "This is our home, and just right for us."

That was what it seemed: right for them. She loved their long living-room: the polished floors, toned rugs, the deep-blue hang-

ings, chairs that were beautiful and comfortable. Then there was
the screened porch off the dining-room, where they had breakfast, friends for tea, cocktails out there on a pleasant evening. It
looked out on a gently sloping lawn, a beautiful old elm; her
flowers, where she loved to work. Their airy bedroom with its
chintz curtains and hooked-rugs; the children's gay rooms.

There was trouble at school about Fred. He'd take things that
belonged to the other children, bring them home and hide them.
She couldn't seem to make him see this was wrong. He'd promise
not to do it again, but he would. His teacher was worried about
it, said she'd never had a case quite like this; didn't know how to
handle it. "Perhaps you can," she said to Norma; "or his father. It's
too bad the way he'll blame things on other children, things he
has done himself. Of course," she added, as if afraid she had said
too much, "he'll outgrow it—with your help."

But she feared Miss Freeman was worried about keeping Fred
in school. The other mothers knew too, as the children knew. It
was terribly humiliating, though they were friendly with her about
it. "It's a job to get them started right," Helen said. "Little Helen
used to take my jewelry and lock it in her doll-house," she'd gen-
erously added. "It seems they aren't born knowing right from
wrong. And if you can't teach it with words—well, there's the
good old hair-brush way, you know."

She didn't want to go the old hair-brush way. She would talk
to Fred about right and wrong, growing up an honorable person
who was trusted and loved; she talked with him as gently and reasonably as she could. Fred would listen, at times with a politeness
that was disconcerting, other times restless, thinking only of getting away.

One night one of the fathers came and said he guessed he'd have
to have Joe's skates back. Joe was raising the roof about it, said
Fred had them. "Kids will swipe stuff," he said. "Have to whale
it out of them."

They found the skates, and Max was furious. "He had skates of his own!" he cried. "To think that a son of mine—!"

He said they had been too easy with Fred; just because he'd been puny as a baby they'd spoiled him. He whipped him that night—too hard. It only seemed to make the boy more sullen.

Surely there was a better way. Why couldn't she reach her own child? She'd just have to go on trying, never lose her patience. If he were ill she wouldn't lose patience with him, and this was an illness of another sort. He'd outgrow it, she would tell herself, outgrow it as he had the physical weakness in babyhood.

She had lost Rosie. This was as incomprehensible as it was sad. But Rosie had never replied to the letter about her "new religion." That just didn't seem Rosie at all, hurt though she may have been. Norma had sent letters wherever she thought there was a chance of finding her. The one she addressed to Rosie's old home in South Dakota was returned. What had happened to the Major family? Dead? Gone elsewhere? Where *was* Rosie? It didn't seem possible they could lose one another like this, they who had been so close. In one way, no one in the world had been as close to her as Rosie. Some morning the bell would ring and it would be Rosie, standing there smiling.

Occasionally she would see a story by Virgil, in the eastern magazines now. They all had that same manner: scoffing, very funny, but usually something would escape, something that had been Virgil (still was?) would come into the story. One of them she didn't like so well. It was about a girl not unlike the Norma Ashe Virgil had known. She married a man worth a million dollars in order to save him from himself, and with truly remarkable speed became the most fashionable and autocratic woman in Pittsburgh. No tender feeling about life escaped into this story. It didn't even seem funny to her, but Helen said wasn't it satirical and amusing, so possibly she was prejudiced.

Of course they had a car now, and one evening when they were driving around town with the children Max slowed before the Pettibone place: a big, pretentious, ungainly house.

"Like it?" he asked.

"What is there to like about it? It's a monstrous house."

"Sorry you don't like it. It may be ours some day."

"Are you crazy, Max? It's the last house in town I'd want to live in."

"Took a mortgage on it a while back."

"You—? But . . . I don't believe I understand."

"It's not so very hard to understand," he smiled.

"But don't they live there? It's the family home, isn't it? Then how could you—?"

"The old man was tickled to death. The bank wouldn't handle it. Maybe it is a bit of a risk, but the interest, my dear, is something pretty."

"Let's not talk about it before the children," she said in a low voice.

That was the first quarrel she'd had with Max in a long time. In the course of it he said: "The less you know about my business affairs the better."

"I'm not going to live on money wrung out of a family's home!"

"Oh, my dear, what money *would* you live on—with your ideas? They want the money, I take the security; that's a simple business proposition."

"I *hate* your simple business propositions!"

"Better not, my darling. You'd have to hate me," he smiled. "These people look on me as a benefactor. They're holding their house—for a while. Now listen, Norma. Mitchell is coming down from Chicago next Tuesday. I want to throw a swell dinner for him. Let's see, we'll have . . ."

Max went up to Chicago occasionally, and sometimes would propose she go with him. But she never had. She just might want to go out and see the University. . . . Too far back—everything so different now. Better not.

They had six years of life in the smart gay set of that town. There wasn't a more popular couple than the Utterbachs. Toward the last she began to worry, as she felt Max was worried. He showed the strain of all he was doing, things he was carrying which she knew little about. One night his lawyer, John Stockton, was there with him, and as she was passing the library she heard him say: "I don't like it, Max. You're getting in too deep." "I can pull out," he answered. "Just another five months and I'll have—"

She didn't want to stand there listening, but when they went up to their room that night she said: "Max, I'd like to live on less money."

"First woman in the history of the world to say so," he laughed.

"Well, I would. You know perfectly well there's something about money worries me. I can get along without Edna. I can manage all right with just Clara."

"Edna!" he scoffed. "Ten dollars a week! Think that's going to get anybody out of a hole?"

"Are we in a hole?" she asked quickly.

"Of course not," he was as quick to reply. "Can't I speak—in a manner of speaking?"

He went on to assure her that times were going to be good now: the war was bound to be good for business. Two months now there had been war in Europe, France and England at war with Germany. How terrible, Norma felt, that we should have come to this place in civilization only to revert to war. Every morning the papers had their terrible stories: death, destruction, suffering of the innocent and the helpless. While her heart ached for the people who were enduring, she was at the same time thankful we were so far away; we would have no part in it. Now Max seemed to think we were going to profit by it. . . .

"I do not want any gains from the suffering of others," she said.

Max said the war was sure hell. The Germans had done it and he hoped the last one of them would be strung up and quartered. Butchery was too good for them. Just the same one might as well be realistic. There were going to be profits. If the war went on American business would boom. He didn't know why he shouldn't have his share. "Just as soon as I work out of this tough spot I'm in . . ."

Tough spot. . . . Then it was true.

She was anxiously twisting the ring on her finger. Suddenly the lights in the stone gave her an idea. She knew Max had paid eleven hundred dollars for it. Suppose he needed a thousand dollars and she went on wearing her ring? "You know, Max, any time things *were* tight—here's my ring. Of course you know I'd be glad—"

He sprang out of bed. "You'd be glad! Norma, do you know you almost *horrify* me? Why, that ring isn't *money*. Don't you know I *meant* something when I gave you that ring? Have you forgotten our talk about it: imperishable—like our love? At least— at least I *thought* it was imperishable. Now you—"

He sat down on the side of the bed, his head in his hands. She went and sat by him, her arms around him. "Max—darling, *please;* you *know* I didn't mean it that way. I just thought—"

He took her arm from around his shoulder, took her hand and looked at the ring. "You know what's in it? Our tears turned to laughter—that's what those lights are. Didn't you know?"

Regarding him, there were tears in her eyes now, and the light of a love imperishable. "Little Joseph is in that ring," he went on; "the smile we never had. And then—God damn it," he burst out, "you talk about selling it!"

"I won't," she laughed and cried. "Dearest! I promise I won't."

"No matter what happens—you promise you won't?"

"No matter what happens, I promise I won't."

"Because I want you to have it as long as you live,"

"Because you want me to have it as long as I live," she repeated as if it were ritual.

"You know, Norma, there are things more important than money."

"Yes," she said softly. And she was happy, for it was Max—*Max*—who had said this. "I was stupid."

"Stupid, will you now come to bed? And stop worrying? When there's anything to worry about I'll let you know. But there won't be. In five months now I'll have it all cleaned up."

It seemed to her she had never loved Max as she loved him that night.

But the time to worry came quickly. They didn't have five months. They had only five days.

One golden October afternoon she was out in her garden when Edna called her to the phone. A man from the office began to talk fumblingly over the wire. "Why, Mrs. Utterbach, I wanted to tell you— Just called up to say—"

"What *is* it, Joe? Is something wrong?"

"Well, you see—hate like everything to tell you over the phone. Is someone there with you? One of your friends?"

"Stop this beating about and *tell* me! Is it—Max?"

"Well—well, yes, it is. You see he went down to the foundry. They were having some trouble there—something broke. Guess you wouldn't understand about that. We've got a rush order and our best mechanic is sick. Max was all upset; then got an idea *he* could fix it, so he—well—"

"You mean—he's hurt?"

"Well, to tell the truth, he is hurt—some. There was a bad explosion. He was sort of pinned-down and— Now don't you worry. They'll get him all fixed up; taking him to the hospital right now."

"The hospital?" She could barely say it. "You mean—it's bad?"

"It seems—course they can't tell yet—thought if you and one of your friends—"

One of her friends! As if any friend in the world could matter— Max hurt. *Max—hurt*. Not badly, surely. That wouldn't happen to Max. He could always . . .

Late that night Max seemed to know he was going to die. His eyes were imploring her to understand something. He could say a little. "In a mess—just now. Little more time—another five months— Do your best, Norma. Tried . . . for you . . . the kids . . ."

"Yes, Max," she said, and said it calmly. "Don't worry, darling. I understand." She never knew where she got the strength for it: able to remain calm while she was losing Max. Only one thing she knew: she must help him—see him through.

It was afterwards she knew she had lost him; it was in the days that followed she couldn't believe it.

They'd loved each other. Through thick and thin, ups and downs, right and wrong—they loved each other. She him—he her. There'd never been any other man for her, and no one else for Max. With all his passionate warmth, his gay vitality, Max had loved her and her alone, even when she exasperated him by not liking things he did. It wasn't often like this, she knew. Something between her and Max couldn't be destroyed—not by ways of man or commandment of God! As life is bruised a million times and begets new life, so their love, bruised at times by differences between them, could always beget new love. It grew stronger in tribulations, was watered by their sorrows and flourished in the sunshine of their joys. It was life itself, and so as strong as life. And now they had come to death.

It was stronger than death! She would rise from this, her own grave, and . . . Max couldn't bear defeat. He wasn't going to be defeated! Somehow, she'd carry on for him. What he had wanted for them, the life he wanted for her, the children, what he had tried so hard to make be—*she* would make be. Somehow. Max couldn't bear defeat.

"It came at a bad moment," their lawyer told her, gently as he could. "He had gotten in pretty deep. Another five months—" He tapped with a pencil and was silent; she never knew what it would have been in another five months. She did know, for he had to tell her, that practically everything was gone.

It made her heart ache for Max; and made her angry, though at what she did not know. Max shouldn't have been treated like this! *Max*, so gay and energetic, always so confident. Again, he was hurt. She must find the way to make it right, as if that would be saving him from the sense of failure which was the very thing he never could endure.

"Of course, you'll have your house," John Stockton was saying. "And there's a little money I think they can't reach. Then there's the old Pettibone place—Max took that over, you know. I believe we can hold on to that, and something might be done with it."

Their way of living would have to change, at least for a time. It was she would make the living now. How? She didn't know yet. She'd do it though! See that the children were brought up as Max would wish—save *that* for him. Not defeat; not total failure and defeat—not for Max!

The children went around as if the sky had fallen, as indeed it had: bright sky he had kept secure over their little lives. They loved him and were grieving for him. How they'd admired, worshipped, their gay strong father. In trying to help them, and struggling to understand all the new things she must deal with, indulgence in her own grief had to be deferred. It waited for her; it did not lessen or go away with the days, the months, the years.

Their friends were kind, but she could feel they were shocked, scandalized by the state of Max's affairs. They're all doing it themselves, she'd think defensively. It was only that Max had to let go at a bad moment and it—came to light. Are Dick Meister and Frank Fielding any better? Only a little richer—something to fall back on. She *couldn't* be against Max; not now! Right or wrong she was with him—oh, *with* him!

There was something in the paper: a plunger, they called him, playing the market with other people's money, defrauding. She could have gone and killed that publisher. She knew him—Max knew plenty about him! His money dealings weren't as righteous as his talk. The hypocrites!

One man who had lost came to see her. "Where's my money?" he cried. "He told me I'd double it in three months. Well, where *is* it? I've a wife and children. I'm a poor man. Are you going to live on here in luxury while my children leave school to go to work?"

He was so angry he could scarcely speak, and he was almost sobbing.

"I don't think there is going to be much luxury for me," she said. "Mr. Utterbach never meant you were to lose your money. In five months he would have—"

"And what do I care about five months?" he demanded. "He's *robbed* me. He's a thief!"

"You stop talking like that about him! And I—I will do the best I can."

But what? What could she do about it—now, without Max? "I want to do all I can to settle Max's affairs honorably," she told their lawyer. "I will pay back all I can."

He shook his head. "You can't. You'll have only enough to start out on."

Helen Fielding proposed she open a school. "I should think you'd be a good teacher, Norma. We'll all send our children and gradually you'll get others."

Teach? Once—long long time ago—someone else had said she'd be a good teacher. . . . But now? Teach as she felt now? No; she couldn't do that.

One evening she walked down past the Pettibone house. His

lawyer justified Max in having taken it. "They wouldn't make any effort to keep up the payments, acted as if they didn't have to. Perhaps they're relieved to be rid of it."

Standing across the street, looking at the gloomy pile, she should think they would be glad to be rid of it. And what was she going to do with it?

Two girls carrying suitcases came along, stopped, looking over at the house. "Is that a rooming-house?" one of them asked.

She shook her head.

"Looked as if it might be. Awful hard to find rooms in this town," she explained wearily.

And that gave her the idea: *she* might use this Pettibone place, a boarding-house.

She walked quickly away, as from an idea more dismal, more fantastic, than the house itself.

But what *would* she do, she kept desperately asking herself in the next week. Certainly she couldn't go home and live on her father; he was too old for new burdens, and there would be no work for her to do in that little town. She had already put up her own house for sale—this dear house she and Max had been proud of and loved. She couldn't afford to live in it. It was in an expensive neighborhood and should bring good money.

So one morning she went to the Pettibone house and walked all through it. It was very large; it was near the center of town and should be good for this purpose. Max would object to her running a boarding-house. But what am I to do, dear? her mind said, as if talking to him. Only for a little time, she tried to tell him, till I can get straightened around.

She was alone in the big dreary house; she threw herself down on one of the beds, sobbed as she hadn't given way since she lost Max.

Her own house sold quickly. Now they'd have to move—go

somewhere. She resolved to try it, telling herself it would only be for a little while; she could get the business going, then sell out to someone else.

Mr. Stockton did his best to restrain her, but she paid back all she could of the money Max owed. It covered only a part of it, but went where it was most needed to take stigma from his name. She was doing something for him, and for her own pride in him. "You're going to need money yourself," the lawyer kept telling her. "There have to be repairs down there, some new furniture. It won't begin paying immediately."

She kept what she thought she would have to have, she owed that to her own children. But it wasn't enough, and the worries about debt began almost at once.

She did not sell her ring. ("Promise?" "I promise." "No matter what happens?" "As long as I live." The love there was between them that night . . .) She kept her diamond.

The day they left their own home, the last thing she walked through all the rooms, seeing Max there—confident, gay. He would want them to stay on here; but how could they? She wished she could make him understand.

She'd made their own rooms down there as attractive as she could before they moved in. At first the children were impressed by the size of the house. They ran all around, Lorna sliding down banisters, Fred investigating.

Then they came back to her and stood there disconsolately. "Let's go home," Fred said. Lorna began to cry.

"Why, children," she said, as brightly as she could, "was that the way your father acted when he had some new thing to do?"

"I want Papa to come *back*," Lorna sobbed.

Oh, my dear, don't I?—don't I? was the thought she did not speak, as she held back the tears she must not shed.

"My Dad wouldn't like it here," Fred said, rather loftily.

No, he wouldn't; she knew that too.

"Well, *I* think," she said, "we're going to have a lot of fun here. Did you know it was the biggest house in town?"

That began her life at Mrs. Utterbach's . . .

*   *   *   *

It was of all these things Norma Ashe, Mrs. Utterbach, had been thinking in those days after her old friend Rosie came to see her. She did not begin at the beginning and in ordered fashion live it through to that present moment, as one might set it down in an account of what had happened; that is not the way of our thoughts. Sometimes she saw a little house on a Texas plain, again she would see the girl who rode on a train through wheat-fields of South Dakota. She heard the voice of the man who had initiated her into the wonder of the world; she saw the love in the eyes of the man she had loved. It had not all opened to her; time dims, and the life of recent past years had warped and corroded. She had not been remembering for the pleasures of remembering happier or more worthy days. She had been trying to find out one thing: how she could be both the Mrs. Utterbach of this boarding-house and the Norma Ashe she also had been. It had seemed important to try and see just where she began to lose what had once been herself. She still did not know—and did it so greatly matter? When?— where?—why, all along the way, perhaps. Life defeats us, she thought, though thought this not very convincingly, made uneasy by a feeling there must be another way. But if there were, she had lost it—and too late now. Desperate worries and petty cares, driven into a corner where one is small and mean when some little spark still lives to make one want to be generous; the canny scheming to get ahead of another that she may not get ahead of you— what vision there?—what chance? We are entangled by a sordid web, and in this we fight—spitefully.

She felt resentments toward old things—an old beauty—that

had waked, would wake, for her. The best she had known she tried to hold out, yet there was an unwelcomed sense of wonder that it should still live, and want to come to her.

I did the best I could, she thought wearily. But knew this wasn't true. Others might say it for her, she knew it was not true; though she tried not to know this too well.

PART III

*I*N CHICAGO things were not going smoothly for Fred Utter-bach. His business had been rudely (he thought most unjustly) interrupted. He was in jail for bootlegging.

He called it a dirty outrage; he had been assured he had protection. Would he have been such a fool as to go into this line if Smith hadn't all but sworn on the Bible he was protected? But here he was, locked up like a criminal, and Smith claiming he was broke and couldn't pay the fine. It was downright dishonest to run a business like this if you couldn't handle the fines. Smith claimed he'd been double-crossed. Boloney to that. Smart guys didn't get themselves double-crossed.

This wasn't going to be good for his future. They'd all be afraid of him now—getting himself pinched. Just as he was seeing a real future for himself, here he gets this set-back. Some fellows got all the breaks. Why, he'd been expecting to send some money to his mother, he honest-to-God had. She'd had it tough, Mom. He was going to be a help to her in her old age, tell her he had a nice little business now (needn't say what it was, she'd be old-fashioned about that) and here was a check and there'd be more where it came from. That's what he was thinking as he read Lorna's letter, just before the damn cops came. As for them—the coppers—they weren't too good to drink the stuff; well then, didn't somebody have to keep it in circulation?

Now take that judge; no decent bootlegger could look at him without knowing he lived on the stuff. Tell by the way he fidgeted he could hardly wait to get home to his bottle. And where did he get the bottle? From a bootlegger, where else? Lousy hypocrites—the bunch of them!

But sitting here sore wasn't getting him anywhere; time to use the old bean if he wasn't going to spend three months in this stinking jail. Have to get hold of some dough.

Of course, there was his mother. Maybe she could raise it somehow. Hike the mortgage on the house, maybe. Guess not, from what Lorna said. The place was about falling into the dump. Crazy idea in the first place: running that boarding-house. He'd never liked it there. How different his future would have been if the old man had lived. He'd be somebody in that town now if his dad hadn't kicked-out. Have his own car: Packard, probably, and that bunch of ritzy dolls that thought they were too good for him would all be eating right out of his hand. Some fellows had all the breaks.

Hettie would go back on him now. That baby wasn't the kind to stick. O.K.—let her; he was getting kind of fed-up anyway—too much talk about getting married. Not for him! A fellow didn't have to get married.

Fine time for Lorna to be acting up; just made it all the harder for him to put it up to Mom. He took out Lorna's letter and read it again.

"Dear Fred: I wish you'd write to Mother. She's terribly upset because I got married. Well, I *did* get married, and what's wrong with that I'd like to know. Haven't I a right to be happy? Mother got married when she wanted to. I don't see why I shouldn't.

"But I feel awfully sorry for her, she's taking it so hard. She isn't very well now, and she's been sort of strange lately. I just didn't know what to make of her; even before this happened about me her mind was somewhere else all the time, ever since a certain lady, whose name I don't know, came to see her. Mother used to know her. Maybe she's been dwelling in the past; I can't tell be-

cause she doesn't say anything. She has had it awfully hard, when
you think how different her life used to be. But honestly, one
reason I got married, I just couldn't stand it: Mother so strange all
the time. I guess you know it hasn't been very pleasant at the
boarding-house lately.

"She was upset because I hadn't told her what I was going to
do; but if I'd told her she would have done everything she could
to stand in our way. She doesn't like George—seems to think he
isn't good enough for us. You know how Mother is, always wanting us to keep up, as if we had more than we have. I really think
she has *false standards*. I suppose it's because her life used to be
different. But you can't *hang on* like that; that's what I tell her.

"George and I have moved out. We have two light-housekeep-
ing rooms up on Milton Street. It's too bad to leave her there alone,
but it would have been just out of the question to stay, Mother
going around looking like death. That would be no way to begin a
marriage.

"I guess you know George. You saw him when you were there
last time—acting so smart. You, I mean. I mean it was you acted
smart. His name is Stanton. They call him Doc—he's with the
School. Maybe you don't like him either, and if you don't that's
just too bad! He's awfully bright, does some teaching, but later
he's going out on his own, and we'll move to Peoria, I think.

"I'm sending this to ask you to write to Mother. Now you can
at least do *that*. Write her a nice letter; tell her it's natural for a
girl to get married, that it's all right. Maybe you could send her
some money. She's been so worried about the bills it's driven her
nearly crazy. You always act as if you were in the money, but I
notice you're always asking instead of sending. I think Mother
may lose the house, and what she would do then I don't know. I
know she wouldn't live with us, even if we were farther along and
could have her. She's very bitter about our marriage; though not
so much bitter as—well, broken-hearted, it seems. Of course that

makes me feel awful—but can you help it if you fall in love and have to lead your own life?

"Now write to her, will you, Fred? She tried hard for us. You *owe* it to her. Yours, Lorna."

Just a peach of a letter to be reading in jail! Lorna ought to be ashamed of herself. She wasn't bad-looking, could have married some money, been a pride to Mom, a comfort. Yes, he remembered the fellow. Kind of a cross between a cheap parson and a slicker. Always shooting off his mouth. He'd never get very far either, not in that two-by-four racket. Lorna'd be poor all her life—the little sap.

He had eleven bucks. Might call his mother long distance, tell her he didn't like the fellow either. That would sort of draw them together, and then he'd get on to this business of the fine. He just hated it like the very devil. He'd always had too soft a heart.

But where would she get the money? If she was about to lose the house, nothing doing there. Then he gave a long low whistle. By golly there was that ring! She must still have it. Once when he'd told her he could get real money for it she'd flared up and said that ring would be hers as long as she lived! That was because Dad gave it to her, down in Texas. Sentiment—naturally a person had sentiment. Wonder some of those cheap-skate boarders hadn't pinched it. He'd told her they would some day, but she'd never listen to reason about that nice little hunk of ice. Pretty good-sized hunk, at that.

Well, she'd listen now. No real mother was going to hang on to a diamond when it meant keeping her son in jail; that just wouldn't be natural. Once he'd asked her what Dad paid for it and she'd said eleven hundred dollars. "He couldn't afford it then either," she'd said. "But then—Max was like that." He remembered how she'd run the ring round on her finger, smiling down at its sparkle. The one decent thing she'd held on to; something she didn't need at all, and not knowing where to turn for her next sou.

"Maybe the trip'll do you good. Little change, you know. Night, Mom. Thanks no end."

He felt much better as he went along to be locked in. Good for Mom! Seemed to take it pretty hard though. Well, she needn't. He'd pay it all back. Then she could get something useful. She sure needed clothes. Pretty silly to wear a big diamond with clothes like hers, hands all rough. He'd get going in Detroit and then she'd have it easier. He went to sleep.

Now Norma Ashe was trying to cross State Street. It seemed impossible—all the cars, the clamor. She stood helplessly at the curb. She had just seen her son—in that place. Her legs would barely hold her up. But she must get across this street. Other people were going now, she'd go along with them, one of the crowd. But a car coming round the corner was right upon her, horn shrieking. She couldn't think which way to move, just stood there until: "Make up your mind, sister!" the driver yelled, and she stepped back to the sidewalk.

A policeman was there. "Bothered about the traffic?" he asked kindly. "I'm going over, you just come along with me. Now we've lost the lights. Just take it easy. Stranger?"

She nodded. "Kind of confusing if you're not used to it," he said.

"Yes." Then, trying to speak more brightly, for he was so kind, "It is, isn't it?"

"Leave it to me. They don't run the police down," he laughed.

When they were on the other side she looked both ways, confused.

"Know your way about?" he asked.

She looked up at the big man. He had a friendly face, he had been kind. She held out her ring finger. "I'm going to try and sell this ring. I was going to go to Swann's first."

He looked at the ring. Then she saw he was looking at her clothes: shabby old winter coat, hat she'd had—how long was it she'd had this hat? She had a sudden picture of how she looked; she hadn't thought much about it before.

"Things were different then," she said.

He nodded. "Things can change. Got to sell it in a hurry?"

"Yes, today. I must have the money today."

"You—you can prove ownership?" he asked.

"Why, of course. My husband gave it to me—twenty-one years ago. That was down in Texas."

"Got a receipt for it? Some kind of papers? Is it insured?"

"It was once. I let it run out. I—I haven't been so well-off lately." But he can see that for himself, she thought.

He was looking at her as if sizing her up. "My husband paid eleven hundred dollars for it," she said tremulously. (Why did she have to *prove* the ring was hers?—ring Max gave her.) "It was worth more than that. He bought it from a man who wanted to sell in a hurry."

"Just like you," he smiled, as if satisfied with his inspection of her. "Well, Swann's is a good place to try first. If they won't take it—under the circumstances—"

What circumstances? she wanted to ask.

"There's a place round on— Here, I'll write it down for you. They won't ask so many questions. Though they ought to," he said, speaking more as a policeman. She looked so bewildered he added: "Lots of hot ice, you know."

Hot ice? She didn't know what that meant. How strange it was —in Chicago.

She walked past the big glittering store twice before she could go in. "Promise?" she could hear Max say. "I promise." "No matter what happens—as long as you live?"

She felt that the clerk who came up to her was surprised to see her in their rich beautiful place of jewels and silver. Summoning all courage she could she pulled the ring off and passed it over to him. "I would like to sell this ring," she said.

He looked at the diamond—at her hand, her hat. "You want us to value it for you?" he asked.

"I hoped you would buy it." Oh, why did her voice have to be trembling like this! As he said nothing, only looking at her, "You do buy diamonds, don't you?" she asked, almost aggressively.

"At times, under proper circumstances," he said with restraint.

"There is nothing wrong with the circumstances. My husband gave it to me—twenty-one years ago, in Texas."

"Texas is a long way off." He smiled and she didn't like his smile.

He took the ring to another man who began looking at it through a glass. She walked down there: would they try to take the ring away from her? They both looked from the ring to her. "Better call Harry," the man who had examined it said.

"Give it to me!" she suddenly cried, and loud enough so the well-dressed people around were looking at her. As they hesitated, "It's my ring! You can't keep it if I want it back!"

"I can assure you, madam, we have no intention of keeping it against your will. We didn't *ask* for the ring, you may remember. You came in here wanting to sell it, and we would like to have our Mr. Watson—"

"Watson—store detective," she heard a woman near her murmur to a companion.

The ring was there, lying on a little piece of blue velvet. She snatched it and slipped it back on her finger. She was near a side door and was out on the street before any of them seemed to know what to do.

She must get lost in the crowd! They'd be coming after her!

But why am I *doing* this? she demanded of herself after she had gone a few blocks. Running away as if I *had* stolen the ring. She had seemed surrounded by suspicion; the ring Max gave her in the hands of cold suspicious people; she couldn't bear it, had to have her ring back!

But what good had this done? She couldn't keep it: Fred, their son, baby—once their baby—locked up in jail. She'd have to go to that place the policeman had written down for her.

Here too there was question of ownership, but they didn't seem to care much about it here. They offered her three hundred dollars. Three hundred—Fred's fine. But he had said he would have to have more: get away, new start. And three hundred!—ring Max had been so proud—

"It's worth eleven hundred," she said.

"Oh, but you can't expect to *get* that for it; not when you're selling in such a hurry." Yes, she had come in breathless; she wasn't doing this well, not at all. He stood there smiling as if he *knew* something; and what was there to know she'd like to ask him! His look made her angry. "I'll not sell it for three hundred," she said.

It ended with her getting four hundred and twenty-five. She came out of the place so weak she almost put out her hand to take hold of a passer-by. Oh, Max—Max!—I wish you were here—help me get home. Home? Where was home? That jail where they had Fred locked up.

Fred said it was a dirty gyp. If they'd let him out, given him a couple of hours, he'd have had seven hundred; nine maybe. "Oh, well, never mind, Mom; guess you did the best you could. And don't you worry! I'll get even with them! I'm going to get even with the whole lousy bunch!"

Now they were in a place eating. It was crowded and noisy, she felt faint. "Why were you in there?" she asked dully.

"Well, I'll tell you—seeing as you've helped me out. I'm in the liquor business—lots of risks."

Liquor business? But this was Prohibition. Oh—*that*.

"That's against the law," she said.

"That law?" he scoffed. "Who keeps it? Do you think your old crowd down in Iroquois City aren't getting their liquor? Is it any worse to sell it than to buy it?"

Perhaps not; she couldn't seem to think anything out.

"It's dangerous to sell it," she said.

"Found that out," he laughed. "Well, I'll be more careful now."

"You're going on with it?" She was speaking as if she didn't much care.

"Sure I'm going on with it. I'm no quitter, am I?"

Fred—her son, sitting opposite her now eating roast-beef. Struggling to keep him alive when he was a baby, she and Max. Max's son. ("Tell you what, we'll send him to Harvard.") She looked into his face, then back to her plate, not liking what she had seen. She wasn't looking into the face of a good man when she looked at her Fred. It began when he was a child . . . something left out of Fred; she wondered a little at not caring more. Lorna married to Doc Stanton. Lorna and Fred: their children. It seemed she had come to the end of everything she had tried to do, but too tired and dazed to care much about coming to the end. It was almost a relief to have it over, nothing to go on for now.

As they were eating their dessert: "Say, Mom, what are you going to do now?" he asked.

"I don't know," she said. *You* don't care what I am going to do, she thought. But what *am* I? she asked herself.

"Like to show you around, but you know yourself this isn't much of a pile. Be different next time I see you; be taking you round in my car next time. But now I ought to be seeing a couple of fellows and then I'll get right on to Detroit."

"Very well," she said.

"You going back home tonight?"

She thought about it and a little to her own surprise said no.

"Think you can't make it, eh? You do look kind of done-up. Gee, Mom, it was good of you. I want you know I appreciate it. You had kind of a sentiment about that ring, didn't you?"

She was silent, her lips pressed together.

" 'Cause Dad gave it to you," Fred went on, as one who understands all about sentiment. "But he would have wanted you to do it. Dad always believed in looking out for the family."

As she did not speak: "Often think how different our lives would have been if he hadn't gone fooling around in that boiler-room. And what was he doing there for heaven's sake? Wasn't his business to fix things."

"Does it matter now?" she asked. Though it had always been Max's business to fix things; always thought he could make right anything that was wrong.

"Well, where will you stay tonight? Here!" he said magnanimously. "You just take some of this money, enough for a couple of days. Get yourself a little rest."

"I don't want *one cent* of that money!"

"You mean—you've got some?"

She nodded. For the trip she had taken money saved for the interest on the mortgage. Now it didn't seem to matter about the mortgage on the house.

"Don't suppose you've got much though," Fred said, looking at her in a special way, canny way, he had. How much *did* she have? A hundred twenty-five wasn't much to start out on in Detroit. Wouldn't have that when he got there. Wished he could jump his room rent, but he had to go out there for his clothes.

Then he had one of his ideas. Now why couldn't his mother take over that room and maybe she could square up for the two weeks he owed. If she were there, taking over the room, he might make a get-away. Pay it all back of course.

"I've got a room out south—on Ellis. You could just take over my place for tonight, or as long as you want. It's not a bad dump," he assured her; as good as your own boarding-house, he was thinking.

So she went with him. She had nothing to propose herself, and it made little difference where she went.

She stayed on there for a week; and then came to know she couldn't go back to Iroquois City. She didn't think out why, too weary to think. Just knew she couldn't go back.

With great effort she wrote a letter to Lorna. "I'm up here with Fred." (What difference whether it was true or not? Might keep Lorna from thinking she ought to do something about her mother.) "I'm not coming back. If you and your husband want to take over the house you can. You can have it for yours. I'll sign it over to you, whatever is necessary. If you don't want it, and I wouldn't blame you, just let it go. If there is any money to be had from it, you take that. I don't want anything more to do with it."

Perhaps Doc Stanton could make a go of the boarding-house. She'd never go back to that town.

Next morning she realized she had only enough money for one more week. She'd have to do something, get work.

This arranged itself with little initiative on her part. That very day Mrs. Hughes discharged the girl who did the rooms. Lazy slut! She'd telephone the agency. One thing, the new one couldn't be worse.

"I could do this work," she heard herself saying. "I ran a boarding-house myself—thirteen years."

Mrs. Hughes looked surprised, then doubtful. "Well, I don't know, Mrs. Utterbach. If you've had your own place, afraid you wouldn't like to work for someone else—not this kind of work. And you don't look very strong."

"You'll find I'm strong enough."

After a couple of weeks Mrs. Hughes said: "Your last name—kind of awkward to be saying it all the time. We're used to calling the girls by first names. Mind if we use your first name? It would be easier for the roomers."

She did mind—a little.

"I know you aren't very young to be called by your first name. It's customary though."

So again she was Norma. "Norma will be up to do your room in just a minute!" "Norma—*Norma*—where *are* you?" "Norma you forgot the towels for third-front. You'll just have to put your *mind* on things."

One day Mrs. Hughes sent her on an errand. "You take the Cottage Grove car and get off at Sixty-third Street. You'll get off just after you cross the Midway. Then you— What's the matter?" she asked, for Norma was standing there as if something had happened.

"You said . . . after I cross . . . What am I to cross?"

"I said the *Midway*. Goodness! Everybody knows the Midway. Great big open place. The University of Chicago is there."

Norma sat down.

"What *is* the matter with you? Don't you feel right?"

"Oh, yes—yes, I feel all right."

"There's been trouble enough here for one day. Now I said something about the University, but you don't go that way."

"No, I understand. I don't go that way."

"When you get off, at Sixty-third, you turn the other way. The University will make it easy for you because you are to go the *other* way."

"Yes—I did. I mean—yes, I will."

She went as in a trance. When she got there she wasn't to turn toward the University; no—the *other* way. That should be natural enough. . . .

But she got off at the Midway, and did walk a little way toward the University. She just stood there in the open where she could see it. There it was at last: The University of Chicago. Gray stone buildings; green roofs, red roofs. Big. Many buildings. Boys and girls carrying books would come along. They went to the University of Chicago. People were still doing that. Young people still going to the University. . . . Abruptly she turned away.

"Did you get along all right?" Mrs. Hughes asked, rather kindly. Norma looked tired, sort of strange. She supposed she really should get a younger person for the work.

"Yes," Norma told her; "I got along all right."

But she hadn't. She was knowing something: knowing that at last she had seen the University of Chicago; and she could know many other things, unless she tried very hard not to. She had been locked in—since Lorna, since Fred; and now those old old things trying to come to life again, as they had after Rosie's visit. It frightened her. Her life had to be just *this:* the rooms at Mrs. Hughes'. She couldn't *live* any other way. She did more work than she need do, wanting to be so tired she couldn't be threatened by— By *what?* It was all nonsense. She would simply stop thinking about it. We had some control over our thoughts, didn't we?

But it was like fighting stars, tides, any other thing over which you have no control. She was all the time knowing it was there— so close—the University, all it had once meant to her.

At last she desperately decided, I'll get this over with! I'll *go* there. All the way this time! And then I'll know, once and for all, it has nothing on God's earth to do with me. *Let* it be there. What harm can it do me when it has nothing to do with me?

She told Mrs. Hughes she believed she'd take her afternoon off this week; she hadn't been taking them, what would she do with them? Mrs. Hughes said all right, perhaps it would do her good.

Of course it would do her good! She'd walk all around there— in and out—and know it had nothing more to do with her than if she had died and were now living another life. And that was the truth of it: died and now living another life. She wasn't Norma, twenty-one years old, who was to have gone to the University of Chicago. She was Norma, forty-nine, who cleaned-up at Mrs. Hughes'.

wo GIRLS were sitting on a bench in the quadrangle of the Building of Modern Languages and Literature at the University of Chicago. They were supposed to be studying German but instead were chatting in English. "Only trouble with studying outdoors," said the one in the light blue sweater and brown pleated skirt, "you forget to study. It's one of those things seems a better idea than it is."

"On a day like this," said the girl in navy-blue suit, running her fingers through her bobbed hair, "we should just— Oh Lordy!" Quickly she put back her hand to keep papers from blowing away, not completing her idea of what they should do on a day like this. "Your date all right for Friday?"

"Joe's going up to Lake Forest, darn it. But there's always Harry. I think maybe I'll wear my white. Do you think that would be rushing the season?"

"The season seems to be rushing itself." She caught a loose sheet just in time and said she guessed they'd have to go in.

"I wish the world were run right. Wish we had to study only in bad weather."

"Old Pumpernickel never heard of weather."

"Hope he gets chewed by a rattlesnake on his trip West."

They laughed a little, not that there was anything very funny, but it was spring, they were young and felt like laughing.

Behind them a forsythia made a soft glow, and in the rich green grass were hyacinths, jonquils, narcissus. The girls too were in their moment of flower, slim and pretty, studying (not studying) here on the green.

"Now what do you suppose *she* wants?" the girl who wished the world were run right asked languidly.

A woman had come slowly through the archway, stood looking out at this green flowering close.

"She hasn't heard winter's gone." The girl's golden hair was blowing in the breeze and with one hand she tried to adjust a bobby-pin, holding her papers with the other. "What's the big idea? Why is she *looking* at us like that?"

The woman just stood there, framed by the arch, looking at them. Her hat was a little awry; the breeze had done things to her hair too, but not things as kindly. She stood so still, looking at the two girls as if she had no idea it was strange to be staring like that.

"Well for Pete's *sake*. Make up your mind, sister."

But she didn't seem to know how to make up her mind. She started to come toward them, as if drawn to them; but again stood stock-still, looking at them in a way they did not at all understand. Finally she turned and moved slowly back through the dim arch.

"*Well*—I hope she feels better!"

"Now she's learned something. She knows just what we look like."

"You know, she made me kind of nervous."

"Just batty, I guess. Looked like one of the scrubwomen."

"Do you suppose she wants an education?"

They laughed lightly.

Two boys were sitting on the steps of the Chemical Laboratory, discussing tennis. They became aware of a shabby woman wrapped up in a heavy coat who was standing near them reading an inscription. She was staring at it as if it were something monstrous: "Ye Shall Know the Truth and the Truth Shall Make You Free." One boy nudged the other: This woman was muttering to herself.

"That's not true!" she said, speaking aloud now, and looking at them as if accusing them of something.

One of them was a well-mannered boy and he rose. His companion got up doubtfully.

"It's supposed to be true," the boy first to rise said with a smile. This boy was interested in all kinds of people, he wanted to know what she would say.

"It is not true," she said tensely.

"Maybe we could chip it out," said the other fellow, ready for a bit of fun.

The woman only stood there looking at them. "What makes you think it isn't true?" the first boy asked.

"I found it out," she said, and turned away.

"Some funny people come around this place," the boy who had been loath to rise said. Sure, you get up when a lady comes. This wasn't a lady; just a batty old woman. "Maybe the truth didn't make her free because she didn't have any truth. The truth doesn't make me very free, I'm telling you. I spent *five hours* yesterday up in that—"

The other boy was looking after the woman who had gone a little way and was now standing there uncertainly. He even took a step forward. "I'd sort of like to talk to her."

"Pete's sake, why?"

"Well, I don't know why—exactly. Think maybe she's got something."

"Sure she's got something. Bats in her belfry. You like to talk to lunatics?"

"Have a hunch she's not a lunatic. Something about her makes me . . . Oh, well"—he gave it up.

This woman they did not understand—this Norma Ashe—wandered about a little longer. "It is *not* true." Her lips would move and some people turned to look at her. "They oughtn't to go on saying it. It's a lie!"

Well, this was over. She'd go home now. One thing was certain: none of it had anything to do with her. Good thing she came, she knew now. She was glad she *had*—gone the other way. . . . Not swept into this: building up the lie!

But somehow it wasn't easy to get away. It was as if she were indeed caught into something, walking in a world that might have been; as if she had come back and was seeing life from outside life. Here she was to have gone. Those two girls sitting back there might have been her and Rosie. When she'd looked at them they *were* Norma and Rosie: across the years, far away, but living there for a moment as if there were no years between. In *that very moment* she and Rosie lived as they had lived before.

Being here now was like a nightmare. She couldn't get out of the nightmare, and it fascinated her too, all against her will it fascinated her: looking into the life you were to have had.

In and out among the buildings as if there were no getting away. Now she had come to the Library, and slowly she went in. She and Rosie had dusted all the books. . . . Not *these* books; they couldn't have dusted all these. Printed page: thoughts. "It must first have reality in the mind." He had said that, their teacher, long ago.

She looked through glass doors into a large reading-room. Students would open the doors to go in, come out. She would step aside, but only to be drawn back, peering at a world that was to have been hers. Long tables, racks; sitting there studying. . . .

She was in the way, surrounded now by a group of young people, caught here amongst these busy students, where she didn't belong at all. She got free and stood a little way down the hall, getting her breath, get more steady for she was trembling. She was standing before a bulletin-board and began to read it, make something real. There was going to be a play: *Antigone of Sophocles*. There was going to be a debate. And—*what? What was this?*

She put her hand out on the wall to steady herself. *Surely* she was making it up! It *couldn't* be there. Wurthen. *Austin* Wurthen. He was going to speak. Austin Wurthen—one of them—world gone—was to speak in one of the halls at the University of Chicago. On . . . ? "The Human Being and Industry."

She began to laugh; leaned there against the wall laughing. People stopped and looked at her; one man came nearer as if he were going to do something about it. But didn't he know how *funny* it was? The laughter became a kind of gasping, a shuddering out loud. She couldn't stop it and this man stepped up to her. "Are you ill? Can I do something for you?"

Do something for her? "No, I don't think so," she said. "Something just struck me—so very funny."

"I'm glad you were amused," he said coldly.

Oh, yes, indeed she was amused, she kept telling herself as she went the long way back to her streetcar, to Mrs. Hughes', where Norma cleaned the rooms. And best of all, she was through! That old dream about the University of Chicago, long long dream and all it was to have meant—all over now. Why, didn't they know any more than *that?* Didn't they know Austin Wurthen *betrayed* the human being ages and ages ago? At last, after all the years, she comes to the University of Chicago; and what does she learn? She learns that Austin Wurthen is to speak—next Tuesday night—on The Human Being and Industry! Why hadn't she told that man how funny it was? Perhaps he would have been amused too. But no, they didn't know. . . . Now she could *laugh* at all she had let go. It was good to laugh, or so she tried to tell herself. . . .

A very good crowd turned out to hear Austin Wurthen. He was quite a figure, a good deal had been written about him: a rich man, or moderately rich, who seemed popping with ideas about the relations of capital and labor. Some people thought his ideas not so good, they smelled self-interest like rot. The unions didn't go for him (not on your life!) and the people who thought he was a fine man said this just went to show how short-sighted the unions were. His own plant, up there in Minnesota, made implements of one sort and another and had prospered under his management.

He said it was to the interests of labor to be friends with capital, and the other way around too—that was his line. His place wasn't closed-shop, this he said was against the rights of the individual. We should think of ourselves as one and work together for the common good. Up at his shop he couldn't always keep them in line for his kind of common good. There was often trouble, trying to unionize. This grieved him; he had their good at heart and had given his life to the true union, he would tell them. An occasional bold one would retort he had also given his life to doing damn well for himself. And why not? he would say. This was America and every man's chance. But he'd not built up his business selfishly; he wouldn't be happy that way was his claim. Where did working men have better wages (quite a number of places could be named) or better homes? He was very proud of the homes he'd built: bathrooms, heat, gardens. The workers had a chance to buy these houses and a number of them had done so. Others didn't like the strings attached. Not everyone could buy; you had to be a *good* boy, feel about it all as Mr. Wurthen felt. And if you took a notion to sell—oh no, except to another good boy. This was one of the stoutest of the strings. But there were recreation-grounds, a nursery, and every little while the place was written up as a fine social experiment, very American. Others said it was paternalism and to hell with it. It seemed quite likely Wurthen would be the next senator from his state—depend on how busy the unions got against him.

The month before a labor leader had spoken there and he had attacked Wurthen. The University believed in giving both sides a chance to spout, as the students put it, so now they were to hear the man who had been scoffed at, and students were trooping in, this evening in late April.

They weren't all students, these were open lectures and people who were interested could come. The place was going to be full. "Hey! Move over there, Bill. Give the lady a seat."

She murmured: "Thank you." Seemed nervous. Maybe she wasn't used to going to lectures. Not a student: too old. Of course there were some old ones, but she didn't look like a student. Wonder why she came, the boy who had made Bill move over speculated. Nothing else to do probably—no money for a picture. Certainly didn't look as if she had money.

No, she didn't have money, but she hadn't thought of going to a picture. And she hadn't known she was coming here, not until the last minute. It was after dinner Miss Ames gave her the coat. "Norma, now this won't hurt your feelings, will it?—but I'm wondering if you could use this coat. There's a little wear left in it and I thought it might sort of tide you over."

She'd taken it up to her room in the half-story above the third floor, an attic with two little rooms partitioned off. She sat down on the cot holding the coat on her lap. A long time since anyone had given her anything. She couldn't remember just when. It was kind of Miss Ames, who was a bookkeeper down town, worked hard, came home tired. It was tan covert cloth. "You can use it as a raincoat, or a spring coat—well, just running around here in the neighborhood, I mean. Wish I weren't so strapped this month, I'd like to get it cleaned for you, and shortened." Miss Ames was very tall.

She got up and put it on. Yes, it was long. The pockets were torn, some buttons off. But that didn't make it less kind that Miss Ames had thought of her.

Then she was putting on her hat and getting out her black silk gloves. Then she knew she was going.

She'd told herself a hundred times that not for anything in the world would she go out there and hear Austin Wurthen speak. Now she couldn't fight the idea any longer. It all seemed to have arranged itself: Miss Ames giving her the coat, Mrs. Hughes going out.

It was the best thing to do, she assured herself, finding a seat in the streetcar. If anything could end things for good and all it would be hearing Austin Wurthen speak, at the University of Chicago, on The Human Being and Industry. And there was something to end, no use denying that. Those two girls, studying as she and Rosie had studied. "Ye Shall Know the Truth . . ." graven in stone. Her trip to the University hadn't been as successful in bringing old things to an end as she had tried to make herself believe. And old things must *not* come back. It would be too ridiculous, too cruel, when all her world had gone. When she herself had gone.

Now a man was introducing the speaker. She didn't look up at the rostrum, but held her hands tight together, looking down. ". . . who believes in social experiment . . . power in his state. . . . A few weeks ago we heard a man who has different outlook. Tonight . . ."

"Fellow-students," began Austin. Yes, that was his voice. More —more suave now, but she knew the voice. There was a little laugh for the "fellow-students." "Oh, but I am. I was once a very earnest student. I have never ceased being a student. I never shall, because that is my true life."

"Boloney," the boy beside her said under his breath.

"I understand you recently heard my old friend Emil Jensen." (Emil *Jensen?* But that was Emil! Had *he* been here too? Emil, one of them but always a little on the outside. The boy they never really knew about—Emil, who lived at their teacher's.)

Was it close in here? Seemed hard to get her breath.

"And I understand Emil took a few cracks at me." There was a spattering of polite laughter; they got bored with that old wheeze of people trying to speak in their vernacular. "Now was that very nice of Emil, for he was an old friend of mine at a college we went to, what you students of this great University might call a jerk-water college, off in the wilds. It hadn't your great buildings and wonderful equipment, but it *had* something, I want to tell you. It was from that little place: poor, hick, if you like, I got the ideals I've tried, in my humble way, to carry on into life."

"You don't say so!" the boy next her muttered. "Now ain't that wonderful?"

A boy ahead turned round. "Lay off him, why don't you? The guy's just getting started."

She looked up at him now as he stood there getting started, smiling at them as he tried to command his audience, this rather difficult audience. Yes, it was Austin. Older, heavier, hair a little sparse now, but she knew that smile. Even though it had changed she knew it. It looked as if it had been used a great deal; a little shop-worn, she thought. It had served many purposes, she could tell.

"So it's too bad Emil took just the cracks he did. We might have stuck together. What he wants is what I want, really. Emil and I should have worked together for the good of all, not spend our energies taking cracks at one another.

"I think the trouble with people like Emil, they get closed-in; get so immersed in one side of it they lose the faculty of seeing all sides around."

From somewhere in the hall came a distinct hiss.

"Now—now, my friend," Austin was saying smoothly, "is that being a very good sport? Sure you aren't a little like Emil yourself: closed-in, not seeing all sides around? It's one of the sad things can happen to us in life, you know."

"Sure it never happened to you, mister?" the irrepressible young man beside her muttered, and again the boy ahead looked around, this time advising: "Hire a hall."

"But I want to talk to you a little while tonight," Austin continued, "about the things I have tried to do, and the things I believe. First of all, I am an *American*." ("Worse luck," her neighbor muttered.) Austin was talking of how great America was: our heritage, obligation. It had a familiar sound—remotely familiar, and all wrong. Their teacher had talked of those things, but from another spirit and to other ends. Austin had no right to say them as his; they were serving him in a way far below the great spirit in which they had been imparted to him.

As she heard his facile words about what had been won for us and how it was now our sacred obligation to carry on and make life what it might become, she tried to stop listening to the prosperous man for whom idealism was but another asset; it seemed betrayal on her part too that she sit here and let him mint an old glory into convenient coins. Was *this* what happened to the idealism of youth? Persuading yourself you still believe it, and trading on it? She didn't look up at him, for she was seeing another Austin, and that well-satisfied man up there would block the way to a young and eager Austin who had glowed with what he believed —and for its own sake, not what he could get out of it. She saw him in the circle around their teacher: his lean and studious face, thoughtful, responsive eyes. "Then you mean—" he would slowly begin, feeling his way into it, wrestling with what he couldn't quite see: asking, to test it, not facilely accepting just because it was thrilling, but paying the tribute of the best tests his mind could give. He had been both responsive and critical, aglow in the search for truth. Once that was Austin.

What became of him?

Could only youth be pure? Was it ever so: the world there to take and change and meanly use what could have made life more beautiful than any dream dreamed in the days before the combat?

And the trickery of it was you didn't even know what you had lost. You grew a little patronizing to the old dream. Adjusted; you were adjusted now. The best of it survived, you'd say—Austin would say. That which couldn't stand the test of living wasn't worthy to survive. That was for people who sat apart, not real men in a real world. That was the history of the human race, Austin would probably say, if he'd thought of it, we took what we could use. The dream was always a little extravagant. Let the surplus go into sermons and poems. She laughed, not quite out loud, but the boy sitting next leaned forward and looked at her. "Fat-head," he said, as if subscribing to an unspoken comment.

These students sitting here listening to the businessman, this businessman with "ideals," what did *they* think? It didn't much matter what she thought. This was their moment: their young un-captured moment. Nothing mattered as much as what they thought. Was it *in* them: dream of a better world? Would they do any better than she and Austin had done? If there were one brave keen dreamer here tonight what would he be in thirty years? A captive? A twister of old truths? Would he say, smiling kindly at his old moment, "Oh, I dreamed the dreams of youth, to be sure. Why, I was going right out and change the world! Well, we don't quite do that, my friends. Large order, you know. But there is something that never dies"—would he stoutly say?—"and I want you to know that I am *still* not ashamed to call myself idealist! I live, to be sure, in a practical world. We make our adjustments." And so . . . was captivity the law of life? Would the yet unborn say, when old, what Austin would say? And where did they *go:* bright brave dreams of youth?

For some time Austin had been telling them about his own "small experiment" with capital and labor. They were a little restive: a few interested, many looked bored, and some of them were listen-ing critically and smiling a little cynically. Perhaps they were more cynical, these students of today; and that was all right—for discarding. But what have you to put in the place of what you see is empty and not for you? she'd like to ask them. Easy enough to smile at what you're on to. What are you going to put in the place of what you have the wit to discard? Smiling is not enough; are you any better than the thing you smile at? Is anything *brewing* in you? Is there, in these days, any such things as—the miracle?

The miracle. . . . Up there in South Dakota, a very small band of people, something had opened and they knew, by revelation, that this was life on its way: they the living moment between a past that had won this for them and a future which waited for them to shape. They knew the secret: that one need not be afraid, not abashed before feeling so great. That set you free. A world shut-in by custom would know, they'd *feel* it as we feel a breeze change the air, that a new spirit was entering human life. "If only a few believe, then life is different. The balance changes, if ever so little, and man will feel it changing and eagerly—"

She came to rudely. What she was thinking was being spoken. He was going to close his speech—with the miracle. How *dare* he, she thought, and stirred as if she must get up and do something.

"I have told you I am not ashamed to call myself idealist. Now I will go further, and in this will I lose my touch with you? Will you feel I have left your realistic world behind when I tell you I am also something of mystic?"

He looked around as if to see—anxious, pretending to be anxious. "Cuts no ice with me, brother," the boy beside her muttered. "I gave you up hours ago."

"May I tell you, just briefly, a little of how this came about, most wonderful experience of all my life? I had a wonderful teacher. I hope you have too, but I've never known a man as wonderful as this teacher of ours. A scholar, and a mystic—though he didn't call himself that. A great intellect, and a man, in his way, profoundly religious. We were his disciples: just a little band of us in a small poor college. We were the chosen—five of us."

He's leaving out Emil, she thought; though it was scarcely a thought and she could barely breathe. He was bringing it into the open, among students, after twenty-nine years! Oh, he shouldn't! Shouldn't be let do this! It was gone—betrayed; don't hold up in sullied hands the best there had been in life! She wished she could stop the words before they came, for she knew just what would come. His voice would break a little. "Words fail me," he would say, and even think that he was moved!

"You could scarcely call him a practical man," Austin was going on; "he thought that *we*—just us—obscure students up there in South Dakota, could make life different. I am afraid he thought it was too easy—"

She was out in the aisle before she knew she was moving. She spoke and did not really know she was speaking. "He never said it was easy! You can't *do* this, Austin! Must you *cash in*—on the miracle? Let it alone, I tell you! Now you can just let it alone!"

There was a moving in seats, a twisting of necks, murmurs. An odd enough figure it was they saw, in a coat as big as a night-gown, hat bobbing, an oldish, bent, run-down woman standing there with clenched fists held high.

But she didn't know that, and scarcely knew that Austin had stepped forward, was leaning over peering at her. Or that a man from the back was moving forward to stop her.

"Austin! Don't you *remember?* Don't you remember—*any-thing?* Don't you know the truth was right there and we—walked away from it? Does that make *it* any less—or him—that you can patronize it now because you—Austin Wurthen—hadn't the brains or the soul or the decency—"

The man had hold of her arm. "Madam, this is no place for you to speak. You are interrupting. You will take your seat or—"

He was interrupted by a number of calls. "Let her alone!" "We want to hear her!" And "We like her better than him!" another called.

"Who are you?" Austin cried through this confusion.

"Who am I?" She jerked from the man who would restrain her, stepped farther down the aisle. "I am one who stood by his grave and heard you say, 'If all of us who knew him are not more for having known him we were not worthy to sit at his feet.' A great brave dream of what life might be, you said. Treasure you said he had. He had given it to us and we were to give it to others. You *meant* it then. Must you *show off* with it now?"

"Bravo!" was loudly called, and the man had hold of her again, and more roughly. "You are creating a disturbance. If you do not subside at once—"

"No, let her speak," Austin was saying. "Let her speak!" went up all around the hall.

This made her know where she was, what she was doing; but she knew it only dimly, and it did not matter.

"It was there then and it is there now! Why don't you tell these young people the *truth?* Tell them the truth and the truth will make them free!"

"Are you—*Norma?*" He said it almost under his breath, but she heard.

"I am not Norma and you are not Austin. Austin—*Austin*—what became of us?"

It seemed she would break then, and the man beside her took firm hold of her arm, trying to turn her around. "This way now."

But she couldn't leave it at that, crying about Austin and Norma. "Yes!" she said to the students. "We did have a great teacher. Something parted—and we saw the truth. We were not worthy. That doesn't mean the truth was not there! Oh—*find* it. Find it for yourselves and *do* something with it! Make the better world Austin Wurthen and I were too poor to make!"

As the man was leading her away, with no difficulty now, Austin called: "Norma! I want to see you. Don't let that lady get away! I want to talk with you, Norma."

She half turned her head and said just one thing. "What for?"

"You are to remain here," her attendant said severely. "We will wait in this office." She shook her head. "It is the least you can do after what you have done to him."

"I haven't done anything to him," she said. "Nothing that will last."

"You are not to leave!"

"Says who?" asked a boy who had come hurrying out from the auditorium. "If she wants to leave, then she'll leave."

She looked at him gratefully. Looked again. Hadn't she seen that face?

He walked outside with her. "I saw you once before," he said. "The other day. You were reading 'Ye shall know the truth and the truth shall make you free.' You said it wasn't so. Remember? You seem to have changed."

"Yes," she said. They had been walking but now she stood quite still.

"Stuff-shirt do it?" he asked.

She shook her head, still standing there so still. She looked up at him. Wonder. That was wonder in her eyes— a great marvelling. "It came back. Suddenly. Suddenly—it was there."

CHAPTER EIGHTEEN

S HE HAD affirmed her faith. Now a door long closed was swinging open. Dreams that remain dreams grow wan. The dream must be constantly won: not ours if we will not fight for it.

When Norma Ashe stepped into that aisle, not knowing she was a figure somewhat comic in a coat grotesquely large, not thinking how she might seem but having to cry out against desecration of an old vision, then the vision was not an old vision but of that moment. She did not do it to gain this for herself, but only because she had to. What might be called an hysterical outburst was the truth in her having its way. When it spoke through her it spoke to her. What had never wholly receded, intermittently lighting her life, was no longer but the beauty of the far horizon. It was the pulse of her: this body which moved and brain that remembered; heart that felt, spirit aspiring. All her life she had been haunted by it; now it was not one thing and she another . . .

The circumstances of her life could not well be worse: sorrow and loss and poverty she knew. She would be called a failure in-deed, she had failed with her own children. She had failed with her-self: her life had deviated. But the truth that was in the dream had not deviated! Too great to be killed by her own years, or by any denying, it rose there above the lives of men, itself unsmirched, itself imperishable. Or it was like the waters of the earth: there to be found.

Through the years of the life of man it has come through in many fountain-heads; the one that was real to her again was the one from which she had drunk. Never before had she seen as now she saw that place where the wonder of what life might be had opened to her. It was lighted and sharp-outlined. Not as that which has faded did she see it now; but like a diamond, imperishable, forever lighted from within itself. If all the rest of the world went it would be there, rising as proud towers rise, against background of eternity, uncaptured by time. In all her other thinking it had not shown its true face; she had looked with some evasions and distortions, a vision 'clouded by self, fears of unworthiness, shame of failure and resentment of that shame. Now all of this fell away; now she could see. And she saw . . .

The movement of man had brought him to Dakota Territory. Man existed because before him had been movement: from inanimate to cell, from water to land, from living in the tree to living on the ground, from cave to the open and to all the continents of the earth. Greece rose and fell, and there was Rome; and Europe. Adventurers crossed the sea and there was a United States of America: all of this, in eternity, not longer than the rising and falling of the leaf in the breeze, but each part of it, while being lived, seeming the whole of life.

First the red man and then the white man came to Dakota Territory, and in a certain year, 1889, one part of the Territory became South Dakota, and men tilled the soil and made the grain grow where once the buffalo had roamed. But man does not live by wheat alone: many of them prayed and some of them read books. There are men who cannot live without learning just as man does not live without food and wife and child. One of these was named MacConnell, a simple and a good man who brooded over this thing that man does not live by bread alone. Now people had their land and here, in these river-valleys of eastern South Dakota, they would live their lives. There was a new national census and it said the frontier was at an end. The frontier was now closed. The frontier: there had been the adventure, the hope. Now life would stabilize; it was going to be made from what we now had. And this simple man saw it as a very important time. We were used to adventure. We would never be content not to open up new things, that was in the blood of the people who were Americans. We would still be pushing on, opening up, and we must open up the right things.

Here in this new land just west of the upper Mississippi Valley were also men from far countries: from Sweden, Norway, from Germany. They too had the blood of adventurers in their veins. Had they not come a long way to what they believed was opportunity for the good life? They had found this distant place, and here they were, side-by-side with older Americans. It was all beginning. MacConnell thought it was a wonderful time and a chance that should not be muffed. The children who were growing up here lived in a region of ancient upheavals. Before there were any children on the earth a mighty force, diabolically playful, had thrown up Badlands and Black Hills. He felt force still latent here: a more benign force that could shape the lives of men. The end of the trail was more than fields of grain and ranches of cattle; more than taking gold from the earth and laying railroads upon it. End of the trail was a chance to shape the better life, a trail unending . . .

There should at once be a school, "higher learning," right *here*. There wasn't any college immediately around, and the young people's folks wouldn't let them go too far, not to places they knew little about. They hadn't the money, and anyway they'd heard about the goings-on at some of those schools. They called the farm boys farmers there, and in a way farmers didn't like. The boys hadn't the clothes for it and the few who went didn't feel at home. They should have their own school, close to the farms and feeling at home. There must be the right ideals, not worldliness and godlessness.

This last appealed to the people he talked to. In his own somewhat profane way MacConnell was a devout man, and he was also a pretty shrewd one. Certainly he had a force as from the earth itself. He gave you no peace once he got an idea. He was all stirred up about his idea of a frontier this side of the frontier, beginning to develop what we now had. He had some money he'd made logging in Minnesota and he was willing to put up a generous proportion of this because, damn it all, did anybody know anything better to do with money?

There wasn't much money immediately around there, but even people who had very little said they'd be willing to put aside something for the future. That was the way MacConnell put it to them: the only sound future was in giving the children a chance to know more than they knew themselves.

He wrung some money out of his church (the central organization) and got most of it from a man in Chicago who'd been born in Dakota Territory, got gold nuggets in Deadwood in '76, but who wasn't a very rich man, for all his gold, because he had lost his only son. "Give back some of the gold Dakota gave you," MacConnell told him, "and give Walter a monument more lasting than granite." As memorial to his son he gave that other boys and girls might have what his boy had only begun to know. MacConnell let no one escape, appealing to the self-interest and romanticism of the farmers, the desire of the church for a more godly institution, the sentiment of a man who has lost his son.

He insisted they call their new school Pioneer College: the right and only name. Wasn't it the business of a name to say what a thing was? "Meaning we are pioneers," one pioneer reflected. "Meaning there will always be pioneers," said MacConnell. "Meaning the frontier is not closed."

None of them knew much about founding a college, but the indomitable MacConnell made it his business to find out, got hold of the people who did know. Pioneer College opened with fifty-six students in 1892. MacConnell—damn it—made a speech. "Our beginnings are small, but so were the first white settlements in America. Our chance is as great as theirs, for we too have a country to open up, a great inner world that can be ours. Boys and girls" (there were only five girls), "you are in a new land and you too are pioneers. You need not be dismayed because you are few. Study your history, as you have a chance to study it here, and you will see you have great precedents. You'll see that this wide land became our home because, always, there were a few men who believed"—he was getting lost· and didn't know just what he was going to say—"why" (he barely held back damn it, when he was wrought-up this seemed so natural a word) "they *believed*, that's the sum and substance of it, and when you believe there's no stopping you! And what do I mean—believe?" he asked, somewhat belligerently, dissatisfied with his speech. "I mean—" then mercifully it came to him and out of his own belief he could say: "America will only be as great as the individual souls that comprise it. You cannot say to yourselves, 'What difference does it make what *I* am?' If you are less than you might be then America is less than she should have been. You have something very important to see to. As important as getting in the crop. Why—" (now he was all aglow!) "it *is* getting in the crop! The courage behind you will have been in vain, the trust and the struggle all in vain, if *you* do not now get in the crop!"

If anyone had written it down it might not have seemed a very good speech. It didn't flow smoothly, but there was fervor in it; it engendered fervor.

Those fifty-one boys and five girls went to work; the business of learning was their business now. They were earnest about it, knowing the value of time, the sacrifices made to keep them here: Mom without her new winter coat, Pop doing the milking and often working alone in the field. There hadn't been strict entrance examinations, higher requirements would have left no students to start out with. Most of them weren't ready for college and some were just plain bewildered, they didn't know how to study. A few got discouraged and dropped out, but more came, and here in this land where the plow was only now turning soil made rich by glacial deposits of aeons ago was an earnest band of young Americans who were going to get educated—come hell or high water!

The building was called Main Building, meaning there would be others. In four years there was another, called Science Hall. The students lived in houses in the town and nearby country, some of them walking three miles, and the walking often about as poor as it could be. No one could charge more than two dollars and a half a week for room and board. This wasn't a law, but woe unto him who tried to transgress it!

The teachers worked harder than the students, not funds for a full-sized faculty. One man taught Greek, Latin, German and English—some religion. Another had history, philosophy, some religion (they thought the teaching of religion shouldn't be all in one man's hands) and sociology. The science teacher taught all the sciences, including mathematics, and some agriculture. But soon the prospectus was saying, "We are enlarging the faculty," and there was another teacher. They were good teachers, Mac-Connell had made it his business to find out about that, and they must have believed in their small raw college, as almost anything else they could have done: preaching, politics, day-laboring, would have been an easier job.

But MacConnell wasn't satisfied. "Maybe it's all right," he'd say doubtfully, "but we seem to be just plodding along. I'd like something would set the place afire!"

"Now Mac," his wife would say, "you just hold your horses."

"I tell you these students are just soberly *learning*."

"Well land's sakes alive, what do you want them to do in college? Raise Ned?"

"Yes!" He smiled. "The right Ned."

In 1896 MacConnell went East on a trip; and he brought back with him a man named Joseph Langley. "Meet the new professor," he said proudly.

And here was the flame! Here the mind to make cold learning burn with life. He made it so important, so dazzling, that some of the students forgot to go to their meals; landladies complained things were going all sixes-and-sevens, oil burning late at night; it wasn't good for them, and ran up the expense.

He was a quiet enough looking man. Nobody would think, to look at him, he'd cause this upheaval. Yes, they would, if they knew what to look for. His body was lithe; his face lean, ascetic. His eyes were alert, as if always watching for something, though this had nothing to do with the conduct of the students, in the usual sense. It had to do with which way the thought was going to turn. Nobody would think of trying to fool him (not twice) about what they knew, didn't know. He'd just stand looking quizzically at this bluffer, hedger, then a smile and the faintest shake of his head, as to say— Oh, come now, you and I know better than that.

When they were dull he'd get so bored it would seem he was going to give them all up. And then he'd cut in—sharp as a razor, and in swift words get them so stirred up it was as if they'd never before known just who they were. He was always surprising them by where he could take them; by golly, by cricket, to think they could *do* this! You'd think they'd get used to him, but it always came as this surprise. He'd take a thing from one twist, possibly something that hadn't seemed important at all, and open from that to a realm they'd not known was there. He didn't follow assigned lessons; it was as if he'd be captured himself, himself surprised by what was there. Then he'd take them with him—spiral after spiral—until they were in this world they'd not known before: a world rarer, electric. He seemed to have all learning right where he could tap it, but a lot of it he didn't do much with; and then it would come—almost a rearing back: yes, like a race-horse. And then he was off.

Other teachers said he was rather disruptive, and some of the students complained too: those who weren't up to it. But he made them alive as they'd never been alive before. "I never know where we are going to *go*," one girl said as she came out from class. "It makes me kind of dizzy."

One day a girl waited for him after class. "I don't think I have a very good mind," she said. "I try, but I get discouraged because I'm so limited. Now that I know a mind like yours I just wonder if there is any use in mine going on."

They were still in the classroom, standing there by the window. "Let's sit down, Laura," he said gently. He was so keen and swift, impatient with many things, with lifeless things, that it might seem he was ruthless and uncaring, but he could be so very gentle with one who seemed in need. Then his face would change, and instead of seeming to be looking into something, in that way that was unsparing, it became the face of one who knew all about you, and cared.

"What you are saying troubles me," he said; "if my mind makes you feel there is no use in yours going on, then mine isn't much of a success, is it?" He smiled, and you always had to smile back when he smiled like that. You wanted to.

"I meant yours is so much more."

"Perhaps," he said honestly. "It's had more chance, for one thing; and then, you see, this is the whole of life to me. I mean—it's all." He stopped, as if thinking of what he meant, and his face tightened, almost as if in pain. He looked at her and for one moment there was open sorrow in his eyes. She didn't understand.

But then he smiled again. "It makes up for everything else. This is my whole world: what we can do with our minds. And I want it to be," he added, almost roughly.

"Has my mind been showing off to you, Laura? Trying to make you feel—"

"Oh, no—no," she had to cut in, aghast to think he might feel she'd meant that.

"I should hope not," he said. "That would be a sorry use to make of anything I have."

He asked her: "Do you know why I came here?"

"No, I don't, Professor Langley. I've often wondered. Because you could be in a place so much better."

"I don't know that there is any better place than Pioneer College," he said. "I met Mr. MacConnell when I was—undecided what to do." Again there was that slight tightening of his face, almost a wince. But he smiled this away. "Don't you like Mr. MacConnell?"

"Oh, yes, I do. We all like Mr. MacConnell."

"I do. I think he has a wonderful idea. It was his idea brought me here—the importance of it to him; because, you see, it's important to me. I'm glad Mr. MacConnell and I didn't miss each other; it makes you stronger when someone else feels as you do. Of course you know what his idea is. That each one of us must be the most he can be. Sounds simple, doesn't it? Many people would say they believe it—and then forget all about it, not do anything about it. But MacConnell—damn it, as he would say— has to do something about it. I like that. Do you?"

"Oh, *yes*. Yes, I do."

"Then how about Laura Schmelling being the most she can be? Don't desecrate, Laura. Never say you don't amount to much. Don't let the horrid little thought sneak into your mind. Chase it out for good and all! We're one, you know: you and I, you and everybody. So please don't pull me down," he smiled. "I mean it. You'll make me feel a failure if you persist in this silly idea you're no good. And I don't want to feel a failure" (a sadness, wistfulness, stole into his face)—"not in this."

He talked to her of how much more there would be for her in life if she used what powers she had to the utmost she could. "Why, that would be success, Laura—that's what success is, making the most we can of what has been given us. And who in the world are you to set limitations to the human mind?" he thrust at her in his more usual challenging way. "You don't *know* your own mind yet. Aren't you taking a good deal upon yourself to condemn it without giving it a chance?"

Laura Schmelling was happier ever after, a little more dauntless. So when faculty, or some of the more pious students—parents, trustees, landladies, would mutter about Professor Langley: he was a queer one, and just what did he believe and what was he teaching them, there was always a pretty solid body of students to say he was the best ever!

Before the Christmas holiday of '97 Professor Langley had to go away on leave. He was sick. They weren't even sure he would be back. Everything was different without him; it was only remembering him: things he had said, wondering what he'd say of this or that, kept them anywhere near the pitch they'd been with him. Though of course they mustn't disappoint him—whether he came back or not. They thought of that too.

He returned the following fall. He looked somewhat different: thinner, and pale; but his movements were the same: quick sure movements of his lithe body, hands that seemed to be expressing his thoughts. And now, more than ever, he seemed in a hurry. As if they must get on with it—didn't have all the time in the world. But though in a hurry he seemed to have an even keener accuracy. He could spot loose thinking (if it came from authorities you were supposed to take as gospel that made him only the more unsparing), would slash, ridicule, then soar from what they

had better leave behind into air clearer, more rare. Sometimes he
seemed the most ruthless, unsparing man in the world. Then he
would get them to laugh with him at what they had demolished.
His humanness balanced his scorn.

Yes, he was indeed different since coming back. They didn't
know just what it was. They couldn't know, as he didn't tell
them he was searching for something. Didn't tell them why it
was so important he find what he sought. And quickly.

He was searching for something among his students. As seniors
that year he had in his History of Philosophy Rosie Major, Virgil
Whitman, Austin Wurthen, Helen Foster, and Norma Ashe.
They were there among fifteen others. And, for one reason and
another, he was particularly interested in these five students.
Came to be—it took a little time to single them out. It wasn't
because of some one thing they had in common he came to feel
in these five what he was seeking. He chose them for a certain
quality in each one of them. There was no doubt about Norma.
When he saw in her clear eyes the response to what he was saying he knew that he had indeed reached, that what was in him
could go to her, would there live and from there grow. Virgil
had imagination, and he could respond to scorn, that needed
scorn for the muddled thinking that cluttered life. Austin was very
much in earnest and had vigor: potentialities. Something of what
he was looking for was in Helen: if Helen saw the thing to do
she would do it. And Rosie. Other students were more nearly
brilliant, but Rosie always made him think of the earth itself.
Could we leave out the earth itself? he would think in thinking
it over. Rosie was goodness and fidelity. Would she not remain
uncorrupted? And these five were friends. They could knit together, perhaps be as one: a little group that would be here when
he was not . . .

One day he asked these five to remain after class. And when
they sat there before him: trusting, eager, alert, he was curiously

diffident. He came down and sat among them, and he looked intently, intensely, from one to another. Then he smiled. There was always warmth—warmth diffusing—when he smiled like that.

"I have a little plot," he began. "It's for just us. I wonder if you will like it."

They were waiting so eagerly; so young. *There;* ready for the most he could give them.

"I would like a few of us to get on faster. It's so important," he said, "we go a little faster. I mean farther. We can't get ahead as I'd like in the classroom. So I've chosen you five, if you'd like to do it."

They were almost breathless in their eager interest. He had them now! Could it happen? Could he do it? As he met the eyes of Norma Ashe he had faith that he could. Something fine and dauntless here: they'd never get Norma down!

"I feel I have something to say to you—to you five. I wonder if you'll give me the chance?"

There was a more tense leaning forward, little murmurs. Then again they waited.

"It's very important to me that I give you the best I've got. You're young. I want to count on you."

"Count on me," said Austin, and the others assented.

He smiled at them. "Well, well, I don't want to make it all so mysterious. I just want a chance to talk to you, you talk to me, out of class. I have an idea we could get somewhere. You know . . . our lives go by. Things take hold of us . . . one thing and another. I want you to be—the most you can be. That's very important to me; more important than anything else in the world."

"We *want* to be," said Rosie, then seemed timid, as if fearing she'd interrupted; he smiled at Rosie.

"I thought perhaps you would come out to my house—say one evening a week, we'll start in like that, and just see . . . where we can get."

Oh, they'd *love* to, they said—five bright, eager, unspoiled young people.

"Now are you sure you would? It means more work—what's called work. Not quite so much time for fun, and fun's fine, you know."

"But what could be more fun than this?" cried Norma. "Do you mind my calling it fun?"

"It's one very good name for it," he smiled. "Are we off then?"

Yes!—a happy eager chorus.

"Then come along to my house tomorrow night. We'll just talk for an hour or so. See where we get."

That began the evenings of those five—the chosen—with their teacher. Others came to know about it and there was some grumbling. It wasn't fair; of course they could get along faster if they were coached. They weren't coached, they said. It wasn't like that. "We just talk. It's more like a little club."

"A club nobody else can belong to!"

If Professor Langley knew about the grumbling he paid no attention. Something else was too important to him. He had none of the usual fears of a teacher about his own position; he had to do it his own way. He was fair to the other students, in class he gave them all he could; this was something outside, different, and very important. He was going to give it to *them*. What he had was to go to his five disciples.

They'd come through the blizzards, in the rain, mud; there wasn't sidewalk all the way to his house (he lived at the outskirts of the little town, in a rather stark frame house). There weren't any of the outer trappings of beauty for this pilgrimage. Usually they'd all come together, along a two-board plank walk part of the way, then into unbroken snow, or the mud. Their laughter announced them before their knock; they'd come in rosy and eager, pull the chairs around the big table—wait for him to begin.

If ever teacher felt sacred responsibility to his students this man Joseph Langley did as he tried to take them into his very thoughts. After the first month they came twice a week. They'd asked couldn't they please? They had only such a little time left here at school. Would it be too much for him? No, it wouldn't be too much for him, and when they were with him it wasn't too much. That came after they were gone, and only Emil, the boy who was there, knew how tired he was afterwards, and why. Emil knew because sometimes the boy had to help him. That was why Emil would hover around, fearing it was going to be too much.

"I don't think they ought to come twice a week," Emil said one night, after the pain came. "They're imposing on you."

"Imposing on me! Why, Emil, they're breath of life to me. Don't you see they keep me going?"

"It takes too much out of you," Emil persisted.

"I hope to God it takes *all* out of me! I want to give them all I have."

"And what about yourself?" demanded the rough, stubborn boy who had come to love this man he helped.

"Oh, you and I know, Emil, it doesn't matter so much about myself."

"It matters a long sight more than they matter! They're like a bunch of kids has to eat up the whole meal."

"Fine! Do you think I want them to go away hungry?"

No, they didn't go away hungry. Or, yes, they did, always hungry for more. It was the way he could bring it to them—dazzling, profound, moving: What life has been, what could come to be. It was a whole of many facets. Often they wouldn't dwell long on what he'd said beforehand they would talk about that night. They'd get on something else, and this would take them: the first living forms of life on earth; the great philosophies. Sometimes it was of faith they spoke, sometimes skepticism. Both were important. Criticism and poetry. Great battles—great mistakes. Often they were speaking of valor: in the sciences, in the struggle to make a world more just. He told them great stories of valor, this man more valorous than they knew. And through it all ran the golden thread it was for them to make life *more*. They were not to be held in the thought they were not important. Insofar as life changed one unseen iota, it changed. The balance was difference, the hope greater. Man should not be ashamed to be consecrated to what life might become. Keep themselves pure, open to the dream, undaunted in the struggle for the better world of the dream.

They talked of the long slow process, how that seemed the way of life and was the theory of history. But we were too much bound by that idea. Always there had been daring ones who found the new way: just as aeons ago, it was only a few of the life forms that lived in the water made that leap to the land. Many died, but a few learned to breathe this untried thing that was air—survived, and so there was man. What was there in them to make them do it, when already they knew how to live in the water? Some blind impulse—call of a far future? They were the great adventurers. And adventurers were needed now as much as then: adventurers who would dare an untried element, give their lives for a distant day.

"I feel," he said slowly that night, "that we are on the brink of something. They talk of the frontier now being closed. *What* frontier? Are we so blind as to think there is only one?" Norma Ashe was sitting nearest him, and he caught hold of her arm and gripped it. She saw the tremor of his face, as though it might be pain; Emil stirred in the background. That passed, and as if something had been won, his face lighted with the vision. "The real frontier is opening. Never was there a time as important as this, *here*, in the United States of America, in South Dakota, in this room. My dear children—"

He had never said that before; he looked around at them and smiled at what he had said. "Yes, you are my real children—and all I have. If I could say only one last word to you on earth,"—he paused, and again Emil stirred—"I would want it to be this: Man does not know his own powers. We have taken the human mind too much for granted. There are not limits to what it can do. The limits are only in our thinking they are there."

He closed his eyes for a moment, said: "Get me a drink of water, Emil."

Norma saw that the water Emil brought back was a little clouded, as if there might be something in it. Perhaps he had to take medicine, so recently he had been ill. They hadn't thought enough about that, for he never spared himself. She was wondering if she should say they ought to go, already it was later than usual. But she could see there was something more he wanted to say.

In the next hour he spoke swiftly, with a passionate clarity; out of an urge, as if he were capturing—for them, and must capture swiftly, while it was still his to transmit.

He said a thought could make a rift in what had almost solidified, in dull thinking almost solidified. It had more power than anything on earth: a thought. Any change must first have reality as idea. We were on the brink of an adventure greater than any along the long way man had come. Let the dim past give you courage! Always there had been adventurers. We were on the brink of knowing what the human mind might become, this the time for which all that was behind us had lived and fought and died. All brave old thinking could be realized and transcended in what now could be thought. Either we did it or we held as naught all that had been gained. He spoke of America. America would change now: no longer the old adventure of fighting savages, taking up land and making new cities. That restlessness and energy were bound to go somewhere. It would go into industrial development, to be sure, and that would come fast, so fast it could threaten everything else. But the best of it: dream of what life might be and fight for the dream—there was the new land and there could rise the noble cities. But it must be *now*, ere we became too set, went into a long sterile time of believing things could not change.

"I see a great vision, more real to me than this room, of what life on earth might be. I see the free happy mind—always wanting to go farther, and able to because of this wanting. I see a people set free: man rising out of his long lethargy and more and more seeing what life can be. Not just intellectual attainment, that's but a means to an end. A kinder, more just people, awake to the potentialities of life and the beauties of the human spirit. A few will see it first—and be it." He looked around at them, changed, and spoke sternly. "So never *dare* think it doesn't matter what *you* are. That's all the hope there is in the world: what you are and can become."

Breaking the silence that followed these words Emil said: "It's almost eleven o'clock." How *rude* of Emil, Norma thought. How *could* he—just now?

"I know," their teacher said. "The time's almost up . . ."

He said one thing more, as if looking into what he could clearly see. "Know more that the dream may grow. Life can rise higher than man has yet had the power to dream. Grow in this power. *Be* the dream. Let it flow in your lives as blood in your veins. And fight! Dare all for what you see can come to be. It waits. It will be."

With no break of mood they at last got up from the table. They were in the presence of something they felt divine, it was as if they could not go from it. And he sat on there at the table. "Guess you know the way out," Emil said.

Then their teacher got up, brushed his hand across his forehead, as if coming from something. "Emil! What's the matter with you? Why, the poor boy must be sleepy," he laughed as he went with them to the door, stood there at the open door as they went down the path.

The next day they heard he had died in the night.

Then they knew they had heard his last words. They could believe now he knew he was giving them his last word. Looking back they could see he fought for it, fought to keep himself that he might give them this word. Yes, he knew. And went on! He *did* it. With death waiting gave them the heart of his truth.

Now it was a sacred obligation to them. He was to live through them.

They went once more to his house, the evening after the funeral, which would have been their usual time to go. They had made no plan for this until, together after supper, clinging together, Rosie said: "Let us go there once more."

This seemed to them a natural thing to do. The rest of it, the services that afternoon, had been for all, for many who knew him less. This was just themselves . . . the nearest.

The door was open and they went in and sat down in their accustomed places. Emil was there, but he did not seem to mind. They said a little. "We will never forget." Or "I think he would like us to be here." "It is as if he were here—still with us." But for the most part they were silent, and they could hear his voice.

It was after long silence they turned to Norma Ashe: she had made a sound—under her breath a cry. And when they saw her face no one spoke—only waited—for it was as if she were looking upon something she could scarcely believe was there, and on her face was a growing wonder, and glory as from that to which she looked.

"I saw it," she whispered, trembling, half afraid, but in her eyes the light of mysterious splendor. "Something parted. I saw it plain. What he told us was there—it is there. I saw it there waiting. Waiting to be."

No one distrusted her words; they were looking upon her face and the wonder of her face let them share what she had seen—diffusing, as a light; hovering over them—so close.

They truly believed something had happened, and they were shaken, as before a miracle, the disciples who sat there after he had gone. And it seemed to Norma, it will one day be said—once it *happened*. To a few people in a room in South Dakota. Something parted and they saw through.

Many wondered why Professor Langley's special students, those five he had done so much for, seemed to feel his death less than the others. Why, they seemed *happy*, as they went on finishing their work at Pioneer College.

Norma and Rosie dusted all the books.

$\mathcal{I}$ N ONE thing a number of people would agree with Austin Wurthen: in the industrial struggle Emil Jensen saw only one side. He saw the side of organized labor. To this fight he was giving his life: fighting not only the grabbing bosses, uncaring of human life, as he said, fighting politicians and injunctions, but everlastingly combating lethargy within the unions in times of prosperity for them, dishonesty of union officials wherever it showed its head. "Let the other side have the crooks," he would say.

He knew the game as few knew it. When he left that place up in South Dakota, homeless again, he'd worked in coal mines and in the steel mills. He early saw injustices and was very soon a trouble-maker. He got mixed up in abortive strikes and came to see the fruitlessness of them. He'd been clubbed and he'd been fired, and he had done a tall lot of thinking. Organization: constant and ever more, that was the answer. No use crying over injustices or getting your neck broken because there was no power behind you. Organized labor—and he meant *all* of it. He drove himself and everyone else. He had no tears to shed for the poor capitalist.

He was an important man now, but he never let up. He was a dynamo. Yet he didn't spend himself on things you couldn't get. He knew what could be had and how to get it. He had no truck with the impossible. He was taut, radical, ruthless—or so they said, on both sides. Many in his own organization fought him as radical. But he was a power. He got results.

No one doubted that he was consecrated to it. The man seemed to have no life of his own, no other life. He'd gone to prison for one fight. He came out bitter, but not so bitter it warped his usefulness. He seemed to know how to manage that: ride his bitterness and not let it ride him. The workers were to have all they could get, and nobody was going to hand it to them on a silver platter. When you got a little go on working harder for more. For God's sake don't let up! The country was rolling in wealth and thousands upon thousands didn't have enough to eat. If he did see outside his work of organizing labor, if he had what another would call the larger vision, it was in the idea that with more power to the workers who knew how to get it one day there wouldn't be any underdogs. When he had time for the luxury of dream it was of that day he dreamed. Mostly he just worked. He had a good salary but not much money. That was his own fault; he was always giving it away. He hated money for the things it was doing, hated the rich because he heard the cries of the hungry. He wasn't hungry himself now, but he had been once, and he had a long memory.

He was a vigorous man of forty-seven. He'd have to be vigorous or he'd be dead. He expected the people who worked for him to be vigorous. A slave-driver. "I thought we were out for shorter hours," a man in his office had the temerity to say. "We'll get ours when everybody else has theirs," he said. Shorter hours; better wages and conditions: security. Wring it out of them!

But a very practical man, he knew how to tame himself when necessary, wasted no energy in futile gestures or windbag stuff.

One May Day he was sitting in his office after the celebration, talking to a boy he'd met out in South Chicago. The boy's father had been killed in the steel mills. Now the kid went to the University of Chicago. That was Emil's doings—under your hat. He didn't know exactly why he'd wanted to do it: something about the boy, and something he, Emil, remembered about a professor he had once lived with, and had seen die. Something he remembered . . .

"Well, so Wurthen took his cracks at you, said he once knew you and you should pull together—"

"Why the dirty hypocrite!"

"Then he went on about the good he was doing—America, heritage, all that stuff they put in speeches; and then he began about a jerk-water college he'd gone to, wonderful teacher he once had—"

"He ought to have had the breath choked out of him!"

"That's what she thought."

"Who?"

"The woman."

"*What* woman? Speak up, man. Put things straight. I don't know what you're talking about."

"The woman who got up and stopped him. Seemed kind of crazy. No—" the boy paused doubtfully; "no, I guess not. Just excited and funny-looking. Seemed out of place. Dressed kind of like the scrubwomen. She said she'd been there, and he was to shut up."

"Been *where?*" He was keen as a whip now, the way he could get, his eyes like the steel he'd once worked in.

"Up at that college. Said she knew all about it and he was to lay off. Her name is Norma."

"*Norma?* Not—Norma Ashe?"

"Don't know about Ashe. Norma, anyway."

"For the love of God," he said very slowly, and to himself. But then he objected. "Norma Ashe wouldn't look like a scrubwoman."

"This one did—sort of. She'd gone to school with Wurthen and started to tell us about it. Then they stopped her."

"And what happened to her?" he demanded.

"I'm sure I don't know."

"You—don't—*know*," Emil bawled at him. "Why didn't you go *after* her?"

"Me? Why, what for?"

"Oh, for Christ's sake. You'll never learn anything!"

"Well, gee, I don't see why I should have. How would I know it was any business of mine?" Then he had an inspiration. "There was a fellow went after her, I think."

"Who's he?"

"Don't know, but he was sitting in my row. He shot out of the hall—nearly knocked us over. Must have been after her."

"And you haven't *asked* him?"

"Well, gosh, Emil, why would I ask him? I don't know him. And how would I know it was any business of mine?"

"It's business of mine," Emil said grimly. He sat there thinking of it. "Norma Ashe," he murmured. "She interrupted him right in the middle of his speech?"

"I'll say she did."

"Gave him hell?"

"Sure did. Kept right on when they were trying to drag her away. Never saw anything like that happen out there before."

Now Emil was smiling. Then sober again. "You say she looked poor?"

"Either she's poor or she doesn't care what she looks like."

"Norma would care what she looks like." His lips closed in a way people had come to dread. "She's poor," he said.

"Tell me every word she said," he commanded, and the boy told it as best he could remember.

"It's Norma, all right. Norma . . . and she remembers."

"You've got to find her," he ordered. "Now you bring her here tomorrow. Understand?"

The boy looked most unhappy. "Why it's easy—nitwit. Get after this guy who followed her out. Maybe he took her home. Now this is the most important thing you've got to do in the world; get me?"

When Emil said "Get me?" you didn't seem to have much choice.

The following morning he had a letter from Austin Wurthen. Twenty-four hours earlier he'd have said a letter from Austin Wurthen cut no ice in his life. It cut ice now.

"Dear Emil," Austin wrote; "I suppose it will just about turn your stomach to get a letter from me, but I think you'd better read on before you tear up in your high-handed way. This is about Norma Ashe." No danger of Emil tearing up.

"A few days ago I spoke at the University of Chicago—and by the way, thanks for the tribute you paid me there. I regard harsh words from you a tribute. Take this good-humoredly, as it's meant."

"You gripe me," Emil muttered, though too intent to give proper emotion to his phrase.

"I was speaking of the old days, which have continued to mean a great deal to me. (Laughing? Well, you needn't.) A woman got up and interrupted me, and after a moment I realized this was Norma Ashe.

"I have never seen anyone so changed—in one way. In another way it was the old Norma.

"She seemed to get me all wrong, as if I were desecrating something, which is absurd. I was only paying a tribute to the greatest experience of my life."

"Yeah—yeah—you fool," muttered Emil.

"But the point is this. She looked poor and she may be friendless. I want to do something for her."

Emil gripped the paper until he had to smooth it out to read on. He was mentally, and profanely, telling Austin to keep his dirty hands off of it. *He'd* do something for Norma, if she'd let him.

"I asked the man who was leading her out" (leading her *out*—

hell of a university) "to keep her there, but she rushed off. I didn't know how to find her, and I had to leave Chicago that night, get up home where we are— But what do you care what we are trying to do for the men who work for us?"

Not a damn in hell, agreed Emil. You stink. You're peppered with stool-pigeons.

"It just occurred to me you might know where she is, or could find out. She looked as if she might be in desperate straits. Think of it! Norma Ashe: that wonderful girl. I hold not a bit of malice, even though she ruined the effect of my speech.

"We've gone our separate ways, Emil, and now we don't see eye-to-eye" (I'd cut out both my eyes first, thought Emil), "but once we had something together. You were in on that too—our teacher and all he meant to us, so maybe we could do this in the name of something we once had. I am in a position now to help an old friend and it will grieve me the rest of my life if I do not have the opportunity. What do you say, Emil? Langley meant a lot to you, didn't he? He was good to you, wasn't he? Your living at the house and all that. Then don't do it for me. Do it for him. Find Norma Ashe and let me know about it.

"I suppose I can't close with good wishes. You don't want them from me. Why do you hate so much, Emil, when once you heard the words of our teacher? It's all been so real to me again, since Norma jumped up and gave me hell—most unjustly. I'd like to talk to her, get her straightened out. And get her some *clothes;* you should have seen how she looked. I doubt if she has enough to eat."

That last got so deep into Emil he couldn't even blow up at the idea of Austin getting Norma "straightened out." A long time he sat there with the letter in his hands, until twice his secretary had said, "Shall we—?"

It wasn't Austin who did something for Norma; or even Emil, not at first. It was a new friend, a very young friend, a student.

Scott Neubolt, to whom she had first said it wasn't true: "Ye shall know the truth and the truth shall make you free." To whom later she said it was true, when he followed her out after she broke up Austin's speech.

He had just walked along with her, wanting to know what she would say. He was like that: lively curiosity about people, always looking for something that might let him in on what it was all about. He had this uneasy feeling he didn't know what it was about: life, the whole business; and he wasn't learning it at the University—not first-hand anyway. People—that was the stuff. How could you write if you didn't know people? Though it wasn't just writing; it was this everlasting curiosity he had, wanting to explore, get to it. Something about this woman had intrigued him since the time she'd stood there saying it wasn't true the truth made you free, said she'd found out it wasn't. People didn't talk that way usually. They just agreed that the truth made you free, even though they'd never given it a thought and didn't care a darn. That was the trouble: all the agreeing, not finding out what you really do think, just too doggone lazy and dumb to find out.

So when she got up and bawled out that pill of a Wurthen he was so excited he couldn't hold back; had to go after her, find out why she'd changed, what it was all about.

After she had said: "It came back," and was looking as if . . . *gee,* as if she were seeing a vision or something, he had to hustle her away from a *Tribune* reporter who was hot-footing it; got her into one of the quads and they waited till the coast was clear. "You don't want to talk to a reporter, do you?"

She seemed dazed. Then she laughed a little. "Me? Oh, no; let Austin talk to the reporter."

"It's his meat," he agreed.

Then they just walked slowly along. He was hoping she'd talk; didn't want to press her, she seemed shaky. Uncertainly he took hold of her arm. She looked up at him and smiled. "You're very kind."

"Me? Oh, no; I'm just out for myself."

"I don't believe it," she said, but seemed preoccupied.

She stopped. It was as if she couldn't take something in. She looked at him but didn't seem to be seeing him. "I wouldn't have believed it," she said very slowly.

He said, "What?" but she didn't speak, just stood there as if something were happening to her. "Wouldn't have believed what?" he asked, quite gently, for something about her . . . you couldn't just butt in.

"The whole thing," she said, as slowly she began walking again. "After so many years," she said.

"How many?" he asked.

She didn't seem to hear him at first. Then, "How many? Oh—many. Almost thirty."

"Wish you felt like telling me about it. I can tell it's something I'd like to hear."

Again she stopped. "You would?" She looked into his face, seeing him now. It seemed an effort to think about it, but finally she said: "How wonderful that would for be me."

"For you?" he laughed nervously.

"You're young. You have it all ahead. If you want to know . . ."

But now she seemed all to pieces, trembling so. He had to steady her with both hands, one arm around her shoulder. He was getting alarmed about it, not knowing what to do; it was as if something, he didn't know what, was too much for her.

"Do you live far?" he asked.

"Rather far. I must get to the streetcar. If you would help me to—?"

"Which streetcar?"

"Cottage Grove."

Still quite some way to go to Cottage. He didn't believe she could make it. He looked back, saw a taxi. "You're all-in. We'll just hop this cab."

"Where?" he asked; she told him where she lived, then leaned back and closed her eyes. When she spoke it was with a little smile. "I haven't been in a taxi for some time." She turned her face and looked at him. "You're kind. And you understand without knowing. That is—very wonderful to me."

"Oh, I'm not so hot," he said, embarrassed.

She smiled as if in denial, but it seemed she wasn't going to say anything more, as if she couldn't.

When they got to the place she remembered him again. "You've been so kind to me. I wish I could do something for you." She pushed her hand back over her forehead, getting her hat more out of place. "Let's see. You—yes, I remember now. You wanted to know . . ."

"About you. I'd like to understand."

"You'd like to understand," she repeated slowly, and it seemed to grow on her; as if it—meant something.

"Another time;" he had the grace to say. "You're sort of all-in tonight."

"So much has happened," she said.

"This where you live? Room?"

"Yes. I work here. I do the rooms."

He was a little taken aback, though disgusted with himself that he should be. "Well," he laughed, "I hope you don't have to do them tonight."

"No," she said, "I guess not till morning."

The driver was looking around. Scott got out and helped her up the steps. "All right if I come another time?" he asked, feeling like a good deal of a fool, but going to see it through if he could.

The door opened just as she was saying: "Oh, *do* come another time." She didn't seem to know the woman was standing there—old frozen-face. "I can't tell you how much I want to see you again. You will come, won't you?" she asked anxiously.

Frozen-face exploded: "Norma! You come in now! *High time*," and she glared at Scott as if he were the devil himself.

"I'll be back!" he called. "Want to see you—talk to you—"

"And I want to—" she was beginning as the door slammed, a good righteous slam.

He paid the driver and let him go, not high enough in funds to ride back home. *Now* what had he let himself in for? Coming to see a cleaning-woman—older than his mother would be if she'd lived—and all run down at the heels. He'd go though. The woman *had* something. Somehow he was all excited.

Mrs. Hughes was excited herself, excitement of a different nature. "Now will you *explain*—what this means?"

She shook her head. "I couldn't, tonight, not even—to him." She spoke "him" quite tenderly. She had her hand against the wall, steadying herself.

"Have you been *drinking?*"

She half-smiled. "Well, in a way."

"*Upon my word*. At *your* time of life! I wouldn't have believed it!"

"No," said Norma. "No, I wouldn't either." But she seemed to think it was just splendid! Why the poor dissolute old fool!

"I'll tell you right now you can't act this way in my house! I don't *run* that kind of a house!"

The words had an oddly familiar sound. Oh! She'd said them herself—at Mrs. Utterbach's.

"Where did you pick up that young man?"

"He picked me up," she said, *smiling*. The woman must be out of her head!

"Isn't he a college boy?"

"Yes. He goes to the University. *Think* of it," she murmured.

"Well that's just wonderful! And he picks up a woman your age and brings her home in a taxi!"

"Yes," she murmured.

"And do you know what happened while you were gone? Running out on me like that when I'd left you here in charge! A couple came would have taken second-floor-back and no one here to—"

Norma had started for the stairs. "And you know something *else* is going to happen? You're going to get out of here tomorrow! You weren't much good anyway, so now you can just spend *all* your time running round in taxis with college boys!"

But it wasn't much satisfaction; the woman didn't seem to take it in. Drunk probably. Dope maybe. That boy was a wrong one. Ought to be informed on—put right out of school!

$\mathcal{I}$N THE morning it suited Mrs. Hughes' convenience to give Norma another chance, as she magnanimously put it. The woman who came for special cleaning hadn't shown up. Perhaps Norma would be grateful and do extra work.

Norma didn't seem to mind. She did what she was told in a sort of daze—effect of last night's dissipation wearing off, no doubt. Sometimes, right there on her knees, *scrubbing*, she'd raise up a little and look as if something was perfectly wonderful! That boy of course. Disgusting! Mrs. Hughes just couldn't make it out: why a boy would want to take up with a woman who certainly had lost any good looks she might ever have had. Though as a matter of fact she looked a little better today: hair different or something. But the very idea of going around scrubbing floors as if you were in church! The boy ought to be tarred and feathered. And what was the matter with those college girls that a good enough looking fellow had to take up with a woman like this? Anyway she was getting a lot of work done; hardly seemed to know she was doing it.

But early next afternoon something happened that just couldn't be put up with! There was a little garden behind the house, and when Mrs. Hughes came back from the store what does she see but Norma sitting out there, right down on the ground by a bed of tulips and things, her hands in the earth, rolling it over in her hands and looking at it. And she hadn't anywhere near finished her work!

"Norma!" she called. "Come right in here!"

But she paid no attention, even when called again she went right on moving the earth around with her hands. In a rage Mrs. Hughes hurried out there.

"Now will you please tell me what you mean—after all my kindness to you—sitting here looking at the flowers? Playing in the *dirt* when you're supposed to be doing Mr. Wescott's room?"

The woman had the impudence to smile. "This seemed more important," she said.

She was crazy—not a doubt of it. No telling what mightn't happen. She'd have to get rid of her; though she'd like to wait till tomorrow when she could have someone from the agency.

"You get right in the house and finish that room!"

She shook her head. "I'm very happy out here, Mrs. Hughes. I'll come in after a while."

Mrs. Hughes was so outraged it was hard to get the words out. "You get up off that ground! You go in the house and *pack your things*. Out you go! *Now*. I'll give you ten minutes."

She got up then, all stiff from sitting on the ground, after the scrubbing. She frowned a little as though perplexed. "Why, Mrs. Hughes, how strange of you."

"Oh, so it's strange of me, is it?"

"To be so angry. I was just thinking how wonderful it is the way things grow from the earth."

Dope. Not a doubt of it.

"Well you can think about how wonderful it is somewhere else!"

"Yes," she agreed. "Yes, I'll do that."

Ten minutes were enough. She had only a few things to put in the suitcase she'd brought from Iroquois City when she came to get Fred out of jail. She was soon down in the hall and Mrs. Hughes was handing her her money. Sixteen dollars; she'd been a little backward because it didn't seem to make any difference to Norma.

"And where are you going now?" she asked.

"I don't know."

"Haven't you any place to go?"

"Not that I know of. But I'll think of something," she said cheerfully.

This bothered Mrs. Hughes—a little. Then she remembered Fred, who'd roomed there before his mother came. Bootlegger he turned out to be—ran in the family.

"Of course you have your son," she said.

"Yes," Norma said doubtfully.

She hadn't heard from Fred, didn't know where he was. Lorna and Doc Stanton. . . . No; not back there. There was too much to think about now. Her father had died soon after she began Mrs. Utterbach's. Aunt Nettie was in an old ladies' home. Her sister lived in the West; didn't even write to each other. There wasn't anybody to go to. But there was the world! The whole great world to find out about—again.

She stood in front of the house wondering which direction to take. This way—that way? It was a crisp fragrant spring day. How beautiful it all was, now that she could see it after so long a time.

As she stood there a young man came hurrying along, stopped before her. "Hello," he said.

It was the boy who had taken her home, the boy who had been kind to her; and wanted her to tell him something.

"I was just looking you up," he said.

"I'm glad you came just now," she told him warmly. "While I was packing my suitcase I was worrying about it—going away without seeing you. I would have tried to find you."

"Leaving?"

"By request," she smiled.

"Well I'll be— Say! It wasn't anything about the other night, was it?"

"Oh, no; not especially. It was more about sitting out in the garden."

"Sitting out in the garden? Is that supposed to be a crime?"

"It didn't seem so to me."

"Well, where are you going?" he asked, suddenly a little uneasy. What was he getting himself into, anyway?

"I was just thinking about that. Should I go this way—or that way? It's sort of interesting, having to make a choice."

The door opened and Mrs. Hughes cried: "Now you clear *out* of here—the both of you—before I call the police!"

"What would she be calling the police for?" he asked as they moved on down the street, he with her suitcase.

"I haven't any idea. It doesn't matter though, does it? I mean other things matter so much more than that."

They walked along; he didn't know where they were going, and apparently she didn't know either. She wasn't worried about it. Funny. Everything about her was funny.

"We might walk over to Drexel," he said. "Sit in the park a minute till you've made up your mind."

"I'd love to do that," she agreed. "I could put my feet right down on the earth, couldn't I? I'd like nothing better than that."

She seemed to mean it. Didn't ask much, did she?

So they sat on a bench in the parked space of Drexel Boulevard. He was trying not to feel like a fool. Some ways it seemed he should; another way he shouldn't. Sometimes when you felt like a fool it was the very time you shouldn't. The woman had something. He was going to find out.

But she began asking questions of him. "Tell me, what is the world like—now?"

This baffled him.

"You see I've been out of it so long. In prison," she smiled.

"*What?* You've been in prison?" Golly, this was interesting!

"Well, in one way—no. Only a prison I made for myself. Now

I'm out. It's so wonderful to be out; I can hardly believe it. Only
. . . I've come out into a world I really don't know any more.
Perhaps you'll make me acquainted with it," she said.

"That's rather a large order," he laughed.

"I suppose it is. But find some place to begin. What do people
think about now? Where *are* they? How far have they gone?"

"Oh, they haven't gone very far. Mostly they just make money."

She frowned; that wasn't what she wanted to hear. "But not all
of them surely. Where are the dreamers and what do they dream?
How is the fight going? I'm just back you see. I'd like to take it up
where I left off."

"And where did you leave off?" he asked. "If you'd tell me that
maybe I'd know where to begin."

"I see," she said slowly. "Yes; we must connect."

Children were playing around with their mothers and nurses.
A tired old man rested on the bench opposite. A friendly dog came
up and she stooped and patted his head. He graciously offered his
paw and she took it.

"I left off believing the world could be different." She spoke as
if feeling her way, looked up at him. "Better, I mean. We were going to do it—do our part. Each one of us was to be the most she—
he—could be. We were to *believe* it could be done. That itself
would be toward the better world of our dream. It must first have
reality as idea."

"Yes," he agreed to that.

"We were not to be afraid, not ashamed. It is so easy to feel
sheepish about aspiration, isn't it?"

"I know what you mean," he said.

"Or alone. There is no need to feel alone. For how do we know
what may not be in the mind of another?"

No one would know what is in your mind he thought; not to
look at you, or not to look at you the first time. And this stirred
him: if dream of a better world could be in the mind of a woman

who cleaned-up at a boarding-house—well, then how *could* one say what might not be in the mind of another?

"Now we are ready. Adventure into . . . what waits."

She was like a convalescent trying out her strength, going slowly, fumblingly feeling her way. How happy is the convalescent!

"Adventure?" he prompted.

And suddenly she remembered how she had said this to Max, sitting on the log; and Max too had said it back to her, waited for her to explain. Twenty—? It was twenty-nine years ago, wasn't it? She wasn't sure; perhaps it was thirty. And after that all those years of her life with Max. It was strange about time. It perplexed her. Her life with Max, nearer in years, seemed much farther away now than what had been just before.

"Sometimes . . . a rift. And we look through."

"Afraid I don't understand," he said. Max had said that, and Max never had understood. That must have been her fault. And Fred. And Lorna.

She hadn't any time left for feeling of failure! It was there to weigh you down, shut you in. There was *this* moment—this boy—meeting him just as she had come out into the world all anew. What was it about him? Oh, yes . . . something he wanted to know. Young . . . wanting to know.

She turned and smiled at him. There hadn't been enough money for the dentist, he could see, but for all that there was something very fine and gallant about her smile. And the clothes didn't matter either; not when she looked at you, when she spoke.

"Say," he said, "where have you been—out of the world—all that? Where were you anyhow?" he laughed.

"Oh, it doesn't make much difference where I was when I wasn't anywhere. It's more important where I was when I was somewhere. Isn't it?" she asked.

"Well, maybe. I'm kind of interested in the whole thing. Why don't you just shoot the works?"

"Shoot the works?" She laughed. "What is your name?" she asked him then.

"Scott. Scott Neubolt."

"And you go to the University of Chicago."

"Yep."

"You see, I'm interested. I was to have gone there."

"You were?"

"Yes; twenty-nine years ago."

"And why didn't you?"

"Oh, that's the other story. Not so important to us now. I thought it was the most wonderful thing in the world that I was to go to the University of Chicago."

"It's all right," he said.

"Isn't it any better than that?" she asked anxiously.

"You can get what you want from it, if you want to enough."

"If you want to enough. . . . And you do want to?" she asked after a moment.

"Well—yes," he said for himself.

"I'm sure you do. You are searching for something, aren't you?"

"Me? Why— What makes you think so?" he asked, feeling a little sheepish.

"I remember," she said softly. "Searching for the truth. All learning is there for you to take from it what is yours. But you want it, not so much for its own sake, as to shape the better world of your dreams."

"Now hold on," he laughed. "I'm not so much as all that. You're talking about yourself, aren't you? What you were; not what I am."

"I'm talking about us both," she said. "I'm happy you have this chance—after twenty-nine years. You won't miss the way, will you?" she asked anxiously.

"It's so important," she went on, as he did not speak (what *is* this? he was thinking). "You can do it scarcely knowing you are doing it. And then you are lost. And then you think there is nothing you can do about it. That is the sad part of the story of the world: captured, and not knowing it while it is going on. Me, Austin, Rosie—I don't know for sure about Virgil or Helen, and I don't know at all about Emil. But now there is you. You won't be captured, will you?"

Why didn't he laugh? He'd feel more at ease if he laughed. Yet he didn't.

"You have it. It's still there. . . ."

"What?"

"Youth. Still there. *You* will . . . bring it to pass."

"I don't know what I am to bring to pass, but I'm afraid I can't do it."

"Oh, but that's the wrong idea," she hastened to say. "Don't let it have that power over you. The right idea is that we *can* bring about what we think should be! You think you are not important because other people feel differently. But how can you know that what is in you—"

"I never said anything was in me!" he broke in almost angrily.

"I say it," she said.

What could he say to her? He wasn't here to be told he was so wonderful. Where did she get the idea anyway? Made him feel like a fool. And yet. . .

"Please believe me," she said, simply and so earnestly, "for I know."

"I'm sure I don't know how," he muttered.

"I don't know either. The miracle, perhaps."

"I don't believe in miracles."

"Oh, I do," she said. "And so do you, if you'd just let yourself know it."

"*What* miracle? I don't even believe Christ rose from the dead!"

"He might have, I think, if he'd wanted to enough. Why should I say he didn't? I know I did."

"You rose from the dead?"

She nodded, put back her head as if to let the breeze go over her face. "Life isn't so easily killed. As a matter of fact we are always rising from the dead."

Darn queer—the way she said it; the way it made her look. He'd like to have a few facts though, straighten it out.

"You went to that college up there where Wurthen went?"

She nodded. Nodded again, and seemed to be looking into something.

"And up there you had a teacher you thought was swell?"

She said slowly: "If by swell you mean the best there is in the world—then, yes, he was swell."

Again she seemed to be—well, looking into it. And perhaps it was pretty raw to prod her, but he wanted to know.

"He died, didn't he? Out at the U you said something about Wurthen speaking at the grave."

"Yes, he died." She didn't seem to care much about this, as if she were thinking of something more important.

"I suppose you felt pretty cut-up about that?" She looked at him as if she didn't quite get the idea. "As long as you thought so much of him," he persisted.

"Oh—yes," she said, but still as if something else were more important.

After a moment she seemed to feel she should explain herself. "He didn't really die, you see. Or we thought not. What he was lived on. He had given it to us. It was to go on through us."

Bluntly he asked: "Well, did it?"

He'd hurt her, he could see, and he was sorry—but darn it he wanted to get somewhere! She sat quite still for a moment; then, just barely, she shook her head, answering no to his question.

As if wanting to turn away from this she turned to him and said with a smile, "That's why you are so important.

"Tell me," she went on before he could object to being called important, "what do you study? What *do* we study—now?"

"I'll bring you the curriculum," he said; and at once felt like a dog.

"I'd love to see it," she replied eagerly.

He was feeling rather sore: whether at himself because he'd said something smarty, or at her because she got something she liked from it, he didn't know. He stole a glance at her as she sat there silent, and then he wanted (couldn't for the life of him have said why he wanted it so much) to know just what she was thinking. What was she *looking* at? And what was there in her could— transform her like this?

"A penny?" he ventured.

She looked at him inquiringly.

"For your thoughts."

"I was thinking of those fishes."

"Oh—come now; you didn't look as if you were thinking of fishes."

"The valorous ones. From water to land. The double-breathers. Don't people still think of them?"

"Well, if they do," he laughed, "I don't believe they get such a kick out of it."

"But why not?" she asked quickly. "How can they help—getting a kick out of it? Just think of those old valorous ones a moment. We owe it to them to think of them. Something in them . . . had to do it. Isn't there anything in us—*now*—has to do it? Has the urge died? Old urge to leave safety behind for the unknown? We too could dare a new element for the future that waits. Surely we are not so much less than they. We too could make the thrust and—" She sat very still. "The thrust . . . I remember," she said under her breath. "I remember those old words . . ."

He thought she had forgotten all about him. But after a moment she turned to him and asked: "You do know what I mean, don't you?"

He shook his head. "Well—vaguely," he qualified it, as she looked disappointed.

"Hasn't it *happened?*" she demanded. "You see, it was to happen right *then*. And so much time has gone by."

"I think maybe we aren't as bright as you were when you were young," he laughed. "Or perhaps not as much in earnest. I sort of half-know what you mean, but I don't quite get you."

She was disturbed, wondering: can't age and youth speak to one another? Do the years of our living make a chasm not to be bridged? Does language itself change and old words not have their old content? Have we no voice to reach ears that are young? She was old and she wanted to speak to this boy who was young; what waste if older could not speak to the young, as their teacher to them.

"It's only that I haven't heard my own voice for so long," she smiled at him. "It's still surprising me. I'll be stronger soon, steady and sure. It cannot be that years are a chasm. Because it's *in* us, you know, in us all; the old old dream transmitted from generation to generation. And now it's so important: on the brink of changes, changed way of life. It's a time ready for it to come in. I mean *now*."

Now? This moment—or twenty-nine years ago? They seemed one.

"Do you ever think about the way things start?" she asked. "Catch on, as they say; spread? One person, then another, then many. If lesser things can do that: a new food, jazz—then can't the greatest?"

"Exactly—in precise words—just what do you mean?"

"Exactly; in precise words," she repeated. "Is that the way we talk now? Well, it's all right; it's a challenge."

The word seemed to help her. "Challenge! That's the way it must come. Challenge to make a better world. Challenge to man to be the most he can be. Just now you challenged me to speak more clearly. You see? There's challenge in you. *You* will make the challenge!"

"Nuts," he said; he wasn't going to fall for all this!

"No. Not nuts. Truth." She repeated the word, lingering over it.

"And who, for God's sake, am I to challenge—and to *what?*"

"Now that's a fair question," she said. "You see, you are very fair."

"Why—" But she broke off, asking him: "What did you say your name was? Will you tell me again? There's so much I'm remembering all at once."

"Scott," he told her.

"Yes, of course—Scott. Now it seems it couldn't be anything else. Now I'll always remember your name.

"Why, Scott, you are to challenge lethargy." She seemed a little uncertain about the word. "That's the word, isn't it: lethargy? I ought to know; I've lived in it so long. Challenge the idea we can't make life what we want it to be! And believe! Believe that what you see can come to pass. Would the vision be there if it had no reality? Challenge the idea we must everlastingly wait. Challenge the long slow process. Do we still talk about the long slow process?"

He nodded.

"It's still there then—standing in the way?"

"Well, if it is standing in the way. Seems pretty sound."

She shook her head. "Not if it stands in the way of—the miracle."

"So we're back to the miracle! And I ask you again—*what miracle?*"

His voice was harsh, she seemed startled. "Why, it's hard to put into words, isn't it?"

"If you can't put it into words it's no good. You're getting out too easy."

She considered this and nodded. "No doubt you're right. Yes;

sinking back into the lethargy, not making the effort to get feeling into words." After a little pause she said, slowly: "It is very very hard though; after so long a time."

She was silent so long he thought now I've cooked it, jumping on her like that. But she turned to him and smiled rather timidly as she spoke. "Scott, maybe you will just *be* there with me. I can't do it unless you try too. If you will just—let yourself be there with me?"

As his face lighted up she went on: "We are not sitting on this bench. We are in South Dakota. It's snowing, I think. Anyway there's a strong wind. We're on our way to our teacher's—five of us. Only now we are six; you are there too. It's muddy, probably. We are all wearing our rubbers. We reach the house; we go in."

And then, as best she could, she told him what happened in the house. As she came into it it seemed to take her and she could speak. The boys sat there without moving. She was lifted by what she was disclosing to him, lifted out of age and sorrow and failure and fatigue. She *was* Norma Ashe again, there with her teacher, seeing the great vision and ready for the fight!

When at last she finished speaking he did not break the silence nor did she. She had been feeling so much, and using every bit of her—summoning—summoning that her words might be right, might be accurate and worthy, that in speaking of it she would not make it less, would transfigure and not betray, so after she had told him, and after that silent time of still living in it, she was suddenly very tired. She only looked at him to see if she had at all succeeded. She seemed satisfied with what she saw.

Then she rubbed her knees. "So much scrubbing," she smiled.

"God!" he exploded.

"God what?"

"*Scrubbing.*"

"Never mind," she laughed. "It's been worth it. Because here I am now talking with you. You're young. It's made me young.

You've given *it* youth. And it needs perpetual youth.

"How foolish it would be for me try to thank you. I haven't any words to thank you." And he couldn't say anything; not nuts —not anything.

But after a little he asked her: "Say, what are you going to do?"

"Me? Do? Well, I'll have to think about that. As you know, I'm just back. I don't suppose I could study now," she said wistfully. "I suppose the time for that really has—gone by."

"Of course you could study! Look at the people who study when they're eighty. But that wasn't what I meant. I mean now— pronto—right away. Where are you going? How are you going to live?"

She laughed. "Oh, I see. Well, I don't know. I haven't had time to think about it, thinking of so many other things."

"Well somebody's got to think about it! Have you any place to go?"

"Not especially."

"You can't just sit here on this bench you know."

"I suppose not. I would be arrested then, wouldn't I?"

"Now take this seriously. It *is* serious. You've got to eat, and sleep somewhere. Have you got any money?"

"Oh, yes." She opened her purse. "See? I have"—she counted it—"twenty-one dollars."

"Twenty-one dollars! Is that all you've got in the world?"

"Why, I believe it is," she smiled.

"Stop *smiling*. This is serious. Don't you know anything about the world?" he demanded.

"Oh, Scott—I know a good deal about the world. Why, my dear, are you worrying about me? Now don't do that. After it's all been so wonderful."

"There's nothing so wonderful about twenty-one bucks!"

He sat there thinking and she moved a little to flex stiff muscles, rubbed her knees.

"My sister is going to have a baby," he said.

"She is? Oh, how nice for her." She thought of Joseph.

"She'll have to go to the hospital in a week or so. She ought to have someone to stay in the house. Only a young girl doing the work, and there are two kids. Two already, I mean." Scott was suddenly very concerned about his sister's household; that nitwit of a Genevieve couldn't swing it all. Ellen had said she was going to get somebody older, responsible . . .

"I think I'll go over to that drugstore and telephone," he said. "You wait here?"

She said she would, but he changed the plan. "No, you come with me. Think we can eat in there and I'm hungry as a wolf."

She got up stiffly and went along with him, sat at a table while he disappeared into the phone booth.

He held the slug in his hand. Now how would he put it to Ellen? It was going to sound phony. Just have to take the upper hand.

"Ellen? Got anyone to stay at the house while you run off to populate the world?"

She seemed surprised—this inquiry from Scott, but said she thought there was someone she could get.

"You needn't bother. I've got it all arranged."

"*You*, Scott?" she laughed.

"Found just the right person—older woman, responsible. Be fine with the kids. I'm bringing her right out."

"Now hold your horses, my boy. I don't know that I want this—"

"Sure you'll want her. Great piece of luck."

"Where did you *get* her for heaven's sake?"

"Oh, I met her when she spoke at the University."

"Spoke at the *University?* Scott! Have you now gone completely off your head? A woman who would speak at the University wouldn't want to—"

"Sure she wants to, just happens to fit in. Bringing her right out —soon as we grab something to eat." He hung up before Ellen could say another word, came back to the table whistling. "It's all fixed. Now what do we eat?"

So it was the new friend—youth of today—welcomed Norma back to the world.

CHAPTER TWENTY-ONE

AFTER Austin had dispatched his letter to Emil he decided that was just time thrown away. Now that he knows I would like to find Norma, any effort he makes will be to keep me from doing it. Just another chance to take a sock. I know why he jumped on me at the University, he thought: opening gun of his campaign to keep me out of Washington. Got it in for me, and on no rational grounds. But then Emil wasn't rational. The chip on his shoulder weighed a ton. He wondered what made him like that.

No doubt he'd had a pretty hard life at one time. Too bad it kept him bitter now when he was doing pretty well for himself. That was the worst thing could happen to a person—get bitter. Warped one; and didn't Emil himself prove a man could make his way in America? But he didn't look at it right. He'd always been stubborn.

He remembered him up there with their teacher, always hanging around. He'd had almost no education himself, but would sit there listening to things he couldn't possible have understood. He was an uncouth boy—terrible manners. Every once in a while he'd seem to be trying to shoo them all out. What business was it of his how often they came or how long they stayed? Seemed to have constituted himself a special guardian of their teacher, hovering around in his lumbering way.

Their teacher liked him: wonder why? Certainly there were students more promising than Emil who would have been glad to live there in the house with him, help themselves through college by doing chores. Funny he should have taken in a clodhopper like Emil Jensen. Of course, he was strong—useful, probably. And he had to admit there was no question of Emil's devotion to their teacher. But he overdid this, fussing around like an old hen; a raw-boned hen, he thought to himself, pleased with the ridiculous picture.

He remembered Emil at the service at the grave. Everything about that long-ago day was pretty sharp in his memory; he'd felt it so deeply, and also felt the responsibility of being the one to speak. Emil stood a little apart from the others, as if he didn't want to mix with them, as if what he was feeling was his own business.

He didn't deserve the treatment he'd had from Emil. Fact of the matter, he'd tried to be good to him. Looked him up the very day after the funeral—thought their teacher would want him to do this; asked what he was going to do and told him he thought his father might give him a job. Emil hadn't taken it in good part, never took anything in the right spirit. Said in his surly way: "Thank you. I'll get along." So going to work in the tough spots was his own fault, and he needn't have been a martyr about the conditions he found. He'd have had a much better life up at the plant.

He'd even written Emil when he saw by the papers he was in jail—ten, twelve years ago that was. He deserved to be in jail: inciting to riot. Emil was against everything Austin himself believed in: doing things peaceably, reasonably, not stirring up hatred but pulling together. Just the same he'd written him, old times' sake, asked if there was anything he could do. Of course Emil took it the wrong way; seemed to think he was being patronized. "There isn't a damn thing you can do for me," he had replied, "and when I get out of here I'm going into the fight in earnest. Fight you and all your kind."

So what could you do with a bigoted person like that, and how foolish he'd been to think Emil might have a little feeling left about the old days. He'd rather let Norma starve than grant any wish of what he called the employer class.

Lord, how Norma had looked. Why, the poor girl—what she must have been through. He remembered how she used to look. However in the world had she let herself *get* this way? He wouldn't have believed it could happen. If she could have it a little easier surely she'd get straightened out in her mind. That was why he felt he had to find her—not one to let an old friend down.

Perhaps Rosie knew now. He'd seen Rosie in New York three years ago, and what a fine woman *she* was. Well, a few of us have come through, he thought. Take Virgil. Virgil had succeeded as a writer. He couldn't get much out of the books himself, never knew just what the fellow was driving at, too much fooling about things that should have been treated more seriously. Just the same he had made a place for himself.

When Austin saw Rosie three years before she hadn't known where Norma was. She seemed sad about it, but wouldn't talk of it much. "Norma would be disappointed in me," she said. "I don't believe I could bear to see her, even if I knew how to find her."

What did she mean, he'd wanted to know; anyone would be proud to claim her as an old friend. She shook her head. "No, Austin, I'm different now. Too much got left out. It would hurt Norma."

He'd tried to tell her that down underneath we never really change, but she only smiled and talked of something else. In one way Rosie certainly had changed. She was a pretty dowdy girl up at school—nice, but definitely country-jake. Now she had money: house on Long Island, clothes. But she was Rosie just the same, and why did she insist she wasn't? People got things twisted. He'd always tried to keep things straight in his mind.

He believed he'd write to Rosie; possibly she had heard from

Norma by this time. Or Virgil might have heard, and Rosie was in touch with Virgil. But before he got around to writing he found he had to make one of his trips to New York. He'd look Rosie up.

They sat out on the terrace having their cocktails, he and Rosie and Virgil. Rosie said her husband couldn't be home, busy in New York. She hadn't asked anyone else, thinking they'd like a visit by themselves.

He wouldn't bring it up, tell his story about Norma, until they'd settled down after dinner. Virgil was a queer one. He made Austin a little uncomfortable: irritating manner, as if he had a joke all by himself. He smiled too much, and at the wrong things. Didn't look like a writer: well set-up, knew his way about. Done well for himself, one could see, but he took things too lightly, sly digs at things there was no sense in taking a poke at. Keen though; not a person you'd be ashamed to introduce.

Rosie was gracious and very charming, but somehow she didn't seem as happy as she should. What did she want for heaven's sake? Lovely home, husband making money, children. Why should it be any effort to be gay? Virgil was very nice to Rosie, almost as if he were sorry for her. That was nonsense.

"Well, well, and here we are," he'd said, raising his glass. "Three of us."

"We will drink to the three who have come through," Virgil said, and as if there were some sort of joke about it. "Virgil— *please*," Rosie remonstrated. So he himself had changed the toast to "Happy days" and the other two didn't seem especially happy about that one either.

During dinner they didn't talk of their old days together. Virgil and Rosie kept up a sort of patter. He talked some of conditions, things he was interested in, and Virgil would look at him in that quizzical way he had. He didn't actually cock his head, but might as well have. They didn't really get together at dinner.

So after the man had brought their coffee into the library, and they'd got it settled about lumps of sugar, he said: "I have something to tell you."

That got their attention—way he said it; there was always a way of getting people's attention. "It's about Norma," he added, and then had them right where he wanted them: Rosie leaning forward in that startled way, and Virgil not doing any funny business.

"I've seen her. She looked—like the poor-house."

Virgil set down his cup, spilling some; he sat with one shoulder hunched away from Austin, as though dodging something.

He told his story, but didn't get the effect he had been looking for. Rosie said breathlessly: "Why, I can scarcely believe it!" But she seemed *pleased*. And Virgil looked more as he used to look out there at school.

"I saw Norma myself," Rosie hurried on, "less than a year ago, and I thought she was—well, the Norma I had known simply wasn't there. I—I gave her up . . . hardest thing I ever did in all my life. Now you say— Virgil! Do you understand? She's back!"

"So it seems," Virgil murmured.

"But what do you suppose happened?" Rosie went on in great excitement. "Austin! Tell us more!"

"Do you realize what I *have* told you?" he demanded indignantly. "I told you she looked completely down and out, and you seem to be *gloating* over it!"

"You bet!" cried Virgil. "Haven't heard such good news in thirty years. You say she got right up there in meeting and—"

"And I'm telling you how she *looked* when she got up there. What kind of people *are* you, anyway? I'm glad I live in the Middle West. Whatever you can say about us, we have hearts."

"Give me some brandy, Rosie," Virgil sang out. "This is no time for coffee!"

"Austin, you don't understand," Rosie said, smiling at him, all excited and happy. "You see—we're so *glad*."

"I see you are," he said grimly.

"Because she's back! Don't you see? She's there!"

"Oh, she's there all right! Right there on the bread-line." His indignation mounted. "Why I thought you'd want to help me find her; get her some clothes—food."

"She has food," said Virgil; "food of the gods. And she's clothed in beautiful raiment!"

"You're talking like a heartless fool!"

"No, Austin," Rosie said, speaking all the time in that breathless way, "we'll come to that, but now we're—"

"I can tell you she didn't look as you look, Rosie," he broke in rebukingly. "She'd had no such dinner as we've had here tonight."

"Oh—us," Virgil said lightly, and waved his hand as if waving them out of the picture. "We're fattened and done for. But it seems Norma . . . Do you mean to say," he demanded, as if he must hear it again and gloat over it, "she got right out there in the aisle, looking as you say she did, not giving a damn how she looked, and told you not to *cash in* on it?" He almost clapped his hands— might as well have.

"She talked very wildly," he said stiffly. "As if poverty may have deranged her mind."

Virgil burst into a rude laugh, and Rosie insisted: "Oh, no, her mind has come *back*. I thought it was gone—gone forever—what was Norma. But something must have happened. Now what could have happened?" she asked excitedly of Virgil.

"I think you are absolutely the most heartless people I have ever known in my life," Austin said slowly. "I'm surprised at you, Rosie." He hoped Virgil got the implication.

He did: the man had the most insulting way of laughing.

And his way of speaking was no better. "But can't you see, my dear Austin, if she could see *right through you*, have the guts to spring up and expose you—"

"Can't you see," Rosie broke in, not giving a hoot how insulting Virgil was being, "that it means she's still *there?* I just can't tell you what this means to me!"

"As to my being 'exposed,'" he turned to Virgil, "as to there being anything to expose in the life I lead—"

"Now, Austin—my dear Austin—don't pull that on *us*," Virgil had the damned impertinence to say. "We know and you know—"

"Let's not quarrel," Rosie cried. "I'm too happy to quarrel."

Awful to be so disappointed in an old friend. He'd always liked Rosie. "If you can find anything to be happy about in an old friend being on the rocks—"

"Rocks!" jeered Virgil. "Norma's sitting at the right hand of God—if you want to call that rocks."

"You're a fool," said Austin, who'd stood enough. "I always suspected it—that damn fool way you write."

"Please, Austin," Rosie said, "we must get together; all be happy together. Now let me tell you—try to tell you—why it means so much to me."

She paused, held up a hand not to be interrupted. "You see . . . I thought it was all gone. Gone out of the world. I can't tell you . . . the emptiness. As if it had never really been at all . . . our life out there, all it meant. I had gone to Norma—not knowing how to live. That is the simple truth," she said simply. "I had to find Norma.

"I found her. Only . . . I didn't. She wasn't there to find. She had gone. *Norma,*" she said incredulously. "I just can't tell you, and don't want to, what that hour with her was like. The emptiness in which I walked away."

She turned to Austin. "So don't you see why it means so much to me? And look! If it can come back to Norma, then why not to me, to you, to Virgil? You do see, Austin? I really feel," said Rosie, in the earnest way she used to speak at school, "that now there is something to live for."

What an utterly senseless way to talk! Oh, no— Rosie had nothing to live for! This beautiful room in which they sat, her whole life with—with worth-while people. Nothing at all to live for!

"As for me," he declared, "I'm just a plain man. I have the ordinary human reactions. When I see an old friend on the rocks——and I do *not*," he turned to Virgil, "mean any damn fool rock at the right hand of God—I'm sorry, just plain humanly sorry, and it is my instinct to try and do something about it. I tell you she hasn't enough to eat, and you're tickled to death!"

He had risen in dudgeon. Rosie got up, a hand on his arm. "No, no, Austin; we'll do something about that, if we can find the way to do it. But we were thinking first of this more important part of it."

"There's nothing more important than not having enough to eat." He was feeling humanitarian and this fortified him in righteous anger against them.

"Maybe she has something to eat," said Virgil. "Perhaps an occasional crust falls from the rich man's table. Don't lots of crusts fall from your table, Austin? Well, where do all those crusts go? I've often wondered."

"You've given me the key to your writing," Austin said, bitingly as he could. "Now I'll understand the stuff, only I won't read it. You have no heart. You'd jeer and jibe at anything."

Virgil said: "I don't know whether I would or not. Perhaps you've ruined my writing, Austin. Possibly it isn't going to be so easy to jeer and jibe." He'd spoken almost dreamily, but finished with a teasing: "Think I could sue you?"

Disregarding Rosie's protests, Austin left. They made him, not only angry, but uncomfortable. He told himself it was because the milk of human kindness was not in them.

When they were alone Rosie and Virgil didn't speak of Norma at first, each thinking the thoughts that came. Then Rosie said, after Virgil had his highball, "I wonder what happened—in between."

"Between?" he asked absently, little disturbing his own thoughts.

"Between the boarding-house, when she wasn't there at all, and this night she sprang up and—"

"And with an avenging sword affirmed her faith," he smiled.

Rosie smiled too, seeing Austin's face as it must have been.

"Rosie," he asked her, very earnestly for him, "do you suppose we were just a lot of dopes—out there in South Dakota?"

"Must you talk that way now?"

"Why not? See what a hold it can take on us again; just the idea that it still goes on in one of us. What is there *to* it? For God's sake just what was it all about?"

"You knew once. You'd know now, if you'd let yourself."

"I'd like to test it some way. Everything has to be tested. It didn't stand up very well, did it? There's Emil—raising all the hell he can. Is that the idea? No, guess not. Norma was the best of us, or so we used to think. She was going to the University of Chicago: dedicated life, carry on the spirit of our teacher, make the world so much better it wouldn't know itself. On the train she meets a guy with sex appeal; has to marry him right quick, so she can sleep with him all in accordance with God's law."

"Don't be horrid, Virgil. She fell in love."

"That's what I'm saying. And everything else—goes by the board."

"We don't know that it did. In fact for a long time she used to write me letters that were very much Norma."

"Well her letter to me was a phony. All mixed up. She left us pretty early in the game, didn't she? This fellow was a go-getter. And she went go-getting along with him."

"You don't know any of those things."

"Now everything else is gone for her—so back comes the old glory to fill the empty life. I'm just trying to get a line on it," he forestalled the objection Rosie was about to make. "What are we so elated about? Can you tell me?"

"I am elated because something I thought had gone out of the world is still there. It reaches me and—brings me life."

"Oh—pooh," he said, not very convincingly.

"I can't *analyze* it, Virgil."

"Then it's no good," he smiled. "Well, I can analyze it, and darned if it still doesn't seem some good. So I'm ahead of you," he had to thrust at her, just because he had the habit of these thrusts.

"We were a bunch of kids more or less hypnotized," he went on. "Rosie, I wonder what he really was," he said slowly.

"He had a lot of power," Virgil mused on. "I'll say that for him. I've known a lot of people whose business it is to communicate, and I've never known anyone had the power, the eloquence, he had. He could quicken the dead. He could— Oh, hell, I don't know— but where did he *get* it? It was as if—pardon my extravagance— as if life really gushed through. But why? I ask you, and while I'm asking I'll tell you. Because he really cared. Upon my very soul I believe he really did."

"I know he did," Rosie said firmly.

"You do? Then why didn't he last longer in your life?"

"Oh, that has to do with—a lot of things," she said sadly.

He nodded. "Just so. Here we'd had this goddam miracle,"— Virgil was making himself another highball—"and then 'a lot of things.' It didn't take, did it? It took, but it didn't last."

"I wish you wouldn't talk that way tonight."

"Of course my case was simple," he went on, paying no heed to her wish. "Simple and not very creditable. I was sore. Hurt. Hurt like hell. I loved her. Lord, yes—I loved her. I thought she was— all those things. That was what our life together was going to be. So when she threw me over I had to throw over the whole works."

"You were pretty awful that time in Minneapolis."

"I was worse than awful. I was ridiculous. So hurt I had to throw rocks.

"So I was out to do the world in. I'd be the *other* side: demon side. I'd puncture where I could. That would show her! Pretty sophomoric," he granted; after a moment he added: "I didn't do very well at it, did I?"

"Not very."

"Care to say why?"

"Because you never ceased caring about the thing you set out to destroy."

"Why, Rosie—Rosie the sage. How can a thing that isn't true sound so wise?"

"It is true."

"I wonder," he said slowly; and after a moment muttered: "Shouldn't wonder.

"Well, let's turn to your case—now that we're leaving me there a flop. You married for money, didn't you, Rosie?" he asked briskly.

"Not exactly," she said. "Not that I knew of."

He laughed, "There's the catch in it."

"I couldn't have the man I loved because he was married. I thought that wasn't right, fought against it. I even took up a kind of new religion, half with the idea that would get him for me, or perhaps would bring me into peace—where I wouldn't want him."

"And the old religion, what we had from our teacher, wasn't that any good to you?"

She was silent a moment before she said: "I guess it made me too alive—what we had from our teacher."

"Now you're getting somewhere. We couldn't be that alive in the world we found ourselves in. Had to cheapen ourselves, day by day, to go on living."

"That's not true! I mean—it needn't be."

"It was with you, wasn't it?"

"Oh—me," she said.

"You didn't matter? There begins the denial. Once you were to have mattered. There's the little germ that eats the bright dream." He laughed. "However, there's always Long Island, isn't there? And what the hell? Now you're rich and complacent."

"If you don't know any more than that," said Rosie, angrily and close to tears, "you might as well go home!"

"I know, Rosie. I was wrong there. You aren't rich and complacent. You're rich and unsatisfied. You haven't got the man you want or the life you want. Poor little Rosie." Virgil was a little drunk—on Scotch and remembering.

"And I'm sorry," he added, and seemed to mean it.

"I know I'm a rather ridiculous figure," Rosie granted. "Seeming to have everything and feeling I have nothing. 'Why the poor woman' the poor could jeer at me. But honest to God, Virgil, money makes very little difference."

"It's over-rated," he agreed; "though so very very convenient."

"That was what hurt me so about Norma when I went to her. She seemed to think because I had money everything must be all right with me. *Norma*—Norma thought that," she said incredulously. "When I walked away from her—a light had gone out of the world."

"I know. I think I know what you mean: a light gone out. How did you happen to marry Dale?" he changed it abruptly, for he would skirt close to things, then edge from them.

"That was after Arthur; when I knew I couldn't have him and still couldn't give him up. I suppose I thought I would forget."

"Kind of raw on Dale, wasn't it?"

"I don't think he cared much," said Rosie, for the first time speaking bitterly. "He never really knew me."

"Tut tut, my dear. That's an old one."

"And true. I'd told Dale about it, and it interested him to see how soon he'd make me care more for him than for Arthur. But he got bored with that, became interested in other things."

"Woman things?"

"Women and money. So I lived that life of money too. You see —I'd let so much go."

"You sure had," he said, not very consolingly.

"Rosie, our stories are sort of shabby, aren't they?"

"Let's talk about Norma's story. Perhaps Norma can still—redeem us."

"Oh, it's late, my dear—pretty late in the day."

They sat there silent until Virgil asked, almost shyly: "Would you like to see her?"

"I don't know," Rosie said. She seemed disturbed, as if wrestling with something. "I can't tell you! I don't know."

"Funny thing—so late in the day—but I think I'd like to see her." He spoke it softly, then added in matter-of-fact voice: "Curiosity, I suppose,"—as if he wouldn't let himself go the whole way.

CHAPTER TWENTY-TWO

So far as Norma knew it had all arranged itself very smoothly about her coming to stay for a while in this pleasant house. When they arrived Scott left her downstairs and went up to talk with his sister. She could imagine it: Scott vouching for her, his sister startled and dubious. "Who *is* the woman? Where did you get hold of her and what did you know about her?" And Scott would say he knew a good deal about her . . .

He must have been persuasive, for Mrs. Hershell sent down asking Norma to come up and see her. She told a little about herself, and soon they were talking about the children, what there would be to do.

She was glad to find Scott lived in this house. That gave her a friend here.

She helped Genevieve with the work, and usually it was Norma took little Ellen to the park. There was a garden, and here no objection to her working in it; she had some spare time in the afternoons. She had tried to read Scott's books, the books he used in school. Just handling them made it a little as if she were at last going to the University of Chicago. But she didn't get very far with the books; it tired her. She told herself this was because she had been away from it all so long. That would come later, when she was more used to things again. Becoming yourself, after so many years, wasn't easy. It was something like being born. You had to let the world take you, grow into it. It was the smell of the earth could take her. All things that grew from the earth seemed to say: Trust us. We are life. We bring back.

The day after she came Mrs. Hershell said: "Norma, we're about of a size. That is when my size is only myself," she laughed. "I have clothes I can't wear now and goodness knows when I'll be able to get into them again. I'd like you to have these things."

So she had clothes now and she was glad to be looking more like herself. It seemed she should be looking herself at this time.

Scott found her out in the garden the afternoon he came home bursting with news. "There's a fellow looking you up!"

"Looking me up?" She was still rather easily bewildered.

"You'll be surprised! It's this Emil Jensen."

She put down the little cultivating fork she had been using. "You mean—*Emil?*"

"Sure. He's been raising the roof to find you. Had a poor guy nearly crazy trying to find me so he could locate you."

"You mean Emil wants to see me?"

"Dead right he wants to see you!"

This too came to pass, the following night. Scott arranged it so she could go. His sister was at the hospital now—false alarm, but staying on; he was going to stick around home that night anyway, he said—run right along with the boy-friend. They'd laughed together at that.

She didn't feel wholly like laughing. She was excited but a little frightened. Emil . . . that boy who lived there. Emil—so close to it. She had always felt he knew things the rest of them didn't know.

Could she but know, Emil was a little frightened himself. This seemed to take him way back: things he'd let go, or so he told himself. Going out to get her he'd bolster himself up. What was he in such a dither about? See an old friend who maybe needed a lift; nothing to get excited about.

What in the world was Austin beefing about? he asked himself as he looked across the table to Norma, here in a German restaurant on Sixty-third Street. Austin talked as if she looked like a scarecrow. Well, she didn't. Dressed all right, it seemed to him. Nice blue suit, good-looking hat, dressed about like the rest of the women. Looked worn though, and if it hadn't been for the way her eyes could light up, the flush of excitement, she'd look pretty old, that was true. But not as Austin had pictured. This Neubolt and his family must have done something for her. Decent people perhaps. Emil was always a little slow in admitting people were decent.

About to begin on her soup, she put down the spoon, looking over at him as if she couldn't believe it.

"I know," he agreed. "Eat your soup. Nothing seems so strange after good hot soup."

"You are used to looking after people," she said. "You looked after our teacher."

"I've looked after a lot of people since that," he said, wanting to steer away from the old things, at least for a while. "That's my business, you know—get people to look after themselves. Some of them haven't the gumption to do it without a good swift kick in the pants."

"And you give the kick in the pants?"

"I'm supposed to be a terrible person."

"I doubt it," she smiled. Still had that smile he remembered. Too bad those two front teeth hadn't been fixed. He was used to noticing people's teeth; teeth could tell you a lot about how people were getting along. And her hands. She'd worked all right.

They talked a little more about him and then he said: "Now suppose you tell me the long sad story of your life."

"Oh—let's not. Other things are more important than my life."

"Once you didn't think that."

"No," she said. "And I don't think it now, not any more. But for a long time . . ."

"Had it tough?"

"Why, I don't know. Yes, I suppose so. The last thirteen years I was poor."

"That's no fun."

"But that wasn't the worst of it. You see—I abdicated."

"How do you mean? You have to speak very plain to me. I'm used to plain people."

"I left. Myself wasn't there at all."

"Um-hum. That's what poverty does; one of the nice little things it can do to people."

She thought about this, shook her head. "It began before I was poor."

She sat there, brows knit, and he just let her try to think it out. As still she didn't speak, "You got married right after you left school, didn't you?" he asked.

She nodded. "And I'm not sorry about that. I loved Max and was happy with him. Only—"

"Stumps you, does it?" he laughed, as again she fell silent and seemed to be looking into something.

"Well, it does," she said slowly. "It seems to me now it needn't have been that way. What happened to me, Emil?"

"I'm sure I don't know," he smiled. "Kind of like to find out, and you're pretty slow in loosening up."

"It takes a little time to loosen up," she said seriously.

"Take your time," he granted. "First pass the horse-radish."

They were quite by themselves in this alcove, they could talk. And after a little time she did talk—beginning fumblingly, as if she didn't know herself what it was all about: Texas, Iroquois City; Max, the children; Max's death, the boarding-house—Fred, Chicago. "So I don't know that we can blame just poverty. Money can do something to you too."

"Dead right it can."

"What about you, Emil? Did you . . . keep it?"

"Keep what?" he asked rather roughly.

"What we had," she said simply.

"Listen, Norma, you don't 'keep' anything. You fight and fight like hell to get what you want."

"But what you want—it isn't for yourself."

"Now you can't glorify me. Don't try it! It all started with my being damn sore."

"At the injustices of the world."

"I hated their guts."

"Hating isn't the way."

"Which shows you don't know much about it! Where did it ever get *you*—not hating enough to fight?"

"Our teacher wanted us to fight; he didn't want us to hate."

"He was wrong there."

She shook her head. "No, he wasn't wrong." She looked at him intently. "And you don't think he was either."

"Say! Don't tell me what I think. I know what I think."

"Sure?" she smiled. "Perhaps you won't let yourself know what you think. You're in this—deep in it—and you won't let yourself see any other way."

"There isn't any other way," he said with his old stubbornness. "Lord, where would I get—running around loving the bosses?"

"I think you love people."

"Now you can just cut this out, Norma. I know just what you're up to. That's my business," he smiled; "keep one jump ahead, know what's going to be sprung on me. You are about to find I have a heart of gold, that it hurts me to hurt anyone. Well, you're wrong. When I can make them squirm that's my reward for a hell of a lot of work."

"But it's not an end in itself, is it? It's to make things better for people who need help."

"I don't like 'need help.' It's not a charity racket, you know."

"You are trying to make the world better. That was our teacher's idea."

"He was visionary—idealistic."

"If I had any money to bet I'd bet you are too."

"I'm hard as nails. I look at it economically."

"Why?"

"You ought to know the answer to that silly question. You couldn't make a go of it under the present set-up."

"I mean, after it's better for them economically—what then? What are they going to do with more money, more time?"

"Do what they damn please with it!"

"You know better than that. What is it? Where there is no vision the people perish. Rosie is rich, and she's not very happy."

"I have no time to weep over the poor rich woman. I've seen too many women didn't have food for their kids."

"I know," she said. "I felt that way about Lorna. I couldn't give her what she should have. It made me bitter. But now I don't want to be bitter. Life is too wonderful."

"Oh, life's just grand. People get sick and lose their jobs and the milkman stops leaving the bottle for the baby. Kids get pneumonia because there's no coal—but oh dear me, let's never forget life's just wonderful! Ever been out of coal, Norma?"

"Yes," she said.

Instead of bing offended by his outburst she smiled at him. "It means so much to me that one of us is doing something."

"You're not by any chance alluding to the hard-boiled baby sitting opposite you?"

"You think you're very practical, don't you, Emil?"

"That I will say for myself."

"Do you ever think—how practical a dream is?"

Before he could get in any scoffing remark she went on: "It's the most practical thing on earth: a dream. The dream comes first; then reality as idea. And then the thrust. Remember how he used to talk about the thrust? Make true what we dream might be."

Her face was all lighted up. How well he remembered it—this same face, sitting there at that other table as their teacher unfolded to them his vision of what life might be. But he wasn't going to be caught into this! The game was realistic. Advance step-by-step, the thing that needed to be done. Jobs, food, plumbing, teeth fixed; children setting out to school in shoes that didn't leak. Sleds—yes by God, sleds to play in the snow. A radio when you sat round the stove at night. Not getting held-up for the funeral. A car to take the whole bunch on a picnic. That was as much as he could see at the moment. If people had more fresh air, time to go to the library, the dreams would take care of themselves. That would come later when there weren't any leaking, stinking houses with rats slinking out of the walls.

He was about to say something like this, but she spoke first. And now she spoke sadly. "I can't understand it."

"What can't you understand, Norma?"

"Why we didn't—go on. One and then another of us let living eat into it. We were captured—so soon. You not entirely. But you see only a little way."

"I see a hell of a long way! All right, I'll admit it. I think so too—he was a great man. That doesn't mean he has to be the whole measure of our lives. You're making him a god. We fail or we succeed according to how close we keep to what he was. Maybe he was inspired. I guess so. He sure gave us something. And when we went out into the real world we changed because we have to live in the world that goes on. If the dream couldn't meet the situation then maybe there's something wrong with the dream. Ever think of that?"

"I have thought of it, and I honestly don't believe it. I think the failure was with us. And I wonder why. Emil, will you tell me something?"

"Maybe."

"Isn't it ever—still there for you? Doesn't it sometimes *stir* in you?"

He shifted uneasily. "I have a lot of work to do."

"You won't answer. I think the answer would be yes, if you'd let yourself be honest."

"I'm as honest as two and two makes four."

"Maybe they don't."

"Oh, come now. Take hold of yourself. Don't you believe in exact knowledge?"

"I believe in—all we don't yet know! We're contenting ourselves too easily, living in what's been handed us. All knowledge is just a working its way to more knowledge, and a lot of it has to be thrown away. The great thing is to keep the path clear. Knowledge can shut you in like walls. Or it can be—a hill to climb, a sea to see. I believe in—the miracle."

"I pass," he said.

"You're just afraid."

"That's one thing they haven't yet called me—fraid cat."

"You're afraid if you see too far ahead you'll think what you're doing is not important. You're afraid of too wide a look. Hence the walls."

"I just keep plodding along," he scoffed.

She took it seriously. "Yes. And that's all right in its way. I mean, it has its place."

"Thank you so much," he said.

"Now, Emil, don't do *that*. We're talking. Two of us are talking again, after so long a time. It means so much to me. As much as milk to your children who haven't milk."

"I doubt that. I doubt that very much, my dear."

"I know it. And you doubt because I talk badly, and that's because I haven't talked for so long. But let me talk on, will you?" She smiled at him in real appeal.

"Sure," he smiled back. "Go right ahead."

"And you won't shut me out?"

"I won't take any of your dope I think is just dope."

"Of course you won't," she said. "Well, to me, it's all open again. As it was up there. That was the great thing he did for us. Almost as if he'd touched it with a wand—he made it fluid. You used to sit in the room, Emil—remember how excited I was? And now again. I'm old and poor and my mind's rusty, but it's as if doors of the spirt were opening, and it's flooding in."

And what good is it going to do you? he thought. He didn't see much of a future for her.

"Harm could never come to me again," she said.

"Oh—*nuts*," he said rudely.

"Nuts?" she smiled. Who else had said nuts? Scott. Scott was young. Scott was going on.

It would go on. It would go on because it couldn't die. It couldn't die because it was *there*, as once she'd seen it, that night after she had seen their teacher's body lowered into the ground. More clearly than she now saw the coffee in this cup she had seen what waited, what could be. We—the disciples—perhaps we just weren't good enough, she thought. Not medium pure enough nor long enough lasting. It couldn't come through. That doesn't mean it was not there. *What?* she asked herself, as she knew Emil would ask were she thinking aloud. Oh—you know, she thought. You know better than you know anything else. More surely than you know Emil's tie is blue you know you were there at a birth, experienced the great moment when there was a rift and the unseen that waited came into the world called actual.

The exaltation of her worn face made Emil angry. "Listen, Norma, get *wise* to yourself."

"That's just what I was doing at the moment," she smiled.

"You're doing nothing of the sort! You're lost in a fog. Why don't you try and *see* the world?"

"But I am! I am seeing. Just then I was—"

"To *hell* with that stuff! You're just—standing in the way!"

"Me? In the way? In the way of what?"

"Of a decent world!"

It seemed to take her breath. "But, Emil—surely not *now*. Perhaps once; perhaps for a long time. But now . . . I'd lay down my life for the world that might be," she said simply. "Gladly—if only I knew how to do it."

And so she would. That he believed. But she'd have to get herself straight first. And all at once he saw a way—a terrible way—to banish an old dream that didn't fit the present pattern. And she became to him all the idealists, the well-meaning dreamers who were worse than the bad people, muddling it up with what couldn't be, making something way off sometime seem more important than everybody having a job.

But he'd kept it to himself all his life: this cruel thing he could tell her now, drastic truth that might put her feet on the earth. No one knew it but him. It had been knowledge that was to die with him, and this had been his own loyalty, which he had thought he would keep forever, and wanted to.

He really wouldn't have done it if right there she hadn't asked for it. "Emil," she said, "I always felt you knew more about our teacher than any of us. You seemed so close: right there in the house, looking after him."

He'd been right there in the house, all right. Yes, he had looked after him. . . . Couldn't he go on doing it? He had guarded so long. He wanted to guard to the end.

But she went on asking for it. "So perhaps you'll tell me things about him you know that I don't know. I'd treasure every word."

It was her face: worn face lighted with wonder, face of one who will worship to the end; her work-worn hands poised there as before the very gates of glory. He could not turn away. He had never seen a face beautiful as hers that moment. And because something in him wanted to pause there . . . be with her . . . it was almost savagely he pulled himself away. The world was real and there was work to do. He'd stamp it out! This much of it he could stamp out. Clear the way. It would hurt, but lots of people were hurt. Hurt to be trapped in a mine. Hurt to hear the kids crying because you hadn't brought home the grub.

"All right then," he said, "here goes. And remember you asked for it." Many people knew his face as it was now: ruthless in the fight, all else shut out, eyes bright and hard as steel.

"Want me to tell you how he died?"

"Why—yes," she said, seeming surprised, and a little frightened by the way he was looking at her.

"Very well, I will. He killed himself."

She sat looking at him as if she didn't know the language he spoke. Then she felt she understood. "You mean by working so hard?"

"I mean by taking an overdose of a drug he had. On purpose."

She didn't speak for too long a time; then she said, weakly yet somehow firmly: "You are mistaken."

"No. I was there. I know all about it. I'm just trying to get you to look at things as they *are*," he said angrily, answering something in himself as well as what he saw in her face.

She shook her head. "No—he couldn't. He *was* life. He couldn't . . ." But she was—sort of crumpling. Maybe this was going to be a hell of a mess. Well, he'd started—go on, get it over with.

"He had a tumor on his brain."

"*That* brain?" After a stunned moment: "No. That couldn't be."

This seemed to help her, though she was looking at him so appealingly.

That was the trouble with people like Norma—wouldn't accept facts if they didn't like them; get out of it by saying it wasn't so.

"I guess those little growths haven't much respect for quality. He knew it ever since that time he went away sick. They couldn't operate, something about the position of it. Perhaps they could now, know more now, but they couldn't then. It would have been one chance in—oh, practically no chance at all. He preferred to do it the other way. Go on for a little while; keep on as long as he could. Had this notion of handing it on to you."

And what good did it do him, he thought—standing all that pain for the times he could still wrench from it? Sticking by it up to the moment he knew he would never do it again as well as he had that night: to go on would make it less, this the moment to go, leaving it while he could leave it at its best. He thought of Austin, what he knew about Rosie; Norma, who'd muffed her life. They were to be the future he'd said, didn't matter so much about himself. Then it had all been for nothing: that truly heroic effort to keep his brain while he could still send it on into the future, as he'd thought. God! how they'd let him down—the bunch of them. And so he didn't care much about the incredulous stricken face of the woman who sat across from him. Let her take it! He could hand her more too.

"Sometimes, toward the last, he had to have a little dope to talk to you. He'd regulate it—just so much, keep him going." Right then and there he could see the man's face: twisted with pain, an effort almost beyond the human to rise out of the pain. This made him savage. "Didn't know you were being handed doped talk, did you? Well, he knew. Sometimes, after you were gone, he'd laugh at you."

Now he had said the very worst he could. Something had taken hold of him and he had to say it.

She seemed to be trying to get her breath. She picked up a glass of water but set it right down again.

She still had some spunk though, there was still fight in her. "Those were the times," she said—waveringly, yet so gallantly, "when he was mastered by what was—hurting his brain. He wasn't himself when he—laughed at us." "Laughed at us" she could barely say.

He wanted so much to help her, so hard to look at her, that he had to go on very resolutely.

"Oh, he was himself, all right. He didn't have crazy spells, if that's what you mean. He just knew the whole thing was cock-eyed."

Painfully she lifted her eyes and looked at him, as if to see whether she had to believe this. And apparently what she saw gave her no way out.

"You do not know what you are doing,"—it was little more than a whisper. "I—I am not as good as Christ. I cannot say Father forgive him—he knows not what he does. You—you are a murderer and a thief," she said quietly, a quiet that frightened him.

"Oh, come now, Norma, it can't be as bad as all that. I just don't want you to spend the rest of your life worshipping one man when there's a present-day world you could maybe do a little bit to make better. Even yet you just might do something, you know. But not up in the clouds. I'm trying to get you down to earth."

Her stricken eyes flashed him a look of such scorn it made him feel a little better; he felt it wasn't fair.

"Sure," he went on, a little more easily, "he was swell. I know that better than you do because I know what he suffered, the fight he made. He didn't laugh at you often," he conceded. "Just once in a while."

"You will stop now, Emil."

"I don't know whether I will or not! God, I used to get sore at you—eating him down to the bone like that."

She put a hand over her eyes. Her head was shaking.

"Oh, hell—I'm sorry," he mumbled. "Here. I can tell you a lot of things will make you feel better. He—"

"I don't want you to tell me anything more—ever. Nothing that came from you could help me—ever."

She started to get up. Even with both hands on the table she couldn't make it. He came around and helped her. She didn't seem to mind his touching her, didn't seem to know he was there. There wasn't any *blood* in her face. What had he done?

Nor did she appear to realize he was putting her in his car. Just sat there—stooped, hands held tight together.

"I'm sorry, Norma," he said, when they were on their way. "If you would let me tell you some more—"

She lifted her hand, shielding herself, as if to ward him off, warding off a blow.

"*Say* something!" he cried when they were near her place; he felt as if he were riding with a dead woman. "You make me feel like a dog."

She did speak then. "You are a dog," she said, in dead voice. But after a moment, in voice very very weary: "No, dogs are all right."

Well—if *that* was the way she felt about it! *Well*—to hell with her then! To hell with her and all her kind!

CHAPTER TWENTY-THREE

NEXT day Emil had to go to Pittsburgh; he had a lot of work to do there and he was glad of it, maybe it would stop this damn thinking. It was growing on him he had done a pretty terrible thing: stripped her whole life, it might be, and that wasn't a nice thought to carry around with you. Especially as he couldn't do anything about it now; she wouldn't let him. This was foolish of her, he could tell her things would make her look at it another way. He'd *meant* it all right he would try to tell himself, but was left with an uneasy feeling about his motives. Too many of his own resentments had spoken when he spoke to her; he was taking it out on something when he struck down this woman who was poor and getting old. She wouldn't call him a dog; dogs were better than that. . . .

He was only trying to get her straight, he would keep telling himself. If she only knew, he'd given up something for her: given up his own loyalty to a man about whom he had more feeling than anyone he'd known in all his life. From the very night it happened, when he took away that bottle, years ago, he'd never doubted he would carry this secret to his own grave. Wild horses—or even the police—couldn't drag it out of him he'd have said. If anything was sacred to him this was sacred. Then he'd spilled it—raw as he could. She needn't think she was the only one who was stripped.

He was hard on the job for ten days, not much time for thinking about anything else. But he was alone on the train coming back, had to take a day train as he must be in Chicago for a conference that night, and there it was . . . the ten busy days hadn't done much good.

He'd see her face: before he told her, after. And he almost heard their teacher's voice. "You did that—to Norma?" He'd counted so on Norma. It was almost as if he—Emil—had wounded the dead. He'd been buried for just about thirty years and it was as if he could still be wounded—he who had been wounded so much.

One night the man had said to the boy: "Why, Emil, I suppose you know more about me than anyone in the world." He talked to Emil; the teacher talked to the boy. It seemed to do him good, it was as if he had to.

He never told the others, the five students who came there evenings, anything about himself. With them every bit of his energy went to what was to go on through them. He was consecrated to this; if ever a man was consecrated he was. Through pain and his own sorrows this lived with singleness of purpose.

But he was a lonely man too, and very human; knowing he would not much longer be talking to anyone at all he talked to the boy who was there. How he trusted me, Emil thought now. Never even asked me not to tell. He knew he was speaking from near the grave; he thought I would guard him dead as I'd tried to alive.

He remembered the first time he saw the man, that day he was still sore from the last beating his father had given him, and exhausted from bumming his way. The teacher took him in and first it was the man took care of the boy.

Emil's mother had left the farm two months before; she couldn't take it: life with Nels Jensen, a brute even when he wasn't drunk. So then Nels took that out on Emil, most killed him. He was a pretty strong boy but his father was stronger. When he left he'd meant to go back some day and beat him up. The teacher talked him out of this, seemed to think he wouldn't get much out of it. Maybe he was wrong there. Every time he got just so sore about something else he was sorry he hadn't gone back and beat up the old man. He'd like to do it now. Dead now probably.

He had to laugh when people got going about how happy childhood was. One reason he could go on working like hell: still so many children who didn't have childhoods. Keep on! For God's sake keep at it: food for the kids, school, security, fun. He knew it was awful not to have had your childhood.

He hadn't been heading for that town where the college was; what was a college to him? He hadn't gone beyond seventh grade, big enough then to be some use on the place. His mother had cried about it, got slapped for her tears. He'd done a man's work ever since he was taken out of school. No, he wasn't thinking about colleges, he was heading for Minneapolis. He fell in with two old hoboes and they'd given him a hunk of bread. That was all he'd had for two days. When they were kicked off the freight he walked though the town—hard to walk, he was stiff and sore. Thought he'd get out to a farm, maybe pick up a little job for a couple of weeks, something to eat, then on to Minneapolis; he'd heard of fellows getting jobs in the flour mills there.

Suddenly he was just too dog-tired to move: been cramped in the boxcar, in between packing-cases. (What was it one of the hoboes had said? "These are not the palatial quarters to which I am accustomed. I am accustomed to the luxury of space." Funny old duck—that hobo.) So he had to lie down, stretch out, stay there till somebody came along and chased him away.

It was the teacher who came. He was carrying books. He stopped and looked down at the big boy sprawled there. "Taking a little rest?" he asked.

"I'll move on in a minute," Emil mumbled.

"Why should you? It's pleasant here." He sat down himself, back against a tree. "Mind if I sit here?"

"Guess you've got more right here than I have," Emil said in his surly fashion.

"Seems to me we both have a right. The earth won't mind if we sit on it, so why should anyone else care?"

That was kind of silly. "Guess somebody owns it," he muttered.

"Then they should be glad to have it enjoyed."

Emil laughed; hurt his jaw to laugh—everything hurt, all over him. "I never found people were anxious to have you enjoy their property," he said.

"No? Well perhaps you've met the wrong people," the man said cheerfully. "I don't own this spot of earth, but I'm renting it now, so we can sit here as long as we like."

After a silence he asked: "You hungry?"

Emil wanted to be proud and say no; but Lord, he was empty all through him. He said nothing.

"Because I am. I've been teaching for three hours. Thought we might go in the house and get something to eat. Then you could lie down on something softer than the earth."

How did he know Emil had wondered then, wondered now—me not telling him, he not asking, how could he know that I was all-in and needed a friend.

At first Emil didn't make it easy for the man to be his friend. He was surly and suspicious, as raw in the spirit as he was in the flesh. He'd never talked much to anyone, seemed it just got you in trouble. Some to his mother, on the sly. It had to be on the sly; his father would take it out on one or the other of them if he knew they'd been talking.

The man didn't seem to mind his gruff answers and sullen silences; just got him something to eat, fixed hot water for the tin tub, without knowing what was the matter with him told him hot water would make him feel better; saw him half-stripped and knew more then, got some stuff and rubbed it on his back after the bath, all the time talking about the wild geese flying south, the buffalo that used to roam this country, how we hadn't treated the Indians right—just talked, but not of Emil.

He put him to bed and told him to stay there till he felt like getting up. He brought him hot milk. "I don't have to be babied," had been Emil's response to this kindness, though he felt like bawling. "Don't you? Well, I do. I'm counting on your babying me after a couple of days."

So he stayed on. Langley said he needed someone there with him; never said you have no place to go.

Perhaps, at first, it was because Emil was unresponsive the man could talk to him. He seemed to want to talk, and later Emil thought he knew why. It was all going to be buried so soon. It was as if he wanted to bring it out into the open, let it live a minute in the light before it went dark forever.

He'd been born in Virginia. Must have been a nice place his folks had down there; flowers Emil had never heard of. Emil's mother had liked the flowers; he'd help her put in seeds, then his father would get mad and tear them out, said there was enough work to do without bending your back for flowers. Folks didn't feel that way in Virginia it seemed, but then they had niggers to bend the back. Professor Langley didn't call them niggers; talked about their songs, a lot of stuff about an old mammy. And the horses!

Then he went to school in Germany. Emil didn't like Germans. The Wickelmanns lived just down the road from the Jensens and they kept themselves to themselves because Jensen got drunk and beat his horse. (Beat more than his horse for that matter.) The Wickelmann place made their own look just so much the worse, so Emil never spoke to them if he could help it, and he didn't see why anyone should go to school in Germany. Langley liked the Germans, liked this Heidelberg. There was a river there.

Seems there were wonderful teachers in Heidelberg. One man knew all about philosophy. Emil had never heard of philosophy, but Professor Langley would just talk along as if the boy did know. And after a while he got interested in the stuff, could understand some of it and even asked questions. They talked while Emil was doing the work, the teacher sitting there at the table, his books before him. Sometimes he got excited and walked up and down the room: the idea, what was real, things you couldn't see were as real as that sink you could touch with your hands. Funny business—kind of interesting.

When he came home from Germany he taught in a college in the South; but they didn't want him to teach it the way he saw it, wanted him to teach the way they thought it ought to be. "I couldn't do that. That would be treachery." He got another place, in the East. But there he was under a man who wanted it all his own way. "I had to be free. You can't bind the truth to anyone's will."

Then he met this man MacConnell, from out West, out here. MacConnell made him think that out here he could be free. And as this was more important than anything else he gave up his place in the big university to come out here where it was all new, where something wonderful might happen. It was too important not to do this, he said.

His wife didn't see it that way. He'd married right after he came back from Germany, a beautiful girl who lived next place to him in Virginia. She didn't like it when he didn't get along in the college down South, thought it was his fault; they paid him and he ought to teach it the way they wanted it. And now he couldn't even get along in the big university. This man, head of the department, was his superior she said, and if he'd just get along with him he'd be promoted and might some day be head of the department himself. "That is one way of looking at it," the teacher said. "That is called common-sense; the practical mind. But the world is too important for 'common-sense,' he'd laughed.

She wouldn't see it his way and he couldn't see it hers. She wouldn't go West with him, said it was crazy—a little place out in the wilds.

"I suppose she was thinking of the future," Emil said.

"But that's just what I was thinking of. How could I sell out the future?"

Well, if he felt it was selling out, Emil had said doubtfully. He was coming to think a lot of the man (you couldn't help it) and there didn't seem much of a future for him here.

Now his wife was married to someone else. He'd loved her. You could tell it by his face, any time he spoke of her.

Sometimes he would talk about things he had done that weren't right, like lording it over other kids when he was a boy down there in Virginia. Once he'd smashed a dam some smaller children had made. It seemed to bother him a lot to think of this, but Emil told him that wasn't anything at all. "But I did it for no reason," he said. "Just to destroy. Just to hurt." Well, for heaven's sake, boys were like that, probably the little kids weren't much surprised.

He wondered what it was in him had made him want to do that. "Cause you were bigger," Emil told him, and this set him off: all the wrong things we did because we were bigger, what the world could be if we wanted to use our power another way.

And once he'd bothered a bird: made it fly out of its nest when it didn't want to. Well, Christ's sake, who hadn't? Funny things to be worried about. But the thing that bothered him was that he wasn't as good himself as his ideas of what the world should be. There was something about a girl in Germany—seems he hadn't treated her right, or so he thought now. Things like this made him distrust himself. Sometimes when he'd been talking wonderfully, that way he could, all carried away about what the world might be, he'd stop as if something had stopped him, laugh at himself— as if he hadn't any right to these ideas.

Then he'd set to work; he was working most of the time, and way into the night, with his books, and making notes of things he was thinking. He seemed in such an awful hurry about it, as if there weren't much time, and later Emil knew why this was.

When he was deep in what he was doing you could make any kind of a noise and it didn't bother him. His face was keen, determined, as one who is after something he has to get. At times it would baffle him and he'd get discouraged. He'd leave it, walk around outdoors; then back, at it again, and after a while it was as if he'd been taken into something. It was there now. Now he had it. Those were the happy times, when he was all aglow.

He didn't talk to Emil about philosophy alone, or only about himself. "You can't stop with the seventh grade," he said. "There's such a lot to know and it's such fun going after it." Sometimes he would look tired when he came home from school, but he'd say: "Now what about my other pupil? Can't neglect the student in my own house," and they'd go at the books he'd got hold of for Emil.

A kid just couldn't be any more unhappy than Emil had been in school; he didn't like being with those boys and girls who knew too much about his old man, who had better clothes and better manners than he had. He couldn't say things in front of them all, even when he knew them, so they thought he was dumb. His new teacher didn't seem to find him dumb. And he seemed to feel Emil had a wonderful chance. "You weren't put through the mill; so little has been spoiled for you." He said it was stupid teaching kept people from being educated, an outrage the way schools could take joy out of learning.

Oh, he did make learning an excitement. God, what a teacher, Emil thought now, remembering how he made it all come to life. Take spelling. In school Emil couldn't get the hang of it at all, but his new teacher would talk to him about words. First he got you acquainted with the word: where it came from, the life it had known, thoughts it had carried. They might touch on geography, history, religions, Greek and Latin and English in the study of one word. Then you were at home with this word. Naturally you knew how to spell it.

And grammar. In school there hadn't been any sense to it, just something they made you do. But grammar had to do with man speaking to man all the long time men had been together. It wasn't something thought up to be mean to you, it was something that grew because there were thoughts to express. Some of it he just needn't learn at all, Langley said; it was good only so far as it was useful, and useful only as it helped you express your thoughts. There were such things as conventions, and many of them were all right because they aided us. Take telegraph operators. Suppose each one took to doing it his own way; they couldn't understand one another. The whole thing about a developed language was that we could the better understand one another. Language had a long history and many a word had the beauty of a polished stone. If you were at home in a language you had a medium for your thoughts, and by expressing them they grew. Words were for thoughts and words could beget thoughts: all so wonderfully intertwined. Books were the thoughts of others. We couldn't meet many great people face-to-face but we could know them through their books. Thus we enlarged our acquaintance, grew richer. Here was wealth just waiting for us. No one need be lonely or poor.

He even persuaded Emil to go the freshman class in American history at the college. Emil had balked at this, said he didn't know enough to go to college, they'd just laugh at him. Matthews was a very good teacher of American history, Langley insisted. Emil must know the history of his country; then he would be proud of his country and want to do his part in making it what it could become. At first Emil could just listen to Matthews talk, that had all been arranged. And they'd work on it together at home.

So Emil went—just to please him. Lord, how he hated going in there that first day. But here he wasn't the son of Nels Jensen, the worst farmer for miles around. Here he was the boy who stayed at Professor Langley's, had clothes as decent as the rest of

them (Langley had seen to that). He'd never forget the first day
he said something in class. Matthews hadn't called on him at first,
but this day he must have seen by Emil's face that there was something he could say. He knew it because they had talked about it
at home: The Bill of Rights; he knew something wasn't in the book
and which the others didn't know. When he'd finished Matthews
said to the class: "That is what makes a student. Digging into it
for yourself, getting all the ramifications, not content with merely
the surface." They turned and looked at Emil. Now he had his
place in that class.

Sometimes when he had to speak to a bunch of strikers he'd think
of that first time he ever spoke to a group of his fellows. If he
hadn't done that perhaps he'd never have done any of the rest of
it, just stayed shut up within himself: no contact, no confidence
for contact.

He got all stirred up about the history of America. He and
Langley would have arguments about it and when they'd differ
Emil even got so he would oppose his teacher, forgetting himself
and finding the words for what he wanted to say. Emil's grudge
against the world gave him a keen eye for injustices. Langley would
say he was too prone to pick them out of the whole, making his
emphasis wrong, not giving proper consideration to what had
caused these things to be. Emil would demand, if they oughtn't to
be what difference does it make what caused them to be? It made
a great deal of difference, Langley would say, not only in understanding history but in shaping the future. To Emil there were
things that stuck out like a sore thumb. One night his teacher
laughed: "Emil, I don't know that you will ever write any history" (they had been talking about the men who wrote history)
"but it wouldn't surprise me a bit if you made some." . . .

"You're interested in economics," the teacher told him, before
Emil had even known there was such a thing. So they went at that
too. . . .

Funny, how things happened; things you hadn't been looking for at all changed your whole life.

Langley told him what it was had changed his own life. It was the look on a woman's face; not a beautiful woman, and he didn't even know her name. It was on the ship as he was coming home from Germany. This woman was down on a lower deck, in the steerage. He had noticed her before because she was always looking out at the water, staring vacantly, it seemed to him. He would have said she was a stolid woman, just plodding through her days. But he chanced to see her just after they sighted land: the new land, America. There was on her face a look of such wonder he felt he'd never known the world at all. He stood looking at the woman who stood there worshipping America. Here were all her hopes, here her great dream for the children clustered around her. She was seeing a vision. She believed. And as he watched her transfigured face, knowing what an arrogant fool he'd been to think this woman stolid, like a bolt from heaven the thought stabbed: *Where else? How many more?* And he too was seeing a new land. . . . Land of the hidden dreams that could transform life.

"I changed," he had said simply. "All at once I knew. Don't tell me it cannot come suddenly. It did with me, and changed the core of my life. In that moment I knew a dream can beget a dream, as it went from her to me. You can call it a miracle, or if it pleases you better, just call it what happened. I resolved to find those dreams in people. Together we would shape the world she believed was there.

"We would have to make America a better land to measure up to this emigrant woman's dream. I thought of the wrongs my country, my family, myself had done: selfishness, unkindness, injustice. Not seeing and not even caring to see. The shame of it almost overwhelmed me; but hope renewed me, for I knew we could make it as fair as we dreamed it might be! And then, as a vista that opens to you, I saw change: something imminent. I saw a people who were ready but didn't yet know they were ready. A time in the history of man when life could realize itself. I saw it fluid: ready to be what we would have.

"So do you still wonder, as I think you did, why I couldn't go on teaching down South there, or in the East, held to what a blind man thought should be told the mind of youth? No; better out here. Ways are not so set. Anything could happen out here. The longest future is in the virgin soil."

Emil said his father lived out here.

He'd laughed at that sly thrust. "Your father is a mistake. Or perhaps a hopeless victim. Let's forget him, shall we?"

"Never," said Emil.

"He wins that way, you know. That way he goes on beating you all your life. Seems to me it would be better to have you win."

"I'll win all right—just to spite him."

"The welts on your back healed up. Your spirit has recuperative powers too. You'll have a lot of fun finding the things to put in the place of resentment. It's so darned interesting, you know."

"What?"

"Good Lord, boy—the whole thing. What I've been trying to tell you. This business of being alive."

"Aren't you sore about *anything?*" Emil demanded of him. "Take your wife. A wife is supposed to go along with her husband. Aren't you even sore about that?"

"Why, I don't think so," he said slowly. "I'm lonely at times. Ever been in love, Emil?"

"I had a girl. Two girls. I just had what I wanted. I wasn't in love."

"That's too bad. Oh well," he said more brightly, "you will be."

"Don't you believe it! Just makes a monkey out of you."

"Be a monkey then—it's worth it." It was that night he said: "When you know there isn't much time left, you think about love."

Almost from the first Emil had known about the times of pain. His face would go all gray. He'd have to stop work, take something and wait till the pain let up. When it passed he seemed so grateful that he could go on, as if the good hours were something given him, something to use happily. The attacks of pain frightened Emil. "You ought to have a doctor," he would say.

One night when it was starting and he knew what he'd have to go through, he told Emil of the doom that waited. Afterwards he was sorry. "I shouldn't have put that upon you," he said. "It was a weakness. We have many weaknesses. Sometimes it's hard to be alone in what you know."

But it was out, couldn't all be taken back. He'd told how he had some time left and was going to use the good hours for what he wanted to do. "Quite easy to call it egotistical," he said; "but we mustn't worry too much about that. It is my belief that I have something to leave." He didn't want it to go for nothing: the feeling that was in him. The times of pain were just time out, worth standing for the hours when he was still there. He wanted to keep trying up to the last: inject it into life. And when there weren't any more good times left, when his mind could no longer give it forth and what he would say might discredit what had gone before—he'd have to be the judge of that, leave before his mind could no longer tell him the balance had changed and—

He'd broken off, as if suddenly aware, in all the pain, that he was talking to Emil; seeing Emil's face he wanted to take back what he had said. Lightly as he could he said: "What rot we talk just because we're having a pain. Forget that last, will you, Emil? It's nonsense, of course."

Emil couldn't forget it, though he too thought, tried hard to think, that that was only the pain speaking. He wouldn't have known how to go on living there by his side if he had to look forward to a day when a lonely decision would be made—and he would no longer hear the voice of his teacher. Yes, we said things; said lots of things we didn't mean, he'd tell himself.

But however the end was to come, it was coming. That much he knew to be true. Emil wasn't used to showing his feelings, that had always been a thing not to do. And the way he showed them now was in anger that such a thing could be. And then in a certain sullen protectiveness.

That was why he resented those five who began coming there evenings. What did *they* know—about the times of pain? Coming here and just eating him up! Never a thought of what he paid for what he gave them. If they hadn't been so wrapped up in themselves, wonderful things they were going to do (which they hadn't done—not on your life), they'd have known that pain was right there with them. Yes, and sometimes the stuff to hold down the pain a little—not too much, that would blur the thoughts as well as the pain, and they must have their sharp edge—sound and full and clear. That was what *he* said; his words those. So he learned how to keep a sort of balance, racing against the time when the balance would be different.

And once in a while—very rarely—it was true that, excited, exhausted, after they had gone he would laugh at them. Though now it seemed to Emil the laughing wasn't really at them at all, but at what was happening, at the way things were. They didn't know there was a tumor eating into this brain, did they? They didn't know he'd had to have pain-killer to talk to them. What did they know about all the things he'd done that didn't fit into his philosophy? Did they think he was a saint, he'd laugh. But that laughing wasn't himself any more than a spasm of pain was himself, and this he hadn't told Norma. Hadn't told her of the fight the man made to give them what he thought could go on through them, fighting against loss, waste—fighting, up to the last.

There were times when Emil had wondered if he ought not tell someone. Perhaps there *was* something could be done, even though he said he'd seen the best doctors. And it seemed he ought to be *stopped:* giving his life away; surely this driving himself, keeping his brain up to the highest pitch, wasn't the way a sick man should be living. And then that other: what he'd started to say and had tried to take back; even suspecting such a thing might happen, as Emil couldn't help suspecting (though he tried not to), and doing nothing about it . . . almost the same as if he were agreeing to it.

Yet it seemed there was nothing Emil could do. This man trusted him, depended on him: depending on the boy who had become his friend to let him do it his own way. And Emil did understand. He didn't understand all he heard talked, but he understood the urge that had to say it; even understood that these things mustn't be harmed. And with all the horror there was in it, there was in it something more wonderful than anything he had ever known in his life or dreamed could be. Valiant was a word Professor Langley used about other things: things that had brought life along to where we now were. And in his thoughts it was the word Emil had for him. He felt, a little uncomfortably, that he was in the presence of something great. He wasn't going to go blabbing around and spoil it all, even though knowing it alone was almost more than he could bear. If *he* can stand it, can't I? he would think. Only, Emil had something else to stand. He loved the man now, and he'd never loved anyone before, not anyone he admired. His mother he'd loved, but she couldn't stand up to things. This man he just about worshipped. And perhaps this was why, all the rest of his life, he'd fought the idea of worshipping. He'd never meant to be like that! (That was why he had taken it out on Norma.)

It was very strange about that night. He had a feeling it might happen that night, and he stayed out of the room; so perhaps he was little better than a murderer. Oh bunk, he told himself now, thirty years later, on the train from Pittsburgh to Chicago. Everything about that night he could see as he saw the gray hair of the woman in front of him, the kid who kept running in the aisle.

After they'd gone, those five: Norma, Austin, Virgil, Rosie and Helen; and when he'd stood a moment at the door looking after them, he came back and sat in the place at the table where he always sat with them. Emil heard him murmur: "I'll never say it that well again." He barely caught the words, and it hadn't been intended he should. And the teacher just sat on there at the table the others had left.

Finally he said: "It's late, Emil. You get to bed. In the morning—" But this stopped him: the morning. . . . He had risen but just stood right there, his hand on the table. "It was nice here tonight, wasn't it?" he said—the way a kid might say it about a nice place he was leaving.

He looked around the room. "Well—goodnight, Emil," and then he went to his own room. No goodbye; sparing Emil that. Went through the door—alone.

Before he himself went to bed Emil almost went in there. Two or three times he had a feeling he must go in. It would have been nothing strange if he had, he often went to the door the last thing to see if there was anything he could do. The strange thing about this night was that while he had an impulse to go, he felt he shouldn't. This should have told him: what he more than half-knew and wouldn't let himself know, because it seemed he shouldn't.

And strange though he always thought it afterwards, he went right to sleep. To keep himself from knowing, perhaps. Keep himself out of the way.

But he woke unusually early next morning, just getting light;

sprang up and went right in there, without reasoning why. And he wasn't surprised to find him lying there as if asleep, but more than asleep.

He stood there at the bedside and knew he was a brave man. That was enough for Emil—more than being a brilliant man, or one inspired. And he knew something else: knew he'd lost the only real friend he had ever had.

But he had things to do, things he must do and do right for this brave man who was his friend. He trusted me, Emil thought. He didn't want to ask for promises, that would make me part of it and put too much upon me. He knew I would do what must be done in order that no one else ever know how it was, no shadow fall upon what he had tried to leave in life. Never asked; just trusted.

He hadn't even tried to make away with the bottle. There it was on the table by the bed, beside it a book written in that funny-looking Greek, this book he often read after he'd gone to bed. Plato was the name of the man who had written it—long time ago, across the centuries, his teacher had said. Had he read a little in it before he . . . went to sleep? The book hurt the boy more than the bottle; so brave to go on being natural. Himself up to the last.

He wished he could have been with him, sat here beside him so he wouldn't have been alone. But no, he wouldn't have wanted to put that on Emil. And perhaps he wasn't alone. He had his thoughts, and this man across the centuries. A great companion, he'd called him.

Emil put the bottle in his pocket. It had been more than half full and now it was empty. He took it out and buried it in the barn. Then he went to a neighbor and gave the word.

Probably it wouldn't have got by in a city. But here they knew Professor Langley had been very sick a little while before (MacConnell knew the most about that). They asked Emil some questions. How had he seemed the night before? Very tired, Emil said; he could hardly get to bed. Did he ever complain of his heart?

Yes, Emil told them, he had bad pain in his heart. They called it heart-failure, and Emil was too relieved to despise them for this sloppy work.

MacConnell took away all his papers. (What did he ever do with them?) But afterwards Emil found a little black-leather note-book. It had slipped in back of a drawer. Or had it been slipped there?—somehow not wanting to destroy it, yet not wanting it found among his papers. This Emil hadn't turned over to Mac-Connell; when he read a little in it he didn't think it had been meant for him. Probably hadn't been meant for Emil either: thoughts he had wanted to express when he was lonely. Emil hadn't read much in it; he felt: he did say a good deal to me, and if these are things he didn't want to say when he could speak, then they're not for me now. But he had always kept the little book among his own things, and when he started on this trip to Pittsburgh, the day after he talked to Norma, for some cockeyed reason he dug it out of his trunk and put it in his bag. It was as if he wanted it with him. The great companion . . .

Now he fished it out of his grip. What was this town they were getting into? Oh, Fort Wayne. Must remind himself to write O'Rouke at Fort Wayne.

He opened the little book. The writing was in ink but the ink was fading. Thirty years was a long time for ink. What did last? Not many things. Thoughts? Did thoughts last? Langley would say they did; but where were his? These were just jottings, little things he had set down from time to time when he was alone.

Often just a sentence. "Karl Marx left too much out." Oh, I don't know about that, Emil thought. If his teacher were here they'd have one of their hot discussions about this.

He read those five names: Norma, Virgil, Rosie, Austin, Helen. Underneath their names was written: "And Emil too." He felt something he'd not felt for years: tears there, ready to come if he'd let them. "And Emil too." He had never known to what extent he was included in what was to go on through those five. He was so far behind; their teacher was getting him ready. Now it seemed he had been included all the time.

Other mentions of him. "Today Emil said . . ." Or "In talking today with Emil it came to me that the flaw in Hegel . . ." On another page, "Emil will fight. The boy has stuff. I hope his father doesn't lick him."

I wonder, Emil thought. I wonder if he did lick me. No, I don't think so. To fight you've got to be sore, and it's right to fight. Langley was too gentle. No, that's not true. God knows there was fight in him. But more love than I've got.

There hadn't been much place in Emil's life for love. He loved his Irish Mary, but she died when he was in prison. Couldn't even be with her when she died, couldn't even say, "Now, Irish-eyes, you cheer up,"—couldn't say any little fool thing to make her smile. God—what a world. After that it hadn't been love. Women sometimes; but not much of that either—just messed things up, had to keep everlastingly at it. Oh, he'd fought, all right.

He wondered now what the teacher would think of his fight. If he were here and they could talk it over, would he say about Emil, as he had of Marx: left too much out? Probably; and what a good scrap they could have about it! "The hell with that stuff—left too much out," he'd say. "Have to do your job—can't go mooning around about something up in the clouds."

Langley would smile: "Why are you so vehement? Afraid maybe you won't believe what you're saying?" (Yes, he'd spot that right away.)

Not on your life! Emil would tell him. I know damn well what I'm saying!

"Then what are you so afraid of?" he'd ask, and Emil would get mad. Oh, they could have a swell fight—now. A feeling of great loneliness came over him . . . they couldn't have their fight.

And because the teacher wasn't there, wasn't sitting here with him to speak for himself, as if in some instinct of fair play Emil let what he would have said come into his own mind, as open to it as he knew how to be.

And by the time they got to Gary he knew that this was a pretty dangerous thing to have done. Something had gone from the teacher to Emil, and he knew it wasn't all—the bunk. And he knew what he had done to Norma.

About to put away the book (maybe he'd give the little book to Norma) a leaf slipped out. In pencil was written: "I am not doing enough. So little time left."

He had to make a fight for it then: a fight not to cry—*him*, Emil Jensen, hard as nails. He'd never cried; not even when he lost his Mary, too angry then to cry. Now he wasn't angry. He just knew there had been a great beauty in the world; and he knew it hadn't died. It lived *now*—outskirts of Chicago—as he closed his grip.

CHAPTER TWENTY-FOUR

REGARDLESS of what may be happening to people, the seasons go their ordered way. Sweet-scented spring opened to summer; summer thinned to fall and fall froze into winter this year Emil Jensen struck a death blow at Norma Ashe. There were no new stars and the old ones had their same places in the heavens. The earth gave of its plenty, babies were born and old people (young people too) died since that day in May when the life that had newly flowed into her ebbed out.

Now the month was January and the year 1929. America was a bedlam of prosperous people: Austin at his manufacturing plant; brokers in New York, including Rosie's husband; Virgil with his new book, the union men for whom Emil drove his hard bargains. Before this year had run its course many would be halted in their tracks. They went their prosperous ways as if this were what life was going to be, sleekly unaware that before they hung out another Christmas wreath would come a cataclysm for years to be known as The Crash. Lives would be different, many would call it the end; yet seed planted in the earth would grow, and no star would fall.

Even Norma Ashe had a modest part in the prosperity of the times, for Doc Stanton and Lorna were making a success of the old Pettibone place. It was succeeding as Doc Stanton's as conspicuously as it had failed as Mrs. Utterbach's. Doc had got hold of some money and changed it into small apartments. Now lodgers could cook in their rooms with no uproar raised. This turned the trick.

And, life being unpredictable, Norma was living in the very place she'd have said she would never be again. She lived with Doc and Lorna, back in the Pettibone house which Max took on a mortgage, which she ran as Mrs. Utterbach's, and which was now full of the people from Doc Stanton's school. Had she been told this was where she was going to spend the last of her days she would have said no, not if the heavens fell. But she lived there now, and the heavens were as usual. One simply doesn't know.

It made no difference to her as it mattered not at all where she lived. She didn't mind Doc Stanton now, or Lorna being married to him. Herself wasn't there to mind.

In those days following her interruption of Austin's speech, after she met Scott (and before she met Emil), those miraculous days when life flowed through her again, she had written to Lorna, wanting to be closer to her daughter.

It was Lorna's husband answered the letter; she received it the second day after her evening with Emil. "Lorna is not at all well," he said. "She doesn't respond to my treatment and I don't want to have in a regular." (A regular would be a doctor.) "I think the whole thing is about you. We're taking over the house, as you offered (and by the way, thanks a million), and will you get the deed fixed up right away, as you said, because I want to put some money into it, got a great scheme for making it into apartments. They'll go like hot cakes—don't know why you never did it yourself. But Lorna can't put any spirit into it because she thinks it's terrible we take over the place while you're doing housework in Chicago. She cries and says you worked hard for her and now you're nothing but somebody's hired-girl. She seems to think she has done you some wrong, though what it can be I can't for the life of me make out. She had a right to get married, didn't she? She's living a decent life and what more do you want? But she isn't happy, and it's a darned shame, because she's going to have a baby.

I think it's swell, but she says children are just ungrateful and what's the use.

"The only thing will do her any good would be for you to come back home. I'll welcome you with open arms—always one to let bygones be bygones. What say, old dear? Better stand by your own daughter, not make a martyr of yourself doing somebody's dirty work in Chicago. We'll make a go of the place; got a lot of the folks at school signed up before we begin. You could help us and that would make a place for you too—darn sight better than being a hired-girl at our age. Lorna frets about your age."

Perhaps she wouldn't have gone because of Lorna. Even thought of her child needing her failed to reach as two days before it would have reached and moved her. She wasn't moved because she wasn't there to be moved. She couldn't know what Emil had told her and live. She would still be counted among the living, but many mistakes are made in that reckoning.

She went in order to get away from Scott. One thing she did still know: she couldn't let Scott know that none of it had ever been true at all. Why he mustn't know this she couldn't at the moment think out; she wasn't thinking things out. She only knew there was one last thing she had to do: keep him from knowing.

When she got home that night, after Emil told her their teacher had laughed at them, laughed at them for believing, it had been hard to get up to her room. Her legs seemed to have stiffened. She got ready for bed quite stealthily, as one afraid of the things around her. She didn't glance around, as usually one looks from this to that and a good deal of the time all around at nothing in particular, but looked only at the thing she had to see: the hanger for her dress, the cover she must put back to get into bed. It was as if she mustn't rouse things, they were not to know she was there. She lay flat on her bed, but as if holding herself up, away from it. She was rigid and made no move she did not have to make. If she even lifted her hand it all might be upon her. It must be as if she were dead; that was the only escape.

She could still make the motions of living when she had to, and as she went about her duties next morning only the truly seeing eye would have known she was moving in a world she had left. There were intrusions, however, for other people were still in their lives. Genevieve, the girl who worked at the Hershells', was alive enough to be crying because Joe, her boy-friend, had a new girl. "I'll kill myself!" she sobbed. "I guess that will show him!" Henry, the little boy, was home from school because he had a sprained wrist. Despite this disability he ran his fire-engine out into the kitchen, kicking over a chair, screaming: "Fire! Fire!" When Genevieve scolded him he began to sing: "Oh, Genevieve, sweet Genevieve—the years may come, the ye-*ars* . . ." Genevieve buried her face and ears in the dish-towel, screaming if Norma didn't stop him she'd go crazy right there before their eyes.

"What's eating her?" Henry asked with interest.

She had kept out of Scott's way in the morning, but that afternoon she heard him call to Genevieve: "Where's Norma?"

She was sorting the laundry. Would he come in here? How could she get away?

He stood in the doorway of the little sewing-room at the back of the upper hall. "Well," he laughed, "how did you make out with the boy-friend?"

Her back was to him, he hadn't seen her face. And as he waited, in that pause there was something she knew with certainty. From deep in her, through stunned layers, it struggled up to warn her: she mustn't let Scott know.

"Oh, all right," she answered, bent over the towels she was sorting, and amazed at her voice. It sounded quite cheerful.

"Talked over old times, I suppose."

She couldn't answer that, pretending to be counting.

"What did he have to say about Wurthen?"

"Oh, he doesn't think much of Austin, you know." She even laughed. Well, if she could laugh, now she could turn and face him.

"Must have seemed kind of funny to you, seeing him after all those years."

"Yes. Yes, it was—kind of funny."

He waited for her to go on and tell him about it. They had formed the habit of talking together and he liked to hear about things: curiosity, youth, the eager mind. She felt pinned in there, it seemed she couldn't run away. Confronted—confronted by youth. Knowing what one knows, and knowing one must keep them from knowing. Better die than say to them faith is something to laugh at. Don't tell them we just make it up. Perhaps he need never know that we are fooled. He might not find out. She couldn't bear to think he would ever be as destitute as she was this moment. The lie was kind.

"What's Jensen like?"

"Well," she said carefully, "Emil keeps very busy."

"Too busy, some people think," he laughed.

"Yes," she said. "I know what you mean."

But you don't know what I mean, she thought. Emil keeps very busy destroying. He takes what one had. With one blow he kills what you thought was there: there to go to, to take from, and in hours of your strength, to add to. Very busy stripping you of that, leaving you just something that moves.

Scott wasn't to know. A little game we played: keep them from knowing. Something blind in you makes you play this game. True to . . . what isn't there. But it was beautiful to believe, while one could.

"I suppose you talked about that teacher of yours."

She started to put her hand to her heart, as if there were a sharp pain there, though there was no pain in her heart. "Yes," she said; and as he waited: "One—remembers him."

"Wonder if I'll remember any of my teachers after thirty years."

"I hope so," she said, and as it seemed she must go on talking: "I hope there'll be one of them worth remembering."

She'd said it because she had to, and was then startled to find it was almost as if she meant it: the hope that one of them would be worth remembering. Why? Certainly she'd been told it wasn't worth remembering.

"Well," he laughed, "if there isn't any teacher worth remembering, I'll just settle for remembering you."

"Oh—don't do that!" she said quickly. "I mean—why should you remember me?"

"Dunno. Must be I think you've got something," he said, casually but a little shyly.

Then, mercifully, the phone rang and Scott went to answer it. *Me* "got something." Stripped of everything—got something. She'd have to get away from Scott. He would make things come to life, she would know what she had lost if she stayed on where Scott was. And then she wanted to laugh herself, as their teacher had laughed: what a barren world it must be if she were one to remember.

He came back excited. "Ellen's had her baby! It's a boy. Mother and child are doing nicely, thank you."

"How—how nice," she murmured.

"You bet! Oh, nothing to raise the roof about,"—this was the Scott on guard against being a softie. "They come thick and fast, you know—sounds like snowflakes, doesn't it? One born every minute they say. Just another mortal on the earth."

This last had engaged his interest. He stood there looking at her, ready for the things this could open up.

Thick and fast . . . Just another mortal on the earth . . .

"Wonder what the world will be like," he speculated, "when this baby is as old as I am. Or your age."

As she did not take this up, "It won't be very different," he said. "We go on doing just about the same things."

He was looking at her—quizzically, but expectant. He thought this would get a rise out of her, as he would say. It was a challenge, as she would put it, would once have put it. She knew the things she would have said just a day earlier, when they were true for her. We needn't go on doing the same things, she would have said. Life could be different: a freer, fairer world. Just a day earlier her imagination would have gone out to meet the newborn in his first hour in the world, welcome and believe in him, think of his chance, his part in making the better world. Perhaps he has brought something with him, she would have said. Perhaps it has entered the world *now*, with him.

But today she and this baby could not meet. He was not of the hope that is limitless and touched with miracle; he did not come trailing clouds of glory. Just another mortal on the earth.

It seemed she must say something. "I hope he will have a very happy life," were the words that came.

Without glancing at him she could see Scott's look of surprise at these conventional words. She didn't need to raise her eyes to know he looked—let down.

"Oh, he'll make out all right," he said. And something seemed to have passed them by.

After a minute he said: "Well, I've got to do some telephoning. Spread the glad tidings."

But still he waited, giving her another chance. And as she did not say it was indeed glad tidings, or that glad tidings should be spread, after a minute he went out, whistling, and she knew she had indeed let him down; and knew she must get away from Scott.

How? How did one make plans? Arrange things?

Doc Stanton's letter, which came the following day, did this for her.

Only Genevieve was at home when she went downstairs with her suitcase and said, "I have to go away."

She didn't wait for the end of Genevieve's surprised inquiries and indignant protests. It wasn't very nice of her, running out on them like that. Where did she have to go all of a sudden? She'd been treated all right, hadn't she? And with Mrs. Hershell in the hospital! The least she could do was wait till Mr. Hershell got home. Or Scott. Scott would be back from the University any minute now.

She knew that and hurried away. She left no note for Scott. She had thought of it, but what was there to say to him after the things they'd talked of together? She didn't want to tell him to have a good laugh. He had said he would remember her after thirty years. Well, he wouldn't. He'd wonder about her for a time, perhaps worry (she hoped not much) and then he'd "settle for" thinking she must be sort of crazy.

She wished she could tell him how much he had at one time done for her. He had been contact with the living moment. Through him had been established (what was the word?)—continuity. But all of that was over now. She'd just have to walk out on him, as Genevieve said.

Back at the boarding-house she found that Miss Pettibone had been obliged to move. The Stantons served no meals and she could not sink to the indignity of cooking in her room; nor could she live in a house permeated with the odors of other people's vulgar taste in food. "She put on quite an act," Lorna told her mother; "said she was driven from her home by cruel mercenaries." How long ago it seemed since she had struggled with Miss Pettibone. The new manager had put Ethel Evans out. Ethel Evans? Oh, yes, the girl who had hurt her knee, couldn't pay her rent, but went on believing in God. They had to pay up the new manager said.

"Mother, it's good to have you back," Lorna told her. "I worried so about you."

She used to worry about Lorna. Lorna was to "keep up," hold her place among the best people. All over now. . . . What social life Lorna had was among the people of "the School"—that place Fred called a phony, and which she had resented. Perhaps it was no more phony than the school she had gone to herself: taken to

a high place, then laughed at. What did it all matter? One thing
was as good as another.

"I realize now, Mother, what you had to go through. Now that
we are the ones to pay the bills I can see why you got the way
you were sometimes. It does hang heavy heavy over your head,
doesn't it?"

It was too bad it should hang heavy over Lorna's young head.
Lorna wasn't strong; she didn't look well now, and a baby coming.
Another mortal on the earth. . . . Max's grandchild, and hers. All
because she met Max on the train, as she was leaving school.

"But we'll get along," Lorna was saying. "George is a good
manager." (Lorna didn't call her husband Doc, and that was nice
of her.) "He has a way with people."

He had a way with his mother-in-law. "Well, Mater," he'd boom,
"your little chick is all right now that you've come back to cluck."

She wished he wouldn't call her mater. The word seemed to belong in another kind of life. Used here it was just another one of the
phonys. Not that it mattered.

Lorna was good to her. "Don't do too much, Mother. You'd
better rest now. You know, I don't want to worry you, but you
don't look as strong as you used to. Sometimes your face is too
flushed, and then again you're pale. Why were you hanging on to
the banister the other day?—as if you couldn't go up."

"Oh, I was just stopping for a minute," she said.

"George wouldn't like it if we had Dr. Grayson come here—
he's unsympathetic to the School. But you could go to his office,
you know, and just not say anything about it."

"I don't need to go to him," she assured Lorna.

She must stop putting her hand to the back of her head. Sometimes it felt so full there; it would press, and there'd be pain in her
head. There were dizzy spells; that was why she had been holding
to the banister. She must be careful, not worry Lorna, Lorna had
worries enough. How different were the things she and Max had

planned for the children. She never heard from Fred. "We'll hear when he wants something," Lorna said. "If the place gets to making any money he'll try to horn-in." He mustn't do that. Let Fred stick to his bootlegging.

Doc Stanton was pleased about having the house. "You're a right one, Mater," he told her, slapping her so jovially on the back she winced. "What's the matter with the old back? Have to get after it, give you some treatments, soon as I can get around to it. And I'll tell you one thing: this is your home as long as you live."

There seemed little doubt of that. This was where she would be as long as she lived. Life wouldn't change again. Nor did she want it to. One day after another, doing what she could to lighten it for Lorna, trying not to let thoughts come in: neither memory of what she had once had nor bitterness in having it no more. Just living along; just another mortal on the earth.

All around her she saw them studying those text-books they had; as earnest as though the goal were true knowledge. Well, why not? One thing was as good as another, she told herself, to shut out a phrase that could haunt her: true knowledge. There were words that were ghosts trying to get back into her life. While she tried to live with much shut out there were times when she knew it was there. It pressed—like blood in her head.

The summer went by and the autumn too had gone when one day Lorna said: "Darn it all, Mother, I'm afraid we'll have to clear out the little store-room. George thinks we could put in another window and rent it. That man is so full of ideas he keeps you jumping. He thinks a lot of the junk could be thrown away and the rest of it shoved into the attic. Most of it is your stuff—things you brought when we moved here."

"Just throw it all out," she said hastily.

"Oh, no, we'll have to look through it. Some of it might be worth something."

"I'm sure none of it is worth anything," she insisted, but Lorna, thinking it was the work she minded, said they'd do it together.

"Mother! Why didn't you use this?" Lorna asked, shaking out a red-and-white patchwork quilt. "People are nuts about these old-fashioned things, and here you just— Oh!" she broke off; "what a shame. The mice have been at it. Gee,"—giving it another shake; "they've eaten it up."

She examined a bit of it. "It's awfully well-made. Such tiny stitches."

"Your great-grandmother made it," her mother said.

"And you just dumped it in here for the mice! I'd like to have had it. I would have had a sentiment about it."

So did I have a sentiment about it, her mother thought. This was the quilt her grandmother gave her when she was married. She could see her adjusting her spectacles, they would keep sliding down her nose as she bent over the stitches at which Lorna now peered. This quilt had been on their bed in that first little house down in Texas: she and Max, their bed. She'd used it instead of the white spread; it was so gay and it came from home. Max liked it too; they used to make guesses on the number of stitches there were in it, those days when they had so much fun. Fun—how far away fun seemed. And love. The nights of love this quilt—knew about . . .

When she'd moved to the Pettibone house, right after Max died, somehow the quilt didn't seem to belong in the boarding-house, nor on a bed in which one slept alone. She'd put it away.

"It will have to be thrown out. Honestly, Mother—" She tossed it out into the hall, seeing her mother's face she left her protest unfinished.

Doc Stanton came in. "How doth the little busy bee—" He sang out, picked up the white sweater in which Max had played golf. "Maybe I could—" he began, and then pronounced "Moths" and threw the sweater after the quilt.

"What's the use keeping stuff if you don't take care of it? This might have done some good to a poor guy who hadn't a shirt to his back," he said reproachfully.

Max had been proud of the sweater. He'd looked so well in it: handsome, gay.

The bending over—something—had made her dizzy. She had to lean against the wall. "You go on down, Mother," Lorna said. "We can finish here."

She didn't want to leave these things for them to handle, throw out as junk, talk about. But she couldn't stoop over again—not right now. "If you'll just leave them for an hour," she said, "I can finish up myself."

"All right," Lorna agreed; but in the tone of one who, even while she humors, means to go on doing the sensible thing.

"Old girl isn't what she used to be," she heard Doc Stanton say in what he thought was a low tone.

No, the old girl wasn't what she used to be. She'd been a girl once, strange though it seemed. She'd been a young wife, a young mother. Joseph—first-born. The baby they had lost; named for her teacher. Some of his things were up there: mice, moths, junk. She hadn't wanted to use all of them for Fred, it seemed they were Joseph's. She had lived with him as she knit the little blue jacket (how tiny it was, she had thought, but he would grow). Dreams of what he would be were knit into the little garment. Doc Stanton would fish it out, say: "I'll be darned,"—for it would be faded now, eaten into. And perhaps Lorna, who was going to have a baby herself, would hold it a minute and say: "Mother might like to have this."

But she didn't want it. The baby and her dreams for him were long gone. She wet a towel and put it to the back of her head.

Later Doc Stanton came in bearing a large box. As soon as she recognized it she cried: "Don't leave that here!" Dear God *no;* she couldn't live in the room with them: books and papers she had brought from school. In that box were her notes: record of what her teacher had said, what she had herself felt in those days. To have them borne in to her now, that past coming to live in the room with her. . . .

"Take that right out of here," she commanded.

The box was heavy; yes, heavy with old faith, dreams, resolution. He put it down with a thud, right close by the bed, right upon her, it seemed; then circled his arms, drew a long breath, breathed out "Whew!"

"Take that out of here!" she screamed.

He stared down at her. "Now you're the grateful one, aren't you just? Here we are trying to make it easier for you and you yell at me as if— These are papers. Lorna said you could weed them out at your leisure. Notebooks—see? Be kind of interesting to you."

He had picked up a notebook to show her, opened it and began to read: "If the energy of the world could be turned to the good the life on this planet can become—"

She sprang up and snatched it from him. "You let my things alone!" she cried.

"Well—O.K. Think I'm snooping, do you? That's the thanks a person gets for trying to be helpful!"

She had sat down on the bed and was gripping the notebook. Her hands were shaking so that the brown-backed book, which had long lain still, was quivering. "You can't make fun of these things," she said. "You are not to stand there and make fun of—"

"Who said anything about making fun of? Why, I was interested. Sounded swell to me. Like to read on—get the dope on it. As a matter of fact, what you wrote there (did you write it?) is just about what I believe myself. 'If the energy of the world could be turned to the good—' You've got something there. It's true."

"Of course it's true!" she cried.

And then couldn't say another word, just sat there. The book in her hands wasn't shaking now; her hands were entirely still. She was strangely motionless, as if stunned, or as if waiting. . . .

Something about her kept him from speaking. What's eating her? he thought as he went out—quietly, for him.

She sat on there without moving. What was that she had said? "Of course it's true," she had said. And said it—as if the truth in her were speaking. Something she had not been able to kill—speaking.

It terrified her.

CHAPTER TWENTY-FIVE

*E*VERY day, through the month that followed, there would come moments when she was on the point of having that box carried to the basement and the papers that recorded old thoughts burned in the furnace. It was unbearable to have them there, right in the room with her; yet she shrank from burning them, as we would turn in horror from the thought of burning something alive. She did nothing about them, but always knew they were there.

"Of course it's true," she had said. Something in her had gone out of control. Something deep in her hadn't been told; it was as if the word had not reached that far: word that it wasn't true and that she had been laughed at for believing. And this sense of something in herself she could not reach, not hers to control, it both angered her and made her afraid. Here was danger, and she powerless. The thoughts which were hers to control moved warily, on guard against what was outlaw.

There were things immediately around her to think about: Lorna having her baby. Quarrels with Doc Stanton engaged one part of her mind. He said there was no need for Lorna to go to the hospital; it was a natural process and why act as though it were a disease. She said Lorna was not to have her baby in that house, and a good deal of the old fight in her came to life in this conflict. She threatened him. She would go to Dr. Grayson and tell him Lorna was not having proper care. Then perhaps Dr. Grayson would take up the whole thing. "What whole thing?" he demanded. The School, she'd told him.

He gave in on the grounds of humoring a nervous mother. But it didn't work out that way. Lorna's time came a little sooner than expected, and in the worst blizzard of the winter. You couldn't see the shape of cars in the street, drifts piled high around the old Pettibone house. Doc Stanton said it would be crazy to try to get to the other end of town. If the car could move at all it would stall in a snowdrift, and fine fix they'd be in then. She looked out at the piling snow and had to agree with him. The wires were down and she couldn't telephone Dr. Grayson; later she got a boy in the house to fight his way through the storm, and somehow, as doctors can—and will—he got there.

"Mother!" Lorna would cry out to her, as one trapped; "what *is* this?" "This is just something you have to do," she would say. "I *can't*," Lorna would moan. "Yes, you can. You will." Through the hours of the night, on into the morning, the pains of labor, the struggle for birth. Lorna grew weaker and whispered she wanted to die. "You can't die. This is life—not death." "Oh—I *can't*." "Yes, you can."

And at ten in the morning there was another mortal on the earth, an infant who would become a woman: go to school, marry, and one day know a night like this. Who would wonder, perhaps, about the meaning of life. And so it went on—on, on. . . . From far in the past to the far future—life went on.

She would have to lie down; there was a woman there now to stay with Lorna. And as she was falling asleep, and in her sleep too, it seemed, she was saying the things she had said to her daughter. "I *can't*," Lorna would cry from her agony. "Yes, you can," she would tell her. "I want to die!" "You can't die. This is not death, this is life." Words she had said to her child: "This is just something you have to do," kept saying themselves over and over to her. . . . She went at last soundly to sleep and woke feeling some change had been wrought in her, something had gone on while she slept. "You *can*," she was saying to herself as she woke.

She was at first puzzled; and then, unwillingly, she had an inkling of what was meant. You haven't tried to understand. You tried only to shut out. You wouldn't go through your labor; the pain was too much and you asked only for death. You thought it an indignity this be put upon you. It was too much to ask and you would not respond. Shunned your ordeal. Life was not to work through you, bringing anguish that understanding might be born anew into the world. But your hour has waited for you. You do not escape. "Yes, you *can*."

One morning when Dr. Grayson came to see Lorna, out in the hall he asked Lorna's mother, "What about you?" He insisted on taking her blood pressure and examining her heart. When he put those things back in his bag he told her: "You'll have to slow up."

"This isn't a very good time to slow up," she replied.

He thought she meant Lorna and told her Lorna and the baby were all right. But that wasn't what she had meant.

She took the medicine he sent her and was as careful as she could be about the things he told her not to do: stairs, exertion. She couldn't do just as he said, a good deal fell upon her right now: attractive things for Lorna to eat, seeing that the rooms were attended to, Lorna's usual duties. A good many stairs to climb, and they did leave her breathless and sometimes dizzy. She rested when she could, for now she could not escape knowing that she was not ready for the end of her life. Something she had to do . . . something that must go on through her, not leave it like this. She had not reached the end of her days because she had not earned the right to go: something she must leave in life. Not to do this would be cheating; it would be betrayal.

She had to understand; and she must bide her time as it was not all hers to do. It had to come through her; when she was ready for it it would enter into her. She a vessel and a thing used. So much of the truth as had once entered into her must not be blocked by her. If she died now there would be a little less light because she had been. The light that was Norma Ashe put out. She had one thing more to do, harder than all which had gone before. Understanding was there to be won, if she could achieve it. She had to look at the thing that had struck her down and perhaps from what had seemed the wreck of her faith . . . Not an easy way we have to go on this earth, but if we are vanquished we betray. She wished for the strength of her younger years, but what strength she had left was hers to use. When it is dark—courage. The light will come.

One morning when she was bathing the baby her thoughts went to what this baby's life would be. They had named her Mary, after Doc Stanton's mother. "You don't mind, Mother?" Lorna had asked. "Your name and mine sound so much alike. Perhaps we should have a change," she had laughed.

Of course she didn't mind, she said. She liked the name Mary. What will your life be, Mary? she thought now, as her hands moved upon this new being on the earth. Not always happy, I know that. But sometimes happy, that I know too. I wish I could let you know some things. I wish I could let you know not to grieve about what is not important. Don't waste the years. They come to an end—so soon. Perhaps a great light will come into your life, making you happy and strong, and you will want to understand. That is the best we have: seeking to understand. The difference between success and failure is there. You are so little now, my grandchild. I hate to think that life is going to hurt you. Will you have courage? Have courage. Baby, do not let them kill the best that is in you. Be pure. Be strong. Be dauntless, Mary. Love the things around you: the flowers, the stars, your fellow-man. So will joy come, and faith. And the other may come too. Oh, I hope so! Your look . . . into the meaning.

She gave the baby to Lorna and, laughing, Lorna uncovered her breast. Just such a very short while ago it was little Lorna greedy at the breast. The breast—the grave; and between the two: our chance.

She went back in her room, pulled up a stool and put her hand on the papers she hadn't until now been able to touch. Once they had been life—pulsing, full of wonder and promise. Perhaps they could evoke life. Was there here a path into what she had lost? Her strength to touch them came from the little child now at her mother's breast. Denial of life must not live so close to the untouched. Hopelessness had no place under the roof of the newborn. "You *can*," she had said to Lorna. Be brave, her thoughts had said to Mary.

She opened a notebook bound in heavy black paper; it opened backward and the pages were ruled. She and Rosie must have bought it at Miss Petersen's store. She didn't remember it at all; of course not, thirty years of living were in between. It was not easy to read, here her writing was finer than usual, as if the lines bothered her and she were trying to keep between them. She remembered she used to wonder why so many notebooks were lined. These penciled letters were rubbed and the paper streaked yellow. Time did that. Time did so many things. She made out: "Thus in the beginning the world was so made that certain signs came before certain events."

What had made her write down these words from Cicero? Had there been a meaning? What meaning? Her teacher . . .

He saw ahead of events, saw the signs of what could be. He had tried to communicate what he saw to them, to her and Rosie, Virgil—

She turned a page, turning from thought of their names. One could laugh at that: entrusting to her, to Austin, Emil.

Their teacher had created a place. He established a kingdom, a place of life into which they could come, from which they themselves were to create. Creation. . . . Creation anew. . . . This can be yours he had said; then laughed at them for entering into it.

Or, had he? She believed what Emil had told her, but there was something more; something she had to know without being told.

She would never be told, yet it was there—there to make hers, if she could. It was hard: to find for oneself the truth behind the denial. But had she not once believed in the miracle?

She took up loose sheets and read something she had written thirty years before. The untidy writing seemed to indicate it had been put down in great excitement, as if fearing a flush of feeling might go before hands could make words. She read:

"Perhaps it will one day be said—After he finished what he had to say he did not at once join his friends but stood looking across the field of grain to the vineyard on the hillside beyond and the grove outside the vineyard. It was as if he were waiting for what he had said to become one with life before he let go of it and resumed his usual way. Then he joined those friends he knew best and they walked away together; but they did not speak of what he had been saying, as if that were still finding its way to them, and he would have it so.

"And perhaps—oh, long long afterwards, when this day was dim in history, but what he had said was alive, because it had made a better world, people then living would wonder— What did the little group speak of after he had finished speaking to them there by the stream that watered the field? Did they at once know the world was different, and was the light of wonder on their faces? Or were they perhaps a little afraid—that they should have been there the very instant it opened and this truth came through into the world?"

She sat a long time looking at it. One moment of her feeling, very hastily put down in words, the act of writing almost too slow to capture. She did not remember it at all, and it was very strange to her. There was no vineyard, she thought. Up there in South Dakota it was not like that at all. Yet I saw it that way. Why?

Light broke slowly, as if fearing too sudden a coming be too much, and she knew why she had seen it that way. In my thoughts it became one with Christ. I was writing about us—and I wrote of him. He was one of us; we one with him. Two thousand years apart—and one.

Releasing tears on her face, she knew then: time does not matter, does not separate and make dead. What has truly lived lives always; there is the oneness of the world, life from first to last. And in this security of the timeless lives hope, live memory and faith. Dream of the better world and the purpose to make it be—that is not of the life that dies. There is the life eternally creative.

But we were to do it *then* . . . our part. We had the dream, ours the will. We were to call upon what waits, summoning into the world of those very days. Our teacher thought. . . .

Our teacher. . . . She sat thinking of him. She heard his voice as he spoke to them; as if they were looking into her eyes now she saw his eyes, saw thought kindle in them and grow. That was reality, she knew now. Of the deathless. All the scoffing in the world could not—

But I do not believe he scoffed, she thought, with some surprise. Did he laugh a little sometimes—at himself, and at us only because he felt he was less than we thought him and less than he would be? Was there sorrow in the laugh, dissatisfaction with self? Do I not grant him the right to a human weakness? Does that make less the light that was in him?

She sat on there in concentration that was painful, her head bent over the box of papers, bent too low, and she felt the strong surge of blood there, but could not stop for that now. Something she had to know, and quickly too, for now she knew full well it must be quickly or could not be at all. Why had it struck her down to be told he laughed at them? It seemed some lack in her own faith. But it came at the moment her faith was strong. Why then had it struck her down?

Because, she thought (thinking slowly, very carefully), we have to believe in the good. I myself wandered far from it, but I always believed it was there. We ourselves may not be good, but if we feel goodness not there—why then should we live? We need it to live, she thought, even though we do not dwell with it all our days and at times are not even aware of our need. The best. . . . Something to which harm cannot come. Something to come home to—for, oh, we need something to come home to. His faith was greater. He could laugh at it, a little, and his security was not shaken. If we laugh at the sun, does the sun go out? Why was it the all-in-all to me that he laughed at us? It was *there*—there secure. He knew that, and perhaps in some weary moment, some sad and lonely moment—pain—blood pounding in his head—knowing his life was not all he would have had it, knowing he had come to the end not ready for the end. . . . Oh! she cried suddenly, both to a sharp pain and to the thought which also stabbed, do I think it so little I think anyone—*anyone*—him—Christ—could destroy it?

Once, in her youth, it had been as if veils parted; she had felt she saw what waits. Now she was herself waiting, there before it again . . . waiting. One moment now . . . it trembled there . . . she knew it was there. In a moment—one moment now—veils would part and . . . Her lips moved. One time more her lips formed words. "This time I will see *all the way*."

There was a thought which moved after her lips could not. I am waiting, her thought said. One moment now. . . . One moment more. . . .

Her head went down, in among recorded thoughts, tracings of the hope and vision and courage of youth. . . . And it was not herself, after an hour, raised her head from the place where it had come to rest.